I0629524

Arthur and the Argonauts

G. H. Lewis

Published in the United States by
Six Ridge Press LLC, Reston, Virginia 20194

www.sixridgepress.com

ISBN 979-8-9856981-3-8 (ebook)
ISBN 979-8-9856981-4-5 (paperback)
ISBN 979-8-9856981-5-2 (hardcover)

Library of Congress Control Number: 2022904414

Chapter One

Arthur Pifflethorpe fell in love. This is not to say he fell in love once and for all, in the tradition we have come to expect from newsstand paperbacks and Hollywood rom coms. Rather, falling in love was in Arthur's nature. The young man had been falling in love for as long as he could remember. His earliest memory was of little Megan Harper teaching him to braid the hair of her doll and the thought that he would like to stay there with Megan forever, learning to braid hair. In truth, the sequence of early memories had grown muddled across time and immeasurable distance, but he wanted this to be the earliest, and that was sufficient to fix it thus in his mind. Arthur was romantic in such respects; indeed, in every respect touching upon his great loves. The braiding of hair had ever since been tied up in his consciousness with his earliest stirrings of devotion to a girl.

Truth be told, Arthur had possessed a doll of his own: an anatomically correct and urologically functional affair of ambiguous race that Mrs. Pifflethorpe had bought in a furor of enlightened feelings about gender roles and sociological liberality in general. He never told anyone about this doll and used it mainly as a squirt gun when left unattended in the bathtub with William. But neither did he throw it away. The doll went some way toward fixing in his mind an empathy with Megan that had not yet come upon his other friends in their relations with girls. Perhaps this connection was what first nudged him along his future course. Perhaps it was some other quirk of fate.

"Left to the middle, right to the middle; left to the middle, right to the middle."

He could still see Megan's rosebud lips forming the words in a porcelain face as yet untouched by sun and wind. Her cheeks were a tad plump and framed by waves of raven-black hair; round spectacles perched precariously on a button nose that had not yet begun to take on the shape it would assume in adulthood. It was the first of many faces Arthur would love and so held a special place among them. It was only with difficulty he remembered them all, there had been so many.

More enduring was a fitful romance with Sloane Villanueva, renewed from time to time during summers at the lake and, sprinkled throughout long intervals between, her occasional reply to an email. By the time Arthur's online persona went silent sometime toward the end of high school, such communications with Sloane and other passing loves were stacked hundreds deep in computer files organized by name and place and date. He reread the happy ones in sad times and the sad ones in happy times, just for the poignancy of contrast. He pored over old drafts in agony over a long silence, wondering what he had said wrong. He mined the trove when at a loss for words, if only in the wanderings of internal monologue.

Sloane responded to his outpourings of the soul, when she responded at all, with vignettes from an adolescent social milieu of which Arthur was hopelessly ignorant. Arthur did not mix with cheerleaders, nor with popular girls in general, at his school at the other end of the state. Sloane was such a girl. It was not that she looked down on unpopular children; she simply did not consider them, the scope of her experiences not having opened her to the inkling that anyone might not be so widely admired as she. Under different circumstances Arthur would almost certainly have faded into the background, but Sloane's summers at the lake had a romantic air about them that demanded a boy to fill the necessary role. Arthur did nicely in this respect. That thoughts of her might consume her solicitous friend, even in the long intervals between summer holidays, was another of those notions that would never have occurred to her.

The only people who commonly registered in Sloane's consciousness were those who fell within a rarefied circle of beautiful, gregarious, and well-born youngsters. By improbable happenstance, far from home, Arthur found himself temporarily cast into this circle. He was thus endowed in her imagination with characteristics he did not actually possess. He felt remorse at not disabusing her of mistaken impressions, convinced as he was deep in his heart that she would have loved him anyway. He idealized the mercies of an undoubtedly virtuous spirit but could never bring himself to anything but equivocal flitting about the edges of the truth.

Most of the time Arthur spent with Sloane was on lazy summer evenings, alone together on a sun-bleached wooden pier, with the last of the day's chop rolling in off the water and a sunset dwindling red to purple to black over pine-carpeted hill-tops. As night fell and voices drifting out from the shoreline faded to silence, they would strip to their underwear, Sloane giggling delightedly all the while, and slip into the black water. Treading whirlpools onto the surface of the lake, Arthur would draw as close as he dared to the panting, whispering, beloved face that emerged damp and goose-pimpled from reflections of a sliding, warping moon. A thrill would shoot through him when he brushed against her. They would lie on the planks, air-drying in the warm night, talking about things meaningful only to the young and watching for meteors and satellites slicing their way across a swirl of stars.

Even then, construction was underway on Beckett Armagast's *Argo*. The mysterious orbiting object was just bright enough to be seen gliding through the sky along its recurrent arc from west to east, west to east. Each summer, it grew larger and brighter until it was impossible to miss, sliding through the blackness like a lighted ocean liner on a midnight sea. Happy hours were spent in speculation over its purpose; indeed, the entire population of the Earth could talk of little else. A consensus held it would be an orbiting playground for the global elite: at best, an aggrandized St. Tropez (sublimely unapproachable by besneakered tourists) and at worst, a vantage from which the fabulously wealthy might observe any regrettable nuclear conflagration. The fringes of opinion had settled upon a manned voyage to Mars. The eccentric billionaire who made the *Argo* his life's work refused to confirm or deny any rumors.

Beneath whispered intimacies, Arthur nurtured the dark secret of his true place in the social hierarchy of adolescence, far below that of the luminary lying beside him in her underpants. With age and experience, Sloane eventually surmised this truth for herself. They parted each August with renewed assurances the friendship would not flag despite the distance, but her replies to his emails tapered off as inevitably as the burgeoning of her body into that of a woman. The final break happened sometime during Arthur's sophomore year, after Mr. Pifflethorpe had passed on and not long before William followed.

Pop psychiatry may suggest that Arthur's long string of unrequited loves had something to do with the passing of Mr.

Pifflethorpe halfway through his high school years. It was tacitly understood in the family—but had never been a point of disaffection—that Arthur gravitated toward his father while William was the unspoken favorite of Mrs. Pifflethorpe. As we have seen, however, Arthur's tendency toward adoration of particular specimens of the fair sex began long before his father's untimely demise. It is also not entirely clear this propensity should be considered pathological. The possibility will be considered in due course.

As a boy, Arthur clung to what moments he could garner between his father's late nightly homecomings from the vacuum-cleaner factory and his plunge into a sleep that rattled pictures on the walls out of plumb with its resonating snore. The family would sit around the dining-room table while Mr. Pifflethorpe drew out his sons with questions about the progress of their schoolwork. He would question them over their respective futures, dwelling for a time on William's boyhood commitment to be an astronaut or on Arthur's inability to formulate any clear plan of action. After dinner, he would sit back in a plush recliner, tug on a wooden lever extending the footrest, and close his eyes as old rhythm-and-blues tracks washed over him from a tape deck arranged on a shelf behind his head. The boys would burrow down into the declivities in his substantial bulk and close their eyes, smelling the lingering odors of the factory thinly masked by the morning's splash of Old Spice.

Mr. Pifflethorpe was a silent and glowering man with a mop of prematurely white hair often mistaken for a toupee in its improbable profusion. Weathered skin of a firm and square-jawed countenance was overhung by black brows that cast in shadow a chin prone to a darkening of sandpapery stubble. Day or night, summer or winter, he dressed in denim trousers soiled about the knees (beyond the best efforts of Mrs. Pifflethorpe) and flannel shirts cut wide and deep to accommodate a great barrel chest. His look was always one of haggard exhaustion. Despite this appearance, Mr. Pifflethorpe was by nature an optimistic man whose dogged steps reflected not the resigned plodding of a Boxer but the obstinate resolution of a blue-collar Dr. Pangloss. Born of immigrants and sons of immigrants in a long and unbroken line that still managed to avoid the inevitable softening, Mr. Pifflethorpe worked. Over long summers, when his beloved wife took their sons away to the lake, the man trudged his daily routine from bed to assembly line and back again, driving up on weekends in a sagging station wagon loaded with supplies.

These weekends bred a panoply of memories that defined Arthur's truncated relationship with his father. Away from the factory, away from the too-small and slightly down-at-the-heels brick house with its never-ending list of needed repairs, Mr. Pifflethorpe existed in a state of being both he and his family felt to be well and truly his. In a one-room cabin on the lakeshore, with its plywood partitions and squealing bedsprings, its propane cooktop and streamlined refrigerator, he would rise before dawn (earlier even than every other day of the year) to wrangle his boys from their bed and motor them out onto the mirrored surface of the lake to troll for trout. He would spend afternoons in a lawn chair, reading from a book about Churchill or the Civil War and sipping hour after hour on the same bottle of flat Olympia beer.

After dark, he would balance a discount Walmart telescope on its wobbly tripod and show Arthur and William strange and distant worlds of rock and fire and gas. Arthur would forever remember Mr. Pifflethorpe's lumbering explanations of black holes and planetary rings. On special occasions, Mr. Pifflethorpe would chuckle as he allowed the boys sips from his plastic tumbler of mid-grade Scotch. He would send them off to the nightly Villanueva campfire and disappear with his wife into the cabin, locking fast the ill-fitting door with its hook-and-eye clasp and pulling closed the curtains. Voices of Etta James and B. B. King on the tape deck drifted into the night. There at the lake, Mr. Pifflethorpe was happy. If he could be happy in that one important place in that brief span of time, he considered himself a happy man.

Mr. Pifflethorpe had been dead for quite some time before the town doctor at last surmised what it was that had carried him off. Indeed, it was not until William fell ill under similar circumstances that anyone had thought to check for underlying genetic disorders. That the gene in question was present in the son (and not in Mrs. Pifflethorpe) was reason enough to extrapolate the cause of the father's death, even long after he had been tucked away beneath the lawn of the town's clapboard chapel. Arthur had also been tested for this virulent sequence of deoxyribonucleic acid. He had been given a clean bill of health.

Arthur's final memories of his brother were from the year after Mr. Pifflethorpe's death. There had been one last summer when Mrs. Pifflethorpe tried her best to keep up the family traditions. She put in extra hours in the months leading up to their annual trip so she might take off the necessary weeks. She rented the same deteriorating cabin and packed the car full of the same fishing poles and lawn chairs and board games. It was not, in the end, the morass of memories that made this the last year they would go to the lake. In fact, the three still managed to find solace in sunshine and old friends. What sealed the break was William's illness that followed soon after and its obliteration of whatever hope remained in Mrs. Pifflethorpe. Her will eroded along with the brightness in her eye, the resiliency of her skin, and even the town itself, which crumbled away along with the vacuum-cleaner factory's dilapidated warehouses and smokestacks.

After many years and many nights out on their pier, that

final summer Arthur at last steeled himself to give Sloane a kiss. It was his first attempt at the enigmatic ritual, and he was far too old to be so caught out. She did not suspect the hopelessness of his inexperience until they were too far along for her politely to divert the fiasco. Teeth grated on teeth in a blind rush to outpace his faltering resolve. He tried far too hard to emulate the devouring passion of the movie stars, who were his only examples of the appropriate way to carry oneself in such circumstances. To Sloane's credit, she played along. She let him have his moment, and then she slipped away. The only sign of her for the rest of the vacation was a voice carrying over the water in the evening—perhaps imagined, perhaps from the end of some other dock where she sat with some other boy. Arthur's spirit was crushed in the weeks to come as realization of his failure dawned upon him. The only thing that could push it from his mind was William's diagnosis and rapid decline some months later.

Mrs. Pifflethorpe henceforth poured all of her efforts into the remaining son. She returned to work in the office of the vacuum-cleaner factory, filing papers until they went the way of the post and answering telephones until they migrated into the jacket pockets of the executives. She put in long hours formerly the province of her husband in order to secure for Arthur his place at the state university. It was not the march of technology that put her out of work at the factory; she was too respected and admired for that, as was her late husband. What put her out of work was the end of the factory itself. She carried home her box of personal effects and switched to two jobs: one at Mr. Underwood's hardware store during the day and another at the diner in the evenings.

The episode preceded the lengthiest gap yet in Arthur's nearly unbroken string of infatuations. But time worked its healing, or perhaps only hurried him along toward what new intimacies might fill the void of all that was lost. He found another girl worthy of his unquenchable love, that most powerful of forces in what must be considered on balance a melancholy life.

This time it was Isabel Weiss, newly transferred in from some far-off and romantic place where she had matured far beyond the petty enthusiasms of small-town life in the Rust Belt. Her father, it was said, was a business consultant hired on to turn around the declining fortunes of one of the town's remaining industrial concerns. Business was big in those days, or at least it was everywhere else. Isabel moved in higher circles.

Yet when she arrived in the whitewashed cinderblock classroom with its tile floor and corroded aluminum-frame windows, Arthur caught a glimmer of fright beneath the glamor. He had a knack for such insights into the secret cogitations of girls. Regrettably, these rarely accompanied intuition as to appropriate ways of acting upon them. Isabel's vulnerability, veiled beneath an imperious curl to lips painted an implausible shade of red, caused Arthur to fall immediately and helplessly in love. His was a heart capable of loving wholly and perfectly on many simultaneous fronts. Indeed, there had been many passing attachments that blinked past Sloane Villanueva's enduring radiance like meteorites against the mounting glare of the *Argo*, which had by then come to rival the morning star in its intensity.

Isabel trod the well-worn path of new kids in school and found a desk by itself to the rear of the classroom. Arthur took an adjacent seat, with no intention of speaking a word. Basking in the brilliance of such a girl was enough, and saved him from potential humiliation made possible by direct engagement. She, however, felt no such inhibition.

"Hey," she said.

"Hey," said Arthur.

"How's Mr. Hibbert?"

"I hear he's OK. I've never had him before."

A restless silence followed as other children filtered in, boisterously reacquainting themselves after the summer holiday. The boys moderated their enthusiasm upon spying the pretty new blonde girl in the back row. They eyed Arthur with contempt.

"You any good at calculus?" She spoke in a voice rising barely above a whisper and avoided eye contact, her gaze darting about the room to measure up each potential ally and each potential rival.

"I'm OK." Arthur was good at calculus.

"I've never taken it before," she said.

"I did pre-calc. It's not so bad."

"Study partners?"

"OK." The leap of joy in Arthur's breast was moderated by a wave of panic. Was that two or three times he had used the term *OK*?

"Have you lived around here for long?" Isabel's eyes continued to survey the room. Mr. Hibbert entered with a step that said he was a no-nonsense type of man. He wore a brown woolen suit with a yellow print tie. A thick mustache was trimmed flush with the corners of his mouth. He settled himself at his desk, casting glances at the chattering students from beneath long, wispy eyebrows.

"All my life," said Arthur.

"Does it suck? I heard the only movie theater just went out of business."

"It's OK."

"What do you do for fun?"

"The homecoming dance is in a few weeks." Arthur panicked at his own audacity, but forged on, his head in a fog. "I run cross-country. The team does a lot of traveling. There's also mountain biking and rock climbing out at the state park, if you like that sort of thing."

"But where do you hang out?" Isabel said. She turned to study him. He held her gaze.

His mind raced. "There isn't much. A lot of kids go to the mall. I think it sucks." Had she used that word already? Had he struck the right balance of acidity and aloofness? He could not get his mind to focus.

Isabel stuck out her lower lip and blew a jet of air that flipped an errant strand of hair up off her cheek. Then she seized the lock and began to twirl it around a manicured finger. Before she could go on, Mr. Hibbert rose from his chair, and the class began.

Isabel was not one to be shy about asking for what she wanted, nor was she often rebuffed. She would certainly get no such treatment from Arthur. She was indeed bad at calculus and felt no compunction about keeping Arthur late in the library to pump his brain on derivatives and the chain rule. Arthur did not mind this one bit. With growing familiarity, his diffidence began to wane. They would lean close over a book, whispering and laughing until shushed by a passing librarian.

Several weeks into the semester, with their first exam approaching, Isabel spoke the words Arthur had been longing to hear. Ms. Landry had walked past their table for the second time, tapping on its surface quietly but firmly with a wooden ruler. This indicated the library was closing.

"I'm hungry," said Isabel, slapping closed her textbook.

"Are you ready for tomorrow?" Arthur asked.

"It's hopeless. I'm hopeless," she replied.

"That's ridiculous," said Arthur. "You've already got most of it down."

"I'm going to fail."

"If you want to grab some food, we can keep studying."

"Do you mind?" Her eyes turned on him, wide and bright, with a look she had found certain to elicit the desired response from young men such as Arthur.

"Of course not," he said.

"How about the diner?"

Arthur did not want to go with Isabel to the diner. His mind ran through possible excuses before settling on the most obvious. "My mom works there," he said.

She blew the lock of hair up off her cheek. "My folks are at my house," she said. "How about yours?"

He nodded, unwilling to test the firmness of his voice.

The matter was settled, and Isabel stood, stuffing textbooks and notecards into her backpack. Arthur did the same. They walked through the gathering night. A low overcast leaked a mist of rain that wetted the pavement until streetlamps reflected from it in diffuse streaks of yellow. Oak trees lining the boulevard shed heavy drops that pattered on the sidewalk and left damp blotches on Arthur's shirt. A row of too-small and slightly down-at-the-heels brick houses sat back from the street on fenced, rectangular plots.

The flush of excitement that had animated Arthur began to subside, replaced by a creeping twinge of shame. Maybe this was not such a good idea after all. He retreated into brooding, and they walked in silence. There was no going back. He turned onto a concrete walk that cut an unimaginative line through a lawn that had returned a good way to its natural state. He unlocked the door as she stood behind him, shoulders hunched against the rain and hands thrust firmly into the pockets of her raincoat.

Arthur's worry eased as he led her into the foyer and snapped on the light. The carpet was getting a tad worn along a path that wound its way through the living room furniture to the kitchen. The ceiling was still encrusted with its unfashionable popcorn. The dining room table stood on legs of chromed metal tubing, and Formica on the kitchen countertops glistened with tiny gold stars. But the home was neat and cozy, the final refuge of a woman to whom the world outside had not been kind. The sofa was new, and a large television was mounted to the wall over the fireplace. Photographs filled gaps in the shelves of a bookcase and lined a freshly painted mantelpiece. Arthur took Isabel's coat and hung it beside his own on a set of hooks behind the door. He led her through the living room and dropped his backpack on a peninsula of countertop as he passed on his way to the refrigerator.

Isabel stopped before the fireplace and stood examining the row of photographs. She paused at one of them. "Who's Buck Rogers?" she said with a giggle. "Is this you?"

Arthur walked back to stand beside her. He stared at the picture. William looked out from the visor of his spaceman helmet, smile stretched to bursting with the joy only a child can understand. Shreds of wrapping paper littered the floor around him. "That's William... my brother," Arthur said.

"I didn't know you have a brother."

"He's gone."

Isabel glanced to Arthur's face. Solicitousness had vanished, and he was far away. She took him by the shoulders, turned him about, and pushed him back toward the kitchen. She perched on the faux-leather cushion of a barstool as he went to the refrigerator to retrieve a cardboard box containing a half-finished pizza. He flipped it open on the counter between them.

"How's this?" he said.

"Perfect." She selected a slice and began to eat it cold. Arthur leaned his elbows on the counter and did the same. Slowly, through a silence intensified by the patter of rain, the mood began to lift. She patted the stool next to her. He slid around to sit.

"Where do you want to start?" Arthur asked between bites, zipping open the pouch of his backpack.

Isabel ignored the question. "Are you going to Homecoming?" she said.

"I hadn't thought about it." Arthur had, in fact, thought about it a great deal.

"Come with me."

The expected flip-flop in his chest was strangely quiet. "OK," he said.

She looked him full in the face and screwed up her eyes as if probing his thoughts. They had stopped eating, and she set aside the nibbled slice of pizza. She rested an elbow on the countertop, her chin on the heel of her hand, and studied him some more. Then she sat up straight and prim, scooched forward on her seat, and leaned close. She hesitated, peering questioningly into his eyes in the instant before she kissed him on the mouth. It was a brief, closed-lipped, dry kiss that lingered for only a second or two before she pulled away, but it lasted long enough for Arthur to feel the soft firmness of her lips and inhale her damp, sweet breath. It was a good kiss, and his previous one with Sloane would be relegated to the status of an anomaly. It was this kiss he would remember as his first.

She paused again, smiled, and began rummaging in her bag for a book.

Chapter Two

I sabel Weiss was not a bad sort of girl. She was not one to scheme about running roughshod over the feelings of others in the name of taking what was hers. She was not one to lie or cheat or steal, at least not more so than the rest of us. Isabel was, quite simply, young. Years later, when she thought back on her brief time with Arthur, she would remember him as a kind and sensitive boy who was incurably naïve in the ways of girls. As such, she could not entirely regret she never came to love him. She would try with all her might, especially after the future laid out for him became widely known. But it all came back to those first weeks in the new school, when she was lonely and frightened and out of her element. Arthur was safe, and whatever well-meaning mothers may say, pretty young women in the flush of impending adulthood seldom fall for safe young men. That comes later.

Even as Isabel began to slip through Arthur's desperately clutching fingers, there was never any cataclysm of realization that she was not the one for him. She played along. She tried to be nice. With one hand, she gripped his devoted (if disconcertingly moist) fingers, while with the other she signaled to a widening circle of admirers that she would only be a moment. If we are honest with ourselves, we cannot hold it against her. Breaking hearts is never an easy thing to do. It was only later Arthur wished she had done it differently, once he could look back on the period as a set piece in time. As that time was passing, he treasured every shred of dissembling affirmation.

Arthur and Isabel's romance carried on for a time in the traditional mold. With admirable self-confidence in the face of mounting evidence that her choice was a poor one, Isabel held Arthur's hand in full view of their classmates and sat with him in the lunchroom. She invited him to her new table when drawn there by the girlfriends that quickly accumulated. She introduced him to the boys who gathered in due course. As Arthur's eighteenth birthday passed and the Homecoming dance approached, she doubled down on this increasingly imprudent sequence of decisions, even as it became evident Arthur was coming to care for her a great deal more than she would ever care for him.

As the leaves began to turn, splashing with gold the foothills at the edge of town, Arthur rode his bicycle through the wrought-iron gates of Bella Vista and over freshly blacktopped streets to Isabel's home. There were no vistas, beautiful or otherwise, in Arthur's midwestern town, unless one counted the rusted grating of a water-tower catwalk that looked out over the railyard. Where the half-vacant strip of Main Street storefronts ended began a regular grid of postwar bungalows that had been the envy of the world in decades gone by. Now they moldered away in pace with the declining fortunes of domestic manufacturing. Beyond, to the west, spread acres of empty factories and warehouses with graffitied walls and yards scattered with wind-blown trash. Broken glass littered empty plank flooring where the shells had not been gutted by fires sparked from the barrel stoves of tramps.

To the east grew up the posher suburbs to absorb what money could still be wrung from that mildewed dishrag of a town. Bella Vista was one such suburb. In it lived the mayor, the county judge, and (ostensibly, at least) a Washington politician laying claim to some vestige of bygone ties to the Land and the People.

Arthur rode past lawns in technicolor shades of green. Sprinklers clicked arcs of spray out over expanses rising to mulched flowerbeds and grand, faux-stone façades. The rear bumpers of Audis and BMWs peeked from imitation carriage-house garages left open in the declining light of an autumn evening. Isabel was waiting for him on the front steps. Arthur left his bicycle resting cockeyed on the lawn and sat beside her. They looked out on a sunset obscured by the row of houses opposite.

"Hey," he said.

"Hey," she replied. Their conversation had not settled into any spontaneous and unaffected rhythm. It never would.

"Are your folks home?"

"Mmm-hmm."

"Everything OK?"

She turned back from squinting at the sunset to look at him. "Of course," she said.

Whether from a desire to do so or in the feeling it was expected, she kissed him. They lingered over it for a bit longer than either of them was entirely comfortable. She pulled back. "Do you want to come in?"

Arthur smiled in response, and they stood. She opened one of a pair of massive oak doors leading into a high-ceilinged foyer and formal living room. A staircase swept upward in a curve, presided over by a brushed-nickel chandelier. Hardwood floors spread through the French doors of a book-lined study and to the rear down a long hallway toward the kitchen. It was in this direction she led him.

"Arthur's here," she called. Her words sounded hollow in the expanse of the room.

A woman in a flowered silk blouse and white stretch-pants peeked around the corner at the far end of the hall. To Arthur she looked young, without the careworn skin he had come to expect in the faces of adults. Her hair looked much like Isabel's, smooth and flaxen. She came toward them, open-toed shoes tapping sharply on the floor.

"Hello, young man," she said. "Please come in, come in." She kissed Isabel on the cheek and offered to Arthur fingers limp and cold. He was not sure what to do with them, having been taught to shake hands with an invariable firmness. He gripped them only briefly before stuffing his hands into his pockets.

"Pleased to meet you, Mrs. Weiss," he said.

"Please... call me Jacqueline."

Arthur felt certain he would never bring himself to call her Jacqueline. Rather, he would resort to uncomfortable silences and contorted turns of phrase to avoid calling her anything at all. He nodded politely.

A table was set for dinner in a breakfast nook across a wide expanse of granite from a French-country kitchen set with commercial-sized, stainless-steel appliances. On the stove boiled a pot of spaghetti. Next to it on the countertop sat a jar of Prego tomato sauce and a plastic bag of ready-mix salad greens. An arc of windows wrapping around the curve of the table looked out over a patio, a flower garden, and yet another expanse of mani-cured grass.

Hardwood flooring ended with a step down into a carpeted family room, where Mr. Weiss sat on a gray, tufted sofa watching television. He was absorbed by the disembodied head of a newscaster who spoke with alarming zeal over a set of scrolling banners ticking off the day's top stories and stock prices.

Mrs. Weiss called to him. "Dear, Arthur's here."

Mr. Weiss' scalp showed through a thinning patch in the dry, brown hair at the crown of his head. He glanced back with a brief look of annoyance. A large, thin nose sat prominently on a boyish face, narrow-set eyes peering out through rectangular spectacles with stylish black frames. His eyes went back to the television as he stood, moving slowly in an effort to balance protocol with his desire to catch the remaining snippet of the story. At last, he broke off and bounded up the step into the kitchen as if he wanted to get it out of the way as quickly as possible.

Mr. Weiss' handshake fell back within the scope of Arthur's expectations, and this time he left his hands out of his pockets, letting them hang limply for a moment before joining them and fidgeting. Isabel stood beside him. He considered placing a hand at the small of her back in a gesture he had yet to try for himself but had always felt conveyed appropriate degrees of decorum and endearing possessiveness. He thought better of it.

"Thank you for joining us, Arthur," said Mr. Weiss. "We've heard so much about you."

"I understand you've been helping Isabel through her first year of calculus," said Mrs. Weiss.

Arthur flushed and smiled. He gave a nod that walked an ambiguous line between polite acknowledgment and looking down at Mr. Weiss' feet. "She's helped me a lot, too," he said.

An awkward silence.

Mrs. Weiss said, "Well, let's sit down to dinner before it gets cold." She had planned little time for chitchat prior to the meal.

. . .

It was not the time spent talking with Mr. and Mrs. Weiss that Arthur would remember of the evening. This may be because he suppressed a memory that did not paint him in his best light. The conversation dragged like a milk cow wading through shin-deep mud, with its only redeeming facet the empathetic glances exchanged between Arthur and Isabel when Mr. or Mrs. Weiss made some comment worthy of their adolescent disdain. What he would remember was the thirty minutes after dinner, sitting uncomfortably on the sofa between Isabel and her father as Mrs. Weiss finished straightening the kitchen. They cut dinner short on the pretext of wanting to watch the announcement that had been foreshadowed in the weeks leading up to an annual shareholder meeting of Armagast Enterprises. Everyone knew of it.

As Mr. Weiss switched on the television, Beckett Armagast was taking the stage. An audience before him was indicated only by shadowed rows of heads at the bottom of the frame. Behind, a floor-to-ceiling screen projected the slowly rotating logo that had come to signify the man as much as it did the company for which he was the founder and majority shareholder. Beckett was of medium build, with a triangular face and forehead mounting upward like a crab-claw sail. The flat top of his enormous head was fringed in short, brown hair combed uniformly downward from the crown. His shirt was collarless and hung open a button or two to reveal a chest thick with hair. A headset clung to one of his ears with a microphone that stretched down over a cheek to end at the corner of lips almost feminine in their voluptuousness. He stood silent for a moment with his hands on his hips as if gathering his thoughts.

When at last he spoke, it was with disarming folksiness. "Welcome. Thanks for joining us this evening," he said, hands still on his hips, head turning from side to side to take in the crowd with an almost proprietorial air. "I'm awfully proud of the team's accomplishments here at Armagast Enterprises. I've been looking forward to this opportunity to share them with you."

He looked down to a clicker in his hand and then back toward the screen as it flipped to a chart full of numbers and squiggling lines. He began to pace the stage. "I won't bore you with the details," he went on. "As you know, we've handily beaten expectations of the Street in each of the last five years, and this year is no exception. We're up 12 percent on revenue and 90 basis points on margin in the last quarter alone. Our automotive division is valued higher than the Big Three combined, and Aerospace has completed its acquisition of Skyrocket Turbofan. Chinese operations grew by double digits in each of the past six quarters. Our contract award announced last month by the Air Force will support the latest generation of ground-based intercontinental ballistic missiles. We're an industry leader in technologies from hypersonics to directed energy, from urban air mobility to global supply-chain management..."

The presentation continued, with images depicting the newest, the fastest, and the shiniest gadgetry from a year of, as Beckett put it, breakneck innovation. After a few minutes of this, he paused in his pacing and turned to face the audience once more, hands back on his hips. "But let's be honest," he said. "None of that really matters. None of that is why you're here tonight... why you've tuned in from around the world... why our little shareholder meeting is playing in prime time. You came to hear what we've been doing up there." He pointed toward the ceiling, and an amused titter spread through the audience. "You came to hear about our banner project that's been consuming headlines for years as surely as it's been lighting up the skies over your heads. You came to hear about the *Argo*."

Beckett Armagast raised his clicker and pressed a button with a melodramatic flick of his wrist. The screen went black and faded in with a video image of the Earth from high above. Music swelled. The blue of the oceans and green of the continents were swirled with obscuring bands of cloud. A knife-edged border of atmosphere separated the riot of color from the crisp black of space. Stars gleamed from the darkness. The object filling the foreground was, to Arthur at least, a letdown after the buildup of not only the preceding comments, but many years' worth of hyperventilated speculation. What he expected was some spectacular rocket ship with swooping tail fins and streamlined nose-cone, poised to streak off into the heavens. This is not what he saw.

What he saw looked more like an oversized aluminum can, somewhat elongated and covered with the lumps and seams and protuberances one would expect on a spacecraft. It rotated slowly on its axis, the end nearest the camera filled by a series of concentric circles around a flanged core obscured in shadow. Providing some indication of the massive scale of the object, a cloud of smaller spacecraft clustered about it like pinpoints nearly lost in the vast expanse.

Beckett let the audience take in the image for a moment before he continued. "As you know," he said, "for the better part of a decade, Armagast Enterprises has led a consortium of corporations committed to carrying humanity beyond what any of us thought possible in times well within recent memory. Along with Griffindale Skyworks, Dalton-Ray Industries, Martinique Aerosystems, and dozens of other partners, we've seized the opportunities made possible by a revolution in space transport. A few short years ago, space was the province of governments. Those who would leverage its ultimate high ground were at the mercy of astronomical costs and long, unpredictable development timelines. No more."

As he spoke, the perspective of the image behind him was slowly changing. Whatever platform directed the camera was moving past the *Argo*, taking it in from every angle. Visible on its rotating surface was a mass of exposed tubing, then acre upon acre of solar panels. A low glass dome bubbled outward from its regular circumference like a blister. Gradually the far end came into view. It too was flat, with a docking port in its center to which was affixed a second, smaller cylinder that must have been some transport unloading its cargo.

"The *Argo* is an unprecedented feat of technology," Beckett said, "but technology alone did not make possible this pinnacle of human endeavor. What made it possible is the relentlessly decreasing cost of access to space enabled by the commercialization of space launch. When Armagast Enterprises made possible the profitable exploitation of space, we fundamentally changed the game. That inevitable evolution was enabled by the irresistible logic of the capitalist ethos..."

A scattering of applause swelled until he was forced to pause, waiting for it to subside. Meanwhile, he turned back to admire his work. The camera's vantage had continued to shift, and the *Argo* was growing smaller with increasing distance. The image panned upward until the surface of the Earth was a thin slice at the lower corner of the frame and the spacecraft was set against a background of stars.

"I guess I'm getting carried away." Beckett chuckled to himself. The audience mimicked him in the sympathy created by his overpowering charisma. He spoke over the ripple of their laughter. "I haven't yet told you what we're doing." He gave another dramatic pause before going on. "Now, I've heard the rumors. I've heard it said we're building the universe's most overpriced hotel, where the rich and famous can cavort beyond the critical gaze of the unwashed masses."

Another pause for the laughter to subside.

"I've heard we're building a military installation that can lob nuclear warheads at will over the surface of the Earth."

More laughter, louder this time and with a more cynical edge.

"They came closer to the truth when they guessed we were sending humanity on its first voyage to Mars."

The carefully managed mood in the room was devolving into excited chatter, and Beckett raised his voice in a mounting tenor that commanded silence. "Well, it turns out Mars is an arid wasteland uninhabitable by any known form of life," he said. "You can have it. We're going here..."

He turned back to the screen and, with a sweep of his outstretched arm, pointed to some point of light lost amid the dusting of stars. As he was speaking, the camera had continued to pan outward until even the *Argo* was no longer in the frame. Now the image began to zoom, magnifying a narrower and narrower interval of sky until only a few hazy specks were visible against the blackness.

"The ability of our astronomers to peer into the heavens has grown alongside our ability to travel there," Beckett said, still facing the screen but with hands on his hips and face turned upward to the central point of light that had resolved into a disk. "They have discovered other solar systems, exoplanets, thousands of which fall within habitable zones like that occupied by the Earth. What you see here is the most promising of these. By the best estimates, it has the right temperature, the right mass, the right atmosphere. By the best estimates, humans may even be able to walk on its surface without the need of pressure suits or air tanks."

He turned back to the audience, which was now silent.

"At current levels of technological advancement, we can be there in less than five thousand years..."

A sharp exhalation of breath emitted from Mr. Weiss's pursed lips, accompanied by an inadvertent mist of spittle. He raised the remote control and switched off the television.

"Well, that was a ridiculous disappointment," he said. "I'll hand it to the man, though: he's made the most of the publicity. Even if that goddamned tin can is nothing but the world's most expensive billboard, he's gotten his money's worth."

"Dear, that's enough." Mrs. Weiss had come to stand behind them and surprised her husband with the rebuke.

He stood and went to her, offering a kiss of apology on her cheek before he left the room. Arthur and Isabel rose from the sofa as well and spread their books on the dining room table to study.

Arthur went home disappointed in his aspiration to see Isabel's bedroom. But it was a disappointment mitigated by Beckett Armagast's revelation. This occupied the place in his thoughts that would have been obsessing over Isabel and the missed opportunity. For him, the stars—the *Argo*—were tied up forever with memories of Sloane, of William, and of his father. Most boys of his age felt some similar pang of awe, having grown up with the *Argo* a looming presence high overhead. It was as if a part of him previously unknown had been suddenly brought into the light.

Arthur and Isabel spoke little the following morning amid the nervous patter of students settling in for a quiz on advanced mathematics. Or perhaps they spoke no more or less than they ever did, and it was only Arthur's hypersensitive consciousness that perceived a difference. He agonized over her coldness. Mr. Hibbert rose to begin, but before he could open his mouth there came a quiet knock on the classroom door. The face of the school's guidance counselor peeked in. Mrs. Quinn was a round and joyful woman. Her tall, stiff hairstyle had not changed since she trod those very halls as a student. A billowing muumuu failed to camouflage her ample girth.

"Mr. Hibbert... I need Arthur for a moment," she hissed in a whisper that approached the volume of casual conversation.

"Thank you, Mrs. Quinn," Mr. Hibbert replied. "I'll send him round as soon as he finishes his quiz."

She thought for a moment. "I'm afraid I need him immediately," she said.

Mr. Hibbert considered this under the scrutiny of several dozen pairs of eyes. He seemed to conclude that the disruption of arguing with Mrs. Quinn would be less than that of allowing Arthur to leave. "Very well," he said.

Arthur rose and followed her out. He accompanied her through hallways lined with steel lockers and banners announcing the Homecoming dance on painted construction paper. Entering Mrs. Quinn's office, he found Mrs. Pifflethorpe seated across a small table from a pair of middle-aged men in dark suits and plain, knit ties. His mother rose along with one of the men, who extended a hand. Arthur shook it. The man was thin, almost gaunt, with a high forehead and oiled black hair. Papery lips failed to conceal a set of teeth badly stained by coffee and cigarettes. A pair of reading glasses hung from a cord around his neck.

"Welcome, Arthur," the man said. "Please... sit."

Arthur glanced to his mother, whose bewildered eyes told him she would follow whatever lead he chose to take. He sat. She and the man retook their seats.

"I'm Harvey Ellison," the man said. "This is my associate, Mr. Lutz."

"Pleased to meet you," said Arthur.

"I'll get right to it," Harvey Ellison went on. "We're from Armagast Enterprises. I suppose you saw last night's announcement?"

Arthur nodded, his mind scrambling after a possible purpose for the conversation.

"We've spoken to your mother," said Mr. Ellison, "and she's

provided us with her permission to offer you a position on the crew of the *Argo*. Do you know what that means?"

Arthur knew what it meant but could not summon a response, positive or negative. After a moment of silence, the man went on.

"You've been selected, you see. Should you choose to accept, you'll be among the first corps of cadets to enter the training academy. This opens the possibility of eventually becoming a part of the crew."

Arthur found his voice. "Selected?" was all he managed.

The man pursed his lips into a beneficent scowl. "Selected... yes. It's quite complicated, you know, and the particulars are not terribly important. We'll have time to get into it later, should you decide to accept our proposition."

The particulars were, of course, terribly important, but Arthur was not the sort to challenge the authority of adults. He looked to Mrs. Pifflethorpe for rescue. She appeared as confounded as he. Mrs. Quinn sat behind a desk at the far end of the room, unsure whether she should pay overt attention or pretend to work.

"You needn't decide immediately, of course," said Mr. Ellison, extending a hand with a small slip of paper. "Either way, you'll first need to graduate. Here's my card. On it you'll find the number to call when you've made up your mind. I should point out that choosing to accept is not irrevocable. The training program will take quite some time, and at any point you may choose to opt out."

They again sat for a moment in silence. The two men glanced at one another.

"Do you have any questions?"

Silence, and with it, Arthur's mind regained function with a furious plunge. Memory flooded him. He saw Mr. Pifflethorpe fussing as he balanced his telescope on a cheap tripod. He saw

William beaming out from his spaceman helmet on Christmas morning. He felt the warmth radiating from the body of Sloane Villanueva as she lay beside him on the dock, gazing up at an expanse of stars.

"Why was Arthur selected for this?" Mrs. Pifflethorpe said. "How could you know anything about him?"

Harvey Ellison again pursed his lips and scowled good-naturedly. "Yes, well... I'm not in a position to comment on the particulars. Frankly, I'm not entirely familiar with them myself. You would need to speak with Al in Human Resources."

Silence.

Arthur saw himself in his bedroom with William, sent there nearly a decade ago by Mrs. Pifflethorpe to await the judgment of their father over some childhood misdemeanor. He saw William hanging upside-down from the bunk bed, going cross-eyed behind the visor of his helmet, laughing, chasing away the dread that gripped him at the prospect of Mr. Pifflethorpe's return from work.

"You'll find all of the information you may require on our website," Mr. Lutz cut in. "Instructions for logging into the nominee portal are on the card."

The men glanced at one another again and stood. It seemed this was not the reaction they were accustomed to seeing.

"Very well," said Mr. Ellison. "You know how to reach me."

They moved toward the door. Mrs. Quinn sprang to her feet to open it for them. After they had passed through but before it swung closed, Arthur found his voice. "I'll go," he said.

The men turned back. "I beg your pardon?" said Mr. Ellison.

"I'll go," Arthur repeated.

"Excellent," the man replied. "We'll be in touch."

Chapter Three

Arthur left Mrs. Quinn's office with silence ringing in his ears, as though he had not yet shaken the water from them after plunging deep into a pool. Mrs. Pifflethorpe had taken hold of his arm in what could have been either a gesture of protective motherliness or sheer dazed terror. At the time, the fact of his mother taking his arm struck him, and even more than the conversation of the previous five minutes made him feel he had stepped past the cusp of adulthood. For the first time, he saw the crêpe streamers and construction-paper banners adorning the walls and thought they belonged back in the halls of middle school. The agitated, fluttering monologue of Mrs. Quinn, who bustled at his mother's opposite elbow whispering a fierce guidance-counselor stream of consciousness into her ear, drifted past him unheeded. All of a sudden, everything seemed so small.

His mother left him at the door to Mr. Hibbert's classroom. Mrs. Quinn's wide smile and round, glistening eyeballs strained to expand themselves into the plump, red flesh of her cheeks as she gripped Arthur's hand in her own and pumped it vigorously.

"Congratulations, young man. Congratulations," she said. "I never had any doubt you would go far." Then looking toward Mrs. Pifflethorpe, she said again, "I never had any doubt."

Overcome, she linked arms with Arthur's mother and hustled her off toward the exit. Arthur turned to face the classroom door. He paused with a hand on the knob. After the thunderous beating of his heart subsided to a manageable level, he slipped in and wove his way between rows of desks to his seat. Isabel met his eyes as he approached, asking an unspoken question to which he could only shrug.

It took time for news of Arthur's nomination to leak out. Longer, in fact, than his agitated mind was prepared to accept. Long before anyone could have heard of it, he began to see admiration or envy in the most casual of glances thrown his way. He carried on the everyday business of life only with difficulty, feeling as he did that the brushing of teeth or mowing of grass was all such a terrible waste of time. He could not concentrate well enough to learn the motivations of Franco in the Spanish Civil War or the historical significance of Jonathan Swift's Lilliputians.

Arthur's distraction did little permanent damage to his academic prospects. It did, however, affect his relationship with Isabel. The brief interval of distance that opened between them, soon to be rapidly closed as he snapped back to her like a stretched rubber band, served to nudge her further toward the conclusion that had already been growing in her mind: Arthur was holding her back. Had he realized she was forming this opinion, he would likely have broken the news of his impending celebrity in a desperate attempt to draw her back. But he waited. When he told Isabel his great secret, he wanted it to be perfect.

That perfection, he imagined, would best be realized in conjunction with some grand and romantic affair. The Homecoming dance was scheduled for the following Saturday. After an evening of engaging banter, of sweeping her about the dance floor with the envious regard of the school turned upon him, of gazing into her eyes across a candlelit table and pouring out their hearts to one another, he would draw himself up, steel his countenance, and tell her that in a few short months he would be heading off to the stars. She would weep and declare her affection and beg he find some way to bring her along on his travels. With fortitude and determination, he would tell her he would look into it.

This is not the way it happened.

The evening of the dance began well enough. Concealed pride swelling in Arthur's breast gave him a renewed confidence that could only be appealing to a girl such as Isabel. Despite the rusted-out wheel wells and sagging springs of his mother's station wagon, he pulled up to the curb of the house in Bella Vista with a smile on his face reflecting joy that would not be contained. He bounded up the walk with a bouquet of carnations in his hand and the pant legs of a rented tuxedo riding up above his ankles.

Mrs. Weiss answered the door. "Hello, Arthur," she said with an indistinct note of compassion. "Come in. Isabel will be right down."

It was as Arthur had pictured it—as everyone pictures these things. He made awkward small talk with Mrs. Weiss, soon joined by Mr. Weiss. Isabel arrived on the landing above and made her way down the stairs in a shimmering green gown with the frills and ruffles that can only be pulled off by the very young and the very old. Her hair was pinned up in ringlets and sculpted locks that hung just so over her temples and revealed the flawless, creamy skin of her nape.

"I need a picture," said Mrs. Weiss, and she arranged them just so, hand placed thus, chin up, turned a little more to the left. "And... smile!"

The ritual complete, Mr. Weiss stepped forward. "I have a surprise for the two of you," he said. He pulled from his pocket a set of keys and held them aloft, dangling them with a faint jingle before his beaming countenance.

"Dad... no!" said Isabel with a manufactured gasp of disbelief. Had he not offered up the Maserati, she had every intention of cajoling it out of him. This kind of thing was not difficult. "You're the best," she gushed, standing on tiptoe to squeeze him around the neck.

It was only after Mr. Weiss had backed the sleek, black sports car into the driveway that the implications of this arrangement occurred to Arthur. He would not be the one driving the Maserati. Isabel snatched the keys from her father's fingers and bounced with a wobbly, mincing jog on three-inch heels to the driver's door. Mrs. Weiss held the passenger door for Arthur, closing it carefully behind him as if to emphasize the importance of exercising the appropriate degree of care in handling the automobile.

Arthur repeated to himself with all his might that being driven to the dance by his date made no difference. But this was the first crack in the image he had formed of the evening ahead. Being driven to the dance by his date felt disconcertingly akin to being driven by his mother. Looking out on the dilapidated station wagon as they glided away in Mr. Weiss' Maserati only heightened the impression that his newfound manhood had been somehow called into question.

It did not help matters that Isabel knew how to drive this sort of car. Heels or no heels, she worked the pedals like a race-car driver and cornered with a firm assurance that thrust Arthur from side to side in his seat despite the grip he maintained on the door handle. Acceleration thrust him back into the heated leather cushions as she burst off the line of each traffic light in a throbbing roar. It hung him against the straps of his seatbelt as she braked to a stop at the next.

Despite the absence of a valet in the circular drive before the school gymnasium, Isabel had no intention of leaving the car unnoticed in the parking lot. This would have been Arthur's last hope of maintaining some degree of mastery over his situation. She pulled to a stop before the doors and swung a sculpted leg out onto the pavement in perfect imitation of a Hollywood star-let. A line of rented limousines and family minivans began immediately to form behind the obstacle, and the clutch of chaperones buzzing about the foyer insisted she move the car. After a brief consultation, it was decided Arthur would move it to the lot. By this time, the admiring scrutiny of the masses had moved on.

When he returned, Isabel had embarked upon the festivities in earnest. Enveloped in the churning mass of her friends, she basked in the light of veneration. White teeth gleamed out from the dimness. Bass echoed amid the cinderblock walls and basketball hoops. A haze of smoke billowing from beneath a disc-jockey table on the stage was pierced by swooping laser beams. Arthur edged his way through the throng to her side and, after several false starts in communicating over the crashing music, received confirmation she would indeed like a Pepsi.

The table of refreshments was crowded with students, and it was some time before Arthur found his way back to his date. When he picked her out through the crowd, a plastic cup of soda clutched in each of his hands, she was swinging her body to the rhythm, surrounded by a hovering bevy of girlfriends who soaked up the covetous gazes of every boy in the room.

Determined not to be put off, he made his way to her. But she was no longer interested in holding a drink, seeing it as an impediment to the quasi-sexual gyrations into which she had thrown her attention. Arthur found a side table on which to deposit the despised cups of Pepsi. At this point he gave up trying to be near her, determining he would not cut an enviable figure alongside the crème of Wilson High School high society. As he had found himself doing so often in the past, he located a dim and unobtrusive space along the wall and watched.

It was toward the end of the evening that Arthur and Isabel again came together. Students were drifting off, and the disc jockey had begun to intersperse the occasional slow song amid a deafening selection of electronica and hip hop. Arthur knew just the thing to tug at the heartstrings of his beloved Isabel. The couple came together once more as Arthur was stepping away from the stage where he had made his request. Every ear buzzed with tinnitus as the volume dropped and the light shifted from strobing white and red to a flood of blue.

Arthur led Isabel to the center of the floor and put his hands on her waist, pulling her close with a self-assurance that surprised even him. The music swelled, this time in a throbbing pulse that had spoken to Arthur's innermost being since his earliest days. It was the music that had emanated thin and tinny from the old cabin at the lake where Mr. Pifflethorpe had once slipped away with his wife. It was, and had always been, the soundtrack to high romance. Arthur and Isabel swayed, cheek pressed to cheek, the scent of her filling his nostrils. The heart-beat rhythm and bittersweet voice of Bill Withers battered at Arthur's soul with the indisputable certitude that there would be no sunshine when she was gone.

Taken through the wringer that evening, Arthur failed to realize Isabel did not share his enthusiasm for old rhythm and blues. Nor did the other young men and women in the room, it seemed. Most had mistaken the interval in the pounding beat for the conclusion of the festivities and spread outward from where Arthur clung to Isabel on the dance floor like a sheen of oil fleeing a drop of dish soap. Eyes deliciously closed and oblivious to all but Isabel, Arthur strove for his practiced slow-motion sway, weight shifting from foot to foot with alternate beats in the rhythm. Isabel disagreed with his vision and rolled her hips in time to the quarter notes. Eventually he relented and settled into a tuneless shuffle that failed to keep time with either rhythm.

He came crashing back to earth as he felt Isabel's body go rigid and her whisper cut through the lingering notes of the song.

"We should get going," she said.

Arthur opened his eyes. Isabel was not gazing into them as he had pictured moments before. She scanned the crowd as it studied them with bemused scorn and made its way slowly toward the exits.

Scurrying to the safety of her girlfriends with Arthur trailing disconsolately behind, Isabel rearranged the remainder of the night's activities. Wouldn't it be great, she asked, to go to the drive-in with everyone else rather than the shabby Italian restaurant that Arthur had selected? He replied that this was a fantastic idea, forcing his face into a mask of delight.

The ride home to change their clothes was a nadir in Arthur's life to that point. He listened half-heartedly to Isabel's excited voice recounting the triumphs of the evening. The ardor of her monologue was surely heightened by desire to paper over the anguish she must have known was obliterating the final remnants of her date's shattered spirit. He kept his face turned toward the window, hiding a glorious tear that slipped down his cheek. He found himself half-hoping she would notice, pull the car to the side of the road, wipe it away, and proclaim a heart-rendingly sincere apology. Words fail to express the torment in his soul. For us, it is like watching a speeding locomotive crashing over a precipice in an old, silent, black-and-white film reel; it seems distant, unreal, and vaguely comical. For the hapless passengers being bloodily torn limb from limb, it is none such.

After an obligatory kiss on the doorstep of Isabel's house, Arthur drove away in his mother's station wagon with a promise he would meet up with her later at the drive-in. He never did.

An unspoken understanding was established that the romance between Arthur and Isabel had ended. With blind cruelty only the young can muster, she tiptoed unobtrusively away as if a lack of sudden movements would prevent Arthur from noticing. They still met from time to time in the library when Isabel's need for help overruled her desire not to lead him on. Once she even invited him out with her group of friends, hoping to draw off his attention on one of its lesser figures and so ease a lingering sense of guilt. Arthur declined. He had taken to shuffling through the halls with as little social engagement as possible, forswearing even glances from other past loves.

His goal was to be forgotten, disappearing into the background only to reemerge someday in the recollections of his classmates when they recognized his face on the television. *Is that Arthur?* they would think. *I guess I always knew he would make something of himself.* But as soon as such a thought forced its way into his mind, he would push it out again, telling himself he never wanted any of these people to remember him.

Remember him they would, and it began when Armagast Enterprises announced the corps of Argonauts to the world. The corporation remained vague on the nature of the criteria involved in these selections, and rumors spread like wildfire. It was all connections, said some, as with admittance to the well-paid ranks of the business community. Being among those who would escape, leaving to their fate the sorry inhabitants of Earth, required knowing someone who knew someone. Others guessed at darker purposes: establishment of a race genetically pure and free from human foibles. Most of these flitted about the edges of the truth, mixing reason with stiff doses of cynicism and conspiracy theory.

Each of these rumors was discounted by the inhabitants of Arthur's little town when they discovered he was among the elect. The son of a poor factory worker who had died of a rare genetic disorder, he was certainly not well-connected or a picture of health. Even those who recalled his brief fling with Isabel Weiss (and fewer remembered this than Arthur supposed) were not convinced he had somehow entered the good graces of her father and thereby achieved acquaintance with anyone of note at Armagast Enterprises. Not a few assumed it was some mistake.

As word continued to spread, Arthur resolved to make one final attempt at reestablishing himself in Isabel's affections. Seated next to her at their table in the library, he looked up from his book and met her eyes.

"You've heard about the *Argo*?" he said.

"Of course I have," she replied. A note of petulance was her way of establishing boundaries.

"I'm going," he said.

"You're what?"

"I'm going. They picked me. I'll be leaving as soon as finals are over, and I don't think I'll ever be coming back." He relished the dramatic finality of the phrasing. He had practiced it.

It took a moment for her confusion to resolve itself. "OK," she said. "Cool. That sounds like fun."

There was a pause while Arthur considered this.

"I don't know if *fun* is the right word for it," he said. "I mean, that's not why I'm going."

"Mmm-hmm." Isabel's eyes drifted back to her textbook. They returned to him with a cold hardness. "Dad says that whole thing is a publicity stunt," she said.

He dropped the subject, and they went back to studying.

Despite the best efforts of the town to disparage the notion of Beckett Armagast creating some modern-day version of Noah's Ark, it became clear this was no mere news-cycle flash in the pan. Reporters shuttled up to the *Argo* amid the stream of rockets lifting off from Florida and California and New Zealand sent back images of steel corridors and banks of computers. The world saw sweeping views of what would soon be farmland, curving upward into the distance with the rising circumference of the ship's outer hull. The mood of excitement spread like a virus from Silicon Valley to Denver to Kansas City.

His classmates' behavior toward Arthur began to change. Standoffishness slowly turned to ingratiation. By the time the packet of admission materials arrived in its bulging envelope stuffed with glossy full-color brochures and minute legal disclosures, he had begun to answer their questions with a confidence outstripping his knowledge of what was to come. He stayed up that night reading every word of the packet's contents.

The last one to come around was Isabel. After Arthur had walked the stage at his graduation ceremony and the school administrators had fallen over one another to congratulate what would surely be the most remarkable alumnus in the school's history, she surprised him in the corridor under the grandstands of the football stadium as he emerged from the restroom. She had been crying there alone, her sniffles echoing amid the stark white glare of fluorescent tube lights and painted concrete. She leaned back against the wall, her robe draped over an arm and her face buried in a hand.

She looked up at him as he stopped before her. She pushed her body erect, wiping tears from her cheeks. He let her wrap her arms around his neck and nestle her body against his. "I love you, Arthur," she whispered, her eyes inches from his own. She kissed him, and he kissed her back.

"I love you too, Izz," Arthur replied.

In the flood of emotion, there was nothing else he could say. His reply was the first time he had said those words to a girl. They faded to inaudibility in the parched rasp of his throat.

Isabel accompanied Arthur and Mrs. Pifflethorpe to the airport when he left the following week. Half the population of the town was also there to see him off. Arthur looked back before rounding the final corner into the terminal. The snapshot in his mind of Isabel standing next to Mrs. Pifflethorpe, surrounded by a crowd of onlookers, would carry him through the months ahead. This and the fact that, deep in his heart, he had to wonder whether the whole thing would really come off.

Chapter Four

There was little in the way of coherent thought passing through Arthur's head as he rounded the corner of the airport's terminal and lost sight of everything he had known. What he experienced was similar to a sharp blow to the head—more stunning than painful (at least at first) and propelling one abruptly into a haze of clouded perception. Every movement was like the beating of his heart or the churning of his digestive system: proceeding on with the business of keeping him alive even as his brain made no substantial contribution to the operation.

Even the novelty of his first time on an airplane could not cut through the mood. The weight of all he had left behind did not come crashing down until long after the commuter plane's engines had run up with a thin whine and dragged the fuselage bucking and straining into the air. He changed planes twice, once to a properly magnificent jetliner and then to a small, high-wing prop for the journey's final leg. Despite a steady drip of adrenaline that left him feeling like a violin string ready to snap, he fell asleep at last. He awoke with a crick in his neck and a damp spot on the shoulder of his shirt. He looked out the window and down on a mountain range that crumpled the surface of the earth into ridgelines and river valleys, snow-capped spires and whitewater canyons, stretching nearly unscarred by human activity to a distant horizon. Nestled in the foothills below, just visible if he pressed his forehead against the glass, was a postage stamp of concrete and steel cut into the parabolic sweep of a hillside that broke at its crest into fissured globules of granite. This is the place where it hit him. This is where he felt truly and completely alone.

The plane bumped to a stop on an isolated strip of tarmac with only a rusted hangar of corrugated sheet metal to suggest it was an airport. Soon Arthur discovered he was not so alone as he had imagined. The Armagast Enterprises training facility—that tiny postage stamp in the foothills of an icebound mountain range—was hundreds of miles distant from the nearest remnants of civilization, which had tapered out beneath the droning engines of the aircraft as Arthur slept. The only people arriving at this outpost were staff and inductees to the *Argo*'s first corps of cadets.

Instructions specified Arthur was to bring with him nothing but the clothes on his back. He and the scattering of passengers had no roller-bags to drag along as they stepped from the still-humming aircraft. They strung out across the expanse of tarmac as they walked toward a motor coach idling just inside the fence line.

The sky was blue, but the sun hid behind a low band of clouds to the southwest, its diffuse light washing the landscape in shadowless homogeneity. Arthur checked his wristwatch. It was two o'clock in the morning; or that was the time back where he had started the day's travels. The airfield's slab of concrete seemed dropped arbitrarily in the middle of nowhere. Beyond a chain-link fence topped with razor wire, black spruce fought up through arctic tundra. Windswept foothills formed a ragged line against the northern sky, obscuring the horizon in an unbroken line from east to west. The humming plane went suddenly silent, and a strange stillness descended, its depth heightened by a light but steady rush of cold wind.

A man drew up to walk alongside him. "It wouldn't seem to have put them out much to pull the damned bus up to the plane, now would it?" he said.

Arthur looked up from where his attention had been absorbed by the pavement before his feet. The man addressing him was a good deal older than he. On a pale, middle-aged complexion mottled with blotches of rosacea, the man carried a look of boyish enthusiasm that clashed with the premature gray of his neatly combed hair. He wore blue jeans and a sport coat over a black shirt.

"I beg your pardon, sir?" Arthur said after a pause.

"Yes... excellent. I've found an English speaker at last," the man said. He huffed and pushed back the panels of his jacket to hike his pants before going on. He was full of nervous tics, his hands rarely remaining still for more than a moment. "The bus —why the hell couldn't they pull it up to the door? It's not like this godforsaken place is busy."

Arthur's eyes flicked down to a clerical collar that encircled the man's neck.

"Father McIntosh," the man said, extending a hand.

"Pleased to meet you... sir." Arthur had never met a priest and was unsure of the appropriate form of address. "Arthur Pifflethorpe." He shook the priest's hand.

"Likewise, Arthur," came the reply. "Aren't you a little young to be here, if you don't mind my saying?" Father McIntosh continued to grip Arthur's hand as they walked. His palm was soft and fleshy.

Arthur did not know how to respond to this question. He shrugged. The priest's grip on his hand was disconcerting, but he was unsure how to disengage. "I just graduated," he said. He was uncomfortable under the man's beaming stare. "They have a need for... clergy... on the *Argo*?"

"So it would seem!" Father McIntosh gave a delighted chortle. "I don't imagine any of us really knows why we're here. Honestly, I have my doubts about whether our new employers are clear on the point. It's quite an operation they've thrown together all at one go. I wonder how much of it is clockwork and how much is baling wire and chewing gum."

"I beg your pardon, sir?"

The padre chuckled again and at last released Arthur's hand. Arthur's palm had grown damp, and he subconsciously wiped it on his pants. This redoubled Father McIntosh's amusement. His shoulders bounced with suppressed laughter, his eyes closed tight, mouth spread in a toothy grin as he enjoyed the private joke. "Nothing to worry about. Nothing to worry about," he said. "Blind speculation, of course."

Father McIntosh followed Arthur onto the bus and took the seat next to him. "Where do you hail from, young man?" he said, rocking side to side to conform the seat cushion to the shape of his buttocks.

Arthur desperately wanted solitude. He needed time to process the thoughts fluttering about his consciousness and refusing to be ordered, stacked, and straightened. It was not to be. He answered the priest's question in clipped tones.

"Well, well, I've been through those parts," Father McIntosh said. He was settling in for a chat and, seeing Arthur was not a talker, determined to fill the deficit of his own accord. "It was a long time ago, and a bit further west as I recall. Dayton? How far is that?" He did not wait for an answer. "I'm out in San Antonio now, or was. A chaplain, you know... military... or was, I suppose. So, I've been all over. It was the Far East before that." A full recount of Father McIntosh's history followed. He had gone into seminary from a small town in rural Vermont and had entered the service soon after, bouncing from one duty station to the next for a decade or more.

The driver finished accounting for his passengers and pulled away, swinging the bus in a circle and off toward a break in the fence line. A gate motored open as they approached. The road beyond cut through spruce forest toward the distant hills. The priest may or may not have been talking to Arthur, but talk he did. His eyes roved over the landscape and the other passengers as he spoke, his hands never ceasing their elaboration upon his words. Eventually Arthur gave up on his effort to appear interested and turned his attention to the scenery passing outside the window. Father McIntosh did not seem to mind.

A layer of tall grass and brambles grew thick beneath the stunted trees, the vegetation thinning here and there into heavy bogs. Green shoots pushed up through dead, brown remnants crushed down by snows of the previous winter. Freshly laid blacktop wound this way and that through the tangle, occasionally offering glimpses of the mountain range toward which they drove. The road's surface had begun to crumble away despite the apparent recency of its construction. Frost-heave bubbled the surface and split it from shoulder to shoulder in great yawning cracks over which the bus had to slow as it bumped past. They had to wait for an orange-vested road crew to pause their work and wave the bus through.

The chaplain had found something amusing in his own monologue and begun to chuckle. Arthur turned back upon realizing a response was expected. "...Baling wire and chewing gum, my boy!" he was saying. "Hope they put more thought into our other means of transportation... heh, heh. If they couldn't account for the permafrost, I don't know how they'll manage up there." He rolled his eyes toward the sky. Arthur gave the expected smile and nod. The chaplain appeared satisfied and carried on. Arthur went back to his window.

Foothills of the mountain range began to dominate the scene. Their destination came into view. It was a cluster of buildings perhaps a quarter of the way up the hillside, just above a low tree line. A complex of glass and steel sank deep into the bedrock behind. To the front it stepped outward onto the rectangular promontory created by a tall, sheer retaining wall of chiseled granite. Above, the hillside was covered with low-growing cranberry and fireweed cut here and there with the gray slashes of rockslides. The road was a narrow ribbon winding its way up toward the facility, cutting more bald expanses of scree into the slope.

"I suppose our man Beckett got a bargain on land up here," Father McIntosh was saying. "A bargain! Have to wonder if he accounted for the cost of travel, not to mention maintaining all of this concrete over eight months of winter. The heating bills! Just imagine! Seems the outskirts of Los Angeles and a good strong fence would have better served the purpose. Not so mysterious, though. There is that. Image to keep up with, and so forth..."

As the terrain began to rise, a view opened over tundra and muskeg dotted with thaw lakes that reflected a pale sky. A glittering band of river swept down from the mountains and spread into the plain, meandering and breaking up into a web of channels and gravel bars until vanishing into the haze.

Reaching the retaining wall, the road paralleled its face as it dwindled to meet the hillside. They rounded a last corner and glided the remaining few hundred meters on a perimeter road separated from the sheer drop by a parapet. Upper floors of the buildings were supported by bare concrete columns that opened up a wide breezeway looking through into courtyard quadrangles of flagstone. Glass-encased stairwells provided access to mirrored buildings framed in steel that rose five or six stories above and downward into whatever floors existed below ground level.

The bus stopped in the center of a small and otherwise empty parking lot on the outermost lip of the promontory. Arthur's eyes, captured by the sweeping view, were drawn back to earth. The bus had stopped. The doors hissed open before a grid of yellow footprints painted out in even rank and file on the concrete of the parking lot. Beyond stood half a dozen men in closely tailored blue jumpsuits with epauletted shoulders, name tags, and insignia emblazoning their chests on chromed pins sculpted into glinting swoops and streaks. They wore mirrored sunglasses in the meager, washed-out light.

It was all very scripted, and quite dramatic. Father McIntosh said so with more than a touch of irony.

It has been said one should beware enterprises that require new clothes, and not rather a new wearer of clothes. The sense of this came over Arthur as he stood stark naked in a bare, tiled room with twenty other men and saw the crumpled pile of their clothing hustled away in a laundry cart. The nakedness was disconcerting. This kind of thing was not done where he came from, not even in the locker room of the high school. There, row upon row of showerheads went unused but for one wrinkled old football coach with a receding hairline and a paunch.

From the moment Father McIntosh found him on the parking apron of the airstrip, Arthur had not had a spare instant to settle his thoughts. The strain was wearing on him. A stream of consciousness from his newfound friend had ended only when the drill instructors boarded the bus and began shouting with incoherent fury. Their desire, it eventually became clear, was that the recruits form up outside the bus, each with their feet on a painted pair of footprints, eyes forward, and arms at their sides. Here they stood for quite some time while raised voices imparted to them the essential nature of discipline to all their future endeavors.

The arrivals were soon herded off into interminable hallways that snaked through the bowels of the complex. From counter after counter, through gaps cut into cinderblock walls, they were issued goods required in their newly begun lives: boots and jumpsuits, toothbrushes and safety razors, book bags and laptop computers. Heads were shorn of hair. Not deigning to move his feet, the barber (if barber he was) spun the chair along with its occupant as he ran the shears up and down over scalp after scalp.

There was a respite as recruits filtered through a carpeted office set with rows of cubicles. These were occupied by crisply dressed professionals who appeared to be lawyers. Arthur sat across a desk from one of these. She recited a memorized litany while flipping through a stack of pages turned to the frantically skimming eyes of her subject. She explained the particulars of nondisclosure agreements, waivers, powers of attorney, and various other provisos should Arthur choose to continue in the program of instruction. Arthur chose to continue despite being hazy on the details. He signed.

The showers were the final stop. Bald and naked, recruits scrubbed themselves clean and dressed in unfashionably snug white underwear and blue jumpsuits issued somewhere previously in the warren of hallways. Through it all, they had been hurried along as if the *Argo* itself were waiting. All went quiet as Arthur was deposited at last in his dormitory room, like a pill into its blister pack on the assembly line of a pharmaceuticals manufacturer.

The room had two bunks along one wall and a pair of desks on the other. At the far end was a set of windows. He tossed two nylon duffels full of gear onto the top bunk and swept back the curtains. The room was on one of the upper floors of the building. It looked out over the magnificent view of tundra, forest, lakes, and distant river. The sun, never having fully set, was on its way back up toward the zenith. He sat and waited, looking out over the view and thinking of his mother and of Isabel.

Adrenaline slowly began to ebb. With it went the numbness that had carried him along with a resolution that would likely have been beyond his means. In its place came an ache. It was the ache that had touched him briefly as he looked down on this place from the airplane. It was not remorse. It was not fear. It was not even second-guessing of the decision he had made (although this played its part). It was an ache defined by cloudiness of perception: a sense that separation from all he loved went beyond simple geography. It was dread that even memories would be lost. Perhaps we do not require so many words to describe the sensation. Arthur was homesick. But only those of us who have loved as Arthur loved can understand the fullness of the word.

Whatever roommate would be joining him had not arrived by the time he was collected for the day's remaining activities. A drill instructor began banging on doors far down the hallway. The banging drew closer and closer until the fist clattered Arthur's door on its hinges. Through the shouting, Arthur was brought to understand he should form up with the other cadets in the hallway. Hustled down a long corridor interrupted at alternating intervals by alcoves and pairs of doors, he reached an orderly's desk at the far end and joined a queue of men standing along the wall.

At some unseen signal, the line began to move. It carried them down a stairwell to the ground floor and across a wide expanse of flagstone. All around were the steel-and-glass buildings of the training facility. In the center was a massive bronze mockup of the *Argo* mounted on a great pedestal of stone. It looked like an altar to a deified can of Coca-Cola. Mountains loomed behind.

Upon reaching a building at a rear corner of the complex, the recruits filed through a set of doors into a cavernous auditorium. Rows of seats sloped down toward a stage set with a single row of chairs along a curtained backdrop. Spotlights and audiovisual equipment hung from trusses mounted to a high ceiling. A balcony of the hall's mezzanine projected out over the rear rows of seats. It was crowded with cameras, microphones, and a crush of reporters. They climbed over seat-backs and elbowed past one another to position equipment for the coming event.

Many men had arrived before Arthur, and more followed with each passing minute. They were directed to seats to the left of a center aisle. Slowly the buzz of conversation built as the crowd sorted itself according to language. The volume of chatter rose. Someone began snoring and was jostled awake. Father McIntosh found Arthur in the crowd. He took the adjacent seat and began an analysis of the morning's activities. Drill instructors? They must have been lured away from Parris Island or Lackland with offers of exorbitant salaries. Surely, they served little purpose but to humor the vanities of a corporate elite who fancied themselves military commanders. The self-important lot had decided they needed discipline in the ranks and set about determining where they could buy it. The man of God was particularly resentful of the head-shaving.

The running commentary continued in a conspiratorial whisper as they watched the auditorium fill. The hum of cocktail-party conversation rose a notch as doors along the opposite wall opened to admit files of women dressed similarly in blue jumpsuits. These were seated to the right of the aisle. What hair remained on their heads was roughly hacked to regulation length. Soon the auditorium was full, and an agitated silence descended, broken here and there by murmurs of dwindling conversation and a hacking cough from somewhere in the rear.

The room fell into shadow as overhead lights dimmed and the stage was flooded with spots. A rippling thrill ran through the audience as Beckett Armagast strode down the center aisle and bounded up a short flight of steps to the stage. He wore his headset and trademark collarless shirt brimming with chest hair. Behind him, a line of five uniformed men and women stepped from the wings and took their places at attention, each before a blue-plastic chair arranged to the rear of the stage. Beckett glanced back and waved them to their seats. He gazed out at the audience for a moment, letting the tension build. He squinted against the glare of the spotlights.

"Welcome, Argonauts," he said at last. He let a rippling murmur flit through the crowd. "I offer my hearty welcome to the inaugural corps selected to be the first in human history to populate other planets... other star systems."

Silence.

"Welcome to the forefathers of the uncountable trillions who will one day fill the heavens. Those of you who succeed here and join the crew of the *Argo* will be heroes... legends... like Odysseus... like Alexander the Great. Christopher Columbus on a scale unimaginable just a few short years ago. Welcome."

Silence.

"The task we set before you, glorious though it may be, should not be taken lightly. We're asking you to set out on a journey from which you will never return." He paused before repeating himself. "From which you will never return. We are asking you to foreswear families... freedom... sunshine... in the name of ensuring that humanity will endure forever. In the name of diversifying our precarious hold on one fragile little ball of rock. Should your mission meet with the wildest success—

success which is in no way assured—you will all live and die and never see your objective attained. Your children and your children's children will live and die as you did: alone in a pinpoint of aluminum and steel in the vast, dark emptiness of interstellar space."

He was working himself up, and the words came faster.

"But what a glorious sacrifice you make. You will be starting a new branch in the human family that will never again intersect with the bloodlines of those left behind. The DNA that shapes your bodies and minds will be the pattern for what will one day—millions of years into a future beyond reckoning—shape bodies and minds that fill the universe."

The curtains to the rear of the stage rolled slowly back to reveal a floor-to-ceiling projection screen. On it was an image of stars on a background of black. It panned in toward the familiar orb of indeterminate blue-white haze that everyone had seen plastered on news reports and media feeds for months.

"Under the precedent set by history's great explorers, we have selected a name for the planet that will be the *Argo*'s destination. We call it Planet Colchis. What you see here are rays of light that left Colchis hundreds of years ago: hundreds of years, traveling at the speed of light. The time it takes you and your children and your children's children to travel that distance will be far greater. In point of fact, we don't know how long it will take to reach this oasis in the vast desert of space. As for any of the explorers of centuries past, there are too many unknowns to calculate such things. Small differences in the speed at which the *Argo* leaves our solar system, small disturbances imparted by course corrections and unanticipated gravitational fields, or any of a thousand other unforeseen factors will have enormous impact over the distances involved in the journey. What is certain is that you will never see Planet Colchis."

A pause.

"Nor your children...

"Nor your children's children.

"The Armagast Enterprises team has combed the known universe for a destination conducive to human settlement. We have built upon research of the world's finest astronomers and astrophysicists. Colchis is our best guess. The unified consensus of the world's greatest minds has determined it is the exoplanet with the highest likelihood of habitability among all the exoplanets we have discovered over decades of searching. The *Argo* may arrive and find an arid and toxic waste. We can't be certain. There is no way to be certain. Should that happen, what crew exists—and it will be a crew for whom Earth is not a memory but a legend—that crew will decide what new course to set. Will they continue on to another destination? Return to Earth? These are circumstances and decisions we have no way of forecasting.

"These are considerable sacrifices we ask of you. Consider them well, for once you set foot aboard the *Argo* a few short months from now, there will be no going back. At any point in time during training, you can raise your hand and step aside. Another will be chosen to fill your shoes. The decision is a weighty one, and I urge none of you to take it lightly. At any time, you can go back to your lives, your families... a lifetime of sunshine and fresh air. Your first opportunity is right now."

He waited. The silence roared in Arthur's ears. A handful of people rose and hurried up the aisles, disappearing through the doors to the rear. There was no conscious line of reasoning that kept Arthur in his seat, but rising from it never crossed his mind.

Chapter Five

Silence descended after the auditorium doors clanged shut behind the last of the departing recruits. Beckett Armagast's hands went to his hips as he let it draw out. "Very well," he said at last. "There will be more. There are some of you right now who have made the decision and don't want to proclaim it publicly. There are more who will make it in the coming minutes, hours, days. So be it. You will speak with the cadre and be home before the sun sets on your loved ones.

"For the rest of you, I'd like to introduce the senior leadership team who will be in command both here at Earth Station One and aboard the *Argo*. Most of those you work and train with here will be among those departing on the journey. We are creating not just a crew, but a society: a self-contained world that will become its own offshoot of human history. The master of that world is Admiral Malachi Demarion."

Beckett turned back as the admiral rose from his seat and stood rigid, staring out at the audience. The brim of a wheel-cap cast shadow over the upper half of a round face that was jowly and mustachioed, with smooth, pink skin and a fringe of dark hair—in need of a trim—that emerged from under his cap. One could only guess at the meaning of each of a myriad of ribbons adorning his chest.

"Second in command: Quartermaster Julia Kumar."

Rising to her feet beside the admiral was a slight woman of dark complexion and a great quantity of black hair tied back firmly in a bun at the base of her skull. Her jawline was well-formed, her mouth below the shadow of her hat's brim a splash of lipstick that settled into a delicate scowl.

"Lane Beauregard, first officer."

The third in line stood; he was tall, thin, and wrinkled either with age or a lifetime of exposure to the elements.

"Atticus Oluwusi, bosun. You will come to know him well in the coming months."

Bosun Oluwusi was short and stocky, the skin of his face so black its features were lost in the shadows cast by the stage lights. He stood oddly rigid with hands clasped behind his back and chest thrust outward.

"And finally: Sakura Sasaki, chief steward."

The final officer stood. She was sturdy of build and nearly as tall as the tallest of the men. The slice of her face that showed below the brim of her hat looked young, almost childlike, but with a curl to the lips that could be taken for contemptuousness.

Beckett thanked them all, and they took their seats.

"You will have many opportunities to hear from your new commanders: their philosophies, leadership styles, expectations. They and their corps of officers will teach you everything you need to know to survive and flourish in the new environment in which you will find yourselves. That training starts now. Our discussions henceforth will be covered under the nondisclosure agreements you signed earlier today, and I ask that the mezzanine be cleared of press."

He waited, pacing the stage and occasionally glancing up

into the balcony, until the reporters had collected up their cameras and tripods and been hustled out.

Beckett went on. "Each of you was selected for particular reasons. Why you were selected is a question I am often asked. My answer to that question is... I don't know."

He paused for a flicker of laughter to fade.

"None of us really knows for sure, with the exception of our human resources department."

Again, laughter filled the void he left open for it.

"Allow me to introduce you to our human resources department. Allow me to introduce you to Al." He turned with one of the dramatic flourishes with which Arthur was becoming familiar. On the screen flashed an image of some fantastical computer system with lights and wires and transparent wallscreens. A crystalline orb in the center was suspended from the ceiling and appeared to house the most important guts of the thing; this was illuminated by spotlights mounted in a ring above. Below it drifted a pool of smoky vapor like a Halloween witch's cauldron filled with dry ice. "Al is our human resources department. As you will discover, human resources are the key to the success of the *Argo's* mission. Hers will be a journey of many generations, at the far end of which her crew must possess a collective genetic composition strong and diverse enough to populate a planet. This is the central problem around which the particulars of our entire enterprise are constructed.

"It is a problem far beyond the computational skills of even the finest human minds. Hence, we created Al. A quantum-powered artificial intelligence of previously unimaginable power, Al has examined the genetic makeup of every human being on Earth for whom online records exist. Each of you, at one point or another, had your genetic code uploaded to the Web. When you did that, and without knowing it, you entered the greatest lottery of all time: a competition to be among those whose descendants will populate the stars."

As he continued speaking, the screen went dark, and the curtains slid closed behind him. "The success of the *Argo*'s mission depends upon a perfectly orchestrated multigenerational plan. The top geneticists and programmers in the world joined together to create algorithms that power AI's intelligence. We have been accused by some of a kind of modern-day eugenics: building a master race of perfect genetic uniformity. This could not be further from the truth.

"The secret to success is maintaining the highest levels of genetic diversity, to avoid the inbreeding and stagnation that plague small populations. Our core problem is optimization of the *Argo*'s crew size: large enough to maintain a viable population and small enough to live within the means of available resources. Using AI's calculations, our scientists arrived at the minimum number of people the *Argo* would need for its population to survive the journey with an acceptable degree of probability. There are five thousand of you in this room today, each of whom carries a small piece of humanity's future right there in your flesh and blood."

He paused and crossed an arm over his midsection, the opposite elbow resting upon it with his chin cupped in a palm. He seemed to consider his words. "Despite my role in conceiving and designing this project," he said in a voice that had lost some of its thunder, "I was not chosen to join you on this great adventure. In one of my life's biggest regrets, I will not be accompanying you on a voyage that is the culmination of human advancement and likely of my entire career. Order, discipline, planning... these are the watchwords that will determine our success or failure. Even I am not exempt."

He was silent for a moment, then his hands went back to his hips. His voice began to rise once more.

"I am not, however, sending you off into the unknown with a simple fare-thee-well. My soul, if not my body, is wrapped up in the ultimate success or failure of your mission. Because among your ranks will be my daughter, Maisy Armagast."

There was a collective gasp. Beckett lifted a hand to shade his eyes and looked out to a point in the audience as a murmur swelled into a chatter of excited voices. All heads turned to where he looked.

Nothing happened. Everyone began shifting, half-rising, turning about, trying to locate the famed Maisy Armagast, for famous she was. Using her father's wealth and celebrity as a springboard, she had vaulted into the stratosphere of stardom. From social media to reality television, from Adam Sandler to Woody Allen, she had worked her way over a brief twenty years of life to the Hollywood A-list. Her latest film was the highest-grossing production of the summer, and her forays into music were beginning to crack the Top 40. No gala or soiree or red carpet was complete without her perfectly formed face and tangle of raven-black hair to fill the cameras.

Maisy disappointed her father's expectations of a dramatic reveal. She never stood to welcome the gaze of five thousand searching pairs of eyes. No one seemed to know where she was. The buzz of speculation rose. Beckett played off the rebuff and carried on, but his irritation was clear to those not absorbed in identifying their idol among the ranks of carbon-copy uniforms and hastily snipped bobs.

"That's right, my only daughter was among those that Al selected to join your crew, and she has accepted. Needless to say, there will be no need for actresses or musicians aboard the *Argo*. She will be learning a trade alongside the rest of you: a trade that will be her life's work as she does her small part—and by extension, my small part—to ensure the success of our endeavor. With my profoundest regret at forever bidding her farewell, I accept this burden as each of your families has accepted your decision to serve a higher calling."

The gloom that had built in his tone vanished in an instant, and he began to pace the stage once more. "That brings us to the second factor crucial to our success. We are not only forming a carefully managed genetic pool... we are not only forming a community... we are forming an economy that must function in self-contained isolation for far longer than any previous economy has survived. For that, there must be work and there must be discipline. Each of you over the next few months here at Earth Station One will learn a trade. You will continue to learn that trade as you ascend to the *Argo* and even as you depart the orbit of Earth. Your life will be devoted to a task upon which the lives of the entire crew depend.

"Soon you will have an opportunity to submit a prioritized list of preferences for the job you will assume. I encourage you to begin thinking about it. Al will account for these preferences as much as possible when he determines the final allocation of responsibilities, but dissent from his instructions will not be tolerated. Your only option, should you not be satisfied with the outcome, is resigning your position."

Now he was pacing quickly. "Success in learning your new role will be necessary for you to continue in the program, but it will not be sufficient. Success of the *Argo*'s mission demands its crew possess the health and fitness to face whatever challenges may arise. You must have psychological strength and fortitude. Training of your minds and bodies will be an important part of your time here.

"Finally, and perhaps the most important, is discipline. Unwavering discipline and obedience will be the final bulwark against the uncertainties that are sure to arise, the challenges you are sure to face. You have already had a taste of that. This is just the beginning. It will grow more strenuous by the day.

There are rules you will follow. Breaking them will carry consequences, up to and including expulsion, and penalties for disobedience here at Earth Station One are the most generous you are likely to experience. Infractions aboard the *Argo* will be dealt with far more harshly.

"Rule Number One—" He stopped pacing and held up a single forefinger. "There will be no romantic relationships of any sort among members of the crew. You will notice males and females have been separated. This state of affairs will persist until we are assured that the importance of this rule has been impressed upon you. The rule is not an arbitrary one: for generation upon generation, the crew of the *Argo* must maintain its genetic viability without growing beyond the limits of the ship's resources. All reproduction will be carefully managed through artificial in-vitro fertilization, with breeding pairs determined by AI in Human Resources. All children will be raised by the community. This rule is inflexible, and violating it will meet with the severest consequences.

"Our time for preparation is short. In less than two years, the planets of our solar system will align in the required conjunction to enable a gravitational slingshot maneuver that will propel the *Argo* at the necessary speeds into interstellar space. At that point in time, you must leave.

"You will be ready."

He was working himself up to a fevered pitch. "I understand as well as you the probabilities involved in this journey upon which we embark. The chance that the *Argo* eventually reaches its destination and finds it habitable may be small. But the payoff is beyond calculation, and so we go. Whether our descendants arrive at Planet Colchis or not, none of us will ever know. But the science of setting the *Argo* off on its trajectory is well established, and the ship is well advanced in the final phases of construction and testing. You will all live the lives of heroes as the first interstellar space travelers. You will travel farther from the seat of humanity than anyone has ever traveled; indeed, farther than any future occupant of Earth is likely to travel. And there is a chance, however small, that your descendants will populate the universe. Think on that as you decide whether the sacrifices we ask of you are too high a price to pay."

He stopped on the edge of the stage, directly in the center, and stared out over the faces. "I'll now turn it over to Admiral Demarion," he said, "to discuss the more immediate requirements of your time here at Earth Station One." Abruptly he turned and stalked off into the wings.

Even Father McIntosh had been silenced by the speech. It was as if a charge of static electricity flickered over the heads of the audience. As the spell faded, Admiral Demarion rose and stepped forward. In a voice crisp and precise, he spoke of the curriculum ahead: of the academic, physical, and military training.

The interminable day and sedative tone of the admiral began to take its effect on the audience as he talked of procedures for selecting professional tracks and the organization of the corps into squadrons and flights. He explained the monetary system under which cadets would be paid in *Argo* Credits that could be used to purchase basic necessities. Everyone would be required to learn English to the prescribed level of proficiency. Above all, Rule Number One would be observed: no romantic relationships were permitted between crewmembers of opposite sex.

Arthur felt the occasional twinge of pride over the course of the afternoon. But as soon as the speeches ended and the lights came up, he retreated back into himself. He left behind a world of strange faces and landscapes. He thought of Isabel. His yearning for her dominated whatever challenges lay ahead. It made them seem small next to the one extraordinary obstacle to his happiness. But there was hope: the composition of the crew was not yet fixed. That their relationship would be prohibited even were she to join scarcely entered his thoughts.

The drill instructors rushed in as soon as Malachi Demarion's final words faded. The cadet corps bounced to its feet at attention before being herded from the hall. Queues formed with noses inches from the backs of freshly shaven heads as they streamed up the aisles and out the doors to the parade ground. They formed up in rank and file and began to march. It was the first of a great quantity of marching that would occupy their time in the weeks ahead. They marched to dinner. Then they formed up again and marched back to the dormitories.

Arthur's roommate had arrived by the time he returned to his room. Ramon Woodard jumped to his feet and shook Arthur's hand with a crushing, two-handed grip. He was a tall and broad-shouldered youth perhaps two or three years older than Arthur. He had wide-set eyes over a square jaw, a shadow of facial hair far beyond his years, and a perpetual grin revealing a perfect set of teeth. With instructions to prepare their room for inspection promptly at Reveille the following morning, they set about unpacking and folding and tucking and polishing.

When the lights went out and peace at last descended, Ramon talked through the darkness. "Damn, boy—Maisy Armagast!" His disembodied voice formulated the thought on everyone's mind since Beckett's speech. "Optimal genetic constitution, I'll say!"

Arthur disapproved of such talk. Or perhaps he only told himself this because he was bad at it. "Yeah, I know," he said. "Wow."

"I had her poster on my bedroom wall when I was fourteen. Do you remember *Homeroom Sweetheart?*"

"Who doesn't?" Arthur replied.

Ramon was not getting the engagement he sought. He changed tack. "No dating. Unbelievable. I'm not sure that's going to work for me."

"You said it."

At this point, one may have expected disappointment to creep into Ramon's tone. Instead, he asked about where Arthur was from. He asked about Arthur's family. In these areas he found more ready engagement. He pulled Arthur out of the reveries that would have drowned him. It became their nightly ritual. Arthur resented the intrusions, but he needed them just as he needed the pointless rambling of Father McIntosh to carry him through those first hours.

Thoughts of Isabel remained his ultimate solace. As he stood in formation in the yard in the weeks to come, staring at the backs of the heads in front as they slowly regrew their ravaged hairdos, his mind was far away. He wrote tortured emails and was rewarded with bright and cheerful accounts that ignored his despondency. She had left their little town for a private university on the East Coast. Her ultimate desire, however, was to join the crew of the *Argo*. Of this she reminded him in clipped sentences fired off from a smartphone as she hurried from one class to the next. Subconsciously or otherwise, Arthur went to no great lengths to disabuse her of the notion that he might be able to help.

Was Isabel sincere in her feelings for Arthur? Did even she know the answer to that question? Millions longed to be among the crew of the *Argo*. Recruitment continued to fill the places of the dropouts. As rumors spread that genetic sequences were the key to securing a place, ancestry analysis ventures were inundated with customers. Waiting lists stretched for months. Hospitals saw a surge in concern over genetic diseases requiring urgent and immediate testing. Mailboxes overflowed with fliers offering low-cost, overnight services. Still, Beckett Armagast refused to confirm or deny any speculation about candidate-selection procedures.

The Weiss family was among those able to circumvent the mounting queues of the desperate. Isabel's personal sequence of nucleotides was dropped into the Web's lake of data to be perused at leisure by Al in Human Resources. But even as the first rounds of dropouts emerged back into society, to be snapped up for interviews by morning newscasts and late-night talk shows, Isabel was not among those chosen to fill their shoes. Her letters to Arthur grew more urgent, even as the demands of life at Earth Station One drew more of his attention elsewhere.

Arthur's daily activities shifted from the painfully monotonous (such as memorization of each agonizing detail of obedience) to the merely painful (such as boxing and the mystifying bloodsport introduced to him as rugby). At last, the day came when substance began to creep into the curriculum. Academic classes began. Rumors floated that the cadets would soon offer up lists of occupational preferences.

Cadets pored over lists of crew stations to be filled on humanity's first interstellar spacecraft. On the lists were requisitions for astrophysicists and nuclear engineers, pilots and heavy machinery operators. The *Argo* would need experts in hydrology and agriculture and animal husbandry. Lawyers would break new ground on the common law. There would be technicians to operate the additive manufacturing equipment and managers to supervise the technicians. There would be managers to manage the managers. Computer programmers would ensure everything from the cafeteria to Al himself operated with uninterrupted efficiency.

Jockeying for jobs began at a quiet simmer as each formulated a strategy for his or her list of preferences. Conversations in the television room and around the cafeteria tables came to focus on identifying the most desirable positions. The posts of astrophysicist and nuclear engineer were marked out for those hired on with the necessary skills. The posts of laundry attendant and line cook fell below the threshold of general consideration. In the middle were hundreds of roles, ranging widely in their levels of scarcity, basic appeal, and consensus over desirability. On these, discussion was hot as cadets formed preferences and calculated odds.

One had to determine the general level of interest without directing additional attention to one's position of choice. Tipping a hand might result in added competition as the role in question rose in the common estimation. One had to identify potential contenders and attempt to steer their deliberation along less threatening lines without revealing underlying intentions. What formed was a labyrinth of duplicity and second-guessing.

Arthur had no relevant skills. He was, by some wide measure, the youngest member of the corps. Unlike most of his peers, he had not even begun studies at university. He possessed little in the way of social awareness or intuition into the machinations of his fellows. He was entirely lacking in the guile required of him. He told the truth. He admitted his ignorance. He openly stated his preferences. He confided the sad story of Mr. Pifflethorpe and poor William. Soon it was whispered that Arthur's genetic code was teeming with imperfections that would be disastrous for the mission.

It may well have been that all of the scheming was for nothing. No one really understood Al's decision-making process. But with alarming rapidity, Arthur slid to the bottom of the emerging social order like a stone to the bottom of a pond. Even as rumors of the magnificent Maisy Armagast haunted the halls of Earth Station One, the name of Arthur Pifflethorpe became a byword for the nether regions of the Argonaut pecking order.

The only friends who could drag him from his despair were Father McIntosh and Ramon.

Tension built as employment wish lists were agonized over and finally submitted. For long weeks, rumors continued to fly. When at last the lists were posted to the bulletin boards above squadron duty desks, no amount of cajoling from the drill instructors could hold back the tide. Crowds lingered for hours as cadets rejoiced or despaired in the company of their comrades. Arthur waited in his room for the clamor to fade. He made his way to the desk and ran his finger down the list. Twice, three times he read over the words printed next to his name: *Waste Management*.

Arthur had been among the last to know. His detractors spread the word with glee and, like poles of a magnet, Arthur Pifflethorpe and Maisy Armagast became opposing forces in the social edifice that organized itself within the corps. And like flecks of iron, the cadets arranged themselves in neat and careful rows with heads pointed toward the specter of the illustrious Maisy and their feet toward our hapless Arthur.

Despite building up for Isabel in his letters the general sense of anticipation over release of the employment rolls, he failed to mention the result and pretended not to notice her inquiries on the subject. As for Maisy, there had been no confirmed sightings of Beckett Armagast's daughter. Among the most conspiratorial circles, it was suggested she had never and would never join the corps. It would be just like her father to spin such a tale in his manipulation of public opinion.

Chapter Six

Months passed, and the brief summer of perpetual sunlight succumbed to the creeping tendrils of winter. A blaze of fireweed sent its crimson flames sweeping up the hillsides. The first snows dusted the hilltops and began their relentless descent toward the campus grounds. It was becoming apparent to all—not least of whom was Father McIntosh —why Armagast Enterprises had chosen the Arctic North as the location for its training facility. Days grew shorter and shorter until the sun made only a brief daily appearance, peeking above the southern horizon before disappearing again and plunging the landscape into an unparalleled depth of night. The sky glowed with stars as Arthur had never seen. Soon the sun would be gone for good.

In phalanx with the darkness came the cold. At the briefest encounter, it froze Arthur's breath in his nostrils and sent icy needles into his flesh. Endless drill on the campus courtyard and forced marches through lowlands clouded with mosquitos drew to a close, and the cadets were trapped within the halls of Earth Station One as surely as if they had been fleeing the vacuum of space. Snow piled deeper until the groundskeepers ceased their futile efforts to plow it away and supplies were brought in via massive steel-tracked Snowcats.

The corps had been over six months at the mercy of the drill instructors. Through it they had seen their world shrink down to featureless corridors and an underground warren of cafeterias, assembly halls, and athletic facilities perpetually echoing with enraged shouting. Windows served only for mirrors as the world outside was plunged into black by an impenetrable bank of clouds that collected along the front range like filth swept into the gutter by a flood.

Amid the gloom, Arthur was awakened one morning to the sound of a fist pounding on his door. This was how he awakened most mornings. Cabin fever and a deficiency of vitamin D affected the drill instructors no less than the corps. These had pushed the drill instructors into a spiral of cruelty, obliterating any scraps of impartiality that may exist among the sorts of minds who would choose such a profession. They circled the weakest of the corps like sharks.

"Pifflethorpe!" *Boom, boom, boom* on the door. "Pifflethorpe! Fall out!"

From the depths of sleep, Arthur's bloodstream was flooded with a surge of fight-or-flight chemicals designed somewhere back in the mists of prehistory. His feet hit the floor before Ramon had even begun to stir, and he crashed into the hallway in a maelstrom of knees, elbows, and unfashionably snug white underwear.

"Is that how you stand at attention?" was the demand that greeted him.

"No, sir!" He strained harder to draw back his shoulders and tuck his chin into his chest.

"Did I tell you not to stand at attention?"

"No, sir!" He strained harder.

67

"Did your mama send a note that says you don't have to stand at attention?"

"No, sir!" The muscles between Arthur's shoulder blades were on fire.

"Maybe you want to tell me why you're not standing at attention?"

"No, sir!" Arthur had responded with the incorrect answer and spent the next several minutes doing pushups and running in place with knees straining upward to connect with the drill instructor's outstretched palms.

"Tell the rest of these worthless maggots to finish up with their mama's teat," the drill instructor shouted at last. Most of the cadre were given to mixing metaphors with abandon. Arthur gathered he was to encourage his fellow cadets to join him in the corridor. At the top of his lungs, he did so.

Soon all were assembled in lines along the walls. After a brief period of clamor in which deficiencies were addressed among Arthur's compatriots, the hall fell silent. Emerging into view at the periphery of Arthur's caged eyes was Bosun Atticus Oluwusi. He almost strutted, with hands clasped at the small of his back and chest thrust outward, the shadow of his wheel-cap obscuring the upper half of his face. His cheeks were pocked with scars, his jawline rounded with an indistinct fleshiness. The skin of his neck bulged over the tight-fitting collar of his dress uniform.

The bosun stopped just past Arthur and pivoted on a heel. He stood at rigid parade rest. Three others, also in full dress uniform, approached and stood before him at attention. The first was a man who would appear middle-aged only to one as young as Arthur. The pasty skin of his face, so common in those months without sunshine, was in the midst of an eruption of acne. It glistened with sweat. Wispy black hairs, missed for some weeks in succession in the course of daily shaving, sprouted from a patch below the corner of his jaw.

Behind him was another pair of cadets, side by side. Arthur knew them by sight; indeed, every cadet knew them by sight. Skyla Sawer and Stanley Waller were the bosun's cadet liaisons with the crew and his lieutenants in all matters disciplinary. The corp's contempt for Skyla and Stanley ran deeper even than that for the drill instructors, traitors that they were to the common cause.

Skyla was sturdy without being overweight and busty without managing to look feminine. Her eyes bulged as if in surprise from a face whose features seemed to be wandering off in disorder, like soldiers just dismissed from formation. Her hair was middle-brown and undyed, desiccated from too much washing and an atmosphere of unaccommodating humidity. Stanley was tall and thick, with pale, freckled skin and a flat, small-featured face that seemed an afterthought to a great, egg-shaped head. What hair remained on its oblong crown was trimmed close and of an unnatural yellow-orange hue that blended with the color of his mottled scalp. He was only slightly overweight, but nevertheless his arms stood out from his sides as if some abnormal accumulation of underarm flesh held them there. His feet were planted correspondingly apart. He looked stuffed.

"Publish the orders," said the bosun in a voice jarringly calm yet audible from one end of the hall to the other.

Skyla raised a sheet of paper before her face, although she seemed to speak from memory. "To all those present, bear witness. I, Admiral Malachi Demarion, in performance of my duties as commander of the *Argo* and its crew, hereby dishonorably discharge Cadet Malcolm Whitaker from the corps, effective immediately. His offense is egregious disregard for Rule Number One. The actions of Cadet Whitaker put in jeopardy the good order and discipline of the crew and place at risk the ultimate mission of the Argonauts. They reflect poorly upon his personal character and cause us to question his ability to maintain a position of trust. To all those present, bear witness."

"Cadet Whitaker, do you have anything to say for yourself?" said the bosun.

"No, sir," shouted Cadet Whitaker.

With that, the bosun came to attention and again pivoted on a heel. The four marched off down the hall to execute the same ceremonials in the next squadron. Arthur could hear preparations echoing around the corner at the far end of the corridor.

The drill instructors took charge once more, and the cadets were given three minutes to dress and make use of the facilities. They descended to the subterranean track for a five-mile run before breakfast, having been informed in no uncertain terms that this was courtesy of Cadet Whitaker.

Life carried on toward a crescendo of madness and drama. The beginning of academic classes had done little to improve the plight of the cadets, who became immersed in study alongside the demands of pseudo-military life. And yet, with the tireless persistence of groundwater seeping through a foundation's cracks, the boys found their way to the quarters of the girls. No one in a position of authority was entirely sure how it happened, but the simple fact was as undeniable as the growing number of females being sent home after coming along in the family way.

At first, with the dogged obstinacy of a Bible Belt preacher, the administration attempted to remedy the situation with threats. The corps of cadets was assembled in the auditorium and berated on their selfish disregard for Rule Number One. The staff vowed that segregation of the sexes would not be lifted until the cadets—one and all—had demonstrated control over their baser instincts. Security was tightened in the corridors connecting the men's and women's quarters. Cadets caught violating the diktat were expelled.

When it became evident these measures were also doomed to failure, the staff arrived at the conclusion that inflexible segregation was only fanning the flames of ardor. Members of the opposite sex remained barred from the respective dormitories, but academic classes were integrated. Rigid schedules were relaxed that had staggered the times at which men and women could dine in the cafeteria or visit the convenience store. Still the ranks continued to thin, and still the cadets endured tongue-lashings as they stood at attention for hour upon hour.

Eventually, without fanfare and without official acknowledgment that Rule Number One had been in any way abrogated, supplies necessary to prevent the inevitable consequences of humanity's most fundamental impulse arrived discreetly on the shelves of the convenience store. From that day forward, the pace of decimation in the ranks of female cadets began to decline. It did not cease entirely, for shelves carrying the supplies in question were inevitably empty within hours of being stocked each Wednesday morning.

While the leadership was willing to make basic accommodation to reality, they would not go so far as to admit a glaring blunder in their scrupulously laid plans. Providing the necessary equipment in quantities to meet demand would have required a supply chain of such manifest scale that the utter hopelessness of Rule Number One would have been apparent even to Malachi Demarion himself. This was clearly out of the question. But chaos had descended upon Wednesday mornings at the convenience store. Soon, a system of rationing was devised under which each cadet was issued a limited quota of coupons. The program was placed under the management of Chief Steward Sasaki.

A black market for coupons accordingly organized itself,

which funneled the monetary resources of the cadet corps from the youngest to the oldest and the supply of coupons in the opposite direction. Having no practical use for his weekly ration, Father McIntosh lived in high style, his dormitory room stocked with all of the most coveted commodities.

Black markets are so called for good reason. Coupons became a target of the petty theft that persisted even among Beckett Armagast's Chosen Few. Pregnancies declined, but instances of cadets caught in compromising circumstances continued undiminished. Addressing these situations fell under the purview of Bosun Atticus Oluwusi, the font of justice in that social microcosm buried in snow. He imagined shame would add to whatever explicit punishments were imposed. For those who managed to evade expulsion, reputations were raised high.

This unforeseen outcome required that penalties be raised, and soon the rate of attrition was again climbing toward unsustainable levels. The black-market price of coupons—and the indiscipline this encouraged—rose to a point even the staff could no longer ignore. Something had to be done. But whatever pragmatism had prompted them into tactical retreat, they were not yet prepared to abandon the field. Chief Steward Sasaki stepped forward with a solution to the problem, announced in conjunction with another public expulsion before the assembled mass of cadets. Discharge of coupons would be tracked, and those whose use of them exceeded reasonable bounds would be accordingly punished.

As night follows day, this created a tertiary market in the services of those willing to execute purchases on behalf of others. The further such activity was removed from the ultimate source of law and order, the more the dealmaking came to resemble the Wild West. Disputes were settled outside formal channels through whatever means the injured parties could devise. The effects on general levels of discipline were far-reaching. Chief Steward Sasaki and Bosun Oluwusi spent many a long hour in conference with Skyla and Stanley, devising new means of bringing the chaos to a close. The clear solution was imposition of stricter discipline. Further examples must be made.

And this is where we return to Arthur Pifflethorpe, sitting quietly in his room, formulating a reply to one of Isabel's letters. Ramon sat behind him with his feet up on a desk, arguing with a friend. Dexter Pruitt lived down the hall, but spent most of his free time in Ramon and Arthur's room. The argument was one they often revisited. Dexter had an obsession with one day being elected president. When confronted with the fact that this would not be a possibility aboard the *Argo*, he proclaimed the whole thing one of Beckett Armagast's stunts. Fame and fortune would be the reward of the lucky ones offered a ticket on that publicity train. He was not fool enough to pass it up. The conversation turned to the growing difficulty of procuring the necessary supplies for biweekly visits to respective paramours across the quad.

Arthur did his best to ignore them. He was disgusted by the subject. He resented the debasement of intersex relations implied by the entire system of credits and coupons and quotas that had reared its head like a leviathan from the deep. He resented being berated for the improprieties of his fellows. His love for Isabel was pure, and it broke his heart that the culmination of such profound sentiments should be bartered like Twinkies (of which convenience-store stocks also tended to run out, although with consequences less dire). When Arthur reached that point in his relationship with Isabel, the planets would align, the angels would sing, and all shadows would disappear forever from the world. Now, locked beneath arctic snows with five thousand lascivious baboons, he must be forever prepared to study in the common area should he return to his room and find the agreed-upon signal for privacy: a blank Post-It note stuck to the whiteboard next to the door. The affair sullied everything he held dear.

As we have seen, considerable wealth was obtainable for those of Arthur's tendency to self-restraint. But he would not lower himself, whatever the profits to be had. Thus, his weekly ration of coupons accumulated in a locked drawer of his desk. Why they did not find their way to the wastebasket is a subject to be pondered, revealing as it may the idiosyncrasies of even the sincerest human souls.

Arthur had managed to shut out the conversation behind him until Ramon poked him with a toe.

"Arthur... Arthur!" Ramon said.

Ramon enjoyed lounging shirtless, as if reveling in the profusion of hair on his well-developed chest. He was at that moment thus unclothed. But whatever Ramon's eccentricities, he was, as we have seen, a boon to Arthur. He was extroverted, loyal, and had cemented his reputation as the squadron wag one day in the showers, by arranging out of sight the outward accoutrements of his masculinity and parading down a bench with legs awkwardly crossed in a sort of nude drag show. Ramon was well liked to a degree even Arthur could not resist. Alongside Father McIntosh, his friendship was the strongest of Arthur's tenuous connections to his fellows.

"Arthur!" Ramon poked him again and he turned.

"Yeah?" He allowed an edge of irritation to creep into his voice. This was ignored.

"I'm out of coupons, dude," Ramon said.

Arthur waved him off and went back to his letter. They had had this conversation before. But Ramon was persistent and was joined in his efforts by Dexter. They worked on Arthur in tandem. His concentration was broken again and again. Frustration mounted.

"Arthur! ...Come on, Arthur, you're not even using them. Help a brother out. Do you want to see Celia sent home? You don't want that on your conscience."

On it went until Arthur reached the breaking point. Without fully considering the ramifications, he opened the drawer of his desk to retrieve the article necessary to end the intrusions into his thoughts. With a sensation approaching that of a clap of thunder, Ramon and Dexter caught sight of the enormous quantity of coupons contained there, and it is perhaps best the expression in which their surprise took form not be repeated here.

"Arthur, you must have ten thousand credits worth of coupons in there," said Ramon. "What in God's name are you saving them for?"

To this Arthur did not have a ready reply. He made one last attempt to shrug it off and return to his letter after thrusting a few of the coupons toward his companions. The damage was irreparable, and the barrage continued. Inevitably, he relented. He spun around in his chair. Ramon and Dexter pestered and badgered, berated and harangued. How could Arthur do this? How many cadets had been sent home because of his selfishness? He should be planning for his future and securing his capital in a safer location. Each of these arguments and more fell on deaf ears.

What eventually turned the tide was Dexter striking upon the subject of Isabel. Arthur's affection for her was no secret, his bulletin board being entirely papered with photographs, at least half of which featured her. Why, Dexter asked, was Arthur saving up? What did he plan to do with all of them? Was Isabel not trying her best to secure a place on the crew? What kind of reception was he planning when she finally made the cut?

If there was truth in this line of reasoning Arthur was not prepared to admit it, least of all to himself. He broke down. The problem remained, however, that Ramon and Dexter were unable to cash in the coupons due to the volume of their recent purchases. Arthur would have to do it. There was no other way.

The following Wednesday, Arthur stuffed his entire stash of coupons into his backpack and went to the convenience store at the appointed hour, his skin burning at the ignominy he faced in the estimation of Ms. Cooley, the cashier.

Arthur had carefully considered this moment and planned it to the last detail. He arrived just as the doors were opening for the day and retrieved a shopping basket from the stack. He walked quickly through the aisles, passing the magazine rack and selecting an issue of *Argonaut Daily* without pausing his steps. Moving at a pace he deemed the appropriate balance between noteworthy haste and unnecessary sluggishness, he continued toward the section in the back containing the goods at issue. With a brief glance behind him to ensure no one was watching, he swept a mass of cartons into the basket and dropped the magazine over them. Then he slowed his steps and drifted casually through the aisles, filling the remainder of the basket with enough unremarkable items to balance the alarming quantity of restricted ones.

Finished shopping, he made his way through a line that had formed before the checkout counter. Wednesday mornings were always the busiest, for reasons that had never occurred to him before this very moment. The fluttering in his chest and heat radiating from his cheeks rose higher with each step he took toward the register. He could not bring himself to do it, he thought. He almost broke from the line and returned everything to the shelves. But he had to go forward. Ramon and Dexter were counting on him. They were his friends, and Arthur could not afford to be prodigal with friends.

It was only when he arrived at the cashier and his basket touched the countertop that he resolved to abort the mission. But it was too late. Ms. Cooley, a pleasant, portly woman in late middle age, greeted him as she always did and snatched the basket from his lingering grasp. With the idle serenity of routine, she began ringing up its contents. It was only when she lifted the penultimate magazine that her eyes grew wide. They came up to meet Arthur's deer-in-headlights gaze.

"Why, Arthur, this purchase will require quite a number of coupons," she said.

Arthur nodded, not trusting himself to speak, and rummaged through his backpack. He pulled out a fistful and laid them on the counter.

"My, my... well, well..." the cashier continued tutting and muttering as she emptied the remaining contents of the basket onto the counter. To Arthur's horror, she separated them from the remainder of his purchases and began, one by one, to pair each carton with its associated coupon. The stack mounted higher and higher. The line grew longer as she worked. He could not pull his eyes from the countertop, as if the urgency of his stare would hasten the movement of her hands.

She finished at last and entered the total into the computer. From its speaker, an insistent beeping noise began to issue, accompanied by a flashing signal on the screen noticeable to Arthur and those behind him only for the alternating shades of light and dark it cast on the cashier's distressingly pursed face.

"Oh, dear. I'm sorry, Arthur," she said, "but I'll need to have this purchase verified by the chief steward's office." She picked up the telephone and punched a number, turning away to conduct the conversation in an undertone.

Arthur could feel the perspiration under his arms soaking

through the fabric of his jumpsuit. The stack of cartons stood before him on the counter, rising nearly to the height of the rotisserie hot-dog oven. He tried to ignore the muttering that had risen in volume from the line behind him. Patrons had by that time extended their queue back into the refrigerated goods aisle. Ms. Cooley's voice had risen to a furious whisper that remained just below the level of comprehensibility. Then it stopped abruptly and she turned back to Arthur, agitation reddening her face nearly to the same shade as that of her customer.

"I'm sorry, young man, but you'll have to wait here. Next, please."

He quailed, nodded vaguely, and set about averting his gaze from any direction in which it could foreseeably capture that of another. The line behind him at last began to move as each in turn stepped around him to ring up their baskets. All the while, the stack of offending contraband stood tall, a beacon of Arthur's humiliation. The still-beeping tone issued from the computer, and the still-flashing warning signal cast its alternating glow over the pile of cartons and the face of Ms. Cooley.

Perhaps half of the accumulated line had passed before the object of the delay arrived. It was Bosun Atticus Oluwusi himself, fully attired in dress blues and wheel cap. He strode through the automatic doors with resolute purpose, hands clenched and chest thrust out.

"Ms. Cooley," he said, "what do we have here?" He stopped before the counter with feet spread and hands clasped at the small of his back.

"A purchase requiring your approval, sir," Ms. Cooley replied, nearly coming to attention as she spoke. She finished ringing up a sale. The customer collected his goods and scurried from the bosun's withering stare.

"My goodness," said the bosun (or something to that effect)

as he stepped forward and fingered the top carton in the stack. He turned his eyes upon Arthur, who forced himself to meet them. "What do you want with all these, son?"

"They're not for me, sir... I mean, they're my coupons, but..." Arthur's meticulous plans had not come so far as this. He was hopeless in forming a coherent response. His mind raced like a hamster on its wheel, straining furiously and going nowhere.

"What's your name, son?"

"Arthur Pifflethorpe, sir."

"Arthur Pifflethorpe. You are familiar, of course, with Rule Number One." The bosun regained his composure after a moment of uncharacteristic discomfiture. This was beyond the scope of his wildest speculations as to the depravity of which his charges were capable. His hands returned to the small of his back.

"I am, sir. They're not for me... I mean, they're my coupons, but..." Again, Arthur ran out of steam. It was over. He would resign at the nearest available opportunity and return home. Maybe they would still take him at the university, maybe not. He would never speak to Isabel or Mrs. Pifflethorpe again. Perhaps he would drive long-haul rigs over the plains to Denver. Micah Olsen's father had done that for a time. It was a respectable position that left one with a ready excuse for being forever unreachable.

"Cadet Pifflethorpe."

As he mused, Arthur's eyes had drifted from Bosun Oluwusi's face to the pile of cartons. They snapped back. He was once again formulating an argument to the effect that the restricted goods were not for his personal use although he was indeed their legitimate possessor. A voice from behind interrupted the line of reasoning. It was the voice of a woman.

"Forget it. I'm sorry for asking," she said.

"I beg your pardon, miss?" The bosun's attention swung to the customer standing next in line.

Arthur turned. At first, he saw only the woman's jumpsuit and cropped hair fading into the background of identically dressed cadets. Then, through a fog of thought blundering about within him like a blindfolded gorilla, he noticed she was quite beautiful. This was the sort of thing Arthur noticed, whatever his state of mind. Her jumpsuit seemed regulation at a glance, but upon further inspection was found to be neatly tailored to the Junoesque form of her body, thus avoiding the usual likeness to a sack of potatoes. Her hair was dark, nearly black, and unlike most was carefully—even expensively—styled to regulation length. The perfect bob threw a perfect bouncing curl over a perfect cheek. On the other side, it was tucked behind a perfect ear. Her eyes were large and round, with black irises that merged with her pupils until they looked like enormous pits standing wide and sharp against sclera white as paper. Her nose was thin, her nostrils some-what pinched, and a pronounced philtrum cut a refined trough down to pouted lips painted in radiant crimson. The mouth stood out from pale skin like a rosebud in the snow. The facial structure formed a triangle mounting upward from a pointed chin and crisp jawline. Arthur found it gnawingly familiar.

"Half of those are mine," she said. "I asked him to buy them for me."

Bosun Oluwusi recovered himself. He knew exactly who this person was, and the moment he said her name the realization flooded Arthur like the warm burn of Mr. Pifflethorpe's whiskey. "He's buying them for you, Ms. Armagast?" he said, fighting back a note of incredulity.

"That's right. He's buying them for me."

"Half of them," said the bosun.

"Yes, half of them." Her gaze was unwavering.

"You understand, Ms. Armagast, that making purchases of restricted goods on behalf of others is prohibited, as is requesting that they do so."

"I do."

"Then why, if I may, did you ask this cadet to buy them for you?"

"I was shy." Nothing in that face would ever reveal a tattered shred of bashfulness. She seemed unconcerned for the incredulity that was surely generated by her words.

"You were shy."

"That's right."

"You realize I will need to take this up with Admiral Demarion and Mr. Armagast."

"Yes, I realize that." The placidity of her face approached the point of iciness but was touched with the faint warmth of humor.

The bosun stood for a moment flat-footed and silent. His jaw churned as if on a lump of bubblegum. His eyes swept over the dozen or more cadets around the store who stood staring in amazement. They ended on the nonplussed countenance of Ms. Cooley. "Please process the transactions... separately," he said. Then he wheeled about and disappeared through the sliding doors.

Ms. Cooley did so with a flustered rapidity that repeatedly left the odd carton clattering to the floor. She eventually managed to contain Arthur's portion within the semitransparent plastic of a shopping bag. Arthur paid and floated from the store on legs that had been entirely forgotten. He was twenty yards down the hallway before Maisy's voice again grabbed him from behind.

"Hey," she called. "Hey!"

He stopped and turned as she swung her hourglass hips

down the hall toward him. Arthur was fumbling with his wallet as she drew up.

"I'm sorry... let me pay you back," he said.

"Forget it," she replied.

"You'll be in a lot of trouble on my account. I really am sorry."

"Relax," she said. "They won't expel me. And if they won't expel me, then they can't expel you."

"Yes, well... I'm sorry. I mean, thank you." Arthur wished he could stop himself from apologizing.

Maisy held out the shopping bag containing the other half of Arthur's intended purchase. "Have fun," she said with a bounce in her voice and a withering wink.

Before he could regain conscious control of his motor function, he had plucked the bag from her outstretched fingers. She smiled at him as she turned to walk away. Even through an obliterating flush of shame, Arthur thought it was a beautiful smile.

Chapter Seven

F ollowing Arthur's encounter with Maisy in the convenience store, reported sightings of Beckett Armagast's daughter multiplied like ants trailing in the footsteps of their first solitary scout across the kitchen floor. The belief came to be generally accepted that she had arrived only recently at Earth Station One. In truth, she had indeed been in attendance as her father attempted to use her for his publicity stunt during the inaugural address to the corps.

Maisy had strongly objected to the plan when it was proposed. The fact that she strongly objected to most proposals put to her by her father led him to believe this particular objection should be classed among the rest and accordingly written off as the contrarianism of a headstrong child. In this instance, however, Maisy's resolution to make her own way aboard the *Argo* was deadly serious.

So serious, that upon leaving the auditorium after the incident, she made her way to the offices of the command staff and demanded she be exempted from the entire first phase of training. It would not be fair to herself or the other cadets, she declaimed at a volume audible throughout the corridors of the facility, now that her father had called her out as exceptional to the common herd. Why, the entire purpose of basic training—the bad haircuts and the interminable marching and the verbal abuse—was to form a team in which no individual was higher than another. That purpose had been irreparably compromised.

It is possible that other considerations strengthened the force of Maisy's objections. Her wish not to disrupt the training regimen also afforded her the opportunity to be excused from the bad haircuts and the interminable marching and the verbal abuse. As in most cases in which Beckett overstepped in managing the mercurial passions of his daughter, Maisy's will prevailed. She spent the first months sequestered at the family compound in Colorado. Once crew stations were assigned and the academic phase of training began, Maisy returned to Earth Station One, slipping in among one of the many cohorts of new recruits brought in to replace the dropouts. The incident in the convenience store became her celebrated debut.

Arthur was the butt of this much-discussed font of hilarity. He came into an unfortunate nickname that does not here bear repeating. The story became bound up in the collective consciousness of the future crew, along with his alleged defective genetic constitution and lack of relevant expertise.

Maisy herself was far above all this. The moment she turned from him and swept away down the corridor, Arthur was already a fading glimmer in her consciousness. She had other pressing matters to consider, such as the roll of her hips as she walked, the angle of her head causing a curl of hair to fall just so across her cheek, and the startled glances of cadets who scurried out of her unwavering path. By the time a circle of hangers-on had formed around her, and the episode came up in conversation, she scarcely remembered it.

Academic coursework had started in earnest, and Arthur had every reason to enjoy himself. Despite his dejection at being relegated to the waste management department, he soon discovered the role was not without appeal. Managing waste was integral to the *Argo's* mission systems. It was the single most important factor driving the ship's design. As a self-contained ecosystem surviving in the blackness and cold of interstellar space for thousands of years, every scrap of waste needed to be recycled. This included the rubbish and sewage that served as a focal point of common disdain, but it also included heat, oxygen, nutriment, and virtually every other material and nonmaterial particle of which one could conceive.

Each vibration of heat and photon of electromagnetic radiation escaping from the ship held no promise of ever being recovered. The only means of replacing them was a limited supply of fuel, and no one knew how long that fuel needed to last. The magnificent tin can was encased in layer upon layer of insulation. There would be no airlocks or observation decks offering sweeping views of the galaxy, except perhaps in the initial phases as Beckett had a never-ending queue of journalists and politicians shuttled up to the construction site. Buried within the *Argo's* walls was a circulatory system that would fight a long and lonely battle against the laws of thermodynamics, soaking up errant fragments of heat and channeling them back to the core. Every shred of waste energy, from the exhalation of a warm breath to friction between the gears of a mechanical apparatus, must somehow be recaptured and returned to a usable state.

Each sordid and seldom-discussed detail of human existence was a subject of Arthur's studies. There was exhaled carbon dioxide to capture and turn back into breathable air. There was excrement to be processed into fertilizer for the *Argo's* acre upon acre of arable land. Urine was reprocessed into potable water. Fluids, minerals, and micronutrients were extracted from corpses, and what could not be directly repurposed was plowed back into the soil. Every imaginable substance that might find its way out of the human body and into the sewage system was explicitly addressed.

The very *Argo* itself—every scrap of metal and plastic and glass and circuitry—would be sure to wear out and require replacement over the course of its journey. Base elements must be extracted, processed, and reused in the manufacturing centers that would churn out new parts and equipment to replace the old. Like a human body passing from youth to middle age and on to its dotage, not a single original cell or tissue would remain, even as life carried on uninterrupted.

Indeed, the *Argo* was not limited to maintaining any particular outward form. The set of physical characteristics optimized for operating within the solar system, with all its debris and heat and gravitational fields, would be quite different from that required in the interminable interval between one star system and the next. Superstructure required for maneuvering and acceleration would be extraneous once the course was set and the ship merely coasting along. Some changes were planned in advance; others would be developed en route. Centuries away from its destination, the *Argo* would likely begin morphing slowly back into a form necessary to deposit its human contents on the surface of the planet Colchis. No one could hope to plan for that yet, so far was it in the future.

All of this Arthur had to understand to fulfill his duties. In addition to job-specific coursework was a core curriculum containing information everyone would need to survive. Each detail of existence had to be relearned. They even studied emergency procedures, although the consensus among the cadets was that these were designed purely to keep them occupied and quiescent up until the moment of death. Once they reached a critical point somewhere out among the orbits of the outer planets, there would be no coming home.

So, while Arthur should have been reveling in boundless oceans of information that at any other time of his life would have captivated him, he found himself nearly friendless, alone, and heartsick. Ramon took every opportunity to drag him out of his reverie. One evening, they drifted into the dining hall late, Arthur having spent the past two hours drilling Ramon on derivatives and the chain rule. They took seats at one of a series of long tables. Rows of buffets lined a far wall. A low drop ceiling felt even lower due to the extraordinary breadth and depth of the room.

"What would you do?" Ramon was saying as he leaned in over a plate of stewed beef tips that the previous day had been served as flank steak. The following day, they would see the left-overs once more as hamburger.

Arthur had no idea what he would do in the circumstances Ramon had described and did not even attempt to answer the question. "What makes you think she'd do that?" he said. "Celia doesn't seem like that kind of girl."

"I didn't think so either, but there it is. It wasn't one of mine. I never use that brand. And even if it was, I wouldn't have stuffed it under the mattress like that."

"Maybe she got it somewhere. Maybe she stuffed it under the mattress."

Ramon smiled ironically as he looked down at his food and shook his head.

"Did you ask her about it?" Arthur went on.

"She said she had no idea where it came from. Reminded me there had been others before I came along. Can't get mad about that."

The look on Arthur's face said he found this reasonable.

"It's been four months," said Ramon. "How does an empty wrapper stay under the mattress for four months? Doesn't she ever change the sheets?" He put his elbows on the table and held his head in his hands.

"I don't know." Arthur took a bite of steamed broccoli and chewed it slowly. Chewing was unnecessary and performed purely out of habit. He swallowed. "All I can say is, I don't think she'd lie to you. Isabel once told me she'd..."

Ramon held up a hand to stop him. "You shouldn't be thinking about Isabel, dude," he said. "Good Lord, Maisy Armagast just saved your ass. It's time to look for greener pastures. You hit the lottery, and you're still living in your mom's basement."

"I'll wish I'd hit the lottery when they send me home to live in my mom's basement," Arthur said.

"They're not sending you home. She was right. They're not going to expel her, and that makes you safe. What you should be doing, rather than sulking and writing all those letters, is living your life. This thing landed right in your lap. That... doesn't... happen." He drew out the words for emphasis.

"I don't see how it changes anything. I can't exactly just walk up to her and say, 'Hey, remember me—the guy from the convenience store?'"

"Why the hell not?" Ramon leaned back in his chair and spread his arms wide for emphasis.

Arthur glanced around the room, startled at the volume of Ramon's voice. "That doesn't work for me."

"It works for everyone. Watch."

Ramon stood and walked to a table three rows down that was crammed with young women in track suits and ponytails. The group bubbled with chatter and laughter. Ramon waded into the middle of it. Within a minute or two, he was seated and laughing along with them. Arthur watched as he ate. Five minutes later, Ramon stood and returned with a broad smile and meaningful look. He sat and continued staring at his friend.

"I know, I know..." said Arthur. "I can't pull that off. You know that."

"Sure you can! It's not hard," Ramon replied. "You know what I was talking about over there?"

Arthur shook his head.

"Beef tips," said Ramon. He let it sink in for a moment. "You're overthinking it. You've got an easy in with Maisy. We see her in here all the time. Here's what you say..."

Arthur let him talk. When Ramon got going on this subject, there was no stopping him. He would never understand.

For weeks after his encounter with Bosun Oluwusi, Arthur waited for the hammer to fall. The worst that came of it, apart from the teasing, was an end to his weekly ration of coupons. This punishment was met with horror by those of his compatriots who did not know him well. Arthur found it a relief. Ramon took care of the rest, disposing of his stock of contraband and refusing to accept a cut of the proceeds, with the exception of a minor remuneration taken in kind.

Spring arrived at last, and with it the long season between arctic ice and summer sun that can only be described as a time of mud. Crisp drifts of snow, unrefreshed from above, moldered away into rotted ice, slush, and dirt. Rivulets feeding streams feeding rivers drained the land of eight months of stored precipitation. They clogged with floes to overtop the footpaths and courtyards and doorsills. With the breaking up of winter, the damage it had inflicted upon Earth Station One became apparent. Ice had completed the destruction of roads. Pipes that had burst months ago at last unfroze and gushed their contents out through ceiling tiles and floorboards. Storm drains were overwhelmed, trash was scattered by hungry animals emerging from hibernation, and everywhere was inundated by clouds of insects.

Earth Station One, for all its grandeur, was not built for the long haul. At the conclusion of the approaching summer, cadets would be shuttled up to the *Argo* for their final period of training prior to departure. Armagast Enterprises had made the sensible decision to conserve resources wherever possible. Planners undershot the necessary period of habitability by some months, perhaps not fully appreciating the brutal effects of an arctic winter. Inconveniences were spun to the corps as valuable training in endurance of hardship. Reporters were no longer invited to the speeches Beckett Armagast continued to give from time to time in the auditorium, the roof of which had begun to leak snowmelt upon the heads of the assembly.

As life returned to the landscape, the corps of cadets at last began to settle into its final form. Those unable to endure the demands of their new lives were gone, the final wave petering out along with the darkness and the cold. The newest arrivals struggled to catch up with a corps far advanced in camaraderie and academic studies. Still, Isabel had not been selected to join the band of Argonauts. The probability she would be selected dwindled with the ever-shrinking cohorts of new arrivals. Arthur was despondent, but had in no way given up on his devotion.

Isabel had no such constitution. Responses to his ever-more-impassioned letters grew shorter and less frequent. Hints of irritation began to show through. The more Arthur pined and yearned and struggled, the more aloof she became, dwelling on the mundane details of daily life rather than the workings of her innermost soul that Arthur burned to see revealed. What Isabel wanted, as we have surely realized, is for Arthur to call it off. She read the writing on the wall but did not want to play the scoundrel and abandon such a tender spirit as it was about to depart forever into the infinite vacuum of space. So, the dying relationship lingered on like a trauma patient slipping into a final, irrecoverable coma.

The calamity that finally tore off the proverbial Band-Aid began in a class on business management. The curriculum for Arthur's field of study was broader than most, as his eventual duties would encompass a wide range of disparate subjects. He learned about chemistry, biology, and engineering alongside more practical courses in spacecraft systems, source reduction, and composting. He and his fellow Waste Management colleagues bounced around between academic departments predominantly occupied by students in narrower fields of study.

Arthur sat one Tuesday morning in a windowless room at one of two dozen desks occupied by idly dozing cadets who would one day go on to fill the ranks of the crew's substantial tiers of middle management.

"...and so," the instructor was saying as he pointed to a process diagram drawn on a whiteboard in various shades of colored marker, "immediately following the Program Planning Review will be the Program Guidance Review. You must remember the PPR always comes before the PGR... wait... or is it the PGR before the PPR?"

He paused to chuckle at his private joke, cleared his throat, and carried on. "But seriously, at the end of the day, it is best practice that those whose duties fall within the wheelhouse of the PGR ensure absolute alignment moving forward. You probably won't have bandwidth for a full deep-dive, so start with the low-hanging fruit. Circle back or take it offline if you don't have time to address the full agenda, but always end with a clear bottom line. You'll need to think outside the box if you expect to leverage all available synergies, so reach out to the team beforehand, and always touch base with each of your stakeholders..."

The door swung abruptly open. The instructor paused to determine the cause of the interruption. Maisy Armagast stood in the doorway with her hands on her hips, surveying the room she was about to enter. Everyone but Arthur, it seemed, was accustomed to the theatrics.

"Excellent that you've joined us, Ms. Armagast," said the instructor. "We were just discussing the Program Guidance Review. Would you like to join us?"

As she paused to consider this, it began to dawn upon those present in the classroom that an extraordinary conjunction had occurred. Their eyes glanced back to Arthur, who had taken a seat in the last row. They bounced to Maisy and back again like observers at a tennis match.

Maisy gave them the spectacle they craved, attuned as she was to her audience. She saw Arthur. Her lips pursed, pushing upward in the center, and an eyebrow cocked over slightly narrowed eyes. She shifted her weight onto one leg in a motion she found conveyed indolence while accentuating the curve of her waistline. After the briefest of pauses, she answered the instructor's rhetorical question with a sidelong glance as she moved purposefully through the maze of students to the back. All the desks were full. She retrieved an unused chair from along the rear wall and sat close beside Arthur, pulling a notebook from her bag and arranging it on a corner of his desk.

Maisy was by this time familiar with Arthur's reputation and her place amid the legends of his boundless ignorance. These things did not change her attitude toward him; such concerns of the masses were far below her. If anything, they formed a connection that could be an asset in the never-ending scramble toward more rarefied strata of fame. This moment would be talked about.

She slid close to Arthur until her knee rested against his. She placed her elbows on the desk, poising a pen loosely between fingers whose tips caressed her temples as she stared at the instructor.

We should note in passing the events that brought Maisy to this place, for it is by no means obvious what set of skills would recommend her to a life of business management. She was not destined to be a midrange bureaucrat, as were most of the other cadets in the room. Al in Human Resources had examined her assets and was, so far as an artificially intelligent machine can be, flummoxed. He churned upon the problem for several milliseconds, which was an extraordinary interval on the scales of time in which he commonly functioned.

It may be supposed Arthur would present the more difficult problem, having brought with him nothing in the way of useful experience. On the contrary. It was child's play for Al to work with such raw material. Arthur had nothing to recommend him to any of the jobs he had requested; these were summarily discarded. Al's algorithm simply pushed Arthur's name further and further down its list of priorities until it had exhausted all the preferences expressed by the remainder of the student body. What was left was the job no one else wanted, and to this Arthur was duly assigned. Maisy, on the other hand, had a substantial online presence from which to draw for Al's calculations. What to do on a starship with a social-media-influencer-cum-actress with pretensions to music?

She would have enormous cachet with anyone in a position of power due to her fame and good looks, but little in the way of actual expertise to offer. She had dazzling communication skills but nothing of immediate importance to communicate. A wildly expensive education provided her with a broad and disparate body of knowledge. But this knowledge could not hope to be assembled by the lessons of experience into any arrangement of practical relevance until long after the period of time in which she could hope to remember it all. Al at last hit upon the answer. He made Maisy a management consultant.

And so we find her sitting next to Arthur, whose mind had

entered the microprocessing equivalent of an infinite loop. Maisy stoked the fires by accidentally brushing his hand with hers and whispering an apology close in his ear. She touched his arm on the flimsiest of pretexts. She giggled with delight at any words that managed to escape his lips. This was sure to make people talk. In Arthur's eyes, it was incomprehensible.

He returned to his room that day with a lingering buzz of adrenaline. With time he arrived at a reasonably accurate assessment of Maisy's designs, and attempted to laugh it off. But his ability to devise an appropriate response was missing some important yet indefinable element. He never got these things quite right. He wrote a letter to Isabel in which he detailed the amusing situation in which he had found himself.

Isabel's reply was delivered the following day. It urged him to come clean about his feelings rather than invent stories about Maisy Armagast. For her part, Isabel never deviated from absolute honesty. So faithful was she in Arthur's love that she would not hesitate to tell him she had spent the previous Saturday night sleeping on a sofa of a friend who had taken her to dinner. Nor did she shy away from sharing that this friend was male and that they had binge-watched old episodes of *Ally McBeal* into the small hours. His name was Porter. It was a hip, trendy name offered *en passant* as a final twist of the knife.

Her reply at last managed to shake the deeply laid foundations of Arthur's faith. He was crushed, and set about correcting his error with the exhaustive explanations and apologies that are the death spiral of intimate relationships the world over.

Chapter Eight

Nowhere to be, nothing to do, and the whole world asleep, or so it seemed. In some corner of the arctic wastes, lying in his bed and staring at the ceiling, Arthur Pifflethorpe faced a world within. It was a world all his own, full of mists and terrors and worries. Everything familiar and safe was far away. Thoughts would not be silenced.

Where was Isabel now? What time was it for her? Would she be in bed? What if she was not in bed? Would she be with him? What were they doing? But he snuffed this line of reasoning as being too painful to consider. And the cycle began again.

Where was Isabel now?

It was twelve days since he had heard from her; twelve days and... six and a half hours, give or take. He was not sure about the minutes. *I think we need to see other people.* Did that mean she *was* seeing other people? Did that mean it was over?

Arthur's reply had received no further response. He had tried to make himself wait before clicking *send*. He had tried so hard. He knew it was best to sleep on it. But there was no stopping himself. Now he ran through the words of his email again and again in his head, imagining everything she may have misunderstood.

I think we need to see other people.

Mastery over wayward thoughts is difficult enough in the daytime as we go about the business of keeping ourselves alive. At night, the mind is a merciless overlord. Arthur could hear Ramon's even breathing below. Knowing he was fast asleep and oblivious to the slow ticking by of the minutes—the seconds—made it worse. Inhale, exhale. Inhale, exhale. Marking time. Dim light shone around the curtains from the streetlamps on the perimeter road. It was not enough to illuminate the deepest recesses of the room. In an effort to snuff out the world and lose himself in oblivion, Arthur removed his T-shirt and tossed it down to cover the luminous red readout of the alarm clock on the desk. The bed's wool blanket began to itch. He pulled up the sheet and folded it over, but to no avail. The fibers must have worked their way throughout the bed.

A niggling itch. First here, then there. Try not to move. Wait for it to go away. Giving up, rustle, rustle... scratch. Relief. Thirty seconds of imagining himself drifting closer to sleep... closer... and then again, somewhere else. That itch.

Where was Isabel now?

Did Arthur sleep? If so, he dreamed of being awake. Consciousness and unconsciousness run together in the deepest nether-regions of hell. There is no escaping ourselves.

The sound of Ramon's breathing.

The distant churn of a Snowcat plowing up the hillside with a load of supplies.

A gray rectangle of light around the window curtain. Amorphous red where the numbers of the alarm clock shone dimly through the fabric of his crumpled T-shirt.

Arthur closed his eyes. The itch, on his nose this time. *Don't scratch it. Don't scratch it. Sleep: will yourself to sleep.* Shift, rustle... scratch.

Was she with him? What were they doing?

Whispering. A glittering giggle, just above the threshold of hearing.

Was he dreaming?

The Snowcat found its destination. Its engine raced for a moment before going dead. The hush of snow shrouded the world in a deeper silence.

A giggle. A whisper, inaudible.

Was it a dream? Was that Isabel giggling? Why was she so happy? What if she was...

What if he was...

No, Arthur was not sleeping; he was fairly sure of it now.

Whisper, giggle.

He was sure of it this time. The sound was coming from just outside the door. He lay there in the dark, straining after sound. Yes, someone was moving outside the door. Someone was whispering just there, just beyond the slab of laminated particleboard, with an undertone of mirth detectable even without understanding the words. It was a girl's voice. Then another. Another... or was that the first again?

A giggle, stifled with a snort. Another furious eruption of giggling.

"Quiet! Stop it!" The words were audible this time, urgent.

"*You* stop it!"

"Is this the one?"

Someone tapped on the door with a fingertip, scarcely audible.

Giggling.

"No no no no no!"

"Hush... he's coming back."

"No, not here!"

"Hey... hey... get up! Not here!"

One of the girls (it was impossible to tell how many there were—three? Four?) began cursing. Voices whispered over one another. Snippets made it through the door here and there.

"Get up! He's coming!"

"Lift her."

"Get her feet."

"He's coming!"

"Go... we have to go. Now!"

"What about..."

"Go!"

Giggling faded off down the hallway. Going. Gone.

Silence.

Arthur listened until the quiet rang in his ears. Nothing. Sleep was forgotten. He sat up and slid to the edge of the bed, dangling his feet over the side. He stopped again, listening. Nothing. He climbed down and crept to the door. Ramon went on sleeping. Arthur laid a hand on the knob and paused again for a moment before giving it a gentle turn. He pushed. It opened an inch or two before hitting some immobile object. Through the narrow gap he could see a pair of legs in the dimmed light of the hall. Someone lay stretched on the floor just outside the door. He eased it closed.

He froze there in the darkness, considering. What to do? Should he go back to bed? Now there was no sense in trying to sleep. *Think. What should I do?* Was the desk officer coming down the hall to investigate? Who was this person outside on the floor? Did she need help?

He was brought back to his senses by a chill wafting over his skin. He was still in his underwear and socks. First things first. Clothes. He went to the closet and retrieved a jumpsuit. He pulled up the zipper slowly... quietly... *don't wake Ramon.* He pulled on his boots and laced them up. Ran his fingers through his hair. Rubbed his eyes. Activity at last set in motion his faltering resolve. He went back to the door and pressed his ear against it. Nothing.

He turned the knob and pushed. Again, it only opened an inch or two before running up against the obstacle. He pushed harder. A groan. The prone body slid on the tiled floor, then shifted its weight of its own accord. Another groan. He got the door open far enough to stick his head out. The light in the hallway was dim, with all but a single bulb in each alcove extinguished. He leaned out past the recess and peered down the hall. At the far end he could see the cadet in charge of quarters seated at his desk in a pool of light. His face was turned down and lit by a dancing glow. He was watching television. He must have been wearing headphones. Arthur looked down. It was indeed a woman stretched out on the floor. She was curled on her side, head pillowed with her hands and dark hair falling over her face.

Arthur pushed harder and squeezed through the gap in the door. He eased it closed. Again he paused, listening. Quiet. He stepped lightly forward and knelt, laying a hand on the girl's shoulder. He shook her gently. A low groan. He froze, looking up and down the hall. Nothing. He had to get her out of here. All the desk officer had to do was look up, and they would be finished. If she were caught here in the men's quarters, she would certainly be punished, possibly expelled.

He peered up and down the hall: *still quiet.* Just across and down a door or two was the restroom. The girl was small. He slid her out from the wall and stepped behind, grasping her under the armpits. She slid smoothly and silently on the tiled floor, her head lolling forward over her chest. He pushed the restroom door open with his backside as he dragged her through. He sat her upright against a wall and bent to peer beneath the disheveled curtain of hair. It took him a moment to recognize the face. It was smeared with green, brown, and black makeup as if she were a commando out on a midnight raid. But recognize it he did. His heart skipped.

How on Earth did Maisy Armagast come to be sleeping outside Arthur's door? The sleeping question we may resolve readily enough. Maisy was drunk, although Arthur was not at the time entirely clear on this point. But how did Maisy come to be dead drunk on the floor outside Arthur's door? It would be some time before Arthur learned the full truth of the matter from Maisy's lips, but learn it he would.

Black market activity among the ranks of the Argonauts was by no means limited to those commodities that had caused so much trouble for Arthur. Of late, some enterprising soul had acquired the means of managing an industrial-scale process of alcoholic fermentation based on spare stocks of potatoes from the kitchens. The product of these efforts was distributed far and wide throughout the corps, passing from hand to hand in vacant breakrooms and beneath cafeteria tables.

Maisy and a small collection of girlfriends had come into possession of a not inconsiderable quantity of this rotgut hooch. Finding occasion upon a birthday or some such, the group resolved to drink it up before it was discovered by Bosun Oluwusi and his cadre of drill instructors. As will often happen in such cases, the subject arose of each girl's recent relations vis-à-vis the opposite sex. Stories were shared, notes compared, and spirits rose higher and higher as the level of liquid in the bottles dropped lower and lower. As in most fields of endeavor, Maisy was not one to be outdone in either the consumption of alcoholic beverages or the telling of tales. She took two drams for every one of theirs and was rewarded by hearty praise and encouragement.

The conversation devolved, as these things will. Nothing good ever happens after one o'clock in the morning, and by this time it was a good bit past this hour. Particulars under discussion grew more explicit and eventually entered upon plans for the immediate future. It was proposed that the girls would do well by securing a plentiful stock of those commodities with which the name of Arthur Pifflethorpe had come to be so closely associated (although it was Arthur's unfortunate nickname, and not the name given to him by Mrs. Pifflethorpe, that was so lightheartedly bandied about). We need not delve too deeply into the logic of setting off in the middle of the night to seek out Arthur's room and finagle from him some portion of his supposedly limitless stocks. The important point was that the whole proposal was delightfully funny.

So, after kitting out in preparation for the hazardous environment likely to be encountered, Maisy and her girlfriends crept off down darkened corridors in meticulous tactical formation. All that could be seen of them were shadows flitting along the walls. All that could be heard was a faint footfall, a whispered breath, and the occasional bout of giggling echoing up and down the halls like birdsong.

They were successful in locating Arthur's door and were fortunate in finding the hallway empty, with the desk officer off on some errand. His return coincided with Maisy's uncontrollable urge to take a nap, right then and there. Supposing (not without some justification) that the daughter of Beckett Armagast would be safer than they should their caper be discovered, Maisy's girlfriends abandoned her to her fate. They found all of this incomparably amusing.

But Arthur knew none of it. All he knew was that he was crouched on the tiles of the bathroom floor, staring into the face of a young lady who was far and away the most famous of the Argonauts. And my goodness wasn't she pretty, despite the gunk smeared all over her face?

What to do?

Maisy moaned, and her eyes came up to meet Arthur's without a glimmer of recognition. Abruptly she turned, pitched over onto the tiles, and vomited a great rancid torrent, the thinnest elements of which began meandering away toward a nearby drainpipe.

Arthur was not entirely naïve in the ways of the world. Sometime between finding Maisy napping outside his door and rinsing her vomit down the drain in the restroom floor, it occurred to him what had brought her to this state. It was not influenza that caused her collapse. She had not been drawn to his doorstep by ineffable magnetism. She was drunk and in the midst of some elaborate prank of which Arthur was most likely the butt.

But Arthur was not one to dwell upon his resentments. It went without saying he would help her. This is just the sort of thing Arthur did, and likely would have done had the individual in question been something other than a beautiful social-media-influencer-cum-actress with pretensions to music. It did not even occur to him—at first, anyway—that helping her would require physical contact at a level previously unimaginable.

Maisy had, for the most part, missed herself in the bout of heaving that emptied the contents of her stomach onto the tiles. But as she pushed herself erect, her hand landed in an errant splatter. She raised the hand before her face to examine this new problem and spent several seconds mulling over an appropriate remedy. She sniffed at it. Arthur watched as he stood at the sink waiting for the faucet to fill his cupped hands. He had been thus shuttling water in an attempt to eliminate the evidence. An instant too late, he intuited the course of her wandering line of reasoning. He released the water into the sink and made a dash for her.

"No no no no no!" he admonished with a rising tone of urgency, but did not arrive in time to prevent her wiping the mess on the leg of her uniform.

"What do you want from me?" she said, looking at Arthur with contempt.

"We need to keep you clean," he replied.

"Hmmm..." she mused. "I suppose it wouldn't do to *mess me up*." She giggled furiously.

Arthur determined he had done enough to wash away the mess. He took her hand. "Come on," he said. "You need to get up. You need to come with me."

"I like it here," she said, pulling way and settling back against the wall. She looked around as if far more interested in the interior of the men's room than in whatever Arthur had to say. Her eyes were captured by a row of urinals on a far wall. "I think I would like to try peeing in one of those." Arthur was relieved to see this observation resulted only in another bout of giggling.

He tried for some minutes more to convince her to stand. Each argument was met with similar justifications to the contrary. This could not go on. Eventually someone was going to enter the restroom. It would be necessary to carry her. Fortunately, the petiteness of her frame recommended itself to such feats of heroism. He cracked the door and surveyed the hallway. The desk officer was still at his station, watching his television program. Arthur went back to her and bent, slipping a hand behind her back and another beneath her knees, as he had seen done. He lifted.

Nothing happened—nothing whatsoever. She might as well have weighed three hundred pounds. This was disconcerting for Arthur and piercingly humorous for Maisy. She seemed to be enjoying it all immensely.

Lift with the knees, he thought.

He crouched, heaved, and this time managed to settle her more or less comfortably in his arms. He was proud at this accomplishment. Only a few short months ago, it would have been well beyond his abilities. It did not, however, go precisely as he had pictured. In the movies, the girl always threw her arms around the neck of her rescuer and thereby assisted him in bearing her weight. Maisy did no such thing. She seemed intent upon her fingernails, and after a grimace of disapproval began to poke at the cuticles.

Arthur carried her to the door and only then recalled that it swung inward. He thought on this for a moment and came to the conclusion that trying to open it with Maisy in his arms was courting disaster. He set her back on the floor. She went on ignoring him and would likely have pulled out a nailfile had she been so equipped. He opened the door, checked the hallway once more, and held it open with a foot as he lifted Maisy again. Maintaining his balance carried him a step back into the restroom, and the door swung closed once more.

Maisy had mercifully switched her attitude from jocularity to disregard. She went on fixing her cuticles as Arthur returned her to the floor. Eventually he did get her out of the restroom and across the hallway into the stairwell. But that was as far as he made it, for at this point he began to distrust the burning sensation creeping up his biceps. This was harder than it looked. He paused to study the flight of concrete stairs descending into shadow and decided against continuing in this fashion. He set her back on the floor while he considered the options. Would she walk, appropriately supported? Could he arrange her piggyback? Would it be necessary to wake Ramon?

His attention was drawn to her once more by the sound of retching. He looked to see she had not been entirely successful in emptying her stomach onto the floor of the restroom. With the new round of illness, her composure was broken. She lay sprawled on her side as if melting, too exhausted even to roll away from the puddle she had made. Her groaning echoed up and down the stairwell.

This new mess would have to stay. The stairwell was not a safe place to dally. He managed to get her to her feet. An arm draped heavily over his shoulders and her head hung limp, hair falling in a curtain over her face. Its tips had not escaped the latest attack of nausea and dangled in damp clumps.

It was thirty minutes or more before he was able to wrangle Maisy back to her room. He knew, as everyone did, to which squadron she belonged. Through months of listening to the banter of Ramon and Dexter, he had learned the best ways to evade security measures between the men's and women's dormitories. Once he had to duck for cover at the sound of approaching footsteps. He watched from the shadows as a curfew monitor stalked past. It was Stanley Waller. The clicking of his metal heel-taps echoed through the corridor. Once Arthur stumbled while lifting Maisy up a set of steps and ran his forearm viciously into the edge of the top step. This brought Maisy to an adequate level of consciousness to direct him the last few dozen meters to the appropriate door.

The room was unoccupied, for Maisy was not one to be burdened with a roommate. In the meager light filtering in around the curtains, he made out a single bed, a desk and chair, a vanity next to the door. A chest of drawers sat next to the closet. A sitting area complete with settee and recliner was arranged near the windows. He closed the door and eased her onto the bed, then went to the desk and switched on the lamp.

Should he undress her? That was what they did in the movies. Her clothes were a mess; he felt it was the gentlemanly thing to do. But he could not bring himself to it. He satisfied himself with tugging off her boots. She shuffled back onto the pillow, curled up on her side, and closed her eyes. What had she smeared all over her face? He should try to get some of it off. In the morning her skin would be a mess of pimples. He found a washcloth and ran the water until it was warm. He soaked the washcloth and wrung it out, then knelt next to the bed and leaned in, pushing back the hair that had fallen over her face.

Her eyes sprang open. He froze, and she gazed into his eyes for a moment. Then the tension seemed to drain away, and she let out a contented sigh. "I know you," she said.

Arthur began to dab at the smear of makeup with the washcloth. She watched him clean her, close and unabashed. Silence descended as he worked.

"I stink," she said after a few minutes of this.

He smiled at her.

"We should take this off."

"Let's not do that right now."

Her voice went down to a conspiratorial whisper. "Plus, I want to show you my underwear," she said. Her hand came up and she began pulling at the zipper of her jumpsuit.

"No, let's leave that on," Arthur said. He took her hand and pulled it away, then tugged the zipper back into place.

"Don't you want to see my underwear?" she said. She reached for the zipper again.

"Not right now, Maisy," he said. "You have to sleep." He took her hand gently, but firmly enough to hold it down until she forgot its original intent.

"I got it in Paris."

"I'm sure it's very nice."

"Do you think I'm beautiful?"

"Yes, you're very pretty." He had done the best he could with the washcloth and returned it to the vanity. He looked back at her. "I have to go now," he said. "You need to sleep."

"But my underwear," she said with earnest intensity. "I got it in Paris."

"I'll see it another time." His hand was on the knob. Turning it. He could hear rustling from the bed. Was she taking off her clothes?

A high whine pulled his attention back. No, she had drawn her knees up and flipped the comforter up over her legs. She lay in a fetal position, her eyes no longer on Arthur. She was staring off at nothing. He paused there to look at her. Then she began to cry.

He stepped back across to the bed. "Hey... hey... what's the matter?"

"I got it in Paris," she said between sniffles.

"I'm sure it's very nice. Right now, you need to sleep."

The crying intensified, and tears were running remnants of makeup down over her cheek. Arthur had been unable to clean around her eyes. "He hates me. They all hate me," she said.

Arthur knelt by the bed once more and leaned in. He could not bring himself to take her hand. "No one hates you," he said. "You're everyone's favorite person. I mean it. Everyone."

"Am I your favorite person?"

"You bet."

"You're lying to me."

"I'm not."

"Beckett hates me. Mama loved me, but I don't see her anymore."

"Why don't you see her? You can see her again before we leave."

The crying had spread from her face to her chest, and her breath caught twice. Her nose was running in a glistening streak down onto the pillow. "She won't want to see me. She doesn't love me anymore."

"Of course she loves you."

"I was horrible to her."

"That doesn't matter. Mamas always love their babies." He

stood and went back to the vanity. He could not find a clean washcloth and did his best to rinse Maisy's makeup out of the old one.

"Arthur..." She never finished the thought, or maybe that is all there was.

It was the first time Arthur had heard Maisy say his name. It was the single memory of the evening that would remain crisp in the years to come. He went back to her and began cleaning her nose and cheeks.

"Kiss me, Arthur," she said in a whisper.

This invitation was not as hard to resist as one may suppose. Even from his current distance, he could smell the odor on her breath. He smiled a smile he imagined to be gallant and went on prodding at her skin with the washcloth. Her eyelids fell, fluttered, fell, and she drifted off to sleep.

He stood and watched her for a moment. The sniffling had stopped, and her breathing was low and even. Her mouth was open, and the damp patch on the pillow begun by her nose continued to spread. He let the sight of her warm him for a moment, then he hung the washcloth on the edge of the sink. He left.

Arthur never told anyone of his night with Maisy. He never even told Ramon, who was still sleeping when he returned. We would like to say his silence was due to some chivalrous desire to be discreet, that in the raillery of manly repartee he resisted the urge to lay Maisy's secrets out for all to see. For all would indeed have seen. Even Ramon could not be expected to keep such a secret, even had Arthur sworn him to it.

No, he kept quiet about it because he could not bring himself to admit his failures. What would they say? All of that, and he had not even given her a kiss, bad breath be damned? He had not even arranged to meet with her again, or left a note on the bureau? Demands that he speak with her in the cafeteria would be relentless. If he tried that, he would surely fail with all the magnificent glory of a thundering space launch. He prayed Maisy would not make yet another joke of it. He could only hope reports were true, and alcohol had a way of making one forget.

Rumors swirled over who had left the puddle of vomit in the stairwell. Suspicions rose further over an unusual smell in the restroom. But these things were not so uncommon and were scarcely reported beyond the halls of Arthur's squadron. Ramon caught an odd scent in their laundry hamper. It had been impossible for Arthur to stay clean while carrying Maisy through the corridors. He made insinuations, trying to draw his roommate into a confession. These were unsuccessful. That was as far as it went.

What of Maisy? She told her girlfriends the entire night was a blank. She had no idea how she had gotten back to her room. Whether this was true or not, they would never be able to determine. Maisy was just as terrified as Arthur that details of the episode would come to light. She had yet to meet a man loath to trumpet from the rooftops their most private intimacies. She waited for the axe to drop in the court of public opinion. It never did.

Chapter Nine

On an evening not long after the incident with Maisy, Arthur sat with Ramon before the windows of their dormitory room. These were opened wide to admit a breeze that would have felt chilly to one who had not spent a winter in that place. It was a mild day in early spring, and the length of the northern days had briefly assumed some semblance of normality on their long trek from solstice to solstice. The sun was low in the sky and cast a conflagration of oranges and reds through roughly broken bands of stratocumulus. It lit upon the lakes, set the river ablaze, and wormed its way into hollows still crusted with lingering snow. The world glowed.

Ramon sipped on a flask of that ill-defined liquid which had recently taken by storm the labyrinthine underworld of Earth Station One contraband. "Drink some," he said, reaching out to offer Arthur a sip.

Arthur declined with a cursory shake of his head before returning his attention to the sunset, which bathed their faces in its radiance. His reticence reflected a drama raging within.

"Here's the thing," Ramon went on, taking upon himself the

declined sip from the flask. "Celia and I never had much in common. Apart from the obvious. She knew what she wanted, and I knew what I wanted, and where those didn't overlap, we just let it lie. Sometimes you need that, but it's nothing to build a life on."

Arthur looked at him. "Isabel and I had more than that," he said.

"What did you have?" Ramon pressed. "How much time did you really even spend together?"

"We were always together," Arthur rejoined.

"Doing what?"

Arthur shrugged. "Hanging out," he said, his eyes again going back to the window.

"Running the clock? Come on, man, that's not what I'm talking about. She's cute... I get it. But what did she say when you asked to do something *you* wanted to do? Did it even come up?"

Arthur gave him a look that said he did not follow Ramon's meaning. Ramon continued to wait for an answer. When it did not come, he pressed, "So, you hung out and... what? Watched television? Maybe you followed her around the mall while she talked about perfumes and blouses and who's dating whom with her friends? Did you ever get her on a mountain bike?" Ramon paused before going on. "What did you love about her? What did she love about you?"

"It isn't about what we were doing," Arthur said. "It was deeper than that. We understood each other. That's what got us through the past year. We didn't need to be doing anything at all. She's just a beautiful person all the way through. I don't care that she doesn't like mountain biking. That's not important..."

Arthur paused to collect his thoughts. Before he could go on, Ramon cut him off. "But it *is* important," he said. "All of those things you used to do before you met her—you did them

111

for a reason. They were you. Did you ever take her out with your telescope? Hiking over in that park you used to go to? Did you drive her to the lake where you used to spend so much time? Introduce her to *your* friends? Was she willing to do any of those things? Or was she annoyed because they were a distraction from what she wanted to do?"

"The lake was too far," said Arthur.

Ramon pursed his lips and shook his head. "You're missing my point, dude. Listen, love isn't some mystical feeling she has about your soul. Love is how she feels about the things you love. If she's not excited about them just because you are, then it's not really you that she's in love with. Those things are what make you who you are. There's nothing more important than that." He corrected himself: "There's nothing *more* than that."

"I think there is," said Arthur.

"Maybe there is and maybe there isn't. It doesn't matter. What matters is what you can see and feel. Everything else is just academic."

"Something has to make all of it mean something."

Ramon shrugged. "Maybe so. But if that's the case, then it has to go both ways. Whatever it is you're talking about has to be connected to the stuff you can see, or it doesn't matter."

"But that's what love *is*," said Arthur. He was having a difficult time articulating what he knew to be true. The sun slipped into the narrow band of open sky between clouds and horizon. Its light reflected from Arthur's eyes as he looked at his roommate.

"Is it?" said Ramon. "Look, all I'm saying is that you need more than common ground. Any two people will have that somewhere. Common ground is not the important thing. There has to be give and take for any two people to spend a life together. You do stuff she wants to do; she does stuff you want to do. You expand each other's horizons. If one of you isn't willing to get their hands dirty on the other's account, then eventually you'll realize what you thought was give and take was really just common ground: the stuff she wanted anyway. Whenever there's conflict, she wins. You'll be the one to do all the giving, all the sacrificing. That's not love."

"You're still missing the point," Arthur replied. "It's not about winning and losing... keeping score."

"Am I? Look... let's say in some alternate universe the two of you got married. Who does the dishes? Who cleans the toilets? You say love is some mystical force that has nothing to do with dishes and toilets. I say love is all about dishes and toilets. If you love someone, taking care of all of life's details isn't so bad because you're taking care of the person you love. If she won't even do something that she knows you like, you can bet she's not going to be cleaning toilets. You'll be doing that, because—in every sense that matters—you care more about her than she cares about you."

"I'm not looking for someone to clean the toilets."

Ramon smacked his forehead with a palm. "But someone has to do it, dude. Someone has to do it. Listen to what I'm saying. Do you want to be her partner, or do you want to be her housekeeper? Do you want to spend the rest of your life following her around the mall, or do you want to grow together? Just think about it. That's all I'm saying."

Ramon just could not understand.

The setting sun drew their attention as its orb was cut by the horizon's even line of blue. Yellows deepened into oranges and oranges into reds. High overhead, everything faded into purple before the encroaching shroud of black. Fifteen minutes later, the show was finished, and the roommates returned to their studies. There was nothing more to say.

. . .

Arthur continued to see Maisy in class, but after that night in her room, she seemed to forget him entirely. The next class period, he took the same desk in the back row. When she arrived her usual ten minutes after the hour, she took no notice of him and found another friend with whom to sit. Arthur did not admit to himself the vague disappointment he felt. After that, he took an empty chair along the back wall and let her have the desk, listening to the lectures with his notebook resting on his knees.

Like all the cadets, Arthur found himself drawn more and more to the magnificent sweep of nature amid which the campus was an insignificant speck. The feeling may have arisen from the need to escape a long winter, and it may have been a final effort to build a stock of memories of all the things they would never see again. The dominion of the drill instructors eased as the months went by and habits became ingrained. Perhaps they too were feeling the grip of melancholy. The corps went about its cleaning and polishing and marching to meals as if they had always lived thus, even as the hollering subsided. Intervals between were filled with circumstances of life, boiled down to their essence.

Unspoken conventions sprang up. On evenings when the skies were not hung with permeating mist, the yards filled with people studying, strolling, or simply lounging about in scattered clumps. The parapet overlooking the plain was lined from one corner of the promontory to the other with cadets leaning against the stone wall, chatting quietly or simply staring out at the view. A footpath cut its way in meandering switchbacks from the yard behind the auditorium up into the hills. It was worn bare by feet finding their way up to the crest of the front range. Atop the massive boulders perched there sprang up cairns and fire rings and the scatterings of litter that have marked the passage of humanity from time immemorial. From that height could be seen crest after crest of earth breaking like waves on a storm-tossed shoreline. The mountain range stretched back to distant summits whose tips barely peeked through vast glacier fields. Rocky slopes were locked beneath thousands of feet of ice, the deepest layers of which had been laid before the dawn of recorded history.

A new camaraderie sprang up where there had been confrontation and competition. No one remaining feared for their place on the crew; or, more accurately, what fear lingered arose not from each other but from within. Departure of the *Argo* loomed. With it came a seriousness, an abrupt lurch into maturity of a culture that had formed over months of feeling one another out. Unspoken was the fact that each cadet, soon to be Argonaut, was caught in the grip of soul-searching. Soon the time for decisions would be past.

Fears had risen among Beckett Armagast and his staff that those final months on Earth would bring a surge in resignations with no time left to train up replacements. They had even debated the wisdom of offering a period of leave for cadets to pay loved ones a final visit. In the end, the exodus never materialized. New relationships tied the crew together with bonds inexpressible in words. Uniting them was solidarity and pride and even a collective hunger to be off. No quantity of bungling by headquarters staff could stamp out the gravity of the situation facing them. No number of silly rules and overbearing authorities and leaking pipes could turn aside attention from their place in history.

Perhaps they all knew this feeling could not last. Perhaps experience had taught them that no human endeavor, however unique, however intense, can avoid the inevitable fate of slipping back into routine. With routine would come boredom. With boredom would come reemergence of the petty passions and viciousness that have underwritten all the world's great sagas. But all this was so new. Perhaps there was the slimmest of possibilities that this group would achieve some great leap in human evolution, would write a new history. These were the unarticulated musings lurking beneath the surface as they stared out on the majesty of nature.

Arthur was not immune to their power. Obstacles that had seemed insurmountable shrank to mere speed bumps on a highway heading off toward interstellar space. Yes, even Isabel began to fall into perspective. What was it that had made her loom so large? Without a conscious change in his understanding of love, without acknowledging what truth may have lain in Ramon's advice, the deep meaning he had read into her every word began to fall away. What was left bored him. He almost regretted the time he had spent distracted from the purpose that now began to assume its proper place in his consciousness. He could not escape the fever that swept his comrades. He threw himself with renewed vigor into learning. He joined study groups that once, not so long in the past, would not have considered inviting him along. He allowed enthusiasm for waste-to-energy theories and economic recycling incentives to push aside feelings of inadequacy. He met his comrades on even ground, if only for a short while.

The leveling caught up even Maisy Armagast. On a sun-drenched midnight in June, Arthur and a dozen other cadets were scattered around the domed pinnacle of granite overlooking the campus, the plain to the south, and the mountains to the north. Someone had lit a campfire with wood from a smashed armchair. Smoke drifted lazily skyward before being caught up and dissipated in a tumble of wind shear whose turbulence somehow avoided the hilltop. Skyla Sawyer sat back from the group, separated by her usual distance from the camaraderie and the conversation. Even her presence could not darken the mood; in her manner were unmistakeable glimmers of desire to be accepted. Arthur sat on the slope of rock facing the mountains along with Ramon and Dexter and two or three other cadets from their squadron. Conversation rose and fell, interspersed with silent staring out over the vista.

Someone passing behind tousled Arthur's regrown hair with a hand. He looked up over a shoulder to see Maisy standing above him.

"Hey, Arthur," she said.

"Hey, Maisy," he replied.

She paused there for a moment to study the view that so captivated Arthur and his friends. Arthur turned back as well, and they looked out on it together. He heard her breathe deeply and looked up again. She caught his eye, smiled, and moved off with her group of friends. Arthur too went back to his private thoughts. Her passing left barely a ripple.

With scarcely a whimper, their studies ended. There was no cramming for exams, no late nights finalizing graduate theses and writing up lab results. Armagast Enterprises had no intention of washing cadets out so late in the game, and put up no final pretense of authority. Soon there would be nothing but time to fill what gaps in knowledge remained. Critical functions —navigation, pilotage, power-plant operation—these were well in hand. The rest would come. The *Argo* was designed to house a population with widely varied abilities and skill sets. Soon it would carry even newborn babies. Final instruction could be managed aboard.

The cadet corps sat through one last series of seminars. They learned the particulars of their coming leap from the Earth's surface up to the waiting *Argo*. The truth of it all, discussed at length after hours spent listening to lectures on thrust vectors and capsule pressurization and abort procedures, was that they were passive participants in the operation. Sealed up like tins of sardines, their bodies would be pitched skyward in a massive cavalcade of fire. Sending five thousand souls into orbit was a magnificent capstone to the decades-long logistical nightmare of construction. Assembly lines that had built cargo freighters were modified to produce passenger capsules and were churning them out by the hundreds.

Arthur's final days on Earth were scripted out in a packet of instructions received from the hand of his squadron's commanding officer. Like the rest of his classmates, he spent that evening in his room, his feet up on the windowsill, alternately flipping through papers and gazing out over the landscape. With no cities to pollute the sky with their light, the vault of stars extended down to the horizon unbroken, like pictures Arthur had seen from the surface of the moon. Contained in the manila envelope he had been given were itineraries and airline tickets and maps. There were bus schedules and hotel reservations and emergency contact numbers. A security pass was already fitted into its plastic sleeve and clipped to a lanyard to be worn around his neck when the time came.

A passenger manifest listed the names of those who would be riding with him to the heavens. He recognized none of them. Following a final period of leave, cadets on that manifest would converge via commercial airlines on an island in the South Pacific, one of many that had spent year after year flinging rockets skyward. Twenty cadets—soon to be crew—would ride an elevator to the rocket's boarding bridge, scramble through a hatch, strap into their seats, and take the first step on a journey that would have no end. There was a numbness that descended over Arthur as he read. He could not have said what was missing from it all, but nagging at the back of his mind was the feeling there should be more.

Carrying identical blue duffel bags with name tags stitched

into the nylon, cadets swarmed the tarmac of the airfield in their final hours at Earth Station One. Departure could not have been more different from arrival. Then, they had been alone and terrified as they stepped forward into the unknown. Now they were a team with shared experiences and hardships, setting off on a great adventure. The crowd buzzed, smiles and laughter papering over the unease.

A line of commuter planes stood at the ready. One by one, they ran up their engines and taxied forward to the loading area. A ground crew set chocks and lowered stairs as drill instructors, still wearing their mirrored sunglasses, shouted out names of passengers and tried to bludgeon order back into the chaos. There was no dampening the buoyant mood. Cadets would return home to be feted in hometown newspapers and on local television stations. They would speak before student bodies in old high school gymnasiums and ride high in the back seats of convertibles in parades down main streets from Boston to Bangalore. They would hug their mothers and visit old sweethearts. There were thousands of stories to be told of thousands of Argonauts, each of whom had his or her own reasons for leaving behind all they had loved. No one on the crew would ask questions about these things.

Arthur arrived back at the little airport to a scene much as he had left it: crowds gathered to set their eyes on the town's only resident within recent memory to rise to national prominence. At the front was Mrs. Pifflethorpe, still dressed in her uniform from the diner and looking astonished at all the attention. Mr. Hibbert was there, as were Mrs. Quinn and a half-dozen other teachers and school administrators who had known Arthur down through the years. The mayor was there, and most of the town council. Even the district's representative to the state legislature had flown in for the occasion, although she seemed more interested in the crew from the local news station than in Arthur.

He took in all of this as he crossed a wide, empty space between the terminal and the security checkpoint's rope line. He embraced Mrs. Pifflethorpe, and she cried. The crowd enveloped him. The mayor stepped forward as Arthur and Mrs. Pifflethorpe drew apart, placing a hand on each of their shoulders and giving a brief speech. Mrs. Pifflethorpe thanked him for his kind words, and Arthur shook a dozen or more hands on their way to the sliding glass doors that opened to the airport's loading zone.

An old Lincoln was idling on the drive. Mrs. Pifflethorpe opened the passenger door and slid across the bench seat to the middle, inviting Arthur to sit next to her. In the driver's seat was Mr. Underwood, owner of Underwood Hardware and Mercantile. Mrs. Henderson from the Society column of the local newspaper stood on the walk and snapped their picture as they drove away.

The three of them had dinner at the Italian restaurant where Arthur had once planned to bring Isabel on their ill-fated Homecoming date. They sat across from one another at a table covered by a red faux-leather tablecloth frayed at the corners. The same fabric, dirty and cracked, upholstered the padded seats of booths lining the walls. A tea candle burned in a little frosted votive, its light accentuating the lines that had grown more pronounced in his mother's face. Light from dimmed gold-leaf chandeliers disappeared into walls clad in walnut-veneer paneling as if into a black hole. The carpet looked like it had been procured secondhand from the hallway of a cheap motel, even down to the frayed seams that ran at regular intervals the length of the room.

Over appetizers Mrs. Pifflethorpe broke the news. "Arthur," she said, placing a hand over his, "Howard and I have become special friends. You've grown up now, and I know you'll understand."

"I know. I understand." It grated that she still saw him as the child who had left for Earth Station One the previous year.

"It's good not to be alone, you know. Your father will always be with us." She glanced at Mr. Underwood for affirmation. He provided it with a solicitous grin and a pat on her forearm.

"I know. I'm happy for you." Arthur *was* happy for her, but he did not want to discuss it. He wanted the memories to be of his father—his family—not of this. He changed the subject: the particulars of his job on the *Argo*, the danger of the coming launch, the friends he had made in training. Conversation was stilted, with Mr. Underwood alternating between attempts to fade into the background and eagerness to please his romantic interest. Mostly Arthur talked, straining to fill awkward gaps.

There was one exchange that would remain with him. It happened toward the end of the evening. Mr. Underwood had excused himself to the restroom, and Arthur had a moment alone with his mother.

She laid a hand on his. "You know how much I love you, Arthur," she said.

"I love you too, Mom." He turned his hand over to squeeze hers.

"Your father would want you to go. William would want you to go."

"Do you want me to go?"

Her eyes welled for a moment. "It's for the best. There's nothing here for you."

"We could go somewhere else." He knew her answer before he said it.

"No... I could never..." It did not need to be said that memories of Mr. Pifflethorpe would always be in that place. She could never leave them.

Mr. Underwood came back across the room with a bounce in his step that said he was trying too hard to lighten the mood. "Who wants tiramisu?" he said as he took his seat.

The week passed quickly, and the next. There was little for Arthur to do during days in which his mother went on working at the diner. Most of his friends had left town after graduation. In any public place, he was thronged with citizens wanting to shake his hand and say a few words. Mrs. Quinn held a question-and-answer session at the high school for interested students. He visited all his old favorite spots, even borrowing the Lincoln to drive out to the lake. He stayed overnight in a tent and went out on the dock where he once swam with Sloane. The sky was overcast, and the water whipped to a chop by a damp wind. The place was dead.

With three days left before his departure, Arthur still had not heard from Isabel. He called her number from his mother's landline. She did not pick up. He stumbled over the words of his message. He told her when he would be leaving. A long pause drew out before he ended with "I love you." He was no longer certain it was true, but the words came out unbidden.

She never called him back. He convinced himself this was due to a tide of emotions that could not be put into words. Deep down, he knew she never listened to the message. Three days later, Mrs. Pifflethorpe and Mr. Underwood dropped him at the airport before another scattering of curious onlookers. He was glad when the tires of the commuter plane left the runway with a side-slipping lurch as it weathervaned into the prevailing winds.

Chapter Ten

Arthur hopped to the nearest hub on the commuter, and from there across the continent. He spent two hours browsing the terminal in Los Angeles, unable to sit still. When the plane finally lifted off and banked westward over a coastline streaked with breakers, it did not occur to him that this would be the last continent on which he would ever set foot.

Arthur saw the ocean for the first time. Its unbroken blue was like the other worlds filling his imagination: vast, empty, and a perfect curving sphere. They climbed and climbed, and when the whine of the engines at last quieted and the plane leveled off at cruising altitude, he felt he could almost discern the bend of the blue Earth rolling away below. The sunset lingered for hours as they chased it across the sky.

It was dark when they touched down. Arthur had not been able to make out the beaches and palm trees as the plane descended. Broken clumps of pinpoint lights provided only a faint outline of the island's shoreline. He had slept but could not say for how long. His head buzzed with the confusion of jet lag and fatigue. The terminal was small and homey, with a vacant tiki bar and tropical flowers growing in pots along the walls. Most of the arriving passengers were tourists in tropical-print shirts and Panama hats. A thatched roof vaulted in rough-hewn timber sheltered three or four luggage carousels from the elements. There was no wall separating the baggage claim from a passenger loading zone and drive bordered on its far side by a golf course. The sun was brightening the eastern sky as he pulled his duffel bag from the conveyor and set off in search of the bus station. Shuttles ran at long intervals at the early hour. He waited for twenty minutes.

The bus dropped him at a fenced and gated resort on the far side of the island just as the sun was breaking the horizon. A circular drive lined with hibiscus and frangipani brought arrivals to the porticoed entrance of a spreading, shake-roofed structure that inside was a forest of massive wooden columns set into a wide floor of ceramic tile. As he stepped off the bus, Arthur looked through a set of glass doors, across a lobby, and out another open rear portico to the sea. A palm-shaded pool deck was scattered with empty lounge chairs. A fringe of grass and gardenia separated the patio from the beach.

Behind a long counter topped in glass stood a smiling receptionist in a red sarong and bikini top, a tropical blossom adorning an ear behind which her long, black hair had been tucked.

"Welcome," she said as Arthur approached. "Are you checking in, sir?"

"Yes. I'm with Armagast Enterprises," Arthur replied.

"Of course, sir. You'll find everyone staying with us at the moment is on their way up." She glanced toward the sky and flashed a wide grin. "Let me say on behalf of our whole team that we're honored to have you staying with us."

Arthur shuffled through his sheaf of paperwork until he found the hotel reservations. He slid them across the counter.

"Mr. Pifflethorpe?" the girl said. "We have you in the Malekula Suite. And I see we have a message for you." She punched at the computer and rifled through a stack of papers on the desk. She handed him an envelope along with a glossy pamphlet. On the pamphlet's front was the name of the resort and a family of beautiful people splashing in the surf, awash in mirthful bliss.

"Your room is not quite ready yet," the girl went on, "but please make yourself at home. We can hold your bag for you. I'll have it sent over once housekeeping is finished. The restaurant's breakfast service will be opening in thirty minutes. There is complimentary coffee in the lounge..."

She ran through a rote litany of amenities. It would, Arthur remembered now, be all crewmembers in this place. Launch would be preceded by several weeks of quarantine. Beckett Armagast had spared no expense, with the press scrutinizing his every move. Arthur's eyes flicked back and forth from the receptionist to the envelope she had handed him. She finished her practiced speech. He tore open the envelope's flap with a thumb and slid out the note inside. Handwritten below the resort's letterhead was his name and a few short lines of text. Mrs. Pifflethorpe had called to say that he just missed a call from Isabel. His stomach lurched.

The receptionist finished speaking and stood watching expectantly, eyes black and bright. She looked like a mannequin advertising swimwear.

"Is there a telephone I can use?" Arthur said.

"Right over there, sir," she replied. "Instructions for dialing out are on the card."

Across an expanse of floor set with rattan sofas and armchairs was an alcove with a console table and a telephone. Arthur dialed Isabel's number and listened as the strange-sounding tone rang in his ear.

"Hello?" Behind Isabel's voice was a distant babble of conversation.

"Hi, Isabel," Arthur said.

There was a brief pause. "Arthur?"

"It's me."

"Oh, my God. Where are you?" Arthur could hear shuffling and her voice far from the receiver saying, "Hang on... I'll be right back."

"Is this a good time?" he said.

"Yes, yes... of course. Just a second..." The chatter in the background faded, and her voice sounded clearer. "Where are you?" she repeated.

"I can't say, exactly." He was not permitted to reveal this to anyone. "An island out in the middle of the ocean somewhere. It's beautiful."

"How awesome," she said. "How long do you get to stay there?"

Arthur did not want to talk about the island. He let her question hang for a moment as he sank into a chair next to the console table. Somewhere behind him, the revolving door swished, and some other guest began talking with the reception-ist. He leaned forward with his elbows on his knees, his fore-head in one hand and the other holding the handset to his ear. He lowered his voice. "You didn't come back."

She was silent for a moment. "No, Arthur. I couldn't come back. You know how things are right now."

"I don't know how things are right now."

She told him. She told him about school, about friends, about life in a new city. She said it all in a bright, chatty voice that told him others around her were listening. She told everyone within earshot, and Arthur too (incidentally, it seemed), how wonderful her life away at college had become.

Arthur found himself not caring what she had to say. "I

wanted to see you," he said when she had finished. "I wanted to say goodbye."

"I know," she said. "Me, too. Things are... like... insane right now." The rhythms of her voice had changed. There was a confidence to it, an overconfidence that slipped into tics and clichés. She was around new people, molded to new social conventions.

"You know that was the last time, right?" Arthur said. "I'm not coming back."

She snapped at him. "This hasn't been easy for me either, you know."

"I'm not saying it is. I'm just saying you've meant a lot to me. You always will. I wanted to see you again." His voice had taken a soothing note that inflamed her further.

"Of course, you did, Arthur... because it's all about you now, right? Arthur the Argonaut, leaving all of us commoners behind as he flies off to save the human race. Well, I have a life too, as it happens..."

"Izz, wait... wait..." He tried to break in, but she refused to let him.

"Don't tell me to wait. I'm not waiting anymore. You want me to wait forever... literally. While you fly off into space with Maisy Armagast."

"Isabel, we've been through that," he said. "I thought we were past it. Maisy is nothing. I don't even know her. It was a misunderstanding..."

"Well, you should get to know her." Isabel's voice had become bright and cheerful once more, any remnant of aggravation gone in a flash. "You'll be spending a lot of time together. I think that's wonderful... really. I do wish we'd gotten to see one another again, and I wish you all the best."

The words were a set piece that stabbed at Arthur's heart

with a viciousness that surprised him. He held the phone to his ear, unable to think of anything to say.

"I have to go, Arthur."

Still, he could think of nothing to say.

"I have to go," she said again.

"OK. Bye."

"Bye."

The line went dead. Arthur sat holding the telephone until a squeal of dial tone brought him back to the present. He returned the handset to its cradle and stared at the wall. His thoughts refused to resolve. He sat for a minute, then another.

"Nothing, am I?"

The words came from behind. Their meaning did not immediately register. Only the sound caused him to turn. Ten feet away, in one of the lobby armchairs, sat Maisy. She lounged back with her arms stretched along the armrests and her legs crossed. She wore cutoff blue jeans and a white cotton blouse unbuttoned to her midriff over a white halter top. Her hair was pulled back in a ponytail that hung over the back of the seat cushion.

"Maisy... I... Hello..." Arthur said.

"Who was that?" She made no pretense over having listened in.

"Isabel," was all Arthur could think to say.

"Who's Isabel?"

Arthur had never referred to Isabel as his girlfriend. It was the word that came to mind now, but he could not bring himself to say it. "Someone I used to know."

"Seems to me you either know her or you don't. There's no such thing as 'used to know.'"

"She's gone."

"She hasn't gone anywhere. We're the ones leaving." Maisy grinned to soften it.

"Right."

"What does she care about me?"

Arthur did not have the energy to concoct an explanation. The fog of jet lag hung heavy over him. "I told her what happened in class. She was jealous."

"Jealous of our torrid love affair? Every right to be, I suppose."

Arthur's lips twisted into a smile. They let it go at that. His eyes drifted from hers and out over the lobby. Apart from the receptionist, who had faded into the background, they were alone in the lingering crispness of morning. "Did you just get in?" he said, hoping she would allow him to change the subject.

She nodded. "We must have been on the same plane."

"I didn't see you. On the bus, either."

"We must have missed each other."

It occurred to him that she had stepped from first class directly into a waiting limousine. "I didn't see you on my launch manifest."

She plucked a packet of papers from the table next to her and flipped through its contents. "I'm on Lift 2N324," she said.

"2N326," Arthur replied. "You'll beat me up."

A corner of her lip turned up as she looked at him. "Know anyone else around here?"

"I don't know. I just got in." He could not compose himself, not having fully processed his conversation with Isabel and now set upon by this girl.

"Come on." She did not ask, she told. She stood and headed off toward the pool deck, hips swinging, perfectly balanced on platform espadrilles. Arthur was powerless to do anything but follow.

. . .

Those remaining weeks of quarantine on an island fringed in sugar-white sand and hung with bougainvillea would, in later years, cast into shade Arthur's other memories of Earth. He would think of Sloane Villanueva. He would think of Isabel Weiss. He would recall even little Megan Harper braiding the hair of her dolls. But all of it would take on a mist of regret when viewed alongside those last few weeks; it would make him wish he had done it all differently. Maisy showed Arthur how it should be done.

She led him to the pool deck, her idle chatter pushing away thoughts that would otherwise have crowded in. They changed into bathing suits in the bamboo shower huts. They arranged lounge chairs side by side and Maisy ordered mimosas from an attendant. The sun cleared the treetops and began to warm their goose-pimpled skin. Waves somewhere off behind ran up the sand and slid back into the sea with a faint swish.

Maisy asked Arthur about Isabel. His tongue was loosened by the unfamiliar drink and the sinuous curve of skin beside him. He talked. Maisy gave a bright, glittering laugh when he told of his ride in the Maserati. With her fingers, she covered a mouth agape with shock and pity when he told her of the dance. He even talked of the long, slow slide after their episode in the convenience store. Maisy's only response, apart from a twisted little grin and narrowed eyes, was to ask what he had done with all the stuff they bought.

The patio and beach filled as the day wore on. More buses arrived from the airport, disgorging their loads of future crewmembers out into the waiting paradise. There were passing acquaintances and a few middling friends and many, many faces that were but vaguely familiar. Well into the morning, Father McIntosh greeted them, brimming with ill-suppressed joy at the libertinism of exposed flesh. The volume rose as the waitstaff shuttled tray after tray of drinks to prone bodies strewn about the patio. As the heat climbed with the rising sun, Maisy and Arthur wrapped themselves in thin cotton robes and shared breakfast in the restaurant.

She was easy to talk to; indeed, he found himself discussing matters that would never have passed his lips upon more careful consideration. Arthur's tale of Isabel lingered and carried, drifting back to Sloane and beyond. Maisy cut in from time to time with her own stories of innocence and lost love, only their subjects were names with which Arthur was familiar: movie stars and musicians and socialites with monetary resources far outstripping their talents. It was nearly lunchtime when they rose from the table. She took his arm as they walked from the restaurant as if it was the most natural thing in the world.

They parted ways to settle into their rooms. Arthur's suite was in an outbuilding flanking the shoreline. It was a thatched structure trimmed in bamboo and reached via a path winding alongside a gurgling artificial stream that spilled out of a pool adjacent to the lobby. Lizards warming themselves on the path skittered off into the bushes as Arthur passed. Banana trees and elephant's ear cast a mottled shade. His room was wide and dim against a glare of light from the sea. It had a kitchen to the rear and a wall of windows folding back to allow breezes in off the water. A veranda was separated from the sand by a strip of coarse grass and potted heliconia. He pushed back the wall of windows and sank into a wicker papasan chair looking out from the porch over the line of surf. People passed on the sand in twos and threes, ambling idly along as they gazed out over a placid sea. He slept until Maisy came to wake him.

Days ran along in a lazy rhythm. In the mornings, Maisy would walk down the beach from her hut and sit with Arthur on the veranda, sipping coffee and watching the sun's first rays shimmering on the waves. After a day or two of this, and without asking permission, she pushed him aside and wiggled down into the cushions next to him. They warmed one another against the morning chill. They walked to breakfast and sunned themselves at the pool until lunchtime, chatting with other members of the crew and occasionally cooling themselves in the water.

In the afternoons, they set about finding ways to fill the time. An entire cohort of launches was sequestered at the resort and not permitted to explore the island. They tried golfing. Neither had any experience with the sport, but they laughed and hacked and drove the cart careening down the fairways amid gales of Maisy's giggles. They borrowed beach cruisers from the hotel and explored the bicycle paths that snaked throughout the grounds. She introduced Arthur to Mai Tais and daiquiris.

The resort crawled with crewmembers equally starved for ways to fill the hours. At first, Maisy was besieged with the attentions of the men. They would send her drinks and splash her in the pool and take Arthur's seat when he stepped away for a bare instant. They would interrupt conversations with strutting confidence and bare chests that put Arthur's meager assets to shame. Maisy turned them away with ready panache. When they were disrespectful of her companion, she drove them off nursing deeper lacerations to their pride. She had made her choice and was not one to second-guess. Eventually the fusillade acceded defeat.

In the evenings, Arthur and Maisy rejoined the herd. The patio was strung with overhead cables and dangling paper lanterns that held back the darkness with its shrieking cacophony of nocturnal insects. Within these bounds was a bubble of well-lubricated bonhomie. A band would set up with guitars and buleadors and steel drums and play long into the night. The party would spill into the hotel pub, and the volume would rise with the advancing hands of the clock. A long bar along the rear wall, lined with row upon row of backlit bottles in every color of the rainbow, would be crowded three-deep. Halfway through the night, the tables would be pushed aside to make room for dancing.

After a night or two of revelry in which Arthur and Maisy immersed themselves in the camaraderie of their fellows until long into the evening, they began to draw back. They would catch one another's eye and slip off into the night. Arthur would walk her to her room before returning to his own and falling into a deep and delicious sleep. Wandering thoughts may occasionally have prevented him from slipping peacefully off, but this is not how he would remember it. If he spent hours tossing and turning, he would awake late to find Maisy standing over him, arms crossed with a mug of coffee sending wisps of steam up over her face. As soon as his eyes opened, she would huff and stalk back to their seat on the porch to await his company.

What was it that drew Arthur to her, spoiled as she was? There were any number of words that might describe her: capricious, self-centered, domineering. Arthur was not so blind as to miss these things. Perhaps the answer is obvious. Maisy was beautiful. Beauty, in the eyes of a smitten young man, shines its light upon every other attribute. Defects transform into advantages. What from a homelier countenance would be irritating presumption becomes the compelling essence of a glittering personality. That this effect persists for no more than ten or fifteen minutes after the final objective has been secured is no impediment to those in the throes of early love. But perhaps, like Maisy's beauty, her unflattering attributes were window-dressing to greater depths of character. Perhaps.

One afternoon, a week or more into the interlude, the inseparable pair strolled together down the beach with shallow waves washing about their ankles. Arthur told her about Mr. Pifflethorpe and William, gone all those years. He told her of late nights at the factory and early mornings at the lake. He told her of telescopes and sagging recliners and old rhythm-and-blues albums. She drew near and hugged his arm to her side as she was wont to do when the conversation grew serious.

"Beckett wasn't like that," she said as Arthur's recollections finally trailed off.

"What was it like growing up with him?" Arthur said.

"I didn't grow up with him."

Arthur turned to meet her gaze, but her eyes looked down to the sand.

"Oh, he came around when he needed something," she went on. "He set up my life to suit his needs: an invitation to the Oscars or the Globes, tours of the sets and mingling with the casts, nights out with producers and directors. I got him into the Correspondents' Dinner the first time he met the President. That was how it went."

"Didn't you want all of that stuff too?"

She shrugged and crinkled her nose, looking off toward the horizon. "I never really thought about it," she said.

"Is that why you wanted to leave on the *Argo*?"

"I guess... maybe." She said it again: "I never thought about it." It was obvious she had thought about it a great deal.

"What did your father say?"

Her eyes came back to him. "He put up a show of trying to talk me out of it."

Arthur's eyes asked what she meant.

She just smiled and looked back down at her feet.

That night at the hotel pub was wilder than most. If you had asked those in attendance, they could not have told you why it was different. Arthur knew it was Maisy. Her moods ebbed and flowed with some mysterious rhythm he would never be able to fathom. Everything and everyone around her was carried along. That night she was high. She chattered and danced and did cannonballs off the diving board. She flirted with the bartender and the band and anyone else who would not make Arthur jealous. She hovered in dim corners with her girlfriends, leaning close with eyes roaming the crowd, teeth gleaming in the light of a full moon as they gossiped and laughed.

They were attuned to her, one and all, consciously or subconsciously. The volume of her voice pushed the volume of the room higher. The enthusiasm of her laughter metered out smiles to all who heard it. She was egged on relentlessly, knowing she held in her hands the fate of the evening. She alone determined whether it would peter quietly out or remain a topic of discussion the following morning. That night she lifted them up.

As the steel-drum band packed up for the night and pop music rose from the stereo system to fill the void, the floor was swept clean of tables and chairs, and dancing began. Maisy left her circle of girlfriends and pulled Arthur from his seat at the bar with Father McIntosh. They danced. The press of bodies grew thicker and thicker as word spread that Maisy was flying. She pulled Arthur into the eye of the hurricane. The music slowed, and she drew him close. It quickened, and she moved with a rhythm that carried him along, self-consciousness forgotten. The room seemed to fall into step. Colored lights spun and bass pounded, and Arthur was carried away.

Long into the evening, the music lulled, and Maisy slipped away to huddle with the bartender over the stereo. Protestations mounted as speakers fell silent and then rang out with the crackle of an old, worn-out recording. There were horns and strings and a melody rising and falling with an antiquated lilt long since packed away and forgotten. Maisy stepped forward with a microphone in her hand and mounted the step to a low stage in a corner of the room. The crowd fell silent, their mood strung taut.

Opening notes lifted and carried, wavered and drifted, silencing ripples of dissent from the crowd. She sang. The words were in French, the audience rapt. She moved like water, her voice silk. She sang of dreams, of memories, her eyes wide and fixed on Arthur through the forest of heads.

The mood of the song gripped her, and she gripped all those who watched. Drinks were quaffed. Eyes flashed in wonder and appreciation. Couples drew closer. It may be true Maisy was no Ella Fitzgerald. It may be true she did not actually speak French and her memorization of the lyrics left something to be desired. But no one whose opinion mattered noticed these things. If she was not on key, she was close enough that the visuals of it drowned the mistakes in a sea of sensuality. She knew how to move. She knew how to entertain. Even the throngs on the pool deck drifted in to see what was happening. Silence descended until one could hear waves washing on the beach when the rolling of her voice fell to its ebb.

She sang, dreamed with open eyes, not looking back. Arthur felt the words, even if he could not understand them. A lull, and a sip from her glass. Eyes caught his again through the heads. Missing him terribly...

At last, the melody trailed off into a mid-ocean quiet that permeated the place, whatever forces of humanity could hold it back for a time. She caught Arthur's eye through a gap in the bodies as they erupted in whistles and applause. She gave him a private little grin, clicked off the microphone, and set it on a table before making her way to him through a crowd that moved aside as she passed. Adulation built until the thump and crash of music came roaring back in. The sea of bodies shifted, rose, fell, and began to seethe once more with untamed abandon.

Maisy pulled Arthur from the press, and they hurried away into the night. The beach was empty and they walked, the sound of the party fading behind. He brushed her hand. She brushed back. He slid his fingers into hers and gripped them. The sensation sent a pounding rush of blood to his head. They stopped on the beach before the porch of Maisy's suite. A pair of lamps cast shadows between the trunks of the palms and across the dimpled sand. She did not turn to enter as she had every other night. She walked out toward the surf, pulling Arthur with her and stopping just above the furthest advance of the waves.

Arthur's life had arrived at a night that at last met the expectations of his imagination. He floated, almost afraid to disturb its perfection, certain it would shatter like safety glass into a million tiny pieces. Maisy looked at him and smiled. She dropped his hand.

"Let's go swimming," she said.

Without waiting for a response, she unbuttoned her cutoff jeans and wiggled them down over her hips. She stepped out of them, and the blouse followed. A permeating warmth washed over Arthur along with the recollection of another time like this one: the memory of Sloane, and their dock on the lake.

But he had not seen this before, because Maisy did not stop where Sloane had stopped back in their years of blushing adolescence. She bent an arm behind her back to unclasp her brassiere and dropped it on the pile of clothes. She bent and slid off a pair of blue cotton panties. The lamps illuminated her skin with warmth, casting perfect, sharp shadows that traced the curves of her body. She stood and held his gaze for a moment more before stepping lightly out into the waves, giggling faintly as she looked back at him over a shoulder.

Arthur worked desperately to see every detail, to file away every sound and sensation and image. Meanwhile, he stood riveted at the sight of her hourglass silhouette animated against the silvery shimmer of moonlight on the water.

He watched her walk away. The water rose to her knees, to

her waist, and then with a sharp intake of breath, she ducked and kicked out into the deep. The waves were at a low chop, still fading with the mellowing night; she had no trouble keeping her head above them. Behind the pool of moonlight on which she floated, the sea spread to infinite black. Her hair pulsed with each stroke of her arms, her head the shadowed center of concentric rings of flashing, sliding light. Arthur could hear the panting of her breath as she turned back, treading water.

Her voice carried in the cool of the night. "Are you coming in?" she said.

Chapter Eleven

A rthur and Maisy's time on the island ended with a rumble that seemed to vibrate the earth with its subaudible throb. Arthur was alone on the beach in the very spot where he and Maisy had stood some nights before. Once again it was dark, and once again the moon glinted off a tranquil ocean. He was charged with energy, despite the late hour. The throb resolved into a roar that blasted over the island like a tsunami. From where he lay on a beach towel, he could see the tops of the trees lit by a flickering orange glow. It brightened, casting sharp shadows through the branches that shifted downward until the outlines of the palms were etched onto the sand. A spectacular pillar of fire exploded into view, at its tip the black cylinder of Lift 2N324.

Arthur watched Maisy go. Whatever sadness there was, it was not the usual sort. They bid farewell only hours before as they had said good night every evening before the doors of Maisy's room: with a sheepish smile and nod from Arthur, who slunk off into the darkness feeling he should give her a kiss but unable to bring himself to do so; from Maisy, no change in manner as she unlocked the door and disappeared (but for perhaps the hint of a cocked eyebrow and a tight grin).

Arthur was sorry their time on the island had ended, but this was not what struck him most. He regretted all the years he had spent chasing love, only to discover that when it finally arrived, it was so simple. He had been trying to force it. When it came, it was as easy as Maisy elbowing him aside as she snuggled down into the papasan chair next to him. It was as easy as her fingers intertwining with his as they walked down the beach toward that perfect, perfect moment.

But he was not sorry to see Maisy streaking skyward atop that pillar of fire now arcing off toward the east and dwindling into the distance. The sight brought him a thrill, for soon he would join her up on the *Argo*. Arthur was starting his great adventure with a girl by his side. She would be waiting for him with the same anticipation that filled him now. The hatch would open with a pop and a hiss, and he would float into the *Argo*'s airlock to find her waiting with that wry grin that said she could read his thoughts, that she had everything figured out.

That little grin said anything Arthur wanted it to say. It said she sang just for him. It said she did not mind a bit if he watched her undress for a midnight swim. It said she knew how he felt, even if he was not quite ready to kiss her. It said she would wait. When he imagined her there in the airlock, she was leaning back against the bulkhead with her arms crossed and her hair floating in a cloud around her head. Of course, he understood she would not, could not, stand like that in zero gravity, but this had no affect on the way he chose to imagine it.

His remaining days on Earth were spent in a fog of not-unpleasant numbness so palpable it almost resolved into a buzzing in his ears. Father McIntosh remained, and when Arthur was not sitting on the veranda of his hut, staring out at the sea, he could usually be found in the company of the priest and a clique of young crewmen who gravitated toward his paternal conviviality.

Late in the morning hours, Father McIntosh would walk stiffly out to his lounge chair on the pool deck—a lounge chair everyone understood to be his—and settle himself as if into the booth of a confessional. He wore baggy nylon shorts with a tropical print, a paunch pushing down the elastic waistline until one marveled at its defiance of the laws of gravity. His ghostly skin must have been slathered with sunscreen because it never dimmed over weeks in the sun. The boys who had no girls to occupy their time established themselves all around, enjoying the priest's uncritical acceptance and a loquaciousness that papered over any deficiencies on their part.

In the evenings, Father McIntosh could be found at his stool in the pub—a stool everyone understood to be his—sipping at a tumbler of Scotch. He would tell indecorous stories long into the night to anyone who would listen as the color rose higher and higher in his cheeks. He always had a kind word and never commented when Arthur slipped away to stew (usually to a particular spot just up the beach, where he would lie on his back and watch the glinting shine of the *Argo* plying the night sky from west to east, west to east).

Days ticked down until it was time for Arthur to pack his bag. He assembled the few items coming with him and discarded the rest in a bin set out for the purpose. A shuttle bus carried him and the rest of the Lift 2N326 passengers to the launch complex. Silence hung heavy as it had on that far-off bus ride to Earth Station One. Father McIntosh was not present to fill the void.

The bus stopped before a gate topped with razor-wire that motored slowly open. A security guard passed down the aisle, checking identification cards and ticking each of them off on a tablet computer that recorded a fingerprint. The bus crossed half a mile of tarmac and turned a corner around a set of blast deflectors before stopping at a bunker complex situated at the base of the launch tower. It felt as though they were being dropped off for school.

Next to a scaffolding and elevator shaft, the rocket was a soaring black column perched over its charred pit. Steam leaked from ports here and there. Emblazoned on its side was the logo of Armagast Enterprises, with its silver swoops and streaks. To the rear stood a massive assembly hangar. A set of steel rails ran beneath the closed twenty-one-story blast doors and out across the concrete to the launch pad. After decades in the business, the company sent off their rockets like Model T's from a twentieth-century assembly line.

A cast of security guards took command. With smooth efficiency and barked orders, they formed the Argonauts into a queue before another set of blast doors, these scaled to human stature. Each was again electronically fingerprinted. They passed into a long hallway set with a row of cubicles, one for each of the passengers. At his cubicle, Arthur was met by a smiling young woman well-practiced in customer service. She chatted with him as she emptied his duffel onto a desk and inspected each item, checking them off on her list of approved equipment. She repacked everything and tossed the bag onto a conveyor belt, where it was whisked off through a portal hung with strips of plastic.

Turn about. Step to the center of the corridor. Face right. And off they went.

In a large, tiled room vaguely reminiscent of a time long ago, the crew stripped bare. Their clothing disappeared down a chute. This time, no one had bothered to segregate the sexes. The workaday feeling made clear that niceties of earthside convention were firmly in the past. This was only the second time Arthur had seen a flesh-and-blood woman without the

benefit of clothes. After Maisy Armagast, the range of shapes
and sizes on display was a fine educational experience. He
largely kept his eyes fixed on the floor in deathly fear of unto-
ward physiological reactions.

Their bodies were scrubbed clean by attendants dressed in
rubberized hazmat suits and wielding long-handled scrub
brushes. New uniforms awaited them on the other side, each
hung neatly in a locker designated by name on a diode reader-
board. Above each uniform was a shelf with a black helmet
adorned with the Armagast Enterprises logo. Dressed once
more and carrying their helmets, they queued for another attendant, who fitted each with a permanent electronic wristband.
These, according to prelaunch instructions, would enable every
on-board activity, from deck access to financial transactions to
location tracking. They were discharged into a waiting-room. It
was all so familiar, so run-of-the-mill. They joked about the
pointlessness of helmets should the launch not go according to
plan. They waited. Arthur slouched down into a chair and,
primed like Pavlov's dog, he slept.

He was awakened by a perky young officer with a face mask
and clipboard who asked them to don their helmets and follow
her. They passed down another set of corridors to a freight
elevator large enough to hold the entire group. Up they went,
doors slid open, and they filed across to the capsule through the
boarding boom's passenger corridor. There were no windows,
no grated flooring. They might as well have been arriving at an
office in some big-city skyscraper. Even the hatch was large
enough to step through with scarcely a stoop.

The central chamber of the launch capsule was cylindrical,
its walls lined with row upon row of bunks accessed by
aluminum ladders fixed to the shelving units with curious
hinges. After a moment of disorder as they milled about
studying the diode reader-boards on each bunk, the passengers

were sorted and tucked away. Arthur listened as a crew of attendants made its way through the compartment. A middle-aged man with a handlebar mustache behind his plastic face shield poked his head into Arthur's bunk.

"Are we all set here..." He pulled his head back out and checked the electronic name tag. "...Pifflethorpe?"

Back in.

"I think so, sir."

The man's hands ran over the straps with rapid precision: fastening, tucking, cinching.

"Bon voyage."

Then he was gone, with just his midsection visible as he checked the passenger above. His belly strained at the zipper of his jumpsuit and pressed against Arthur's shoulder. It was the last person Arthur would speak to who was not heading off with him into space. He had begun taking note of these lasts, ordering and filing them away. He reached back into memory for ones that had passed unregarded. The train of thought had an eerie unreality to it.

Finished strapping down the passengers, the attendants departed. Arthur could hear the hatch clang shut and bolts slide home. He guessed at the purpose of a series of mechanical noises that reverberated through the hull; this one was probably the access bridge drawing back, that one the pressurization system humming to life. His ears popped.

Whatever strangeness there was to his situation, it could not overcome the routine of unpredictable fits and starts. Again, they waited. No one had thought to provide them with a countdown or any other means of determining how long it would be until liftoff. Or more likely they had thought of it but deemed it an unnecessary expense. The only means of communication was a red emergency call button.

The bunk above was a foot or two from Arthur's face.

Fastened to it with aluminum rivets was a zippered cloth pouch. Arthur opened it and examined the contents. There was a laminated sheet outlining the emergency procedures they had been required to memorize. There was a packet of motion-sickness bags and a pair of earplugs. The pouch also contained a glossy magazine with articles about *Argo* entertainment and dining facilities. Advertisements showed pictures of goods available for purchase in the Crew Store. Reading so close to his face was uncomfortable, and he fitted it all back into its pouch.

Time strung out as he lay there. Perhaps the weather had turned, or some malfunction had been identified. Bodily functions were provided for by way of plastic bags stored away in the zipper-pouch, or it would have been an uncomfortable wait. He wondered how the ladies managed such things. A pair of crewmen began to chat about a cricket tournament capturing headlines in some far-off corner of the world.

Then, without warning, it began. It started with a hum and a whine emanating from somewhere below. Voices fell silent. The hull shuddered and shifted, and the whine was drowned by a low and rising vibration that grew in intensity until it could only be described as violent shaking. Arthur was thrust back into the cushions with startling intensity. The force grew and grew and continued to grow for a period of time far longer than he thought possible. It held him there, pinned to the bunk.

With no clock to measure the time, Arthur could not say how long it went on. It seemed like an eternity. There was a kick and a jolt and the force pressing him downward—or what felt like downward—renewed itself with sudden vigor. *That would be separation of the rocket's booster stage*, he thought. They went on accelerating. Another kick and another jolt; still pressed downward, but with less force now. It almost felt like they were back on Earth. Then, with a deafening clap of silence, it ended. Arthur was weightless. So strong was the contrast that it almost felt like powered deceleration, like he was being thrown forward against the straps that held him down. He lifted a hand in front of his face and practiced moving it about. It felt strange without the pull of gravity. They waited. Someone above him laughed.

More waiting, and the aggravation of not knowing where they were or how long they had been traveling began to set in along with the nausea of weightlessness. From here and there came the sound of crinkling paper as passengers retrieved motion-sickness bags from their pouches. Congestion clogged Arthur's head. Heaving rose in his abdomen, and he fought it down. Clicks and hisses announced capsule course adjustments that tumbled his inner ear. He heard someone retching. The smell began to spread, and with it a contagion of vomiting.

The nausea was unstoppable, and he heaved again and again into a paper bag. From all around came similar noises. The ache grew even as his stomach emptied. He filled one bag, then another, depositing each into a receptacle on the wall designated for the purpose. Arthur was in misery. This was not how he had pictured space flight. He wanted to take back every poor decision of the previous year. He wanted his feet back on the ground.

At last, there was another mechanical hum and whine that was closer—there, just behind the bulkhead. The bunks seemed to shift, spread, and collapse against the walls of the capsule, pulling their occupants with them. The passengers were now spread out over the walls, looking across at one another like men and women painted on the wallpaper. Someone lost his grip on a sick bag. It floated out into the void, slowly spilling its contents in shifting globules that drifted like jellyfish on an ocean current. Odor of renewed intensity produced another round of heaving from the passengers. There was another click and hiss, and Arthur's ransacked inner ears were tossed once more into disarray. They were spinning, and a slight pull pressed them outward against the walls. The drifting bag and its disgorged contents began moving toward a crewmember who lay in its curving path. She cursed in some unknown language and snatched the bag out of the air, seizing it by the lip and swishing it about, trying to catch the former contents of her shipmate's stomach before they landed on her.

Arthur's stomach had at last begun to settle when there was another jolt, a sliding rasp, and a violent shudder. A hiss of escaping air. They had arrived. There was no hatch to climb through, no dramatic entrance. The entire ceiling of the capsule —or what they had come to think of as the ceiling—split into triangles as it folded back. Behind it was another round door that folded back in turn. Then another. Behind that was a long tube, somewhat wider than the capsule itself and lined with tracks and cables and fluorescent lights stretching off into the distance, shrinking in perspective down nearly to a point.

Maisy was not there to welcome him. He knew deep down that this had been too much to hope for. Clinging lightly to the wall in the microgravity was Bosun Atticus Oluwusi. He lifted a hand in greeting. Simultaneously, everyone's buckles unclasped, and the straps fell loose.

"Let's go, squids," the bosun said. Or that is what Arthur thought he heard.

On any project of such vast scale, it is impossible for designers to think of everything. The *Argo* was no exception. The great tin can contained a series of concentric rings, each comprising a deck, that spread outward from a central core that housed the engine at one end and the primary docking port at the other. Transport vessels joined the docking port at the end of a long tube running through the axis (after initiating a spin to match the ship's rotation, as Arthur had experienced). This tube, ending at the power plant's firewall, served as a convenient means of transporting arriving materials throughout the ship.

Lying at the center of the massive rotating vessel, the axis tube was a superhighway of sorts, allowing movement of large quantities of material at near-zero gravity. At intervals along the length of the cylinder were access shafts allowing personnel and equipment to be carried to the appropriate deck via lifts. As successive decks spread outward, artificial gravity imparted by the spacecraft's rotation accordingly rose. At a point near the outer hull, gravity precisely matched that on Earth. This was the location of the everyday crew quarters.

The problem was that each deck sat at a slightly different distance from the axis of rotation. Each accordingly experienced a slightly different effective gravity. This differential was, of course, calculated with precision in advance. Inner rings were set aside for storage and machinery and other uses requiring either low gravity or low levels of daily occupancy. What was not foreseen were effects on the human body of this arrangement. In the outer reaches of the vessel, it was not a problem; one got used to the minor changes with relative ease. Toward the center, this was not the case. Not only did one experience a slow, nonlinear drift toward the outer walls that made locomotion a challenge, but one also had to contend with an alarming radius of rotation that scrambled otolith fluids and produced noticeable differences in gravitational force between one's head and one's feet. The end result was a violent tumbling sensation producing waves of nausea as if the ship were designed expressly for the purpose.

This was the welcome each new arrival received upon first setting foot on the spacecraft that would be their permanent home. Atticus Oluwusi, inured to the sensation or perhaps merely skilled at disguising his discomfort, watched with a satisfied smirk as the new batch of crewmembers contended with violent disorientation. He had seen this many times before and never tired of it. That their stomachs were at this point largely empty meant the bosun need not fear a mess that may have spoiled the fun. Like contestants in a dizzy race, they flailed and pitched. They pushed off the walls with undue vigor and were sent tumbling into empty air, twisting and reaching and grasping at nothing. At last, they understood the purpose of the helmets as they careened off one another and the walls of the capsule, now conveniently padded by the launch bunks. This went on for some minutes before each managed to secure a grip and make his or her way hand-over-hand into the axis tube.

"This way," said the bosun. He turned about and leaped upward into the tube, floating with a long, arcing bound that eventually brought him back into contact with the wall. It was effortless, even with an old-fashioned clipboard in one of his hands. He stopped and turned back, watching as his charges followed in bumbling, tumbling confusion. Arthur would find the moment a fitting metaphor for the turn his life had taken.

Some semblance of normalcy returned when they reached the access shaft. The bosun punched at a control panel, and a door in the wall of the tube slid open. The drop to the floor of the lift was disconcerting to see, but each of them stepped off and floated gently downward, coming to a rest in a pit that looked much like a freight elevator but for its open roof. The roof slid closed.

"Brace," was all the bosun said. He took hold of a webbed strap fixed to the wall. Quicker-thinking crewmembers did likewise, among whom was Arthur. The rest were tossed to the top of the compartment as the lift started downward. The bosun held the same cryptic smirk as he watched them scrambling back down and taking hold.

The lift moved slowly, gravity increasing perceptibly as it did so. It took some time for the vertigo to ease. The ride lasted several minutes, and when the lift at last came to a halt, Arthur felt as if he were standing back on the surface of Earth. This time a set of doors on the side of the compartment slid open.

The bosun led the group down a long corridor that bent upward almost imperceptibly. The walls looked like brushed steel fitted with rivets and truss supports and access panels. The floor bore a striking resemblance to the linoleum in the old kitchen of the Pifflethorpe home. Numbered doors opened at regular intervals to either side. They looked like any metal door you would find in any Midwest industrial facility. Arthur had seen many like them. Beside each was a small keypad and proximity reader, presumably activated by an appropriately encoded wristband. As they walked, the bosun explained the numbering system on the doors: first the deck number, then a letter indicating the nearest spoke, then the number of the room itself. Over time, he assured them, one learned to navigate to one's destination based on its room number alone.

They turned a corner, then another. Signs on the walls pointed off toward various points of interest: *Auditorium, Cafeteria, Stair*. Other crewmembers occasionally passed, but the corridors were largely empty. The bosun talked all the while, explaining the layout and locations of important facilities. They crossed a plaza lined with darkened booths closed off by sliding screens, then a mezzanine looking out over a wide floor set with tables and chairs. It looked like a food court. Arthur looked again. It was a food court. They could have been in a shopping mall in any number of old hometowns.

They passed from the mezzanine back into a corridor. They descended a flight of steps and passed through a set of sliding glass doors into a lobby with a long desk on the far wall. The man behind it stood as they approached.

Bosun Oluwusi stopped before the desk and turned back. He raised his clipboard and read off three names. "These are the crew quarters for Argonaut Squadron Seven. This is your CQ desk. Petty Officer Lin is currently the officer in charge of quarters. He will take it from here."

The named three broke off from the group. The rest continued on. They visited more lobbies with more sliding glass doors and more CQ desks. With half a dozen left in the group, they arrived at a squadron with a large, blue 4 on the wall. A man stood from behind the desk. A stone settled in the pit of Arthur's stomach. He knew this man, and he knew what the bosun would say before he said it.

"Pifflethorpe... Wheeler... You are assigned to Squadron Four. Petty Officer Waller will take it from here." The bosun had scarcely finished speaking before he stalked off, trailed by his remaining ducklings.

"Seaman Pifflethorpe... Seaman Wheeler..." Stanley Waller looked them over. This was the first time Arthur came to understand he had been assigned the rank of seaman. "You've been assigned to Squadron Four. I'm Petty Officer Third Class Stanley Waller. You can call me Petty Officer Third Class Stanley Waller." He chuckled quietly. His teeth looked like baby teeth but for their parchment hue. His eyes settled on Arthur, who determined it was his turn to introduce himself.

"Arthur Pifflethorpe," he said, extending a hand.

"I know who you are," said Petty Officer Third Class Stanley Waller. He turned and walked off down a hallway. The apparent inability of his legs to touch one another imparted an awkward, zigzag quality to his gait. Arthur and his companion followed.

Stanley (for Arthur was soon to learn he could dispense with the formalities) stopped before a door and waved Seaman Wheeler forward, gesturing to indicate he should swipe his wristband on the access panel. When he did so, the lock released with a click. Stanley pushed on the door, and it swung open to reveal a compartment that looked much like their old dormitory back at Earth Station One. They must have gotten a quantity discount on the furniture, for it too looked the same. Something that could not have been a window was set into the far wall. It seemed to look out on a quiet residential street lined with oak trees, lawns, and small red-brick bungalows.

"You can settle in," Stanley said. "Your bag should be along shortly. The cafeteria opens in..." He looked down at his wrist-band, which also served as a timepiece. "...forty-five minutes. You're probably hungry." He chuckled to himself again. "After that you'll begin in-processing."

Seaman Wheeler stepped into the room as Stanley continued off down the hall with Arthur. They arrived at his door and followed a similar procedure. When Arthur was at last alone in his room, he sat on the bed and stared at the wall-screen. On it was the house where he had grown up, the house he had left some weeks ago in the sole care of Mrs. Pifflethorpe. Someone had clearly come up with this idea as a way of easing the transition. Its effect was disconcerting. It felt as if he were looking at his home through the window of the Wileys' house across the street. It just made him sad. He did not know how to turn it off, so he drew the curtains that hung to either side.

He sat back on the bed, and a familiar ache began to swell in his chest. He had pictured it all so differently: portholes with God's-eye views of Earth spinning slowly against the black of space, the vast bulk of the *Argo* topping the horizon and drawing slowly near. He saw himself looking over the shoulder of a pilot as he steered them to the docking port with a joystick. He saw a ship buzzing with people, each hurrying off to accomplish some critical task. A command bridge with banks of blinking lights. Wheeled robots whizzing through the halls and catwalks looking out over colossal and mysterious machinery.

Instead, it was this. Gut-wrenching nausea as they were

tossed about like packaged goods in transit. Empty halls and closed-up shops not yet populated with all those yet to arrive. A cold and impersonal greeting from a man who looked like a petulant egg and clearly had a streak of assertive conceit. The only personal touch was a picture on the wall that had been pulled down from the Internet, probably by some automated computer algorithm. He was hungry and dizzy with hypo-glycemia.

And above all, no Maisy. Surely she was squirreled away in some other room in some other featureless steel hallway, forlorn and hungry and missing Arthur with comparable intensity. Against all odds, he would seek her out. He would open the door to find her sitting on the bed, weeping. His shadow would fall just so across the floor, drawing her eyes up to him. He would sit and fold her in his arms. Her tears of sorrow would change to tears of joy as she dampened the shoulder of his uniform.

Or perhaps not. No, she was probably reclining in a lounge somewhere, socializing with all of her new best friends. Or on the command deck, dressing down Admiral Demarion for the rough treatment she had received en route. She would not be alone in her room, missing anyone. She would surely not be thinking of Arthur.

A thought struck him like a charge of electricity: Who among his shipmates had seen her undress when her lift cohort was scrubbed down for launch? Did others know she had a perfect dusting of freckles hidden under the hemline of her tiny blue underpants? She probably did not care a bit if they knew. She probably had no scruples whatsoever about undressing in front of people. Arthur was not so special. She kept no secrets for him. He was unused to the twinge of jealousy that gripped him, but was not one to be consumed by such things. Soon it dissipated and he just felt profoundly, profoundly alone.

Chapter Twelve

Arthur was among the first waves of Argonauts to arrive aboard. This left him time to wait before the grand ceremonies and fist-pounding speeches that would formally inaugurate the next phase of the glorious adventure. It was an anticlimax. His first lunch in the cafeteria was a dispiriting affair. It looked like any high school cafeteria back home, with a sneeze-screened serving counter and food that had been sitting in its warming trays for far too long. The scattering of early arrivals commiserated over the uncomfortable ascent, discussing nausea and vomit as they ate steamed broccoli and refried beans. Maisy was not among them.

In-processing was equally disappointing. The skeleton crew managing the process had been aboard for years. This, for them, was any other Monday morning. Their air of boredom sucked from the atmosphere whatever charge of excitement may have existed. Arthur was issued bedding and undergarments and half a dozen different uniforms. He joined small groups for expanded tours of the ship, which included zone access instructions and warnings over prohibited areas.

He was assigned the rank of petty officer third class at the same time he was issued uniforms stitched with the appropriate insignia. However Stanley had made it sound, there was nothing notable about the ranks carried by most crewmembers. They were as changeable as one's clothes and corresponded to a set of assigned duties. The ship's senior staff—drawn largely from the ranks of the world's military forces—had insisted upon some outward mark of hierarchical authority. Those who were really in charge—weighing in from the boardrooms of the project's major corporate sponsors—thought such fussy particulars an encumbrance to optimal utilization of human resources. What resulted was a compromise that made no sense to anyone.

Academic studies were far from complete. Arthur accumulated a stack of books so large it had to be wheeled about in a cart along with the rest of the personal equipment he collected. Mentally and physically exhausted after hours spent pushing this cart about the ship, he arrived at last at a nondescript door in a nondescript corridor somewhere up on the ninth deck. Gravity was noticeably weaker. He stopped before the door and compared the room number stenciled on its aluminum surface with that on a sheaf of papers in his hand. Yes, this was the correct room.

An elevator chime sounded down the hall. He turned to look. A wheeled cart much like his own emerged, followed by a woman. She nearly lost contact with the ground at the first few steps and had to cling to the cart to hold herself down. She saw him watching and cast her eyes to the floor. She turned her cart toward him. They were going to the same place.

"Good afternoon," she said upon drawing up. "My name is Wei. You are also an apprentice with the Department of Waste Management?" Her accent was crisp and precise. Black hair hung limp to her shoulders. Porcelain skin gave one the impression she was far younger than was likely the case. Arthur would never reach the point where he felt comfortable asking her age.

"Arthur Pifflethorpe," he said, extending a hand. "Pleased to meet you."

"Pleased to meet you."

An air of awkwardness hung in the air. Both were on edge. Wei looked to the door and back to Arthur. Arthur looked to Wei and back to the door. He shrugged, raised a fist, and knocked.

A cry of "Enter!" found its way through from the other side. Arthur swiped his wristband and pushed open the door. The pair left their carts in the hallway and stepped inside.

The headquarters of the *Argo's* Department of Waste Management was a mess of clutter. The sound of clicking keyboards and shuffling papers was muffled by upholstered partitions. It was difficult to tell the size of the room due to the profusion of cubicles crowding a long central passageway. Beige walls matched an industrial low-pile carpet. The color of this carpet was only distinguishable around the edges. In the center it was worn down nearly to the backing and stained with ground-in filth. It struck Arthur as odd that they had installed old carpet on a new spacecraft. Then it hit him: the *Argo* was by no means new. He had been watching it grow for nearly a decade, ever since those days at the lake with Sloane. For years, people had been passing up and down this corridor, sitting at these desks, typing away at these keyboards. Maybe these very same people.

A man seated in a cubicle at the opposite end of the passageway leaned back in his chair to see around the adjacent partition. The face was leathery and spare, with thinning light-brown hair and a smear on the upper lip that must have been a mustache.

"What can I do for you?" he said.

"Arthur Pifflethorpe, sir," Arthur replied. "I just finished up with IT. Petty Officer Garza sent me here."

"And your friend?"

"Petty Officer Third Class Yao Wei, sir," she replied.

Confusion flickered over the man's face. He disappeared back into the cubicle. "Come on down," rang out.

Arthur looked into the cubicles as he passed. Desks were piled so high there was scarcely room for computers: stacks of paper, file folders, pencil cups, trash left over from lunch, food left over from lunch (some of it not today's, by the look of it). Scattered everywhere were discarded machine parts. Half or more of the cubicles were occupied. The people were seated on swivel chairs shoehorned into gaps between yet more piles of paper and file folders and machine parts. It seemed as if at any moment one such accumulation might collapse and bury its occupant forever, like the tourists one reads about who dig holes on the beach. Backs hunched over computer screens. Hands pounded at keyboards or rifled through stacks of paper.

Arthur and Wei reached the end of the passageway and stood behind the man who had greeted them. He was pounding on his keyboard along with the rest.

"Of course, of course... I'm on it now," he said under his breath, taking a few last violent swipes at the keyboard. He spun around, his knees deftly missing a stack of dented computer servers. "Welcome, Pifflethorpe! Yao! Glad to have you. We can use the help, as I'm sure you can see." He waved a hand to indicate the chaos around them.

"Yes, sir," said Arthur, turning to survey the mess.

"Welcome aboard," said the man. "I'm Chief Petty Officer Dulka. I'm the supervisor up here." He extended a hand stained with grime. Arthur shook it, followed by Wei.

"Pleased to meet you, sir," Arthur said.

Wei half-nodded, half-bowed her concurrence. A self-conscious flush rose in her face.

"Didn't realize you'd be up so soon! Damn, but time flies!" Petty Officer Dulka smiled to himself and shook his head. "Not to worry... we'll find a place for you in here somewhere. In the meantime, we'll give you the grand tour. Bentley!"

Another head tipped back into the passageway. This was heavily coiffured, with a thick, black mustache tapered to waxed tips. Arthur hoped he would not be required to grow a mustache. He had tried it once, with dispiriting results.

"Give these pips the grand tour!" said Petty Officer Dulka.

Bentley rolled backward into the aisle, then stood and pushed the chair back where it came from. He stepped forward to shake their hands.

"Happy to ditch the paperwork for an hour or two," he said with an accent as hard to place as the color of his skin. "Come with me." Bentley turned on a heel and strolled off toward the door.

Thus, Arthur began his duties in the Department of Waste Management. He and Wei were shown to their lockers and a supply room filled with hardhats and pressure suits and tool bags. Ladies' showers to the left, men's to the right. Academic classes would accompany on-the-job training.

The two were apprenticed to Bentley, a senior technician who had been aboard for years. Beside him they learned how to run water-purification systems and replace ventilation filters. They fixed broken pipes and unjammed trash-sorting equipment. For the simpler tasks, Arthur was sent out alone. He spent a large portion of his time trudging the halls with a toilet plunger, tracking down the sources of angry telephone calls to the facilities operations center.

His favorite job was composting, for this brought him to the agricultural ring. For the time being, most food was brought to the *Argo* via cargo lifts, but it would not be long until the first crops matured and the ship began approaching self-sufficiency. On the outermost deck, situated directly atop the hull and its hundred feet or more of impact armor, radiation shielding, and insulation were the farms.

Dropping down on a scaffolded elevator screened with wire mesh, one looked out over acre upon acre of crops growing under ultraviolet lights in the ceiling thirty meters overhead. Beams and trusses of the ship's superstructure interrupted the vast space here and there, but for the most part it stretched away in every direction toward the closest thing the Argonauts would come to a horizon. Along the axis of the ship the ground was flat, ending at the bulkheads at either end of the enormous cylinder. In every other direction, it curved gradually upward until one's line of sight was interrupted by the similarly curving ceiling. This view was occasionally broken by translucent bulkheads running the length of the ship and dividing the outer ring into zones. These allowed for varying climates to suit a wide range of crops.

Fields grew far more than wheat and soybeans and potatoes. There were fruit orchards of every sort imaginable, from temperate to tropical. There were vineyards and strawberry patches and bean poles. Sprinklers and drip lines provided precisely calibrated rainfall to bananas and coffee beans and hops. An army of mechanized plows, seeders, and harvesters operated of their own accord, running on a schedule determined by the world's finest agronomists. The diet of the Argonauts would be primarily vegetarian, this being far more efficient. Some small amount of meat was provided for, however, for reasons of morale as well as recycling nutrients back into the soil. There were pens with pigs and chickens. There was pastureland with cows and sheep and goats. Tanks held fish, ducks, geese, and a wide variety of crustaceans.

This was no replica of Earth's hills and shorelines and forests. Everything was cultivated in racks and pens and tanks providing only the precise volume of space deemed absolutely necessary. But even so, it was a relief to descend that caged elevator to the surface of the outer ring. Everywhere else in the ship, one's perspective was demoralizing: four walls, a ceiling, and a floor. Even the largest rooms—the food court, the auditorium—were of a scale limited to what one might find back on Earth. Ceilings illuminated to resemble cloud-strewn skies and wall screens with magnificent vistas sounded better in theory than they were found to be in practice.

A poor proxy it may have been for the open skies of Earth, but it did not take long living on the *Argo* for those open spaces to become a necessary release from the claustrophobia forever nagging at the back of one's mind. In spare moments, Arthur would pull a tattered paperback from the leg pocket of his jumpsuit and stretch out on the grass to read. The lowing of cows, gurgling of irrigation systems, and chatter of Argonauts playing frisbee in the sheep pasture would lull him to sleep.

Only in the fields did one achieve a full appreciation for the scale of the task set upon by Beckett Armagast and his corporation. Building the *Argo* required far more than steel and aluminum and titanium. Base elements were tossed aloft by rockets to synthesize everything from water to fertilizer to fuel for the thrusters. Seeds and saplings and crates of bewildered chicks may have been easier to transport than adults of the species, but all the biomass of full-sized organisms had somehow to reach the *Argo* before the animals could be expected to thrive and multiply. There were tricky items that people talked about: nuclear reactors and quantum computer cores and entire manufacturing centers transferred into orbit. But then there were the simple ones that likely presented an even greater challenge. What unimaginable quantity of rocket fuel had been expended sending up acre after acre of dirt? Nothing about the ship was particularly advanced. What struck Arthur looking out over the farms was the sheer scale of the task. It was a marvel not of technology but of logistics.

Interspersed among Arthur's duty hours were classes. He and Wei were often together for these, along with a handful of other new arrivals. They studied the ship's waste-management systems, even as they toiled as apprentices to those who had built them. The men and women working alongside them during the day would be instructors for the evening's lectures. Arthur's employment was no desk job. Paperwork was for the Petty Officer Dulkas of the department. He heaved and toiled and sweated for hours on end before showering and eating and hurrying off to class. He studied long into the night, the ship's ambient light being programmed to mimic the regular rising and setting of the sun.

The population of the *Argo* grew with each passing day. Hallways and lounges and cafeterias filled along with the classrooms. One by one, shops and restaurants began to open, and a nascent economy sputtered to life. Many of the same problems that began at Earth Station One presented themselves aboard the spacecraft. There were thefts and squabbles and disciplinary actions. There were bureaucratic bottlenecks and outright insubordination. There were irreconcilable differences that could only be settled by the legal department.

But some lessons had been learned. The coupon system was discarded, and the Crew Store stocked with adequate supplies of necessary commodities. Locomotion was monitored via wristbands. Computer algorithms flagged suspicious conjunctions between individuals of the opposite sex. Supervisors and desk officers were kept on call to interrupt questionable activities and ensure that appropriate precautions were being taken. It did not take much of this before the crew learned to exercise an appropriate degree of care in managing potentially reproductive activities. The impenetrable musings of Al in Human Resources largely dropped from common debate even as, beneath the surface, his mystique continued to grow. He took on almost mythical overtones, his continued existence offering up questions no one was yet willing to ask.

Admonishments repeated again and again during regular assemblies of the crew warned of the increasingly severe consequences for violations of the rules, Rule Number One being the most important of these. Sending perpetrators home remained a possibility, but the cost of doing so had grown exponentially. Penalties were accordingly raised. While proximity to the earth-side population excluded corporal punishment from the realm of acceptable measures, it was darkly hinted that the crew approached a time when such things would be entirely at the discretion of Admiral Demarion and his staff. The *Argo* was fitted with a brig. This was highlighted as an extravagance that could be easily repurposed should more definitive expedients become necessary.

Arthur's new routine formed slowly over the course of weeks and months. The time he spent with the Waste Management journeymen brought them into a friendly professional rapport. He tracked down Ramon and Dexter via the ship's online directory. They resided in far reaches of the ship and organized their daily activities according to widely divergent schedules. They were occasionally available to meet up for a meal or an hour or two of online video games, but no longer fit neatly into his life. Looming over all of it were unrelenting thoughts of Maisy.

Arthur's association with Maisy had thus far been limited to learning where she lived via the ship's directory. He had been too consumed by self-doubt to visit her, and continued on in the hope of an accidental encounter that would convey an image of confident detachment. Expecting this to happen at any moment, he waited. But a day went by, then another, and nothing happened. It was like sinking into quicksand. By the time he realized something was wrong, a glimmer of doubt had crept in about the depth of her feelings. Perhaps she did not want to see him. Perhaps he would seem needy. The more time passed, the harder it became.

A month or two passed before Arthur happened upon an open secret circulating among the more exclusive cliques of the social hierarchy. The discovery was not a function of any personal connections with such people. It was his job in the Department of Waste Management that brought Arthur to knowledge of the observation deck. A call to the facilities operations center took him there in an unoccupied moment of an otherwise busy afternoon.

One gained access to the deck via an unobtrusive corner of a rarely used passageway and a lift that carried one down through deck after deck, out over the chasm of the outer ring, and through the layers of defenses lining the hull. The observation deck was not a permanent feature of the *Argo*. It would exist only so long as the ship was able to replenish the energy that leaked from it like a window left open in the winter. Thereafter it would be closed off and dismantled, its materials recycled back into the ship. For the time being, however, it was a marvel.

The observation deck had been constructed not for the purpose of filling the crew's leisure hours but to create a suitable impression upon the reporters and dignitaries who visited at the invitation of Beckett Armagast. It rose like a great blister from the outer surface of the ship, enclosing a space roughly the size of a mid-tier sports stadium. Its shell was composed of a spider's web of trusswork supporting monstrous panels of tempered, multi-pane, reinforced glass.

Given the rotation of the ship and the resulting incidence of effective gravity, one did not stand upon the surface of the outer hull and look up at the heavens. Rather, one was pulled down toward the dome itself. This complication was addressed by the construction of an intervening deck upon which one stood and looked down at the view. This deck was composed entirely of reinforced Lucite. Everything that could be so composed was so composed: the tables, the chairs, a dais at one end. Everything was nearly invisible but for a bare minimum of electrical equipment, sofa cushions, and superstructure.

The effect was spectacular, as if one were floating free in the vacuum of space, looking up at the curving surface of the *Argo* and down on the slowly rotating panorama of a star-strewn universe. The sun, the moon, and the orb of the Earth rose at regular intervals over a steel horizon and marched slowly underfoot before setting once more. Someone had thought to bring a telescope. It rested on its tripod with the lens pointed down at the floor.

There was no lock on the door, no restrictive wristband access fitted into the lift. The only thing that had thus far kept it the exclusive domain of the highest social echelons was their unwillingness to discuss it openly. Someone, of course, must have been the first. There was never any doubt who this was.

It was on his first errand to the observation deck that Arthur at last happened upon Maisy. The elevator doors slid open, and there she was. She lounged in a plush wingback armchair far out in the empty expanse, her feet up on an ottoman, chatting with an accumulation of friends among whom she was the unquestioned center of attention.

Arthur saw her. She saw Arthur. She smiled and gave a little wave with idly waggling fingers before going back to whatever she had been saying. Arthur returned the gesture, unsure of whether it was observed. Unmindful of the awe-inspiring majesty around him, he hurried past with his toilet plunger, hoping to make it into the offending restroom before the flush rising in his cheeks became apparent to all the world spread out below.

What was Maisy's reaction to the sight of Arthur hurrying past with his toilet plunger? He would speculate long into the night over this question. It would occupy his thoughts as he hosed out trash compactors and cleared grease traps in the kitchens. Perhaps she was waiting for him to make the first move. Was it all up to him? Had he already blown his chance? It was also possible their fling had been just that: a fling. Arthur was the sort that plunged toilets; that sort of man was not a realistic prospect for the likes of Maisy Armagast. She had had her fun and moved on. It was up to Arthur to do the same. Then there was the possibility she did indeed feel for him but was prevented from acting on her feelings. The specter of Al in Human Resources and Rule Number One loomed.

Since asking her was out of the question, Arthur mulled and stewed and fretted. There were few with whom he could discuss the possibilities forever churning through his mind. Ramon would listen when their schedules aligned. This was rare. A more reliable confidant was Father McIntosh.

The padre had set up shop in the Office of the Chaplaincy alongside accommodations for the Muslims and Buddhists and Hindus and half a dozen other world religions. The fellowship of mostly introverted young men that gravitated toward him began once again to coalesce (the women leaned Buddhist for reasons mysterious to Arthur). The priest was a reliable source of advice on subjects ranging from academic ethical dilemmas to sorrow over absent mothers, all delivered in the utmost confidence.

After hours, Father McIntosh would decamp to the food court. Having bid farewell to his beloved Scotch, he settled upon the passably drinkable bootleg hooch that flowed seamlessly to fill the void. His evenings vied in popularity with the observation deck (knowledge of which began to spread) and the football pitches chalked out among the sheep and cows of the outer ring. Arthur had held a special place with Father McIntosh from their earliest days.

Not long after Arthur's encounter with Maisy, he sought out Father McIntosh at his station in the food court. This was far back in a corner, behind one of the enormous cables supporting the floor and beyond the casual gaze of any passing security guards who might object to the contents of his crystal tumbler. He flatly refused to drink spirits from the unobtrusive paper cups common among the crew. Arthur sat next to him and they looked out over the crowd. He opened his cafeteria to-go box on the table before him. (Why pay in the food court when the cafeteria was free?)

Father McIntosh waited for Arthur to speak. He sat in silence, chewing. In the distance, Maisy entered and began picking her way through the throngs of people, laughing and chattering with a pair of girlfriends. Arthur's eyes followed her.

"What's on your mind?" said Father McIntosh.

It was a moment before Arthur answered. "The Spoke G compactor is down," he said. "It's been a crazy week."

Father McIntosh glanced at him, his face blank. He sipped at his glass. Silence drew out.

"It can't go anywhere," said Arthur at last.

"Why's that?"

"I don't think she's into me like that."

"If I'm not mistaken, the two of you had grown quite close."

166

Even the padre did not know precisely how close they had grown, but he had his suspicions.

"It was our last few weeks on Earth. It was the island. Everything was different."

"And different is a bad thing?" Father McIntosh's point was often just beyond Arthur's grasp.

Maisy stopped before a young man who had risen from his seat to speak with her. She flashed a smile and placed a hand on the young man's forearm as she leaned in to be heard over the din of the food court. A great quantity of stone settled in the pit of Arthur's stomach. He set down the spork that was halfway to his mouth.

"She has her pick," he said.

"And this was different on the island?"

Arthur continued to stare. He could never get anywhere with Father McIntosh.

The other foil for Arthur's conversation was Mrs. Pifflethorpe, although with her he would never think of discussing Maisy. Indeed, Mrs. Pifflethorpe was but a phone call away. Soon after his arrival, Arthur had discovered he could pick up the handset of the little plastic phone in his quarters and dial up his mother —anyone on Earth, in fact. It was all bizarrely mundane, without even the odd international dial tone he had experienced on the island.

It is not uncommon, of course, for earthly communications to make use of on-orbit assets in connecting one corner of the world to another. There is no reason whatsoever the *Argo* could not, while in orbit, be as connected to the global information grid as any other satellite. The reality of the situation went farther. The spacecraft, in various phases of development, had been orbiting for a decade or more. This arrangement resulted in large quantities of on-orbit real estate residing conveniently at the terminus of a complex, well-developed, and highly efficient supply chain. Beckett Armagast spotted a revenue opportunity. For years he had been selling a host of telecommunications services from equipment temporarily bolted to the ship's outer hull.

The project had become a massive profit center—inadvertently, it seemed, only to those less familiar with Beckett Armagast. The *Argo* collected overhead imagery and monitored weather patterns. It served as the primary computing and storage node for a network of thousands of other orbiting objects. It beamed pop music to soccer moms in minivans and monitored the globe for nuclear missile launches. The acreage of available space and ultra-low cost of access were irresistible lures to entrepreneurial spirits.

As a matter of fact, the global community of satellite-services consumers faced something of a conundrum when it came to the impending loss of their preferred on-orbit resource. An enormous amount of capability would disappear with the flick of a switch that fired the *Argo*'s engine and sent it rocketing off into the infinite black. This global community was at that very moment involved in a massive, worldwide effort to mobilize resources and arrive at alternative solutions. At the center of this storm of economic activity was Beckett Armagast.

Arthur's ability to chat with Mrs. Pifflethorpe would not last forever. But it would be quite some time—years, in fact—before connection was altogether severed. In the meantime, fidelity and bandwidth would diminish as the ship sped off on its journey. As soon as the spacecraft left Earth orbit, transmission lag times would begin to increase until real-time conversations became impractical. Communication would then be limited to text and recorded messages.

The next significant transition would occur after the *Argo* had executed its first sweeping acceleration maneuver through the gravity well of the sun. It would speed off into the outer reaches of the solar system, past the orbits of Mars and Jupiter and on toward Saturn and beyond, stealing away some small fraction of each planet's angular momentum as it slingshotted past. As it proceeded, the ability of the *Argo*'s solar panels to collect energy from the receding sun would approach the threshold where they could no longer replace that lost through electromagnetic transmission. Communication functions would begin to shut down. Transmission to Earth, as with any other activity that caused the ship to lose energy, would be prioritized and metered out based on a dwindling capacity to replace it. Functions such as Arthur's missives to Mrs. Pifflethorpe would be the first to go.

Eventually all transmission would cease, and the *Argo* would be capable only of receiving messages. Thus, for some years more the Argonauts would be kept abreast of activities back on Earth. Technological advances and other important tidbits would be sent along to help the spacecraft on its way. Television broadcasts and similar entertainments for the crew would also be among the last to go. Early on, Beckett Armagast had announced that Armagast Enterprises would cover the cost of monthly content-streaming services for the crew right up until the point communication ceased. This relative pittance would put him at the center of creative production and broadcasting circles for years. It would stimulate a surfeit of *Argo*-themed programming that would come to dominate the medium for a time.

But once the *Argo* ceased transmission, it would grow increasingly difficult for even the high-power antennae available on Earth to locate and transmit to that infinitesimal speck. Beams would tighten as transmission patterns gained up, throwing their limited power further and further into the heavens. As beams tightened, they would strain for adequate range to reach the *Argo*'s quietly listening receivers. But this would also make it more difficult for them to hit their target. Eventually, maintaining alignment would become impossible. The *Argo* would be on its own.

Chapter Thirteen

Lift 34R12b docked with the *Argo* a little more than three months after Arthur's arrival aboard. With it came the final load of crew and equipment prior to departure. The *Argo* was far from complete, but it would never be complete. It was engineered as something approaching a living organism, with its crew forever building and dismantling and building again. Repair and refurbishment had begun in some corners of the ship even as construction was still underway in others. Technology had advanced far beyond the projections of the earliest designers by the time the final fittings were installed and the final panels bolted into place. At some point, a line needed to be drawn. Beckett Armagast drew that line at Lift 34R12b. Construction was officially finished.

Before the assembled crew in their dress uniforms and a forest of cameras, Beckett hailed the accomplishment in terms both grandiose and deprecatory. No expense was spared on speechwriters well practiced in availing themselves of the latter in order to accentuate the former. Floating on the Lucite stage of the observation deck with a blue-green Earth spinning by below his feet, he all but proclaimed himself the Savior of

Mankind. The crew was called to attention as he formally bestowed command upon Admiral Demarion and his corps of staff officers. He announced the precise date of departure a scant eight months in the future. The conjunction was fast approaching, and the *Argo* could wait no longer. The speech left one and all with a renewed sense of purpose and a proud tingle in the spine.

All, that is, but Arthur. His mind was far away, his eyes not on the speaker but on the floor—through the floor, really, to where the landmass of North America spun by beneath his feet. He found the East Coast beneath the white swirl of a gathering storm. He followed it up to the beckoning finger of Cape Cod, then inland. Past the mountains, below the sprawling blobs of the Great Lakes. There—just there—must be where Mrs. Pifflethorpe sat, probably in the recliner in the living room, watching the ceremony on channel 507. Just to the right—there, by the coast—is where Isabel would be. Sloane—where was she? Probably in that same town at the other end of the state that had once loomed so large in his imagination. He could not pick it out from the bland, featureless expanse.

When his eyes came back up, they still did not go to Beckett Armagast, who had lowered a raised fist to grip the edges of a Lucite podium now clouded with mists of saliva. No, Arthur looked to Maisy, whom Beckett had positioned in the front row. Below hair tucked behind an ear, Arthur could see the line of her jaw where it turned up toward a perfect, downy earlobe. He pictured her in a very different place: standing on the beach in the moonlight. All those months gone by, and nothing. Even if she were to return to him, what could come of it? Sterile loneliness, and death somewhere out in the black of space? Perhaps he never should have left home.

The Argonauts were called to attention. At a barked order, they saluted as one. Then the crew was dismissed and hustled off toward the emergency stairwell by security forces directed to clear the room for Beckett and his distinguished visitors. Arthur watched for Maisy in the press of bodies, but to no avail. She doubtless had joined the command staff and Beckett's collection of world leaders for a round of drinks and chitchat.

The date of departure ticked nearer, and the crew came to terms with yawning uncertainty while dealing with the petty annoyances of life aboard. There were everyday conveniences no one had thought to stock in the Crew Store (fingernail clippers were one example that created quite a sensation). Identifying such an oversight and retooling the manufacturing centers to accommodate took days. Even the most advanced spacecraft in the known universe had finicky internet service and hot-water tanks that ran out in the middle of the morning's shower rush.

Then there were the desk officers, the bane of daily comings and goings throughout the ship. They seemed selected by Al in Human Resources explicitly for the attribute of officious self-importance. They monitored attendance logs and enforced cleanliness regulations and acted upon tipoffs of suspicious wristband conjunctions with all the zeal of children on Christmas morning. Among this cadre, Stanley Waller was first among equals. Even his peers occasionally felt his efforts were carried to excess.

One evening, not long after Taps, Arthur returned to his room from the showers after an afternoon wheelbarrowing manure from the cow pasture to the first officer's rose garden. Such tasks were not officially the responsibility of the Waste Management Department, but Petty Officer Dulka often received this type of request from the staff. When Lane Beauregard thought of cow manure, he thought of Waste Management. Petty Officer Dulka was not one to contradict him.

Arthur changed into his track suit and dialed up Mrs. Pifflethorpe for a video chat. As her image resolved on the screen, a knock sounded on the door.

"One sec," Arthur said to Mrs. Pifflethorpe. He looked toward the door. "Come in."

Wei entered. Arthur was expecting her.

"Thanks, I loved it," she said. She held out a paperback book. Arthur took it.

"It's great, right?" he said. "Come in." He turned the computer so its camera took her in. "This is my mother... Mother, this is Wei."

"Hello, young lady," said Mrs. Pifflethorpe.

Wei stepped forward and half-nodded, half-bowed a greeting. Her face began to flush red. The door swung closed behind her.

"Arthur has told me so much about you," Mrs. Pifflethorpe went on.

That was as far as she got, for just then a knock sounded on the door.

"Come in," Arthur said. The door had begun to open before he could get it out.

Stanley stepped halfway into the room and peered about as if expecting an ambush. "Right then, Pifflethorpe..." he said. "Having visitors after hours, are we?"

"Ah... no... well, yes," said Arthur. "We work together. She'll just be a moment."

"Mmm..." Stanley screwed up his face as he considered this.

Arthur turned back to the computer screen. "Mother, this is Stanley," he said.

"Good evening, young man," said Mrs. Pifflethorpe's freezing, skipping, buffering face. Someone walked up behind her. Mr. Underwood bent to place his face in the frame and waved. He moved off.

"Good evening, ma'am," said Stanley. "If you'll excuse us, just a quick official matter to clear up." He turned back to Arthur and glanced from him to Wei and back again as he spoke. "After hours, you know... and with the door closed. Irregular, I'm afraid. I just received notification at the desk. Need to check that all's in order."

"Yes, we're fine," said Arthur. "She was just saying hello to my mother." Again, he gestured toward Mrs. Pifflethorpe to ensure the fact of her presence was not missed.

Stanley was undeterred. "Need to verify proper stocks on hand," he said. "Safety first, that's the important thing."

The shade of red in Wei's face continued to deepen. Arthur moved toward the door in an effort to take the discussion into the hallway. Stanley stood firm.

"I don't think that'll be necessary," said Arthur. "We're colleagues. She's heading right out."

"Yep, yep... understood," Stanley said. "Just need to verify you're properly provided for, and I'll be right off. Rules are rules, you know. Can't be having any accidents. Human Resources isn't ready to in-process any new baby Argonauts, if you know what I mean." He chuckled to himself.

"I don't have any because I don't need any," said Arthur. "This is Petty Officer Yao. You can call up to Waste Management and talk to Chief Dulka..."

"Hmm..." Stanley cut him off with a grunt of disapproval. "No stocks on hand. Hmm. Young lady, you'll need to come with me, I'm afraid. Pifflethorpe, this will need to be reported, you know. Rules are rules. Must have stocks on hand when we've got ladies and gentlemen alone unattended. I'm sure you're aware. No accidents... babies, you know... not required at the moment."

Wei was gone by the time Stanley trailed off. Stanley raised a finger as if to make one last point, paused to look after the retreating Wei, and hurried after her.

"Well, my goodness," said Mrs. Pifflethorpe. Then she asked Arthur about his day.

The hurricane of the Argonaut rumor mill continued to gather pace, with the subject of Stanley's lecture on everyone's minds. Whispering raged over the algorithms that would be used to determine breeding pairs. How would this be accomplished in practice? Would such things forever be executed through sterile medical procedures? What if the pair preferred to do it the old-fashioned way? Would this be permitted? Was marriage out of the question? Who would be responsible for raising the resulting offspring?

The truth is, no one knew—or no one in a position to reveal such details to a wide audience. The official line from the senior staff was that plans were still under development and would be announced in due time. No one believed this. "Due time" was taken to mean a period sufficient for degradation in communication channels to render feasible the censorship of transmissions back to Earth.

Arthur did not enjoy this topic of conversation, whether or not his mother was present. He found the subject distasteful. It was not only the lascivious overtones; it was the very fact the topic had to be confronted. Such things were not to be planned for. Such things resided somewhere out in the mystical haze that formed his understanding of conjugal relations. He knew, of course, that the Grand Plan of AI in Human Resources was coming. He knew he would be a part of whatever scheme was devised. But by not thinking about it, he carried on under the illusion that his dream of everlasting love remained within reach. His head was planted firmly in the sand, and the crew's insistence upon speculation dragged it repeatedly into the light.

Even as Arthur despaired of ever being with her again, the

subject of Maisy was thrust upon him again and again. The manner in which she was discussed by the male crew was distasteful. That any among them held out the possibility of fathering a child upon the great Maisy Armagast was fodder for many an after-dinner conversation. Arthur excused himself whenever such discussions threatened, but they were impossible to avoid altogether.

Even Stanley, champion as he was of Al's Grand Plan, was not immune to flights of fancy. Three nights after his introduction to Mrs. Pifflethorpe, Arthur was sitting a graveyard shift at the duty desk. This was a common punishment for minor violations of the rules and had been meted out by the bosun's staff when Stanley filed his report. The penalty was intended to serve the dual purpose of giving desk officers a break from their duties, but Stanley required no such break. He hovered about, chatting and tut-tutting and peering over Arthur's shoulder to offer suggestions on the best ways to carry out the duties of a desk officer.

"Mmm-hmm," said Arthur. This was the third or fourth time in a row he had said it.

Stanley was growing noticeably disappointed that Arthur did not acknowledge the wisdom of his suggestions with a suitable level of enthusiasm. A new thought occurred to him. He had just the thing to ingratiate himself to a fellow crewman. The coolest among the crew could talk of little else in those days.

"Know who came by the other day?" he said.

Arthur shook his head and returned his eyes to the computer screen, hoping Stanley would give up and go to bed.

"Maisy Armagast," said Stanley.

Arthur could not avoid the jolt that brought his eyes back to Stanley's face. Stanley noticed it. He let his eyes drift off as his body sagged toward the countertop upon which he rested his elbows.

"Came by?" said Arthur. "Why did she come by?"

Stanley's lips pursed contemplatively. "Yeah, it's happened a few times. Just passing in the hall, but too often to be coincidence."

"When?" said Arthur.

"Oh..." Stanley drew it out. "Last time was a few days ago. She wants to say something, of course, or why would she keep looking in? Can't blame her, really." He paused to let this sink in.

"Can't blame her for what?"

Stanley tried to smile while pressing his lips firmly together. "I probably shouldn't get into it," he said. His look said he very much wanted to get into it. He swallowed his disappointment when Arthur did not press him. "She's a pretty girl, but we gave that up, right? If we were back on Earth, who could say no? As Argonauts..."

"Say no to what?" said Arthur.

"Hmm..." Stanley toyed with Arthur like a cat with a mouse. "She didn't need to ask... we both understand."

"Do you know her from somewhere?"

Again, Stanley's smile was cryptic. "You could say that."

Arthur let it go. Stanley had never spoken to Maisy, that much was obvious.

Maisy continued as the vortex of a social tornado that began once again to swirl among the Argonauts. She neither avoided Arthur nor seemed to make any effort to seek him out. She was friendly when they crossed paths, saying hello in the corridors or giving a wave when their eyes met across the lunchroom. The intimacy developed during their time together on the island seemed to have vanished.

But unbeknownst to Arthur, he had similarly begun to swell in her thoughts. What could possibly be occupying Arthur's time? Did he have a sweetheart? Was it that Wei girl? Why didn't he just tell her about it? She, of all people, would not be jealous.

She would be perfectly fine with it.

It would not bother her a bit.

She found herself forswearing her usual band of admirers in the food court to eat supper in the cafeteria. This was a sensible financial decision, she told herself. She must learn to manage money now that Beckett was no longer supporting her. There was no sense in paying for meals at the food court when dining in the cafeteria was free.

Maisy never went out of her way to sit with Arthur. The demands of her social life were pressing. He would understand if the sensitivities of her devotees must be tended to. But with their schedules synchronized, she could not help noticing he tended to depart the cafeteria at precisely the same time each evening. It did not matter with whom he was talking or the amount of food left on his plate.

The mystery consumed her. One evening, she slipped out of the cafeteria after him and followed along as far as his squadron lobby. It was then she realized with a flash of anger that she had been duped. Maisy Armagast did not chase after boys, and certainly not bashful garbagemen from decaying Midwest industrial towns. Obviously, Arthur had planned all of it. Why did he not just talk to her? Invite her to his room after dinner? He was leading her on. Toying with her. She was furious.

For his part, Arthur had taken her disregard at face value. Why had she taken to eating in the cafeteria if not to be near him? Why go out of her way to be near him and not come over?

The only conceivable answer was that she wanted to make it clear that Arthur was nothing special. The manner with which she engaged those around her had taken on an almost frenetic air, as if she wanted all the world to see how much she was enjoying herself. The only possible explanation was that she had taken up with some other man and wanted Arthur to move on.

Getting to sleep meant taking his mind off Maisy. Each evening, he had taken to joining Ramon and Dexter and half a dozen other Argonauts spread throughout the ship for a round of online warfare, spattering enemy soldiers with immoderate fusillades of machine-gun fire. After supper on that final day, at his usual time, he tore his eyes off his beloved Maisy and returned to his room.

Maisy watched the door to his room click shut from her position beyond the glass partition of the squadron lobby. She was not spying on him. Their paths had conveniently aligned. Nevertheless, she waited until Stanley stepped away from his desk before stealing down the corridor to Arthur's door. She pondered and dithered. The blood rose in her face as she peered up and down the hall, expecting a door to open at any moment and someone to ask what she was doing.

This was ridiculous. This boy was not worth such a fuss. She would simply talk to him. As soon as Maisy's knuckles had touched the surface of Arthur's door, she reconsidered the wisdom of her plan. It would be better to speak with him in a more public setting. After all, there were the wristband monitors to consider. Tomorrow, perhaps, or next week. She had only knocked once. He had probably not noticed. She was turning to go when the door opened. Arthur stood rooted to the spot wearing nothing but a terrycloth robe over his underwear. A silence drew out.

"Hi, Arthur," she said at last.

"Hi, Maisy," he replied.

Silence.

"I just thought we might catch up." *What was she thinking? Catch up? She could have spoken to him any number of times in the cafeteria.*

"Yeah, sure... I was just about to..." He got halfway through the thought before the image of himself playing video games in his underwear made him taper off into silence.

Maisy's embarrassment was on display to anyone who might happen by. She stepped forward into the room and the door snapped closed behind her. They stood looking at one another. Before either could think of anything to say, another knock sounded on the door.

Stanley had returned to his desk. Not long after settling into his chair, he received notification of a suspicious wristband conjunction just a few steps down the hall from where he sat surveying his dominion. One of the wristbands belonged to none other than Maisy Armagast. Arthur's door had hardly snapped shut before Stanley was leaping to his feet. He covered the distance at a dead run.

At the sound of the knock, Arthur stepped past Maisy and opened the door.

The only person who wanted to be in the room at that moment was Stanley. He announced the purpose of his visit. Maisy made a passing comment upon the nature of Stanley's parentage as she excused herself. She retreated with a nonchalance only slightly disturbed by unbecoming haste. Stanley followed, afraid of missing his chance to bring the incident before the proper authorities. Women like Maisy respected a man in a position of command.

It was not long before Stanley returned, having failed in his attempts to capture Maisy's attention and not possessed of sufficient self-confidence to accost her. He leaned against the doorjamb with a cool sangfroid.

"Hey," he said.

Arthur looked at him.

"That Maisy Armagast is something else," Stanley said, or something to that effect.

Arthur could feel his blood coming to a quiet simmer.

"We have a thing, actually," Stanley went on. "You probably didn't know that." He directed his gaze down over his physique as if to accentuate the point. "We were both on Lift 2N324, if you know what I mean."

Arthur's blood reached a full boil.

"Know what I call her? ...Freckles." Stanley chuckled to himself. "If you're nice to me, someday I'll tell you why."

The young man was not so bad really, although it would take Arthur quite some time to realize this. Stanley tried to emulate the popular boys and could never get it quite right. He desperately wanted friends. He had always wanted friends. Was this not how it was done? Male bonding? From the moment he saw Maisy's universally acclaimed form scrubbed down with a stiff-bristled brush, he knew it was his ticket to the Big Leagues. He had been watching for an opportunity to drop his trump card. For Stanley, the *Argo* was an opportunity to start afresh—to recreate himself in the image he had always imagined possible if only he could shake off the legacy of past mistakes. But that never works. New places, even spaceships headed off to distant star systems, cannot change who we are.

Chapter Fourteen

The *Argo* stood at the lip of a precipice. Below was the seething surface of the sun. Above was the expanse of interstellar space. Up is where it was headed, but first it would go down.

Among the factors critical to success of the *Argo*'s mission was speed. Over the hundreds of light-years it would travel, the smallest differences would magnify into centuries spent drifting through black and frozen emptiness. Every joule of energy expended in acceleration would be that much less to sustain the crew on its voyage. Thus, the colossal engine built into the core of the ship was not its sole means of locomotion. The amount of fuel that would be required, by itself, to accelerate the spacecraft to anything approaching an adequate velocity would be far beyond what it was capable of carrying, even should all other functions be stripped away to make room. More than half of that fuel would be preserved in anticipation of eventual deceleration millennia hence.

An initial tap of the accelerator would tip it out of Earth orbit and send it plummeting toward the sun. On the way it would fly to Venus and slingshot past. Mercury it would skip, unable to approach so close to the sun, but it would expose its solar panels and other collection devices to the searing radiation, gathering up and storing away whatever could be captured. Some months later, it would return to where it began, zipping past the Earth to gather yet more speed before rocketing off into the outer reaches.

Mars would be omitted from the itinerary due to lack of proper alignment, but Jupiter and Saturn would receive visits, each quicker than the one before as velocity mounted. Not long after passing Saturn, the *Argo*'s speed would reach a point where it was no longer possible to decelerate, drop into orbit around one of the outer planets, and eventually return to Earth. They would be committed to leaving forever.

Uranus they would also miss due to improper alignment. Neptune would be the last the crew would see of their home solar system. In reality, they would never set eyes upon its tremendous blue orb. Neptune would be just an image on a screen, the observation deck having been long since packed away and sealed off as the crew retreated within its cocoon of insulation. Soon after, most of the external cameras would close down to save the heat dissipated by their mechanisms and circuit boards.

As the day for departure approached, the crew set to work battening down anything that might be disrupted by the acceleration. Livestock were rounded up and locked in their pens. Covers were rolled closed over aquaculture tanks and library shelves. Dishes were packed in Styrofoam and anything with wheels was strapped down. None of this touched much upon Arthur's duties. There remained kitchen scraps to be carted off to the composter chutes and worn-out electronics to be disassembled and sorted, but if anything, he was relieved by the distraction that gripped the upper echelons of management. His free moments were not filled with make-work tasks someone thought would be educational.

For a time, he was press-ganged along with the rest of the nonessential workers. He spent hours packing away test tubes and beakers and petri dishes in one of the laboratories. By and large, however, such chores required less time than forecast. No one stepped forward to volunteer surplus man-hours, and front-line supervisors did not press the issue. For them, keeping everyone busy was nearly as onerous a task as securing the *Argo* for departure. It was sufficient to look busy when anyone of note passed and to fill status reports with irrelevant commentary. For the first time since he had come aboard, Arthur found himself starved for things to do.

Maisy found herself in the same position, although this was more common in her line of work. She was, like Arthur (like the entire crew), struck by the immensity of what was to come. It could be argued that she had far more to lose by leaving Earth behind. In neither place would she lack for attention or the basic necessities of life. She would enjoy entrée into the highest circles of power and perquisites not available to the rank and file. She would always be a celebrity, for people will always need idols over whose lives they can speculate and pass judgment. But Earth was a deep market for gregarious beauty, and who knew to what heights of stardom she may have risen? How many wealthy, famous, and even royal husbands she may have attracted over the course of her life? These were the thoughts she mused upon when members of her coterie were startled to find her sitting alone and staring off into space.

The occasion was, as most would later agree, a letdown. All were directed to report to duty stations and strap in. Blood ran high. Few duty stations were provided with the necessary straps. Arthur's cubicle in the Department of Waste Management certainly was not, although he moved the towering piles of file folders and machine parts into a less precarious arrangement. Despite the complaints, this did not in the end present a problem. The great jolt and furious straining that had been envisioned turned out to be little more than a low vibration passing through the walls that may have risen to the verge of a shudder before settling back. Forces of acceleration never rose above what one may have experienced in an underpowered minivan heading west out of Colorado Springs. The *Argo* had an enormous engine, but the *Argo* was an enormous ship.

Following the engine's firing, much of the equipment was left stowed away in anticipation of maneuvers to come. There were a few days that followed of unpacking the essentials. It was quite some time before the crew settled back into its routine. Numbness pervaded them all. Encounters between old acquaintances were less boisterous, games of poker less contentious. The atmosphere in the food court and cafeterias had never been so subdued. It was not uncommon to come across shipmates conducting business in hushed murmurs. At all hours of the day the observation deck was filled to capacity, but the festive mood was gone. Most sat staring out at the receding ball of blue and green as it dropped slowly aft, spiraling away against the rotation of the ship and shrinking into the distance.

It would be a few weeks before bandwidth dropped off along with communication fidelity. Skipping and buffering of video feeds slowly increased but they did not immediately terminate. Phone calls were filled with interruptions and awkward pauses, but for a time continued largely as before. Arthur maintained his interactions with Mrs. Pifflethorpe and the few other friends with whom he had remained in intermittent contact.

One day not long after their episode in Arthur's room, Maisy happened upon him on the observation deck, reclined on a sofa and staring off at the receding Earth. Without needing to be told, Ramon slid down to make room for her. She took her place at Arthur's side, their hips and shoulders pressed together as of old, fingers interlaced. In hindsight, neither ever doubted they would arrive at this place (although hindsight can be a poor judge of eventualities). They picked up where they had left off.

There was no cataclysm in Arthur's relationship with Maisy —no midnight trysts and losing themselves in perspiring flesh and heavy breathing. The mood of the time did not allow it; regardless, it was not Arthur's way. Those with such predispositions to self-doubt rarely enjoy the torrid kisses and postcoital panics that spice the lives of brasher souls. They think, they wait, they plan, and in the end, they wish just once they had simply jumped. That those brasher souls often wish they had done more in the way of thinking, waiting, and planning rarely registers in the minds of young men like Arthur, so prone to regret.

Even Maisy could not drag it out of him. But truly, she would not have wanted to. She had never known such peace in her relations with young men. The very simplicity of it was a shock. Their approach to her had always been so polished, so predictable, so stilted and overconfident. Arthur was just *there*. It felt to her like he had always been there. She never knew it could be so easy.

Life settles into rhythms in even the strangest of circumstances. It did so for Arthur and Maisy as they set off toward their universally acknowledged doom somewhere out in the black emptiness. Maisy's admirers, none of whom honestly believed in his heart he would be the one to win her over, accommodated Arthur's presence with surprising grace (at least when Maisy was present). Petty jealousies abounded, but never

rose above the level of mild irritation. Maisy was the unquestioned arbiter of discernment and sophistication. If she chose
Arthur then there must have been more to him than met the
eye. His reticence became quiet confidence. His naïveté became
authenticity.

They would lie together for hours on Arthur's bunk
watching television, occasionally interrupted by Stanley's
dutiful inspections. At first, Stanley was transparently bitter
over Arthur's triumph. But when he continued to find the
couple fully clothed and largely unentangled, resentment
turned to smugness in his knowledge that the rumor mill had
overestimated their level of intimacy. Maisy remained open for
business. He was not about to encourage competition by
divulging this to a wider audience.

At the conclusion of each evening together, Arthur and
Maisy would stand for an awkward moment, allowing discussion of their schedules for the following day to peter out into
silence. Maisy would linger for a moment more, watching
Arthur wrestle with himself. She would give him a smile to
carry him through the night before she turned to go.

There had to be a first kiss. It took time before Arthur was
able to work himself up to it. Maisy watched it all with faint
amusement and no small measure of impatience. The kiss
finally happened one day in a cherry orchard in the temperate
zone of the outer ring. The trees were among the first planted
and were taller than most, reaching high enough to spread a
canopy that offered privacy from the farmers and maintenance
crews that bustled about.

Arthur had not planned it out, or no more so than he had
planned any of his previous misfires. Maisy finished early her
day's work of translating a plan of business-process reengineering into PowerPoint slides. She asked around until she
found Arthur raking rotted cabbage into a garden plot. They

walked together past the aquaculture tanks, past the sheep pens and pastureland. The cherry orchard was among their favorite spots, and that is where she led him. Trunks of the trees were the thickness of a man's forearm. The uppermost branches obscured the tops of the pair's wandering heads. The ground was overgrown with weeds whose seeds were smuggled aboard amid truckloads of soil for which Armagast Enterprises had paid top dollar under the assurance of its absolute purity. Briars grew in tangled mounds here and there.

Maisy led the way, her body twisted sideways to slip between the rows of trees and to grip the hand of Arthur trailing behind. Reaching the center of the orchard, they dropped down into a circle of undergrowth crushed flat by frequent visits. They sat side by side, legs outstretched. Trees formed leafy colonnades stretching away in curious geometrical patterns. Spreading branches nearly closed overhead. They talked about translating a plan of business-process reengineering into Power-Point slides.

Arthur's heart began to pound, as it always did in such circumstances. As he sat beside her there in the orchard, it at last became unbearable. Who could say what finally tipped the balance and made him lean over and kiss her? To all appearances, the touching of their lips had a casual, almost offhand feel to it. Arthur went blind with the surge of chemicals flooding his bloodstream; but looking back, he would be proud of the way he carried it off. He had avoided the colliding teeth and manufactured passion of past misadventures.

The kiss lingered for only a moment. Maisy smiled, broad and close, and ran a hand over Arthur's cheek. She shifted to lay on her back with her head in his lap. Arthur toyed with a lock of her hair, which had grown longer since the early days. Together they looked up into the branches and very nearly felt themselves back on Earth.

It would be quite some time before Arthur would be prepared to take more advanced steps in his pursuit of Maisy. This did not bother her overmuch. The sense among all the Argonauts was of a superabundance of time, with nothing at the end of it but a slow fade off into blackness.

How could this state of affairs progress but badly? Even as Arthur and Maisy fell deeper in love, machinations were underway for execution of the Grand Plan to propagate the *Argo*'s new branch of humanity. This plan did not account for love. Love would lead to resistance, to conflict, to offspring that did not conform to the prescriptions of AI in Human Resources. Love was a remnant of human frailty that must be crushed out.

Arthur's duties gave him knowledge of a wide and growing inventory of quiet nooks where he and Maisy could meet for moments of solitude. Storerooms adjacent to busy cubicle farms were the best, as the wristbands usually failed to discern they were alone together. Arthur's access was among the most permissive allotted to crewmen of his station. Even when duty did not call him to remote corners of the ship, he would spend long hours exploring. He learned the *Argo*'s secret corners from prow to stern.

The wristbands themselves proved less of a nuisance than had been imagined. The *Argo* was not long past its initial gravity-assist maneuver around Venus when the crew experienced its first fatality. A fifty-year-old industrial mechanic dropped dead of a heart attack as he emerged from the restroom on his way back to the line. With this, Arthur and the rest of the Waste Management journeymen were instructed in procedures for recycling human remains. Disconnecting the clasp on the poor fellow's wristband was as simple as applying a small electronic key stored in a cabinet of the morgue.

It was not long before duplicates of this key entered into circulation. The original was back in its place before anyone knew it was gone. Duplicates remained rare, approaching the status of legend among the broader crew. But the Waste Management journeymen were among the fortunate. The profession was widely looked down upon, and the group stuck together. Arthur had little trouble securing a key for Maisy.

So, while to the watchful eye of the ship's computer Maisy sat quietly at her desk or asleep in her bed, she and Arthur would slip off together. Ever so slowly, Arthur's explorations widened, this time on terrain of a more personal nature. In many respects, the adventure was as new for Maisy as it was for him. She had never been with a man so utterly bereft of experience. She relished the opportunity to train him up as she would want a man trained.

"Don't do it that way. Do it this way..."

"Not quite so wet... yes, that's better..."

"Oooh, no no no... that tickles..."

Arthur threw himself into his studies. He was spared the embarrassment of fumbling with unfamiliar buttons and zippers and clasps, each of which was addressed in Maisy's curriculum.

The death of the mechanic crystalized for the ship's officers the realization that Al's master plan must begin soon. This presented a challenge, as the *Argo* had not yet completed its final swoop past the home planet. Armagast Enterprises had no desire for the (as some may have perceived it) draconian measures to become widely discussed. Internet firewalls were strengthened. Airtime was limited and rationed to fit the capacity of a temporary army of censors employed to monitor interactions in real time. It was an all-hands-on-deck exercise for which Stanley Waller volunteered with enthusiasm.

Meanwhile, a test case was initiated. Al spit out his first recommendation for optimal genetic recombination. The feared crisis was postponed when it became clear the young lady selected would be a willing participant. As for the men, they would never know for certain whose children were whose (although as things progressed, some resemblances would prove indisputable). In each round to come, dozens would be called to perform their duty. None would be told which were the lucky fathers. A firestorm of whispering began, with midwives, geneticists, obstetricians—anyone who might possess insider knowledge—achieving new heights of celebrity and gaining admission to Maisy's exclusive circles.

Life carried on. The observation deck reopened as the *Argo* rounded the sun and began its outward voyage. Near to the inferno, it had been closed to avoid exposing the crew to retinal damage and unsafe levels of radiation. Upon reopening, it was filled to capacity each evening with crewmen too-long locked away from the glories of the universe. Lounge furniture was ransacked from lobbies and break rooms across the ship and carried there to meet the demand. Even so, most of the visitors simply sprawled on the floor, face-down, staring out at the stars.

One evening after his dinner in the cafeteria (Maisy was not yet ready to begin breaking Arthur of his thrift), Arthur came to the observation deck in response to an invitation from Father McIntosh. Over a game of chess, they entered into conversation on a subject of recent concern to Arthur.

"You're young. Enjoy yourself. Someday you'll wish you had." The priest said the words as he dropped a knight into the center of the board.

Arthur considered this with a look approaching dismay. "You really think so?" he said. "I thought that kind of stuff wasn't allowed."

Arthur was conflicted by the progression of his relationship with Maisy. The inflexibility of certain thresholds had been drilled into him from childhood, and these thresholds were being rapidly approached. Maisy seemed to have no compunction about breezing past. In fact, she was impatient. Father McIntosh was the only one Arthur could trust with such confidences.

"I thought we were talking about happiness." The priest paused in his studying of the board to meet Arthur's eyes. Behind him, the wash of the Milky Way spun by under the line of the ship's hull. "If you want advice about the preservation of your everlasting soul, that's a different matter altogether."

"They're not the same thing?" said Arthur. He countered the knight with a bishop.

The priest laughed heartily. "Oh, my boy, you've much to learn," he said.

"So, you think I shouldn't worry about it?"

"I didn't say that." The priest's eyes were back on the board.

"Then what do you mean? Yes or no?"

"I think you know the answer to that question." Father McIntosh sipped on his drink. He castled.

Arthur thought for a moment. "What do I tell Maisy?"

"What have you decided to do?"

"I haven't decided anything."

The priest shrugged. "Well then...?"

"Well then...?" Arthur was inviting the padre to continue, but he seemed to consider the matter closed. These conversations always ended like this. Arthur could never say why they were a help to him. He advanced a pawn and tried again. "What about Rule Number One?"

"Planning a family, are we?"

"Of course not. You *are* a priest, right? You *did* go to seminary?"

"Indeed. You'll find few so devoid of illusions on the matter."

"But you're not answering my question."

"Perhaps we should leave this discussion for another time."

"I beg your pardon?"

"Perhaps we should leave this discussion for another time."

The priest could be so infuriating. Then Arthur realized his friend was not meeting his eyes. He was looking past Arthur, his gaze rising as it followed the countenance of someone stepping up from behind. A hand ruffled Arthur's hair.

"Arthur, guess what?"

He turned to see Maisy standing over him. She was not alone.

"Hi, sweet..." He swallowed the word. "What's up?"

Maisy stepped around him and took one of the two empty seats at the table. A woman who had arrived with her took the last. Arthur and Father McIntosh did a simultaneous double-take. "I've got dirt," Maisy said. She introduced her companion, though they knew her by sight. "Skyla, this is Arthur... Father McIntosh. Guys... Skyla Sawyer."

They shook hands all around. The skin on the back of Arthur's neck prickled as he touched her, but he fought the feeling back down. Animosities from Earth Station One seemed so petty now that they were embarked on their mission.

After an exchange of pleasantries, Maisy got down to it. "Skyla works in Human Resources."

Arthur and Father McIntosh both looked up from the chessboard as Skyla's eyes went down to it. Who worked in Human Resources besides Al?

"Who works in Human Resources besides Al?" Arthur asked.

Skyla glanced at him with a look of annoyance but did not answer.

"We just met," said Maisy. "We're setting up HR with business processes to support program execution."

"Execution of what?"

"Their business processes," Maisy replied testily. "I just said that."

Arthur considered this. Father McIntosh had gone back to studying the board. He retreated with the knight.

"What's the dirt?" Arthur said.

Maisy looked to Skyla, and Arthur looked back to the board.

Skyla had become engrossed with the game. Maisy prompted. "Know why Beckett was in such a hurry to clear us out?" she said.

"The conjunction?" Arthur's eyes said he supposed the obvious answer was incorrect.

Skyla spoke at last. "Nope." Her eyes stayed on the board. As Arthur sat watching her, she moved a piece for him.

Maisy stepped in once more. Skyla and Father McIntosh carried on with the game as she explained. The conjunction, it seemed, had less to do with their immediate departure than had been supposed. There were, in reality, many possible arrangements of the planets that would allow for an acceptable slingshot maneuver, the next being a mere eighteen months in the future. This one would miss Jupiter and Neptune but pick up Mars and Uranus.

Despite her air of indifference, Skyla would not be deprived of the opportunity to divulge the good bit. She cut in. "The real reason was Al," she said.

"Al?" said Arthur.

She pulled her attention from the chess board at last. "Ever wonder how he got all that DNA data?"

"From the internet."

"Do you think it was posted for anyone to see? Where did he get yours?"

Arthur thought for a moment. He said, "I guess it was in my medical file."

"Exactly."

"So, he stole it," said Arthur. This was partly a question and partly an attempt to process the claim.

She went on. "Al has a quantum core. That doesn't just lend itself to genetic recombinatory forecasting. It makes him good at..."

"Hacking." Father McIntosh said it as he shifted a rook.

"Hacking," Skyla concurred. "Codebreaking."

"So, Beckett wanted us gone before this was discovered," said Maisy.

"Yes and no," said Skyla. "People already figured it out. Armagast Enterprises never officially acknowledged its selection methods, so lawsuits were out of the question, absent concrete evidence. Organizations that were hacked—which included pretty much everyone—preferred to keep it quiet as well. Mr. Armagast needed to get the data before cyber-defenses caught up with his quantum capability. At that point, he wouldn't be able to get anything new. All the old stuff would start to age out. He had to get us out of there quickly."

Everyone thought this over as four pairs of eyes stared at the chessboard.

"Does it really matter now?" said Arthur.

Skyla looked up at him. "Does all of this seem a little thrown together? Does it feel like they've really thought everything through?"

It was a rhetorical question. Her point had been made. The game went on for two or three moves as they continued to sit in silence.

Father McIntosh at last broke the lull. "Why is he called Al?"

Skyla shrugged and reached for Arthur's queen. "That was just a mistake. In the early days, someone was explaining to Mr. Armagast the capabilities of our new artificial intelligence systems. He saw the acronym and thought the second letter was a lowercase *L* instead of an uppercase *I*. No one wanted to correct him. For a while, he was the only one calling him *Al*. Then people who hadn't been in the original meeting took it up. There was no going back. I think Mr. Armagast still thinks we intended to call him *Al* from the start."

Chapter Fifteen

In the Argonaut's final view of Earth's oceans and continents, the ship streaked past somewhere outside the altitudes of the highest geosynchronous satellites and somewhere inside the orbit of the moon. The home planet would never again loom as large as it had from orbit. So much had the *Argo's* velocity increased, the Earth's motion past the dome of the observation deck would have been clear to the naked eye had it not been disguised by the ship's rotation. Each time the blue-green marble rose from the steel hull, it corkscrewed a few dozen meters aft until at last it spun away behind them, tumbling through space as if caught in the *Argo's* churning wake.

A long, slow burn from the engine was underway. Hysteria about powered maneuvers had become a running joke, and there were no more large-scale efforts to prevent things sliding about. The kitchen staff did not bother to pack up the dishes; it was sufficient to exercise caution when opening the cabinets. Things were occasionally broken: a glass would slide off a table to shatter on the floor, or someone would forget to set an emergency brake and a golf cart would roll off down a corridor. No one paid much attention except for the Waste Management staff. Arthur was busy for a few weeks.

The crew crowded the observation deck at all hours of the day and night, some even falling asleep there until roused by security guards and packed off to their beds. With alarming rapidity, the Earth shrank into the distance. As the sun's radiance also began to fade—although more slowly—they got their first taste of the blackness to come, entering a long interregnum between waypoints on their journey. It would be a year or more until they reached Jupiter.

Importance of relations with the population of Earth waned. Attention of the ship's officers turned to more pressing matters. Discipline had grown woefully lacking. Beckett saw no need for undue strictness which might stir up acrimony with his shareholders and an admiring public. This resulted in an explosion of intersex mingling that overwhelmed the monitoring capabilities of the Rule-Number-One notification system. All but the most dictatorial of the desk officers had ceased responding to alerts forever pinging their computer screens. Most muted their speakers in an effort to circumvent the nuisance. Laxity spread until it was common to see couples snuggling up in public spaces. Security staff would do little more than stroll by from time to time and demand a visible degree of separation. Not long after they passed, the sweethearts would be back where they started.

One Saturday evening after supper, Arthur and Maisy sat together on the observation deck. Saturdays were a workday like any other aboard the *Argo*, and they looked forward to sleeping in the following morning. Such thoughts raised in Arthur's mind the vision of waking with Maisy beside him. This was the image fixed in his mind as he rested his chin on top of her head and looked out over a panorama of stars. They sat with their feet dangling over the edge of the Lucite deck. Maisy was between his legs with her arms folded over a rail of the safety fence. He held her close against his chest.

"Tomorrow's Sunday..." Arthur mused aloud.

"Mmm-hmm..."

"Do you think anyone would notice if you didn't sleep in your room tonight?"

Maisy cocked her head. "Are you asking me to sleep over?"

Arthur had not thought through his question before he asked it, and was not prepared for it to be put so starkly. He retreated into confusion. She let him stew.

"Come with me to the orchard," she said after a moment's pause.

They hurried off, hand in hand. Their bower was stocked with a picnic blanket, snacks, and several other necessities that Maisy kept ready in a knapsack hidden away in the weeds. There was no time to dig them out. They had scarcely reached the cover of the trees before they were stripped to their underclothes. They tumbled down in the grass.

This is the point at which Arthur's enthusiasm usually began to wane at the urging of his conscience. Maisy wiggled away and jumped to her feet. Before he could catch hold, she was naked and giggling, flitting off through the trees. He chased. She let herself be caught and in the tousle relieved Arthur of his remaining clothes. Then she was off again, Arthur in pursuit. If their frolicking was heard by any of the agricultural staff in the adjacent fields, it was never reported. Such things were common enough in those days.

Maisy did not sleep in Arthur's room that night, but the devil-may-care attitude continued to creep up on them. They would stop by one another's rooms without bothering about the wristbands. Stanley came to tolerate this, enjoying the opportunity to banter with Maisy. His confidence did not allow him to suspect the extent of the liaisons going on behind his back. He convinced himself that they were simply friends. Maisy encouraged his advances. Ambiguous flirting with anyone showing interest (and many who did not, just for the fun of it) was an old habit supported by the feeling that rapport with Stanley would serve her well when the permissive environment inevitably ended.

This was a gross miscalculation on her part. It is a rare man who can maintain a friendly relationship with a woman of Maisy's comeliness and charm without falling prey to his imagination. It is a rare woman who is not occasionally surprised by the propensity of men to do so. Arthur must also take some of the blame for the turn of events. His good nature worked upon Maisy until she began, in her lighter moments, to see the world through his eyes. She assumed the best. She wanted to be nice.

Stanley's growing affinity with Maisy redoubled his self-confidence. He was a once-bullied young man coming into his own, with all the blossoming of buried self-regard this implies. Life in the squadron may have gone on largely unchanged in his absence, but he convinced himself that he alone directed its symphony of bustling activity. Like a Ferrari owner faced with traffic and speed limits, he cherished the trappings of power whatever his ability to affect outcomes. Even as he was quietly judged for the shamelessness of his vanity, he quietly judged others for the gauche earnestness with which they pursued lesser aims. Energized as an aspiring participant in the widespread descent into dissipation, Stanley looked upon the ne'er-do-wells around him with uncharacteristic liberality, even magnanimity.

Then everything changed.

The lapse in discipline accompanying the *Argo*'s final public-relations blitz was addressed by the command staff in their monthly operations review not long after the Earth had fallen permanently astern. Atticus Oluwusi was emphatic that the situation had reached catastrophic proportions. Examples needed to be made. Dark hints were the only proposals to which he would commit himself until he had gained a better sense of the mood among his fellow officers.

"What, exactly, do you propose?" Admiral Demarion asked from his seat at the head of the bridge's conference table. The bridge had no panoramic windows with sweeping views of the galaxy. Prows and sterns being largely irrelevant to one drifting along inside an enormous tin can, it was buried in an office complex in the center of the ship. A screen on the wall was designed to project an image out the front of the ship, but the spin had proved disconcerting. The video feed was taken down and replaced with a still image of the stars, updated whenever someone thought to do so.

"Only that discipline must be reasserted with the utmost urgency," Atticus replied. "Examples must be made."

"Can you give us an example of what kind of example you would like to make?" There was no hint of irony in the admiral's voice.

Atticus considered his words as he adjusted himself in his seat and leaned forward to rest his elbows on the conference table. As he was raising a finger to emphasize his point, the first officer cut him off.

"Now, Atticus, it's not as bad as that. The first in-vitro has come off without a hitch. We've seen no unplanned... incidents. Reinstatement of the nightly curfew will be adequate to address the situation." Lane Beauregard was the most sentimental among them. In truth, he had considered a dalliance of his own before being disabused of unfounded impressions by the object of his attentions.

"I beg to differ, sir," said the quartermaster. She, like the bosun, had no patience for such things. "The tone has been set. There are certain... influential persons... who have been encouraging the lawlessness. As long as this is allowed to continue, the situation can only deteriorate. It's only a matter of time before Al's plans begin to unravel."

"Only a matter of time." Atticus had left his finger in the air throughout the exchange. He now lowered it and formed a fist by way of emphasizing the point. He was not yet so confident as to thump it on the tabletop.

The admiral sighed. "We never should have brought her along," he said. "We should have stood firm when Beckett proposed the idea. It could only cause trouble."

"The situation can be turned as quickly in our favor, sir," said the first officer. "She leads public opinion. When she's brought back in line, the rest will follow."

The admiral looked askance at him as if he were not so sure. He adjusted the tilt of his wheel cap.

"Who has she taken up with?" the first officer went on.

"I don't know... some teenaged trash collector." Quartermaster Kumar knew that Arthur was no longer a teenager, but her contempt overtopped its banks.

"Which is why we needn't concern ourselves," said Lane Beauregard. "The moment she meets the least resistance, she'll move on to weightier matters. That will be all the example we'll need."

"We must at least discuss the possibility she does not," said Atticus. "We can't very well cut off her communications with Earth before we've even cleared the asteroid belt. She's integral to Mr. Armagast's plan. Revenues are up threefold since the announcement. They love her as much on Earth as they love her aboard."

"This can't be what Mr. Armagast meant when he said to keep her happy and posting to her media feed. His public-rela-

tions campaign can't come entirely at the cost of the mission."
Julia Kumar was appealing to the admiral.

Atticus continued to make his case. "Three days ago, a desk officer in the squadron of the young man in question saw Ms. Armagast sneaking out at two o'clock in the morning. For reasons we have not yet determined, the system had not notified the CQ desk of the encounter."

"Has the system been checked?" The quartermaster, it seemed, had not yet been informed of this breach. She did not like to be caught off guard in front of the admiral. "Has the encounter been verified? Is this desk officer certain she was not there on some other errand?"

"It seems the evidence is thus far circumstantial, but she had not been known to enter the area for any other reason than to visit... what's his name?"

"Petty Officer Third Class Pifflethorpe," the chief steward supplied. "Arthur Pifflethorpe."

The bosun knew well this name, but he had not yet drawn the connection. He worked his jaw for a moment before going on. "...than to visit Petty Officer Pifflethorpe. We've yet to identify any glitches in the notification system. The desk officer in question was quite agitated. He divulged a history of questionable behavior on the part of Ms. Armagast and this boy going back months, perhaps even before launch."

Again, the chief steward spoke up. "As a matter of fact, we had an incident with this young man back at Earth Station One. It appears he is—or was—at the center of a contraband trafficking ring that might have lent itself to the present... disorder."

"We all remember that debacle," said the quartermaster. "We'll regret bowing to Ms. Armagast's manipulation."

"We'll need more than circumstantial evidence to raise this issue with Mr. Armagast," said Admiral Demarion. The tone in his voice said he had arrived at a conclusion. "That is the course we will need to take, should punishing Ms. Armagast become necessary. Monitor it closely, Bosun."

"Yes, sir."

"And institute the lights-out curfew from Taps to Reveille. We'll keep an eye on the situation."

"Yes, sir."

"And the surveillance cameras, First Officer Beauregard— how are we proceeding with manufacture of the surveillance cameras? Will they be ready by the time we switch to text-only communications for the crew? I'm blind on my own ship."

"Thus far we're on track, sir."

"Very well." Admiral Demarion steepled his fingers in front of his chin and turned his eyes down to the agenda printed on a sheet of paper before him. This indicated the matter was closed for the time being. They proceeded to the next item.

Stanley was devastated by the incident under discussion among the command staff. Earlier the previous day, Maisy had spent upwards of three and a half minutes chatting with him as she passed his desk. Her errand had not even been a visit to the Pifflethorpe boy. She was merely passing in the hallway and saw fit to drop in. He had floated through the remainder of his shift. He even contemplated taking his first steps toward reciprocating the feelings Maisy was obviously developing for him. Compassion, if nothing else, demanded he indulge the poor girl's obsession.

So, when that very night he saw through the dimness at the far end of the corridor the unmistakable swing of Maisy's shapely posterior retreating through a rear exit, he was cast from the highest of highs to the lowest of lows. He was not on shift at the time—merely returning from the restroom—but nevertheless he rushed to the CQ desk to check for notifications of illicit wristband conjunctions; the desk officer on duty had seen nothing.

Had anyone of note passed the desk?

No, not since Taps.

Stanley was unable to sleep for the remainder of the night. He turned the vision over in his head, working himself into a frenzy of indignation. In the end, he could do nothing but pass the report up the chain of command. It *had* been her. He *knew* it was her. Why would she be there after hours but to visit Pifflethorpe? All her friendliness had been a sham. He had been used. Duped.

At the same time Maisy's rapport with Stanley went sour, her relationship with Skyla Sawyer took a similar turn for the worse. The two had grown close in the preceding weeks, or so it seemed to Skyla. In the great game of musical chairs that constituted the *Argo*'s early social milieu, Skyla imagined she had at last secured her place among the highest echelons of Argonaut society: admittance to the inner circle of Maisy Armagast. This was only to be expected. Her mother had provided the firmest assurances that Skyla's future was a bright one. It had been to her dismay that rising to the top ranks of Earth Station One's cadet corps had failed to earn her the acceptance of her peers.

Skyla had never been a popular girl. She was, however, exceptionally intelligent. In this oldest and cruelest of curses, she had come of age understanding that her own worth was far above that credited to her by the peers whose acceptance she craved. Hopelessly inept at sports and a perennial reject from her high school's cheerleading squad, she had thrown herself into those extracurricular activities reflecting more mature notions of individual worth. She was the Honor Society president two years running and the leading lady in every dramatic performance of the Thespian Club. She organized the school's annual canned-goods drive.

Upon graduation, she delivered the valediction and went on to attend a well-regarded private girls' college. From there she moved on to the Ivy League to complete her master's thesis in biomedical engineering. Still not prepared to decide upon a permanent occupation, she was admitted to the country's finest postgraduate program in molecular biology and genetics.

While Skyla's life had gone from one academic success to another, her social life markedly failed to keep pace. As years went by, relentless encouragement from her mother began to turn upon the subject of boys. Surely there were some nice post-graduate colleagues with whom she would like to engage at a more personal level? But no matter what her marks in organic chemistry, the boys were simply not interested. Not long after the granting of her doctoral degree—and before she could find employment and move out of her mother's house—Skyla was notified of her nomination to join the crew. She accepted without a second thought.

Nevertheless, when Maisy had happened upon Skyla in the break room of the Human Resources Department, her friendly advances were met with skepticism.

"Can I help you?" was all Skyla could think to say. She said it with no undetectable degree of scorn. In Skyla's circles, Maisy was as outwardly despised as she was privately idolized. Even the loudest proponents of this conflicted position would probably have been unable to say which feeling predominated.

"Maisy Armagast," she said in reply to Skyla's question, and extended a hand. The daughter of Beckett Armagast immediately set about flattering the sensibilities of the *Argo*'s deputy assistant geneticist.

We are already familiar with the outcome of the conversation. What may be less clear is how Maisy came to enter upon it. What was it that brought her to wander into the break room of the Department of Human Resources on a Tuesday afternoon and introduce herself to Skyla? It was a combination of things.

Most directly, it was at the urging of her immediate supervisors within the Department of Managerial Consultation. Somewhat at a loss for ideas on how to apply their considerable abilities aboard an interstellar spacecraft, they had imparted to the department's rank and file the necessity for, as they put it, creative ideation. Those aspiring to promotion, a group which of course included Maisy, set about identifying appropriate subjects for the team's ministrations.

In her research, Maisy happened upon an organizational diagram of the Department of Human Resources. She was surprised, as most of her fellow crewmen would have been, to discover the department's staff included more than just a computer named Al. Her surprise redoubled when she found Skyla among the list of employees. So began a fortuitous confluence of means in the pursuit of divergent ends.

It had recently been announced that the first participant in the staff's scheme of Argonautical reproduction was with child. The rumor mill spun at a furious pace. Maisy felt some responsibility as the hub upon which it turned, and had for some time been seeking insider knowledge that she could bring forth. What better way to accomplish this than forming relationships within the Department of Human Resources? The department was likely also in need of management consulting services, given the nascency of its remit. Establishment of sound business processes to support program execution was just the thing.

Despite her hesitation, Skyla became a ready participant in Maisy's scheme. She brought forward the proposed plan of business process reengineering, to wide acclamation. Maisy soon introduced her to Arthur, Father McIntosh, and thereafter to the remainder of her clique. Skyla began frequenting the observation deck and made herself comfortable in the circle of sofas and bean-bag chairs unofficially reserved for the in-crowd. She regularly joined Maisy for meals and relished being pumped for information by the constellation of Beautiful People that gravitated to her. There was a time when this would have played out as these things always play out: with the flavor-of-the-month quietly fading back into obscurity as the herd's transient interests wandered off. The consequences of this particular affair would be less innocuous.

Skyla played it well at first. She resisted the impulse to tell too much too quickly, holding back vital bits and pieces of the story with which to string along her audience. She started with less pertinent revelations such as the massive theft of personal data perpetrated by Armagast Enterprises. Slowly she moved on to items of more pressing interest. What genetic attributes of the young mother had led Al to select her? Could women with similar characteristics expect to be next? Who among the first cohort of donors was the father? The answers to these and many other questions were divulged in hushed tones upon reassurance they be held in the utmost confidence. But eventually, the well ran dry.

Maisy did not abruptly turn Skyla away with the callousness that may once have predominated. She made halting and unpracticed incursions into the field of interpersonal decency. She included Skyla in conversations that had moved irretrievably beyond her narrow field of expertise. As in Maisy's interactions with Stanley, her lack of experience blinded her to the damage inflicted upon that sensitive constitution by the crushing of long-cherished dreams. Slowly, Skyla went the way of the latest streaming television series upon which the crew furiously binged before being sucked away into the next passing fad.

Skyla's permanent ascension to the stratum of the social elite was not to be. These people did not want to talk about science. They did not want to play chess or debate the nuances of ethical theory. As soon as her usefulness subsided, it became clear to all that Skyla was as bored with them as they were with her. This reality did not assuage the grief Skyla felt at being cast aside. Maisy became the focal point of an inundation of bitterness.

Cataclysmic turns of events are rarely the result of a single thread of causation twisting and turning through the weft of history. Thus it would be for the future of Arthur's love affair. Thus it would be for Maisy. What all led up to the final momentous decision even now looming before them? Surely, it was Arthur's sortie into the echelons of beauty and fashion. It was Maisy's corresponding introduction to humility and decency and the mess she made of it. It was Stanley's unrequited passion and Skyla's shattered hopes. It was the politics of corporate boardrooms and military commands. It was the simple churning of artificially intelligent algorithms and the human bias that will forever plague them.

At the same time Stanley's revelations were reaching Admiral Demarion's staff, Skyla was giving up on evenings with her fickle new companions. Rigorous enforcement of the nightly curfew was announced, along with imposition of the permanent operating system for reproduction of the *Argo*'s crew. Notification arrived in the Department of Human Resources that nomination of the first full cohort of maternal candidates was required. This notification passed from the director to the chief scientist to Skyla where she sat at Al's terminal, tending to the day's administrative minutiae.

The algorithms governing Al's selection process were not so autonomous as may be supposed. Al was certainly capable of selecting from scratch a pair of ideally suited mates from among the crew. He was also capable of taking a female recommendation and finding an appropriate male to match (or vice versa, for that matter). There were no firm rules about this, so new were the procedures. Few understood this as well as Skyla Sawyer. She would be entirely within her rights to execute the order as she saw fit.

The tortuous development of Skyla's character had imparted to her the importance of exercising her entitlements. She looked for every opportunity to make a point when she knew it must be supported by the authorities, like a bicyclist who insists upon riding in heavy traffic. At the flashing prompt on her screen, Skyla typed a name: Maisy Armagast. Al took this recommendation to heart and thought long and hard over Maisy's optimal genetic pairing. It would be beyond the realm of credulity to presume that of the thousands of possible matches he arrived at Arthur Pifflethorpe. No, Arthur was not even among those selected to the donor cohort that would provide the required degree of paternal ambiguity.

Although no one but Skyla, Al, and a few other select individuals would know it, Maisy would carry the child of Aditya Patel, petty officer second class and sous-chef in the main kitchen of Deck 3, Spoke F. Admiral Demarion, Bosun Oluwusi, and the rest of the senior staff were delighted by the turn of events. They did not think it necessary to inquire into the origins of the remarkable coincidence.

Chapter Sixteen

Conceiving of a plan to reestablish discipline aboard the *Argo* proved easier than its implementation. A host of loose ends had to be tied up prior to accomplishing the command staff's ultimate goal. This goal was wresting psychological control of the crew back from the young woman who had become the uncontested maven of public opinion. In the words of Admiral Demarion, Maisy Armagast was a Pied Piper leading the Argonauts off into decadence and abandonment of their duty. She must be stopped.

The plan was multifaceted, with each set of objectives overseen by a member of Admiral Demarion's senior staff. The bosun was the most visible and enthusiastic participant. At his instigation, rigorous enforcement of the nightly curfew came into effect. No one was permitted outside of his or her squadron after Taps without appropriate permissions coded into their wristband. Security officers would conduct spot-checks. This restriction affected even those, such as Arthur and Maisy, with illicit means of removing their wristbands as it dramatically cut the number of crewmen out after hours. It became impossible to blend in with the crowd.

Accompanying the curfew was a crackdown on mingling between the sexes. It was no longer left to squadron desk officers to use their judgment in reporting unauthorized wristband conjunctions. The system was centralized, with all reporting funneled through the security operations center. Infractions were logged and tracked. Each automated notification required a written status report including findings, actions taken, and referral to home-squadron commanders for appropriate disciplinary action. The new rules nearly overwhelmed the capacity of the desk officer corps until they began to take effect and incident rates declined.

Despite the grumbling provoked among the crew, this was not altogether unexpected. These were, after all, rules that had always been in ostensible effect. Everyone knew that they would eventually come back into force. More controversial were additional measures implemented at the direction of Quartermaster Kumar. She announced that throttling of the ship's bandwidth in transmissions to Earth would begin immediately. Outbound messages of an unofficial nature would be limited to textual formats.

Once again, everyone knew this was coming, but no one expected it to arrive so soon. The quality of video links had been degrading since the gravity-assist maneuver that brought them back into close proximity with Earth, but the system was far from unusable. The explanation provided by the quartermaster was that the ship must begin to husband its resources. It was broadly understood that messages in textual format were far easier to monitor and censor. Those testing the limits of tolerance found transmissions touching upon controversial topics were far less likely to reach their destination. Officially this was put down to parsimony with the *Argo*'s energy resources.

Not long after restrictions on transmission came into effect, the quartermaster announced the most inflammatory yet of the staff's new measures to reimpose discipline. A date was set for permanent closure of the observation deck: a date mere weeks in the future. Again, the announcement was couched in terms with which it was difficult to argue. The deck was an enormous waste of energy, like a leaky faucet spewing precious heat out into the darkness. The crew need not worry: full panoramic views would be streamed in real time to each crewman's private television for as long as external cameras remained operational. Insiders understood that it would actually be quite some time before the ship's energy losses would begin to overwhelm the capacity of the solar panels. Rather, the deck was a focal point for the whispering and conniving and fraternization lying at the core of disciplinary deterioration. It had become, to repeat a term then in common use, something of a meat market. This fact was not lost on the officers.

A final measure arrived more quietly, but the firestorm it loosed cast into shade all previous efforts. First Officer Beauregard began installation of the *Argo*'s surveillance system. Questions swirled as soon as the crew began to notice nondescript video cameras appearing in shadowed corners and opportune vantage points. What was their purpose? Did the command staff not trust its own crew? Were they setting up some kind of Orwellian police state?

Such questions were waved aside with justifications comparable to those provided all along: this was a preplanned step in the phased approach to bringing the *Argo* up to full operational capability. The cameras were nothing to worry about. They were simply a safety measure. Who could argue against safety? Each new instance of disorderly conduct and petty crime was cited as vindication. They were all One Team, One Crew: the Argonauts, setting off into the Unknown!

Full-color posters proclaiming slogans to this effect, inclusive of stirringly prolific capitalization and emphatic punctuation, began appearing in public spaces. The management consultants were kept busy designing a comprehensive program of strategic communications. With it came the utmost efforts of Chief Steward Sasaki to divert the attentions of the rank and file into more salubrious pursuits. More streaming services were added to the bill of fare, free of charge. Social events were scheduled and carefully choreographed: intramural football leagues and hobby clubs and group cooking classes in the cafeterias. Despite what were undoubtedly the purest of intentions (it had to be admitted by all who knew her that the chief steward was a delightful human being), the social calendar began to take on a tinge of paternalism that only heightened the mood of disaffection.

Arthur and Maisy were enthusiastic participants in speculation rife among the crew over where all of this was headed. Neither suspected the locomotive was bearing down upon the very spot where they were being surreptitiously tied to the tracks. Apart from a mounting accumulation of inconveniences, the pair carried on largely as before. Arthur missed his evenings cuddling with Maisy on his bunk, but truth be told, he was conflicted on the matter. He had become starved for sleep. Maisy would chastise him roundly when he had the temerity to suggest the television program she selected did not justify the fatigue he would endure the following day.

Why did he have to be such a baby?

Didn't he want to spend time with her?

He was not so foolish as to point out she rarely needed to be out of bed before nine o'clock. After all, she was right: Arthur was *not* a baby. He *did* want to spend time with her. But he was always so tired.

Arthur's job continued to pull him off to unfrequented corners of the ship. Maisy's more meager responsibilities rarely prevented her from slipping away to meet him. They packed lunches to be shared in the banana groves. Maisy would wear a string bikini beneath her uniform and strip down to sunbathe in the tropical light of the ultraviolet lamps. He would read to her from the latest paperback to take up residence in the leg pocket of his jumpsuit as sun conures flitted among the branches. Some birder on the planning committee had thought them a nice touch. Maisy would drift off to sleep behind her enormous sunglasses.

They crept into the dairy pens and laughed themselves to hysterics over attempts at milking the cows. At Maisy's instigation, they even attempted amorous gymnastics, of a sort, in a storeroom high up in the inner rings, where effective gravity approached negligible levels. Both found it a better idea in theory than in practice. The nausea attendant upon such environments was an insurmountable obstacle to setting the necessary mood.

They were forced to take precautions as surveillance cameras proliferated, but avoiding detection was not as difficult as may be supposed. The security staff had no way to monitor all the video feeds at all hours of the day, nor was the system meant to cover every square inch of the ship. It was designed more as a means of retroactively identifying perpetrators than of preventing every conceivable infraction. Despite Admiral Demarion's hopes, the psychological effect quickly wore off as the system's practical limitations became apparent.

The gradual tightening of the noose carried on for month after month, the above-mentioned disciplinary initiatives following one upon the next and each taking quite some time to bring to full effect. The crew's last view of Earth was a fading memory. Missives to loved ones were limited to brief, grammatically erratic emails banged out in spare moments when feverish realization swept the crew that some important date, such as Christmas or Mother's Day, had come and gone. Such milestones had little meaning anymore. Anything resembling inter-personal affection was pushed back below the surface, into clandestine encounters in back rooms and quiet corners. Things had nearly settled back into something resembling an acceptable routine when the proverbial shoe dropped.

It happened on an afternoon much like any other. Arthur was sorting rubbish to be reprocessed into polymer for the addi-tive manufacturing center. Maisy was presiding over an ice-cream social in the cafeteria. Under normal circumstances she would never have been caught dead at such an event, but she was required to demonstrate at least cursory efforts at contributing to the chief steward's campaign of strategic communications. The event was well attended as those things went, word having gotten around that Maisy would be in atten-dance. Fans who pined over her from afar had been deeply affected by closure of the observation deck where she had regu-larly been on parade for all to gawk upon. Nevertheless, it was irrefutably an ice-cream social. She hovered about, fretting over the magnitude of the debit from her stock of social capital.

It was with a mixture of trepidation and relief she received word via First Officer Beauregard's personal aide-de-camp that she was to report immediately to his suite of offices on the fourth deck. She declined to accompany the overeager young man for the time being, pleading she must first see to the execution of the chief steward's wishes. Maisy Armagast did not follow errand boys about like a whipped puppy dog. But over the course of the following hour or two, she drifted toward the staff offices.

By the time she arrived, the first officer appeared to have forgotten his summons. He left her waiting in the lobby for ten minutes as he finished typing away at his desk in Maisy's full view through an open doorway. At last he picked up the plastic handset of the telephone on his desk and punched at the glowing keypad. The phone rang on the desk of his aide-de-camp.

"Send her in," she heard the first officer say, both through the door of his office and small and tinny from the speaker of the aide-de-camp's telephone.

"He'll see you now, Ms. Armagast," the aide-de-camp said.

She rose and swept into Lane Beauregard's office, taking a chair across the desk from him before he could offer it.

"Ms. Armagast, thank you for coming," said the first officer. He immediately chastened himself for the comment. It was she who should be expressing an appropriate degree of supplication. Apart from a brief pause, the thought was not distinguishable behind his weathered countenance.

Maisy nodded acknowledgment. Things were as they should be.

"I have wonderful news," First Officer Beauregard went on. Again, he stopped. He was already off to a bad start. He was so ham-handed at discussing subjects such as this. Perhaps that was why his third wife had divorced him. Perhaps that was why he was sitting on the *Argo* at that very moment. Existential questions passed through his mind in a familiar flash. How did people manage the task of talking to women about womanly things? He would never know.

Maisy raised an eyebrow, inviting him to continue.

"After our trial run, the full plan of reproductive propagation is ready to begin." He felt this roundabout introduction would convey the thrust of what was to come. It did not.

"Yes, Mr. Beauregard, we addressed that issue some months ago." Always being called *Ms. Armagast*, Maisy never thought to address the officers in any other fashion. The practice took on an air of affectation that sparked their ire, but neither could they bring themselves to call her anything else. "The process review is complete and the playbook on file with the Department of

Human Resources. Is there some problem?" An ill-defined question was niggling at the back of Maisy's mind even as she said it. Why would the first officer bring this directly to her? It should be taken through the appropriate supervisory channels.

"Ah... no..." said the first officer. "That is not the issue at hand. You have, you see... ah..." He trailed off.

Again, she raised an eyebrow.

He gave up on trying to be tactful and let fly. "You have been selected as a participant. Isn't that wonderful?"

There was a moment of silence that was partaken of by the three or four members of the office staff who had been eavesdropping.

Then Maisy exploded.

What she said does not bear repeating. She would remember little of it. Needless to say, it was lengthy, shockingly profane, and delivered in a tone of voice audible some distance down each of the hallways leading from the suite of offices. It concluded with the firm assurance that the first officer was sorely mistaken and that Beckett himself would hear of this.

Beckett, of course, would not hear of it. She had no way to reach her father through the impregnable firewall that had been constructed and tested and reinforced over the previous months. She was on her own and entirely at the mercy of the command staff.

Stalking from the office, she disappeared into the labyrinth of corridors. As ascertained sometime later, her wristband monitor tracked her back to her office. Then there must have been some kind of glitch, for no one could find her there. Her image was captured on various surveillance feeds, but she must have studied the locations of the cameras in advance. Eventually the sightings tapered off without providing a clue as to her final destination.

The news was all over the ship by the time it found its way

to Arthur. He contained his emotions for long enough to reach his quarters. He had grown skilled at this over the years. There he found a blade of grass cast as if inadvertently on the floor. He found Maisy in their nest in the cherry orchard. She was curled in a ball on the picnic blanket, eating a granola bar and crying more bitterly and (quite frankly) unattractively than he had ever seen her cry. Mascara was smeared across her cheeks, and crumbs clung to her upper lip. In that moment, Arthur knew he had never loved anyone so furiously in all his life.

Upon closer inspection, it became clear that Maisy had long since cried it out. Disappointed that Arthur had not discovered her in the sharpest pangs of agony, she had renewed the fervor of her weeping as he approached. This facsimile, she felt, did not convey what would have been conveyed had he experienced the genuine article. It irritated her. She had gotten hungry waiting for him, and he caught her in the middle of munching on a granola bar. This further detracted from the poignancy of the image.

She need not have worried. Arthur's distraction over the news swamped any subtleties of unspoken dialogue. He was more crushed than she was. After all, Maisy in her innermost heart had to admit it was not an unmitigated disaster. She and Arthur still had a reasonable chance of prevailing over their oppressors, or so she supposed. Assumptions about her ability to manipulate those around her had not caught up with the new circumstances. And the catastrophe would do wonders for her reputation. It would be quite some time before anyone discussed anything but the tragedy she faced.

Arthur sank into the grass behind Maisy and spooned her, his kisses on her neck and earlobe communicating his desire to assuage her grief where words could not. His position behind her carried the added benefit of hiding his own tears. He had learned long ago that girls did not look upon displays of emotional ardor with the sympathetic pathos he had once imagined. He and his beloved lay together, feeling one another breathe.

At last, Arthur felt the need to speak. "I love you, sweetheart," was all he could think to say.

Maisy sat up and turned to face him, cross-legged on the turf. "You love me?" she said. "Is that *it*? Do you understand what's going on here?"

"Of course I do." He sat upright to face her.

"Of course you do?" she retorted. "How could you possibly know how I feel? Have you ever been forcibly impregnated?"

Arthur had not the foggiest idea how to respond.

"Well?" Maisy said at last. "Have you?"

"No."

"No, you haven't. So, you don't know how I feel, do you?"

"No, sweetheart, but that isn't what I..."

"Then what could you possibly have meant by it?"

"Just that I'm here for you... whatever you need."

"Whatever I need. I need to not have to carry a stranger's baby as part of some sick effort on the part of Admiral Demarion to make a point with the crew. Can you help me with that?"

"Maybe, but..."

"Maybe? I need more than maybe. You're the one who put me here. If you hadn't insisted on getting so lovey-dovey right out in front of everyone, I wouldn't be in this position."

"But wait, I don't think we..."

"You don't think you brought this on me? You might as well have dropped it in the suggestion box. Can it not be all about *you* for just one minute? Can you consider *my* feelings?"

It carried on like this for quite some time. The only person who would be baffled by the tenor of the conversation was

Arthur, who took her arguments at face value. He set about trying to justify himself and convince her he had no such intentions. How could she blame *him*? Did she really think he had any objective apart from helping her?

No matter what his protestations, they were turned back upon him with renewed fury that only mounted higher the more he tried to tamp it down. He never suspected that, even in his bumbling incompetence, he gave Maisy exactly the comfort she needed. She needed to lash out; she needed to fight; she needed to tell her persecutors exactly what she thought of their schemes. They were not available to listen, so Arthur would have to do.

Finally, Maisy's fury began to ebb. She was inundated with a wash of emotion that pushed aside carefully reasoned logic. She returned to him. Soon they were touching, then embracing, then sitting facing one another, she seated in his lap with legs wrapped around his midsection and their foreheads pressed together.

"I love you, Maisy," said Arthur. "I love you more than anyone I've ever loved."

Maisy felt Arthur was the first man ever to arrive at such a sentiment. "Oh, Arthur," she said. She kissed him with his face held between her hands. "I love you, too. I'm sorry I lost it."

They whispered, they petted, they soothed for twenty minutes or more. It built toward an irresistible crescendo.

"Let's get married," Arthur said. The words were out before he had considered them.

He succeeded in startling her for a moment. Then she seized his face once more and kissed his eyes, his cheeks, the tip of his nose, and then his mouth. In the time it took her to do so, she had considered the matter and decided upon a course of action.

"Yes," she said.

"Yes?"

"Yes."

"When?" Arthur's tenuous command of the situation once more yielded to the force of his beloved's personality.

"Now," she said.

Once the decision had been made—and Maisy was not one to revisit decisions—discussion turned to practical matters. The *Argo* was not provided with means for executing the contractual particulars of matrimony. Quite the contrary. Maisy was not overly bothered by this, arguing they might then and there embark upon the only bit of the whole overblown production that really mattered. This she contended with an urgency that nearly overwhelmed Arthur's principles. Nevertheless, he insisted that there were certain forms to which one must adhere.

His ability to impress this attitude upon Maisy surprised even him. Soon she took it up with her own surge of vehemence. She would show them all. Arthur and Maisy would be well and properly married, and then there would be no going back—no denying the facts on the ground. They would set a moral and legal precedent that would forever govern the world of the Argonauts. But how, precisely, would they go about accomplishing this? The captain of the ship was the usual representative of authority under such circumstances. Turning to Admiral Demarion was out of the question. The only person to whom they could appeal for help was Father McIntosh.

Going by way of seldom-frequented machine rooms and access corridors, they made their way to the Office of the Chaplaincy. The padre had embarked upon his evening tipple but had not yet departed for his after-hours station in the food court. While Maisy freshened up in the restroom, Arthur laid out the idea for his old friend. Father McIntosh thought it a splendid idea.

It took the priest quite some time to assemble the necessary vestiture and liturgies and supporting staff. In the end, the resident imam was called as witness, and the rabbi imparted upon to sing a hymn or two. Arthur initially set about discouraging such trivialities until dark looks communicated the substance of Maisy's wishes. He arranged himself in a quiet corner as preparations were set in motion. The receptionist barred the door as a dozen or more occupants of the office suite set about arranging the ceremony. It was great fun and addressed what for all of them had become a creeping suspicion that their function aboard the *Argo* would, with time, grow redundant.

Maisy took care to mind important sensitivities. They procured a glass upon which to stomp at the conclusion of the nuptials. This detail was much appreciated and fussed over by the rabbi. A thrice-repeated "qabul" was appended to the usual "I do." Maisy's hands and forearms were decorated with all of the intricate patterns in henna that time would allow. One of the hymns was replaced at the last minute with a meditation on mindfulness. A white dress was not to hand, but Maisy bore the misfortune along with the weight of her persecution.

When at last Arthur stood with his bride before the assembly, he came to see the wisdom of Maisy's pronouncements. It all felt very official, and in the stories that would percolate through the crew in the coming weeks it would take on a splendid aura of finality. The wildest hopes of the chaplaincy were far exceeded. Attendance at religious observances would surge, and this would not be the first covert wedding to take place under the noses of the command staff. In truth, the ceremony dragged on a bit, so diverse were the traditional forms to which Maisy had acceded, but in the end, a swell of pride engulfed Arthur as he said the final words and kissed his beloved before the assembly. They were man and wife.

Arthur had often imagined this moment. Were he one day to achieve his fondest aspiration and take Maisy as his own, he must be prepared to give her the most glorious honeymoon to be had. In performance of his duties, he had come into possession of a fragment of knowledge held by precious few occupants of the *Argo*. While the observation deck had been locked, had not been decommissioned and sealed off. As had been widely suspected, this was not yet necessary. No one had gotten around to it. The lock was no match for him. Thence Arthur led his bride. Having let himself and his companions through the final access-control point, he disconnected his wristband and left it in the care of Father McIntosh, who flushed and fretted as he sent the couple off to consummate the great event.

It was all Arthur could have hoped. Alone together amid the unimaginable sweep of the churning universe, with the sun shrinking away behind and Jupiter yet a speck in the distance, they spread out a great pile of sofa cushions on the polished Lucite floor, among which they tumbled down together.

Bodies entangled, noses touching, they breathed one another's breath.

"Hello, wife," said Arthur with a burst of joy that spread over his face.

"Hello, husband," Maisy replied, mimicking his smile.

"Wife, wife, wife." Arthur was astounded at the sound of the word on his lips and the gravity of all it implied.

Maisy smiled again and kissed him to put an end to the foolishness.

Arthur was prepared with a hard drive containing all his favorite music. He connected the Bluetooth to the deck's public-address system. Maisy made the selection. They floated away to the honeyed rhythms of Bill Withers, and even with the sunshine faded to a pale reflection of what it once had been, Arthur was at last certain this girl he loved would never, ever be gone.

Chapter Seventeen

So unexpectedly brief was Arthur and Maisy's encounter (at least to our young newlyweds) that neither of them could have suspected it met with such unmitigated success. It would be quite some time before they would understand the full ramifications of that afternoon—before they would understand the impact of what was, even as they cuddled, churning away somewhere down in the mysterious depths of her body. They had broken the unbreakable Rule Number One and had done so far past the point of returning to a place where spontaneous procreative activities were an acceptable pastime. For now, lying in one another's arms, suspended over the infinite depths of the universe, this was the furthest thing from their minds.

"Is that how it's supposed to go?" said Arthur. He could not prevent his fingertips from tracing lines over her skin. It tickled, and from time to time she would smack them away.

"I think so," said Maisy, unwilling to dampen his spirits. "Don't worry about it. We'll have lots of time to practice."

"So, it wasn't good?" He did not want to ask such questions

—he rebuked himself even as he did so—but holding them back was beyond his power.

"It was perfect. You're perfect."

A pause.

"But did you have fun, too?"

"Of course, I did."

A pause.

"I just ask because it seemed like..."

And so forth. Eventually she succeeded in easing Arthur's self-doubt or at least driving it beneath the surface for a while.

"I want to ask you something," she said.

"Of course," said Arthur.

"Why didn't you swim with me?"

He knew exactly what she meant. "What do you mean?" he said.

"On the island, our last night alone together. Why didn't you come with me?"

Arthur had studied her question in finely grained detail. It was a question he had asked himself again and again, relentlessly—in the night, in the day, in idle moments, and to the detriment of urgently pressing activities. "I wanted everything to be perfect," he said.

"It wasn't perfect?" She looked down, letting her eyes follow her own fingertip, which now played over his chest.

"Everything in its time. I didn't want to miss anything by going too fast." Ten minutes later, he would change his mind on this answer. Then he would change it back.

"Did we miss something?"

"Mmm..." Arthur's noncommittal mumble was as ambiguous to him as it was to her. In the rational corners of his mind, he was convinced the decision had been the right one. What if he had gone with her? Would they be lying where they were right now, or would he have wrecked it all, as he had so many times in the past with other girls? With equal conviction, it was a decision he would regret deeply and profoundly to his dying breath. How badly he wanted the moment back. How badly he wanted that memory.

"I couldn't stop thinking about it." She spoke now in a whisper meant only for him, even though they were as alone amid a vast and empty nothingness as two human beings could be.

"Me neither."

"We'll never get it back."

"I know."

"All of this will be gone soon, too." She said, looking out into the universe.

"I know."

For a moment, they both went on staring down at the stars. Then Arthur laid his head on her chest. He listened to her heartbeat and breathed her smell. They closed their eyes, and whether or not they slept, they would never remember.

Even as Arthur and Maisy lay in one another's arms, the firestorm they had ignited was sending its first crackling sparks out into the dry tinder of the *Argo*'s crew. Following upon the heels of the disciplinary crackdown and rumors of Maisy's selection to the reproduction program, their marriage prompted a flurry of speculation over the likely response from Admiral Demarion. Opposing attitudes coalesced, with one side voicing full-throated support for a campaign of resistance and the other warning of yet more security measures sure to follow. In the coming days and weeks, until Maisy resurfaced and beyond, whispered opinions would develop into ideologies nearing the point of full-blown factions.

Whether a given Argonaut would fall into either of these camps was determined largely by the status of their personal lives. Whatever the claims of Armagast Enterprises about the ability of humanity to rise above emotion in pursuit of loftier aims, Argonauts continued to meet and fall in love. Those with sweethearts sided by and large with the romantics. Surely, they said, a solution could be found to the problem of the crew's propagation that would account for intimacy and personal relationships. The individualists, loners, and stoics tended to opinions of the more scientific bent, whether from reasoned principle or perhaps only bitterness.

Admiral Demarion and his staff had only just begun to feel these tectonic plates shifting beneath their feet. Following Maisy's outburst in his office, the first officer called an emergency consultation of the senior staff for that very evening. Arthur and Maisy's wedding had taken place as preparations mounted and plans solidified. Word of it reached the command staff during their conference. They arrived at the unanimous decision that Maisy must be confined to quarters without delay. She must under no circumstances be permitted to interact with the crew, either directly or through her abundant intermediaries.

Arthur would be interrogated to determine the level of enthusiasm with which he had participated. He was likely a mere pawn in her game, plucked from a crowd of ready admirers and used as the instrument with which she would make her point. Surely there could be no genuine romantic attachment between Ms. Armagast and a sanitation engineer (moonlighting as a black-market dealer in contraband) who scarcely met the crew's minimum age requirement. If this was indeed the case, they may be able to co-opt Arthur to the side of reason and thus deflate the surging revolt before it gathered steam.

Protocols of coordination and execution followed in due course. Minutes of the conference were transcribed and distributed, decision points documented. Relevant regulations and authorities were identified and cross-referenced. Notification was sent to the security operations center demanding Maisy Armagast be immediately remanded to quarters and Arthur brought in for questioning. By the time the command staff could thus assemble, discuss the issue at hand, and arrive at a decision, events had already begun to slip beyond their grasp. Arthur and Maisy were long since embarked upon their honeymoon. By the time the order was issued for Maisy's arrest and the necessary documentation drafted, reviewed, and certified, consummation of the marriage had created new facts on the ground that would hopelessly complicate the proceedings. By the time the rank and file of the security forces were notified and set upon their task, it was long after Taps.

Neither Maisy nor Arthur were to be located in their respective quarters. Despite a search of Maisy's office, neither she nor the wristband beacon indicating her presence there could be located. Arthur's wristband signal somehow indicated his presence in the private quarters of the Catholic chaplain, who was found alone and in a frightful state of inebriation. Confusion abounded, orders were issued and countermanded and reissued, and it was long into the night before the admiral made the decision that it could all wait until morning. After all, no one was going anywhere.

Sometime in the small hours, Arthur and Maisy emerged from the afterglow of their sequence of hastily made decisions. They talked and concluded the state of affairs could not long be sustained. They would need to eat. Security forces would be searching for them. The observation deck was not provided with bathing facilities and, whatever fantasies Arthur had held about the activities of the preceding hours, they tended to accelerate the accumulation undesirable bodily odors. Maisy was in need of a toothbrush, and Arthur suspected the same of himself.

Her disheveled state left her irritable, much to the bewilderment of her eager and accommodating new husband.

Maisy insisted they begin by dressing themselves. They then discussed the matter in depth. What were they to do? If Maisy was caught, she would surely suffer the foulest indignities at the hands of Admiral Demarion's staff and the abominable Al in Human Resources. They did not yet realize Arthur's similar predicament, not appreciating the irresistible force of the rumor mill that had spread news of their disobedience from one end of the ship to the other in a matter of hours. But they suspected, sooner or later, he would also fall under scrutiny.

They agreed upon a course of action. Maisy must remain hidden away for the time being. It fell to Arthur to reconnoiter. What was the mood on the ship? Had any decisions been announced by the authorities? Could they count on support from the crew? Arthur must provide for Maisy's basic necessities. The restrooms and water fountains of the observation deck remained functional, but Maisy would need fresh uniforms and her makeup kit. A hairbrush and skin moisturizer went without saying. Socks. Underclothes. Washrags and a towel. She was nearly out of a particular class of feminine products. Could Arthur stop by the Crew Store and pick up another package? (The blue box, not the green one; could he remember that?) She sniffed discreetly at her underarm and asked that Arthur add deodorant to the list. All of this fascinated him. He understood, of course, that women experienced the same unmentionable bodily functions as anyone, but until just then had never appreciated the fact. There had remained some shred of doubt over the possibility that Maisy could smell anything other than lovely.

Their stash of snacks from the orchard would hold her over until Arthur could find breakfast. He slipped out and returned momentarily with the knapsack. Their bower in the orchard was agreed upon as the drop point, should Arthur be unable to return. He jammed the lock to the observation deck's emergency-access stairwell, allowing her to pass in and out unimpeded. At last they sat side by side on a sofa, staring off at the universe and nibbling on granola bars. There was no more putting off the inevitable. He kissed her goodbye with the firm, casual air that once characterized Mr. Pifflethorpe's farewells to Mrs. Pifflethorpe. It was another kiss he would think on with pride.

The corridors remained mostly empty as he made his way to the Office of the Chaplaincy. The hour was still early, and few were up and about. Father McIntosh was not yet in. Arthur settled himself on the sofa and dozed for an hour or two.

When the padre arrived, he had largely recovered from the previous night's celebration. He filled Arthur in on the evening. After Arthur had fled with his bride, the wedding party had set themselves to the traditions of post-matrimonial revelry. They relocated to the food court. Toasts were drunk to the pair, and speeches lauded their virtues and compatibilities. The size of the party grew as word spread. Carousing only ended when official inquiries into the whereabouts of the bride and groom made it clear that observance of the sacrament had not been well received by the senior staff.

Arthur pumped Father McIntosh for information.

Had the priest been interrogated?

No, not that he could recall, although recollections of the evening had grown hazy.

What were people saying about Maisy?

The padre referred Arthur to his previous statement. It seemed he would be of little further use. Arthur retrieved his wristband and thanked the priest. He set off in search of supplies.

Obtaining access to Maisy's quarters was the easiest of Arthur's objectives. His permissions were nearly unrestricted in the dormitories, so long as a room's occupant had not made use of the deadbolt. He did his best to suppress a thrill as he rifled through Maisy's toiletries and underclothes for the specified articles. Such things had a wonderfully comfortable feel to them. A glimpse into his new wife's cupboards and drawers—all her womanly secrets laid bare—renewed the glow of affection forever hovering about the edges of his consciousness. That whole world was foreign to him. One by one, he collected the requested articles into a duffel bag.

He had greater difficulty in obtaining the necessary items from the Crew Store. Blue box? Which blue box? There were several different blue boxes, each of the specified brand, each offering varying assortments of benefits. He stood toying with the stubble on his chin as he studied them. He leaned in to read the fine print. He stood back to survey the field. This carried on for quite some time, the color rising in his cheeks all the while. Eventually he settled on a packet (the selection would prove incorrect although this would not, as we know, matter) and checked out under the searing scrutiny of the cashier.

Arthur made it as far as the cafeteria when he began to suspect something was amiss. Hallways and public spaces continued to fill with morning traffic as he completed each of his errands. In the feminine products aisle of the Crew Store he had expected whatever sidelong glances he received; but upon leaving, the looks persisted. Was everyone watching him? As he made his way down the cafeteria's buffet line, filling his tray of to-go containers with food for two, it became clear he was indeed a subject of scrutiny. Gossip spread like a virus in the close quarters of the ship. *There was the boy who married Maisy Armagast.*

He was loading cartons of food into a plastic bag when Ramon approached. "Dude... what are you doing here?" he said.

"What do you mean, 'What am I doing here?'" Arthur replied. "I'm getting breakfast."

"They're looking for you. Everyone knows."

"Everyone knows?" It took Arthur a moment to process Ramon's words.

"Buddy! You got married!" Ramon embraced him and slapped his back. "Maisy! I didn't think you had it in you."

Arthur could feel dozens of pairs of eyes upon him. Hair bristled on the back of his neck. He lowered his voice. "You know what they're going to do to her?"

"Everyone knows."

"Everyone knows?"

Ramon just gave him a look. Arthur's eyes continued to sweep the room. They did know. Overtly or otherwise, they watched him, one and all.

Stanley and Skyla fell firmly into the camp of those appalled by Arthur and Maisy's rebellion. As each opposing side closed ranks, these were among the most enthusiastic volunteers in the effort to safeguard the long-term viability of the Argonaut population.

Skyla threw herself into organizing the first round of procreative pairing. Maisy Armagast and the main kitchen's sous-chef on Deck 3, Spoke F, were not the only scheduled match. For each of the four other women, there were dozens of men who had to be called up. Feeling among the ship's officers and within the Department of Human Resources was that beginning the program in earnest would ease worries generated by widespread misinformation. It would set Maisy and Arthur apart as dangerous radicals. Skyla scheduled medical appointments and coordinated resources. In her spare time, she drafted pamphlets for the chief steward's campaign of strategic communications, laying out the requirements and benefits of successful management of the *Argo's* genetic stockpile. Dissent from Al's Grand Plan would endanger them All!

What was it that so fired Skyla to bring Maisy to account? It was not simply the acrimony generated by a snub. Skyla was an intelligent young woman who was used to disappointment. She was not generally one to hold a grudge. No, the source of her zeal ran deeper. At its core was a nagging certainty she had done wrong. The needling of guilt manifested in an overreaction of blind fury, its objective to bury away the scolding of conscience.

She was entirely within her rights to offer up anyone she chose as a candidate for reproductive pairing. That was her job, her responsibility, her very duty. Regulations did not specify means through which Al would arrive at his conclusions, so long as he was allowed to operate as designed. In starting with Maisy Armagast, she was entirely within her rights. Her flurry of activity snuffed any sneaking suspicions that contradicted this perfectly reasonable conclusion. She made a name for herself among the officer corps, with the cadre of Human Resources supervisors lauding her efforts far and wide. The praise cemented a veneer of certainty that she had made the correct decision. After all, she was entirely within her rights.

Furor over the Maisy Armagast Affair rocketed Skyla back into the limelight. Her previous contributions to the debate over reproductive procedure made her a go-to source among the social elites to whom Maisy had introduced her. With her patron faded from view, Skyla took on a presence of her own. Leaderless, Maisy's clique began to disperse and coalesce into new patterns of deference and approbation. In this emerging constellation, Skyla found her place as the guru of the reactionaries. Even those who sympathized with their former leader turned to Skyla in foraging for the latest cud upon which to chew.

Skyla told herself it had been only a matter of time until she rose to this rightful position of prominence. Really, it had nothing to do with Maisy. Mrs. Sawyer had impressed upon her daughter from the very beginning the inevitability with which Skyla would come into her own. She was too smart, too capable, too all-around wonderful of a human being to go long unnoticed and unacknowledged. Conversely, the Maisy Armagasts of the world were destined to fade away, so thin was their substance, so tenuous the foundations of their popularity. Playing out before Skyla's eyes was the solemn prediction of her mother, drilled into her from childhood.

Although she had not crossed paths with Stanley since arriving aboard, the two carried on in symbiotic parallel. Where she blossomed into the intellectual heart of the pro-establishment faction, he became its self-styled fist. Ill content to fritter away his time conducting lights-out checks and reviewing visitor logs, Stanley set himself upon ascension from a mere desk officer to the ranks of the full-blown security forces.

Such promotion was not remotely within the realm of possibility. No one with a shred of understanding for the demands of policework would consider entrusting such a man with the stamp of official authority, let alone a sidearm (or their space-borne equivalent: stun-guns guaranteed not to damage the ship with an errant discharge). Stanley would not be deterred. When his oaths of loyalty and commitment—voiced during a series of interviews following his late-night sighting of Maisy—failed to stir recognition from his superiors, he took matters into his own hands.

His efforts began with the corps of CQ desk officers, nearly all of whom were comparable in their commitment and parochialism. He called for constitution of a professional association and organized a convocation to inaugurate the body. He stood on a chair in the cafeteria and waved a fist in the air as he called upon the patriotic sentiments of his colleagues. In their hands was held the ultimate success or failure of the entire *Argo* enterprise. They were the first line of defense against fraterniza-tion and comparable forms of malfeasance. The desk officers held a sacred responsibility to safeguard the well-being of the universe's first branch of humanity to step beyond the bounds of their home planet. This august responsibility was no less than epoch-making in its momentous import.

The group gathered before him in the cafeteria first mumbled vague assent, then applauded Stanley's foresight, and ended by cheering his thundering rhetoric, much to the amuse-ment of the cafeteria's remaining occupants. These observers spread far and wide the tale of Stanley's ascendancy. What began as a humorous anecdote related over rounds of poker and cups of hooch grew in the coming weeks into rumors of a full-fledged militia.

Whatever the powers entrusted to Admiral Demarion and his staff, they were faced with the reality that more than half the crew sympathized with the dissidents. Even as the admiral reit-erated the zero-tolerance nature of Rule Number One, he weighed the currents of popular opinion. He was faced with the challenge of nipping a nascent rebellion in the bud while not stirring broader discussion of human rights and such nonsense. He had to—ostensibly, at least—accommodate the demands of both sides while steering the majoritarian whim toward the cause of the crew's ultimate survival. That, in his mind, was the final objective. Nothing less than catastrophe would result from repudiating the preeminence of AI in Human Resources.

Stanley's militia provided convenient means for Admiral Demarion both to have his cake and eat it. Even as his command staff gave lip service to the cause of interpersonal sentiment, it threw the full force of its efforts into a campaign of propaganda. The security forces, while doing their utmost to apprehend Maisy, were bound by the constraint of maintaining broad support among the crew. They were, after all, grossly outnumbered and armed only with nonlethal weaponry. Barred from overt means of suppressing nefarious activities, they left such things to Stanley and his contingent of desk officers.

Stanley's army was no regiment of thugs in brown shirts and jackboots. The aura surrounding them might be captured in any number of nicknames by which they came to be known. The Dork Brigade was one such that adequately captures the tone of surrounding discourse. Nevertheless, they became a significant impediment to Arthur and Maisy's designs. It was difficult to move about the main deck without attracting their notice. Off duty they were as dangerous or more so: one could never be sure who was watching and listening. The slightest violation of regulations was promptly reported, and soon the outfit began taking matters into its own hands. Known dissenters found themselves the subject of unremitting scrutiny and rigorous enforcement of technicalities. One could not live long aboard the *Argo* without falling afoul of some rule or another; this provided wide latitude for making lives miserable.

Where was Arthur as this juggernaut gathered force? He began by allowing Ramon to pull him to a seat in the cafeteria where they could discuss the matter in full. He could not go back to the observation deck. This would lead the authorities straight to Maisy. That they had not already detained him implied they were waiting and watching for this very purpose. Surely the authorities had picked up his trail as soon as he donned his wristband and passed before the waiting lens of a surveillance camera.

Arthur gave instructions in hushed tones: Ramon must bring the supplies to the cherry orchard in the outer ring and leave them wrapped in the picnic blanket hidden away in the center of the grove. Ramon set out, leaving Arthur to finish his meal. Unsure of what else to do, he showed up for work on time. No one treated him differently than on any other day. His morning duties were carried out under a cloud of paranoia.

At lunchtime, Petty Officer Dulka informed him that in two hours he must break from scavenging manure from the cow pasture and attend an appointment with the bosun. At last Arthur's fears were realized. Should he run for it? Should he pretend nothing was wrong? Should he lie? Tell the truth? He was utterly unprepared to entertain such questions or to act upon any conclusions. Escape was out of the question, as was capture; his beloved was relying upon him. Would they lock him in the brig? Confine him to quarters? For all he knew, summary execution was not off the table. Still his legs carried him forward as on that first day so long ago when he set off through the terminal of a tiny little airport in a tiny little town. How insignificant that all seemed now.

Was it bravery that carried him on? Was it the cowardice of a sheep led to slaughter? Even he could not tell the difference, so clouded were the inner workings of his mind. He watched himself introduce himself to the bosun's aide-de-camp and seat himself in the waiting room.

Arthur left the bosun's office thirty minutes later with a sense of profound disappointment unlike any he had expected. Did he matter? Did any of his actions affect the world around him? He had arrived convinced he would be perceived as nothing less than a modern-day Benedict Arnold. Instead, Atticus Oluwusi was preoccupied and seemed irritated Arthur had interrupted whatever task should be receiving his full attention. He was scolded for his little stunt of staging a ridiculous mock wedding. Surely, he realized he was simply a pawn in thrall to a dangerously subversive young woman? The bosun thought better of a strong young man like Arthur. He had checked the files. Arthur's employment records were impeccable, his academic marks slightly above average. He had a bright future aboard the *Argo*. He should think long and hard before throwing it away to suit the whims of a capricious girl who was obviously using him. He realized this, didn't he? Maisy Armagast? Did he really think she cared for him?

"Now, let's put this whole affair to rest," the bosun said in conclusion. "Are you aware of Ms. Armagast's whereabouts?"

Arthur managed a shake of his head to the negative that appeared to be taken at face value.

"Very well." Atticus' eyes went back to his computer screen before he had even stopped talking. "I'm confident you will report any further contact. That will be all."

For a moment, Arthur remained seated, unable to process what had just happened. Only when his interrogator lifted his eyes to peer at him pointedly did he rise from the chair and excuse himself. He gave a deferential half-nod, half-bow that came out unbidden. When he reached the hallway, the feeling of shock turned to one of affront. Was that *it*? Did they think so little of him? Were they really so foolish, or was Arthur really so inconsequential?

In the coming weeks, Arthur, Ramon, and Father McIntosh built their fellowship of trusted associates. They organized resistance to Skyla's propaganda, the expanding scope of Stanley's espionage, and the command staff's surveillance. Between them, they kept Maisy stocked with necessities and out of sight of the authorities. Whenever the opportunity presented itself, Arthur slipped off his wristband for a visit. They talked, they gazed out at the universe, they practiced relentlessly at being man and wife. No, Arthur realized, he had not done it correctly the first time. But Maisy was a patient teacher.

This could not carry on forever. The command staff

continued to expand its search for the deserter. The security forces continued to monitor her consort. Stanley's militia redoubled its efforts. Skyla buzzed around the medical ward to ensure all proceeded according to plan. And then, of course, there was the clock ticking away within the biological machinery of Maisy's body. One day when Arthur came to visit, she sat looking at him with a quizzical smile. He paused and looked a question at her. Still, she silently held the little grin.

"What is it?" he said.

Chapter Eighteen

"What is it?" Arthur said again. His wife continued to smile at him. A pause and then again: "What?"

"I'm late," she said.

"Late for what? You need to stay here. They're looking for you."

"No... I'm *late*."

Still nothing.

She gave up on being playful. "I'm pregnant, Arthur. You're going to be a daddy."

There was a moment of stunned silence before Arthur launched into an outpouring of emotion that some may consider unbecoming of a spaceman and an Argonaut. He laughed, he wept, he plucked his bride off her feet and spun her about until she demanded he stop at once. After jubilation ran its course, she settled him in their nest of cushions and let him coo and pet as she steered his attention back to the issue at hand.

"I can't stay here," she said.

"Is it a boy or a girl?" said Arthur.

"How could I possibly know that?"

"I just thought maybe..."

"You've been to health class, right? You understand how this works?"

He waved it off with a smile and a laugh. His joy would not be deterred, nor could he resist reaching to rest his hand on her abdomen. She shooed it away.

"I need you to focus, Arthur," said Maisy. "I can't stay here."

"Why not? It'll be a while yet, right?"

"Of course, it will. But we have to time this properly. We can't wait until our hand is forced. Sooner or later, they're going to find me."

He shrugged a vague acquiescence. "What will we name it? He? She?" He laughed again to himself and let his eyes wander down over the stars. Jupiter's point of light was beginning to swell as it spiraled toward them over the bow of the ship. The largest of its moons were just visible. "How about Thebe?"

"No."

"Europa?"

"No. And what if it's a boy? I don't think we should worry about that right now."

"Right. I get it. What do you think we should do?"

"I don't know. That's why I'm asking."

"What if we went another way with it?" Arthur's gaze was drawn in a circling sweep below them as his eyes followed the swirling current of the Milky Way. "Antares."

She scrunched her lips and widened her eyes in frustration. "You've got to be kidding me. Stop."

"Arcturus."

She lunged and pinned him to the floor, legs straddling his midsection, hands on his wrists. He let her have her way, radiance beaming from his face. His exultation was seeping into her. She leaned forward until they were looking into one another's eyes through the tunnel of her falling hair.

"We're going to have a baby," said Arthur. Then again: "We're going to have a baby."

She was captured, and her joy broke loose. She kissed him as well as one can kiss through a smile that refuses to be deterred. Then she collapsed beside him with her body curled around his. "We're going to have a baby," she repeated back.

They lay there for a time as thoughts pulled back from their dancing, fluttering heights. They were having a baby. But Maisy was already scheduled to have a baby, and it was not supposed to be Arthur's. What would Admiral Demarion say when he discovered his plans had been preempted? What would he do? More to the point, what would Arthur and Maisy do? Arthur returned to her initial question. The answer emerged ready-made. It was the only answer at which Arthur could arrive.

"Skyla... Stanley," he said, musing, his idea crystalizing even as he spoke.

"Huh?" She looked up at his face without taking her cheek from his chest.

"We need to deal with the Skyla-and-Stanley problem," said Arthur.

"What do they have to do with it?" Maisy asked. "Admiral Demarion and the security forces are the problem."

"Are they?"

Maisy rolled to her back, and Arthur lay on his side next to her. She let him unzip her jumpsuit and lift the hem of her undershirt to play his fingertips over the skin of her belly.

Arthur went on. "They haven't even arrested me. I've been going to work every day like nothing is out of the ordinary. They're treating our wedding like it was some kind of prank. They just want it all to go away."

"Maybe so, but apparently part of making it go away is knocking me up."

"I already knocked you up."

"So you did."

They smiled at that.

"Their problem is the crew," Arthur said. "Listen, Skyla was right: this whole mission was thrown together on a shoestring. With no disrespect to your father, it's a publicity stunt."

"Disrespect away." She turned her head to look into his eyes.

"It's not *Brave New World*. It's not even *1984*. I'd say *Animal Farm* at best."

She smiled again.

"They have no way of putting down the crew if everyone is against them. Skyla and Stanley are our problem, not the bosun and the quartermaster."

"What do we do?"

He told her. It was obvious, really. Theirs was a battle over worldviews, not regulations. There were the lovers and there were the fighters. Admiral Demarion and his staff were beholden to these currents churning their little lake locked away from the ocean of humanity but in no way distinct from it (at least, not yet). Bringing Skyla and Stanley over to the side of the lovers was as simple as helping them to find love.

Maisy's face took a baffled look. "Who would fall in love with Stanley?" she said. "Who would fall in love with Skyla?"

Arthur watched her as realization dawned.

"Oh..." she said, drifting. Then with emphasis: "Oh."

"What do you think?"

"That could work."

The devil, of course, was in the details. Well suited they may have been, but Stanley and Skyla moved in different worlds. They had not crossed paths since their cadet days, and could not reasonably be expected to do so. And it would take more than putting them in the same room together. So thick were their calluses, so impregnable their defenses, that intervention by the gods themselves would be unlikely to pierce those shells.

But Arthur had an idea.

The assault began the following day in the food court, where Stanley took his meals alone. Whatever his acclaim amid the ranks of the desk officers, he remained a solitary man. Loneliness was cause and effect of an all-consuming anxiety bubbling just beneath the surface. There was more to the formation of his militia than righteous indignation or patriotic fervor. Stanley wanted friends. It was only after he had succeeded beyond his wildest dreams that he came to see how isolated a position of command can be. Troops do not want to socialize with their commander, admire him as they may. Nor did his prominence translate into cachet with the ladies. Those with whom he commonly mixed were captured by the hardhearted principles he espoused, overawed by his position of power, or entirely uninterested (this last group, of course, was the preponderance). For all his astounding success, he remained alone.

He scarcely deigned to glance up from his reconstituted scrambled eggs when Arthur took a seat across from him.

"Hey, man," said Arthur. This was not a form of address Arthur commonly employed, but he felt it would conform to Stanley's conceptions of fraternal banter.

"What do you want, Piff?"

Arthur shrugged and set about squeezing a pool of ketchup into a vacant space at the corner of his pile of home fries. This complete, he said, "You heard anything about Maisy?"

Stanley aborted the bite he was about to take and lowered the fork back to his plate. "I thought you two got married?" The question dripped with contempt.

Again, Arthur shrugged. He tucked into his omelet, avoiding Stanley's gaze.

Stanley considered this for a moment. That was all the time

it took to formulate a firm grasp of Arthur's situation. "Got tired of her little game, did she? I could have told you that would happen."

"Just wondering," was all he said. He took a mouthful of fried potato.

"I tried to tell you, Piff. You should have listened. She was playing both of us. Whenever you weren't looking, she was all over me. I was close to falling for it, too—I'm not going to lie. It takes experience to see what's really going on with that kind of woman."

Arthur swallowed hard. "We did get married, you know. Ask the padre."

"Sure you did, Piff." Stanley went back to his plate of what passed for eggs. Arthur let it settle for a moment.

Then he said, "How would you do it, Stanley? If you were interested in her, I mean."

Stanley sat up straight and let his gaze drift off into an ambiguous distance. "You've got to let them come to you," he said. "Chase too much, and they just run away."

"I thought you weren't into that stuff."

Stanley's contempt again spilled over. "We gave it up, Piff. We all gave it up. That doesn't mean I don't know how it's done. Anytime I wanted to, I could do what you do. But the Argonauts have a higher calling." He leaned forward with elbows resting on the table bestride his plate. "I could have had Maisy. I could have had just about anyone I wanted. That comes with being an officer. Don't worry—you'll get there one day."

"A desk officer?"

"Whatever." He took another bite.

"I just ask because they say she turned herself in. Walked right into the Human Resources Department and demanded to speak with the supervisor."

Stanley blanched and nearly choked before regaining his composure. "It's like I said, Piff," he said. "That whole thing was just a game. None of us are going anywhere, so we might as well play by the rules. She must realize that, too." Even as he said it, he was rising to his feet and collecting up his tray.

"Are you finished?" said Arthur.

"Yeah, I've got to get going," Stanley replied. He turned away.

"Hey, Stan..."

Stanley paused and looked back. "They call me Stanley," he said. Stanley's mother called him Stanley. He had grappled for years with the best way to impart this preference upon those who chose to disregard it. This was the phrase he had settled upon, and he used it often.

"Right... Stanley," said Arthur. "What's with the Freckles thing?"

Stanley laughed—slow, deliberate, humorless. It brought him back to the table, where he set down his tray and straddled the bench as if only dallying for a moment. He tried his best simultaneously to tuck his chin and tip his forehead back toward the ceiling. "Let me tell you what..."

He proceeded to tell Arthur what Arthur already knew, but he did it with supreme relish and undisguised gratification at being turned to for such manly repartee. He leaned in. The pace of his speech quickened. The odor of sour coffee and not-quite-eggs wafted over Arthur's face. Arthur watched him as if with interest, taking great gulps of orange juice to prevent chewed potato from sticking in his throat. He chuckled at all the right places, closed his eyes, and shook his head in admiration. Stanley was a hero.

"Freckles..." Arthur mused once Stanley had finished. "That's great... Freckles. Wish I could have been there."

"Listen, man, I have to go." Stanley stood once more. This time he would not be detained.

Arthur watched him weave his way through the tables, dump the remains of his lunch into the waste chute, and depart in the direction of the Department of Human Resources. Arthur checked his wristband for the time. Hopefully, it had been enough.

Arthur was right: there was nothing Admiral Demarion and his staff (with the possible exception of the bosun) would have welcomed more than having the whole mess disappear. Hard as they tried, it had gone from bad to worse. The *Argo* had not even reached Jupiter. Already they were facing disobedience verging on mutiny and, perhaps worse, the collapse of Al's Grand Plan, which was their only hope of handing off the mission to their successors in any kind of acceptable state.

It was about more than Arthur and Maisy's unsanctioned marriage; that could be played off with relative ease. It was about precedent—about the danger of emotion getting the better of the cold force of reason upon which everything depended. It was about chaos versus control. This marriage could be the proverbial camel's nose under the tent.

But what to do? A swift disciplinary response would have cowed the will of many a young crewman. With Maisy Armagast, this was impossible. She held the passions of the masses in those tiny little fingers and knew how to bend them to her wishes.

So, private opinions of the matter tended toward accommodation. Undoubtedly, Maisy would be amenable to reason. Given that no strict legalities had been observed in the marriage, laughing it off or just pretending it did not happen remained possibilities. If she would agree to keep quiet about her little garbageman, they would agree to pretend the ceremony never took place. As long as everyone adhered to the spirit of Rule Number One in respect to its practical applications, all may yet be well. And it went without saying that the Office of the Chaplaincy would be given a stern talking-to.

Alas, it was not to be, for even as Admiral Demarion's unease was dissipating with the passing weeks of relative quiet, the fruit of Arthur and Maisy's disobedience was growing larger. Along with the baby—and perhaps even more important —was their hardening resolve and the plan taking shape through the dangerous medium of pillow talk.

That plan emerged from the hazy mists of Arthur's subconscious even as Admiral Demarion was changing into his blue cotton pajamas with gold ribbing and large plastic buttons. As Arthur and Maisy were discussing it, he was settling himself into his bunk and drifting off to sleep. As Arthur was taking his seat across from Stanley in the food court the following morning, the command staff was assembling around the bridge's conference table for their weekly staff meeting.

Moments later, Maisy would retrieve her abandoned wristband from a niche in the floorboards beneath her office cubicle. Lights flashed on computer screens of the security operations center as she made her way through the corridors toward the Department of Human Resources. Before the signal could be verified via video feed, she had knocked on the jamb of Skyla's open office door and leaned against it with a faint expression of distress. Skyla spun around to take her in.

"Maisy!" Skyla said. She put her hands on the arms of her chair as if to rise, then thought better of it and leaned back to study the visitor.

"Good morning, Skyla," said Maisy. "I hope I'm not interrupting anything."

"No... come in." Skyla motioned her toward one of the

chairs arranged around a small table in a corner across from the desk. "Where have you been?"

Maisy sat upright with elbows on the armrests and hands clasped before her. "I've been hiding on the observation deck," she said after a pregnant pause. "They haven't closed it up yet. Listen... I need your help."

Skyla's countenance was steeled for battle. It relaxed a barely perceptible fraction. "OK... tell me," she said.

"I have a problem..." Maisy fumbled at it. "I need your advice... You understand Al's plan, right? The mathematics of the reproductive assignments?"

Skyla tried her best simultaneously to tuck her chin and tip her forehead back toward the ceiling. "As much as anyone, I suppose," she said. "Why?"

"What would happen if..." Maisy trailed off before beginning afresh. "What I mean is... how important is Rule Number One, really? I mean, over a thousand years, Al can work around one or two deviations, right?"

Skyla's eyes narrowed. "Why do you ask?" she said.

"Well... I mean... there are five thousand of us, right? Everything doesn't have to go absolutely perfectly. There must be some room for error. After all, he can't predict the exact outcome of any particular combination. He's just guessing, too, to some degree?"

Confrontation again crept into Skyla's face. "Why do you ask?" she said again.

Maisy released her clasped hands and laid one of them on her stomach. She tried to summon a tear, but this was beyond her theatrical capacities.

"You didn't." Skyla almost hissed the words.

Maisy could not have picked a confidante who would be more horrified by this particular breach of protocol. She saw that now, but it was too late to go back. "You could put it into the computer, right? See what the outcome might be? Maybe it will be OK?"

"You little floozy," said Skyla, or something to that effect.

Maisy did not feel it worth pointing out that the child in question was, in fact, produced within the legitimate bounds of matrimony. Instead, she said, "It was an accident... really."

Skyla's response to this does not bear repeating.

"But you must be able to help," said Maisy. "Couldn't you just check with Al? Maybe one tiny slip doesn't matter."

"It's that little garbageman, isn't it? He must be the one. And you, of all people."

Maisy was trying to work upon Skyla's better nature. She underestimated the scope of the affront to an overeducated and prematurely empowered geneticist when faced with such a revelation. Maisy's suggestion was a direct challenge to the import of her entire life's work. *Doesn't matter?* One might as well ask if Skyla would devote her life to designing crossword puzzles. Maisy grappled for some way to draw her back.

She was saved from the necessity of further comment by the arrival of Stanley. He nearly burst into the room before drawing himself up and looking from one woman to the other as he tried to smooth the rumples out of a uniform that in his haste had gone into disarray. His eyes settled upon Skyla and lingered there for a moment. "Hello, Skyla," he said.

Skyla's fury began to dissipate as she took in this new arrival. Her hand went of its own accord to a stray lock of hair and tucked it behind an ear. Her back straightened from where it had hunched over as if preparing to spring at the fiend sitting across the room. "Hello, Stanley," she said, rising and extending a hand.

Stanley briefly gripped it in his own. "It's nice to see you again," he said.

"Likewise..." Skyla's hand went back to the lock of hair.

Stanley drew himself up. He made an effort to suck in his paunch at a rate slow enough that it would not be noticed by either of the women.

"The restroom is right down the hall on the left," said Skyla.

"I'm good," said Stanley.

"I've just gotten some disappointing news from our Ms. Armagast, here." Skyla's face returned to its scowl as she turned her gaze back on Maisy. They both studied her for a moment as she did her best to look contrite. "We've had a violation of Rule Number One."

The wrath that briefly flitted over Stanley's face resolved into a more appropriate strain of indignation. "Is that so?" he said. "The command staff must hear of this immediately."

Skyla stood, the better to look down upon Maisy and confer with her new ally. They discussed particulars as if Maisy were an object of furniture. Skyla would take the news to the bridge, where Admiral Demarion's weekly staff meeting would be getting underway. Stanley would convey Maisy to the operations center for confinement.

Admiral Demarion's profound wish that Arthur and Maisy's bout of insubordination die quietly away was snuffed as Skyla stormed into the breach with all the fierce intrepidity of an Audie Murphy. She flew through the corridors of the *Argo* with head thrown back and arms pumping furiously. She burst in upon the command staff's morning meeting in full assurance that the subject consuming her attention would be the sole topic of conversation for anyone who was anyone. They had been discussing reports of persistent backups in the fourth-deck latrines; this quickly fell by the wayside.

Skyla rested her clenched fists on the conference table. "Maisy Armagast is already pregnant," she said.

There was a moment of silence as the senior officers processed this new bit of information. Skyla was pleased with the response, supposing it reflected the gravity of her pronouncement. In reality, it arose in no small measure from surprise that she could be so presumptuous as to burst in upon their staff meeting.

"Thank you, Petty Officer Sawyer. We will discuss it. Will you excuse us?" Quartermaster Kumar said the words, jumping in before Atticus could send Skyla off on less gracious terms.

Skyla hesitated. In picturing the situation, she had imagined it would unfold quite differently, perhaps even resulting in the officers scooching down and pulling up another chair so she could join the discussion. Instead, they sat awaiting her departure. She complied.

The command staff set about debating an appropriate response to the fresh circumstances. It carried along lines similar to those before. Perhaps the whole episode could still be swept quietly under the rug. Surely one small deviation from Al's Grand Plan would not be catastrophic over the centuries to come. Surely Maisy would be amenable to obscuring the paternity of her child from the general population of the ship. The system was, after all, fortuitously designed to do this very thing. All she had to do was keep her mouth shut. A few weeks' discrepancy in due dates would surely go unremarked.

What they neglected to account for was the reaction of their informant. Even as they debated difficulties associated with disguising the parentage of Maisy's child, Skyla was carrying forth the mission she laid out for herself—the mission that, somewhere in her addled exultation, she imagined they had set her upon. Clearly Maisy's behavior would provoke outrage from the crew. Clearly, they would see that their future—that the success of the entire enterprise—depended upon a swift and unequivocal response. The pregnancy could not be allowed to continue. Skyla never considered any other course of action within the realm of possibility.

She set about implementing orders she felt certain would issue from the convocation of the *Argo*'s command staff. Medical resources must be marshaled. The procedure to terminate the pregnancy must be scheduled. Maisy's appointment for fertilization via sanctioned means must be shifted to a later date. One and all must understand that the leadership brooked no dissent on matters so vital to the survival of the Argonauts. Even as Skyla set in motion the wheels of the medical establishment, she told anyone who would listen of Maisy's behavior and the response soon to issue forth from Admiral Demarion and his staff. Not a few of them hinted to Skyla that perhaps the ferociously brutal nature of this response may create more problems than it solved. Skyla was in no condition to pick up on hints.

By the time the staff actually arrived at their conclusions and set about transcribing and distributing the minutes, documenting decision points, cross-referencing relevant regulations, and sending notification to the operations center, Skyla's vision was a *fait accompli*. Arthur and Maisy's unauthorized child would be sacrificed for the good of the mission. Those who did not yet know it would get the news within a matter of hours.

Rumor spread like water bursting forth from a ruptured dam: Maisy was pregnant, and Admiral Demarion was putting an end to it. From the font of Skyla's waggling lips, it roared through the admiral's administrative staff and the front office of the medical ward. It inundated the corps of doctors and the highest ranks of the bureaucracy. It swept away the meager official pronouncements trickling out from the command staff's morning meeting, all of which were quickly retracted when the reality of the situation became clear. From there the gossip branched and spread, running in rivulets and side channels down the cafeteria tables and through the lounges and break rooms. It spread and slowed as it percolated out into the general population, like water soaking into an arid lowland plain.

For the command staff, there was no turning back from the course Skyla had set. Schedules were cleared, the meeting reconvened. Debate was furious. Lane Beauregard declared they might as well execute the young woman, so far as the likely response from the crew was concerned. It would mean mutiny. Even Quartermaster Kumar could not entirely disagree with this assessment. While none were prepared to back the wisdom of Skyla's course of action, the bosun was willing to address the facts on the ground. The cat was out of the bag. Equivocation would signal weakness and invite further insubordination. The admiral sided with him.

Arthur meanwhile had finished his breakfast and returned to his room to await Maisy's arrival in accordance with their plan. He waited and waited. Something was wrong. Sometime after ten o'clock, Ramon heard the news from a colleague as he paused to secure a Diet Coke from the refrigerator of his office break room. Moments later, as it happened, Father McIntosh would be informed of the command staff's decision by the chaplaincy's secretary. The first thoughts of both were that Arthur must be found. He could under no circumstances be allowed to receive this news from anyone but a friend.

However earnest their intentions, Ramon and Father McIntosh were powerless beside the ruthless efficiency of Stanley's army. Within moments of first contact, the rumor reached the supervisory level. It skipped from squadron CQ desk to squadron CQ desk until someone thought to pass it to the central supervisory board (Stanley was a vigorous organizer). From there it blasted out to every computer monitor across the network, flashing into Stanley's inbox just as he was returning from the operations center where he had deposited the prisoner.

Even as Ramon was hurrying through a transverse corridor of the third deck and waiting at a spoke lift clogged with pre-lunch traffic, Stanley was rocking back in his chair with his hands clasped behind his head, breathing a sigh of blissful contentment as a smile spread over his face. Even as Father McIntosh was directing cancellation of his daily sojourn in the office confessional, Stanley was rising to his feet and turning toward the corridor to Arthur's room. Neither of Arthur's friends made it even to the squadron's entrance before Stanley was pounding on his door.

When his knock received no response, he raised his voice to be heard through the door. "I say... open up, PO3 Pifflethorpe."

Another sequence of raps.

"I say... open up. You'll be wanted at SecOps. No doubt they'll be along shortly."

Still nothing from Arthur.

Stanley's voice lowered a notch and he leaned close to the door. "What were you thinking, Piff? Did you really think they'd allow this kind of thing to go on?"

As we have suggested, Stanley was not bad through and through. We must judge a man in his entirety, not based solely upon cherry-picked low points. Nevertheless, this was not among his finer moments. The rate at which he had been carried away by his newfound power was alarming.

"Do you think Al would let Maisy go to any old ragpicker?" he said. "Well, he won't. If we're going to make it to Colchis, we have to be more careful than that. That Maisy Armagast is prime stock. I'm on the list, you know—the list of donors for this round. Did you think you could cut the line?"

Arthur's hand was on the knob.

"Well, this nonsense is going to end. The medics are already prepping her, I'm sure. They'll have everything back in order in no time."

Arthur did not kill Stanley. That was not his way. Neither was Stanley one to acknowledge the vagaries of chance that allowed him to go on breathing in and out, for a lesser adversary may not have permitted it. No, when Arthur opened the door, he simply pushed past the desk officer and walked away down the hall.

"I say," said Stanley as he grappled with a response to Arthur's abrupt departure. His dominion relied to some degree upon mutual consent, or the threat of force imposed by higher powers. When these failed him, he was at a loss. He watched Arthur go.

Arthur passed Ramon and Father McIntosh in the hallway. Without breaking stride, he slipped his disconnected wristband into Ramon's ready grasp. Then he was gone. No one knew the forgotten doors and hidden passageways of the *Argo* like Arthur Pifflethorpe.

Chapter Nineteen

Leaving Stanley behind in the hallway of Squadron Four, Arthur found himself once more in a state of drift. Where would his feet carry him but back to the place where it began? Seated cross-legged in an expanse of transparent emptiness, he corkscrewed alone through the universe, waiting for his thoughts to resolve. Perhaps his subconscious was inching toward a plan of action: a daring rescue of his beloved and their child. He would slither through the dark recesses of the *Argo*, drop unexpectedly from a ceiling tile, overpower the guards, and so forth. But let us be honest with ourselves: Arthur did not have that in him. Any insight he possessed into the problem had been applied; any strategizing of which he was capable had been set in motion.

He waited, and Maisy came to him. As everything began to come apart, she knew where to find him. She approached from behind, bent to kiss the top of his head, and sat cross-legged behind him, back to back, mirror images looking down on the universe and letting its grandeur draw out their thoughts.

"Well, I made a hash of that," she said at last.

"Did you?" Arthur said.

"It seems that way."

They considered this.

A few minutes later, Arthur spoke again. "I thought they got you."

"They did. They do. They've got both of us, and they know it. It doesn't really matter, does it?"

"How did you get away?"

"I didn't."

"No, really."

It was not difficult, not for Maisy. The crewmen in the security operations center crumbled before her will as surely as the crew of Odysseus before the will of Circe. Had the duty officer been a woman, there was a chance she would still be locked away. He was not, and she was not. Confident assurance, a little vague flirting, and confusion compounded by a lack of official orders from the bosun was all it took. But she did not want to get into it with Arthur. She shrugged. Arthur felt the gesture against his back and did not press the question.

"Do you think they'll find us here?" he said.

"Yep."

"Maybe we shouldn't stay."

"You're right. But it's nice."

"It is nice."

They spun onward through perpetual night.

"Do you think we have time?" he said.

"Good grief, Arthur," said Maisy. "Is that all you think about?"

He let it go. It was a bad idea.

Their legs began to ache. Picturesque as all of it was, no one past the age of kindergarten can sit like that for any length of time. Maisy got to her feet and offered a hand to Arthur.

"Did you get everything set up?" she said.

"Mmm-hmm." He took her hand and she pulled him to his feet.

Even as Arthur and Maisy sat there in the dark, the world around them was dissolving into chaos. They knew this; it was part of the sublime pathos of the moment. They had cast the dice and had only to wait as they bounced and tumbled.

Stanley's army notified its commander at once when it became known Maisy had not remained in custody. Even as Stanley raged, he knew deep within that incompetence was to be expected. If you wanted something done right, you had to do it yourself. Why—oh, why—would they not just put him in charge? He set off to find Skyla. In her, he had found a kindred spirit who would stand beside him in his crusade against the forces of indiscipline and ineptitude. She alone had the determination to say what needed to be said, to do what needed to be done.

Admiral Demarion and the bosun had no desire to end a pregnancy by force under the magnified scrutiny of the entire crew—and this, the only person who passed for a celebrity in their little world. What better way to create a *cause célèbre?* What better way to fuel the fires of revolt? That Maisy managed to slip away on her own was a convenient coincidence. That she remained at large was due to the complicity of the admiral. The official order for her arrest remained unissued. The strategy for the time being was deliberate ambiguity. Everyone wondered what to do. Some security guards searched, unbidden. Others sat at their desks, laughing at the chumps who continued searching and at the command staff's wherewithal to botch everything it touched.

What the command staff needed was calm. Calm would come only with time.

The crusade remained primarily the province of Stanley Waller and his desk officers; however, even this had gotten complicated. He put his militia on high alert but informed them in no uncertain terms that their commander had the situation well in hand. Why did he not call an all-points bulletin on the fugitives? Organize a squad to accompany him? Call up his reserves? Send everyone off to turn out drawers and peek under beds? His reasons for not doing so will become clear as we focus in on where he was and what he was doing.

Stanley was with Skyla. He sat in her office, commiserating over interminable bureaucracy and the incompetence of anyone managing to rise above the rank of chief petty officer. They digressed into personal histories and laughed over petty enthusiasms of lesser souls. They reminisced about their cadet days. They sympathized over their fellow Argonauts' inability to appreciate the responsibility resting upon the shoulders of professionals who would abandon the pursuit of personal pleasures in the name of the mission: in the name of humanity. Here they were, cast together, the only ones who understood the gravity of the situation. All could yet be lost. The weight of five thousand years of history yet to be written was carried on their shoulders. It was all up to Stanley and Skyla.

"We have to find them," Stanley said. "We can't count on anyone else. It's just you and me."

Skyla concurred wholeheartedly. Then she said, "I know where they are."

"I beg your pardon?" said Stanley.

"I know where they are. Maisy told me where she's been hiding out."

He waited for it.

"They're on the observation deck," she said. "That's where she's been all this time."

"The observation deck is closed."

"They haven't sealed it off it yet. No one knows. Somehow, they got in."

Stanley rose and began pacing the room. "We have to bring them in," he said. "I don't trust the security forces to do it. They couldn't even keep her locked up when we delivered her to them with a little bow."

"Maybe we'll need backup," Skyla said. "There are two of them and just two of us."

Stanley waved it away as he stopped at the far wall, turned, and paced back the other way. His eyes roamed over the room as if searching the recesses of his brain. "No, no," he said. "You don't need to worry about that. Pifflethorpe is no fighter, I can tell you that. He'll come along quietly enough when he sees he's been outmaneuvered."

"Are you sure?"

Stanley paused to look her in the face. "If he puts up any trouble, I'll handle it," he said, and continued pacing.

"What about Maisy?"

Again, he stopped. This time he retook his seat and looked at her earnestly. "Swear yourself to secrecy," he said.

"I swear," she replied. Her whole life had been nothing but study, study, study—laboratories and computers and textbooks. This was all quite thrilling.

Stanley unzipped his fanny-pack and reached inside. From it he pulled a pair of handcuffs. He reached in again and pulled out another.

Skyla gasped. She was uncertain what prompted this gasp. What was so incredible about handcuffs? Nevertheless, the sight set her tingling. "Where did you get those?"

"I've got friends," he said. Indeed, everyone had friends in the manufacturing centers—even Stanley. The ship was rife with contraband.

"You think we should do it?"

"We have to do it. We've no other choice."

Skyla found herself struggling to catch her breath.

The observation deck's emergency stairwell opened to a shed backing up against a rear corner of the sheep stables. Stanley and Skyla descended via the steel cage of the agricultural ring's auxiliary lift and made their way around the fenced border of the paddock. It was full of sheep, the pasturage opposite having been emptied to accommodate a game of ultimate frisbee. Stanley strode confidently along the perimeter road with Skyla bustling at his side. He eyed the frisbee contestants with scorn. He eyed the sheep with suspicion.

They drew up before the shed. Stanley raised a hand for silence. Delighted hollers and shrieks drifted over from the pasture. He backed against the wall next to the door and beckoned her to do the same. He tried the knob. The lock had been jammed, and the door swung open beneath his touch. He gave his companion a knowing glance and slipped inside. A moment later, his head emerged, and he motioned for her to follow.

The stairwell was lit by flickering fluorescent lights on every other landing. Stanley and Skyla moved from light to dark and back again as they zigzagged down into the recesses of the ship's outer hull. Every ten flights or so, a set of safety doors provided buffer against any catastrophe that might befall the controlled atmosphere of the observation deck. Down and down they went. At last, they arrived at the bottom. From there one could look up the center of the spiraling staircase into the gloom above. The steel floor was crusted about the corners with dust and spilled soda pop.

Skyla's hand went inadvertently to her chest as if to becalm a fluttering heart. She watched Stanley edge open the final door and peer out into vast and empty space. He really was quite brave.

It was dark, the only illumination provided by the panorama of stars rolling by below. Their glow revealed the wide expanse of Lucite floor, now nearly empty of furniture. Far out in the center was a solitary pile of cushions, a wing chair, an end table with a lamp (currently switched off), and a plush, eight-foot beanbag. Light rose and fell with the eddies and currents of the galaxy turning past.

Skyla followed Stanley forward, step by slow, deliberate step. She clung to his arm. He allowed it despite the impediment it presented should defensive maneuvers be required. The charge of adrenaline was like a drug. She had never felt so willing to discard the convictions and obstinacies of her youth. Stanley, for his part, suppressed the crashing rhythm of his heart. Against all reasoning to the contrary, he found himself hoping beyond hope they were alone. He had never felt so betrayed by his own passions and yet refused to let the wish die.

They reached the center of the room and stopped before the nest floating out over nothing. The far reaches of the floor faded into obscurity, heightening the effect of vacuous infinitude. Then, rising up so slowly they never noticed when it began, came the faintest strains of music. Had it been there all along? In Stanley's poised concentration—nerves strung taut like the steely musculature of a Navy SEAL—it had gone thus far undetected.

"Is that Percy Sledge?" Skyla whispered, so close Stanley could feel the wind of her breath on his ear.

He raised a hand for silence, his head cocked. Percy Sledge indeed. The volume was creeping upward until the strains were unmistakable. Yes, it must have been there all along. He stood rooted, struggling with all his might to pull his attention back from where it was relentlessly dragged by the grip of Skyla's hands on his arm, her moist breath on his ear, the dulcet tones of Percy Sledge. All depended upon maintaining discipline. He must rely upon his training.

"I believe it is," he whispered back.

"Stan, I'm frightened," said Skyla. She was unsure whether

it was fear or some other emotion that made her heart crash and blood pulse audibly in her ears.

Stanley gave her a look sure to restore confidence in his ability to protect her.

The music swelled. Percy Sledge told Stanley that he would sleep in the rain if this girl told him that was the way it ought to be.

Indeed he would, thought Stanley. *Indeed he would. But that would have to come later. First came the mission. Always the mission.*

From where they watched in the dim recesses of the deck's perimeter, Arthur and Maisy saw Stanley step away from Skyla and turn in a circle, peering into the gloom. The song was fading.

"It's not working," Maisy whispered.

"What do we do?" Arthur whispered back, thumbing through his playlist. "How about Sam Cooke?"

"Sam won't do it," she whispered. "You know what it has to be."

"No, Maisy. No."

"You have to."

"No..."

Percy had faded nearly to silence.

"You have to."

He looked into her eyes, begging her not to make him do it. She ran a hand over his cheek and gave him a kiss.

She was right. They had no choice. He tapped on the title beneath his hovering thumb.

The music had ended. Now it rose once more, throbbing like a heartbeat.

"Did someone leave the music playing by accident?" Skyla whispered. She had drawn close once more to whisper in Stanley's ear, her grip regaining its place on his arm.

"They must have. What an awful waste of electricity..." His voice trailed off as he caught her eye. He had not meant to do so. He turned his head as he spoke, as by chance she brought her gaze back from where it watched the stars spinning by. They listened for a moment, gazing into one another's eyes. The throbbing voice of Bill Withers spoke to Stanley's soul, telling him what his world would be like if he ever let Skyla get away.

Ain't no sunshine, thought Stanley. *That's right. That's damn right.* No force in the universe could have pulled his eyes from Skyla's, not even all the legions of the enemy creeping up behind. Skyla pulled him closer. Their faces were fading from bright to dim as a spiral arm of the galaxy set over the line of the hull. They kissed.

Human beings are primed to see disaster. So devoted are we to seeking it out that we fashion our histories into sequences of tragedies strung out like cherished pearls. From there comes our terror of a future in which we see only opportunities for everything to go horribly wrong. We walk a tightrope, our highest aspiration that we may avoid dashing ourselves to pieces on the rocks below. What friend of ours is time? It is to be resisted: wrestled into submission and bent to our will. At all costs, we must safeguard against the breaking of the dam, for who can return the waters to their former place? Who can undo the damage?

Time runs on cycles beyond reckoning. Amid shattered, muddy remnants, hands rebuild. The flood dissipates. Sodden land dries. Molecule by molecule, water evaporates away and floats up to the sky. Gales send it on an eddying course around the globe and back again. It howls over oceans, crashes in on salt-sprayed beaches. It screams through lowland forests, bites into the mountainside and rises: slowing, cooling, condensing, falling as rain. The rain collects in cataracts that froth and foam into rivers coursing downward to refill the reservoir once more. Thus, decades hence, all returns to where it began. Yet we remember only disaster. We nurture such memories.

From these comes our need for heroes to storm the gates, heroes to fight angry gods. From these comes our need for a hand when we slip from the tightrope. And what kind of hero is Arthur Pifflethorpe? What could the radiant Maisy Armagast, the brash Isabel Weiss, the popular Sloane Villanueva see in a reticent, inward boy forever thinking and planning and never striking out with conviction? Just once, will he not rise to the occasion? Just once, will he not win the girl with that valor sure to be lurking somewhere inside? Or is love the most he has to offer?

Arthur and Maisy slipped away from where Stanley and Skyla embraced amid the spinning universe. Music played on as they eased closed the door behind them and trusted to the only thing Arthur knew. They could only wait upon the turning wheel of time: allow feet to plod onward, undirected. Wait they would—in their nook in the orchard, in the storerooms of the upper decks, in the gaps and crannies and dusty corners. With Arthur's knowledge of the *Argo*, they may well have lived a lifetime amid cracks and seams, shipboard rats for a new millennium. Left to his own devices, Arthur may have thus gone to ground. For Maisy, such a life never entered into consideration.

No official policies of the command staff would be rescinded, no orders countermanded. There was no sweeping reconsideration of the *Argo*'s founding principles. Rule Number One stood inviolable and Arthur and Maisy subject to its ineluctable logic. Like the *Argo* speeding off on its one-way journey to the heavens, the chain of reasoning proceeded. Falling away from the straight and narrow path of reason would lead to failure. All must yield before the ultimate consummation of human progress, before the cold calculation of AI in Human Resources.

And yet, love blossomed. Can that be entirely discounted? Arthur may have had no vision of an endgame back when he and Maisy set his plan in motion, but neither was he firing blind. He was not predisposed to trust in his own ability to govern cause and effect, but neither was he powerless. His faith was nebulous, mystical. It was not the faith of a warrior. It was the faith of an assembly-line technician in a vacuum-cleaner factory. Such is love. Such is life apart from fairy tales.

Arthur and Maisy waited and watched. They sat together among the grass and the tree trunks at the fringe of their orchard, out of sight of the contestants and spectators gathered in the sheep pasture. Arthur sat upright and alert. Maisy sprawled beside him, gazing up into the leaves, musing on what had passed and what was likely to come. The frisbee match concluded. The players caught their breath and shook hands and drifted away in twos and threes. Silence descended, broken only by the distant hum of automated farm machinery.

Arthur laid a hand on her thigh. "Here they come," he said.

Maisy sat up and followed his eyes with her own. The door to the access shed cracked. From the darkness emerged a set of fingers gripping the door, then a nose, then the face of Stanley Waller peering this way and that. He disappeared back into the darkness. Then the door opened wider, and he stepped through. He stole to an edge of the wall and peered around it—then to the opposite and did the same. He went back to the door and held it open. Skyla emerged furtive and blushing, smoothing her hair and tugging at her jumpsuit as if it were a skirt to be straightened. Maisy failed to suppress a giggle. Arthur hugged her close. "Shh..." he breathed. They watched.

Stanley almost crouched, so tightly strung were his nerves, so earnest his need to defend his sweetheart. His eyes darted and strained into the distance. He guided Skyla forward, his hand on the small of her back. She let herself be steered, bustling with a satisfied grin. She was not so caught up in the intrigue but appeared taken with her companion's enthusiasm. His manner eased as they achieved an inconspicuous distance from the shed. Away they strolled: two passing acquaintances out in the fields for a breath of air.

In the days to come, Arthur and Maisy would catch word of them from time to time. Father McIntosh, sworn to confidentiality in such matters, may or may not have seen Skyla popping by the chaplaincy for a visit with the Methodist pastor. Ramon happened upon the pair dining together in a quiet corner of the lunchroom. Now and then, Arthur and Maisy would steal back to the observation deck for an hour or two of stargazing and like pursuits. They could never be certain, but on occasion it seemed their little nest had been disarranged since the last time. News from Arthur's old squadron held that Stanley had been seen putting his feet up on the desk and flipping through the *Argonaut Daily* while on shift. His army was starved for causes stirring enough to justify fist-pumping speeches. Their interests were, for a time, captured *en masse* by a craze for the latest multiplayer online video game to sweep the ranks.

Pressure from this quarter eased, but all was not well. Admiral Demarion saw his opportunity. He had achieved his modicum of calm and resolved to end the matter once and for all. With Maisy dropped from sight and her persecutors lapsed into inexplicable contentment, the meandering course of public opinion found other outlets. It was the perfect time to bring in the outlaws and stuff them away until the matter had been permanently closed and the crew had lost interest.

Subtly, the heat began to rise for Arthur and Maisy. Sweeps by the security forces became more organized, although still limited by the need to remain beyond notice of the crew. Low-gravity decks near the axis tube to which the lovers had at last begun to acclimate were no longer outside the realm of occasional patrols. Maisy's wristband was discovered in its hiding place beneath the floor panels of her cubicle. Surveillance cameras proliferated. It was becoming increasingly difficult to circumvent checkpoints and jimmy locks.

Although it had been fun for a time, the sneaking about began to wear on Maisy. It was not her way. Arthur saw it, attuned as he was to her moods. Indeed, a block of granite may well have attuned itself to Maisy's moods.

With all the lying about, she was putting on weight; didn't Arthur think so?

Of course, he didn't think so. She was perfect. And even if she did gain weight, it wouldn't matter one bit.

So, she *had* put on weight. Why didn't Arthur just say so?

No, no... that's not what he meant at all.

There was no need to beat about the bush. She just wanted an honest opinion.

That *was* Arthur's honest opinion.

Then why wouldn't he come out and say it?

Matters over which they argued grew pettier and pettier. The periods of time she made him wait before making up grew longer and longer. He could not do anything right. Whatever the romance of it all, a man and his wife were not intended to live their lives squirreled away in broom closets. In pursuing love as an end, Arthur was well-practiced. In experiencing love as a beginning, he was lost in a howling wilderness. Few loves would have survived it, and certainly none so young as theirs. This was, in the end, what drove the moment to its crisis. It could not continue.

How long would it take before Stanley and Skyla were inextricably entangled? Who could say? This was the essence of Arthur's plan, the next domino that must fall. But the only evidence it had worked was circumstantial. It was possible that in turning to a supposed ally, they would be walking into the arms of an enemy. They had no confirmation the soup had finished its cooking, but to the table it must go.

On a Wednesday morning several weeks after her reacquaintance with Stanley, Skyla was late to work. She arrived rumpled and out of breath. She had never been so late before and, strangely enough, did not feel particularly out of sorts in consequence. This feeling had overtaken her more and more of late. She must not let it get out of hand. But if she missed the morning staff meeting, so be it. All would carry on without her. She would read over the minutes.

Besides, she had other important matters to attend to. The first full cohort of reproductive candidates was progressing step by step through the department's freshly engineered set of business processes. Matters had been complicated by the Armagast woman, but she would eventually turn up. After all, she had nowhere to go. All must progress as ordered from above. Skyla would do her duty, provide her recommendations, assure appropriate coordination between Human Resources and the medical staff. Beyond that, it was out of her hands. A shame it had come to this, but she had other things to think about.

There was a moment of surprise as she approached her office and saw beneath the closed door that the light inside was on. Had she forgotten to turn it off the previous day? Quite possible. Over the past week, she had found herself eyeing the clock as five o'clock approached. This brought her thoughts to Stanley and sent them drifting off. Her face, once so prone to settling unbidden into a scowl, shone with a lazy half-smile. She was both surprised and not surprised to find Arthur and Maisy waiting in her office. Maisy sat in the same chair where she had sat weeks before. Arthur had taken the seat next to her. Their conversation appeared to have ended abruptly with Skyla's arrival.

Skyla drew up short. She considered being angry and then thought better of it. This had once been her go-to reaction, but lately it seemed to expend too much effort. And truth be told, she had come to doubt deep in her soul whether she was the one with a right to be angry. The veneer of certainty that smothered her doubts had cracked.

"Good morning, Maisy. Good morning, Arthur," she said. She deposited her tote bag on a side table and seated herself behind the desk.

"Good morning, Skyla," said Maisy.

Arthur nodded.

"Everyone's been looking for you," said Skyla.

Maisy knit her brows. "Everyone? My, my... well, I hope we haven't put you out."

Skyla considered whether this was the appropriate moment to attack but decided to let it go. It felt nice, strangely nice. She had never been one to let things go. Her thoughts again drifted off until Maisy brought them back.

"Is there something you needed?" Maisy said.

"Needed?"

"You were looking for us."

"Well now, you know very well what the trouble is," Skyla replied.

"I suppose we do," said Maisy. "As a matter of fact, that's why we're here. Things ended so badly the last time. Surely we can all discuss this like adults."

Was Maisy implying Skyla was not an adult? Whatever. She let it go. "I'm afraid I can't go against the admiral's orders," she said. "I've passed instructions to the medical staff and, quite frankly, I'm finished with the whole business. You'll have to take it up with the admiral." What she told Maisy and Arthur was the same thing she regularly told herself. But trying to wash her hands of the affair was inevitably accompanied by a lump rising in her throat.

Arthur lifted a finger in preface to speaking. He had found this helped with the propensity of others to go on speaking over him as if he were not there. Indeed, Skyla had nearly forgotten he *was* there. "That's just it," Arthur said. "We'd like to take it up with the admiral, but first we need your help."

Skyla considered asking Arthur why he felt the need to be present. It would be delicious watching the boy try to explain his relevance to the whole sorry situation. Weeks before, she probably would have taken this approach, but at the moment it seemed unnecessarily cruel. Besides, some might say she owed him a good turn.

"My help?" she said.

"That's right."

Skyla waited for him to continue.

Maisy and Arthur had agreed he would ask the question this time. Perhaps woman to woman it had come across as too confrontational. Maisy understood these things better than he did.

"We were wondering," he said, "how difficult it might be to have a word with Al."

"Have a word with Al?"

"That's right—see what we can do about clearing up this whole business as amicably as possible. It would seem Al is the one best placed to address it."

Skyla had never really thought about that. She asked the questions, and Al provided the answers—very simple. "I had never really thought about that," she said.

"Do you have an interface?" Arthur asked.

Skyla spun around the monitor on her desk so they could see its screen. Called up was Al's interface window. "You can't do it from here," she said. "Only the engineers down at the quantum core have full access."

"Can you take us there?"

The question hung in the air for a moment.

Skyla shrugged. "I guess it couldn't hurt," she said. The lump in her throat began to dissipate. It felt wonderful. Besides, it was not strictly against regulations. And she had never been to the core.

Chapter Twenty

There were two places on the *Argo* where Beckett
Armagast had most loved to bring visitors. Surely, he
enjoyed watching them tumble and vomit in the axis
tube. He got a kick out of projecting images of Klingon warships
onto the wall-screen of the bridge. In a great coup, he had
secured a James Beard Award winner as head chef for the officer's mess. All of these touched his pride. But his tours
inevitably lingered in two places. One of these we have seen: the
observation deck with its unspeakably magnificent panorama
that never failed to strike dumb even the most garrulous politicians and critical journalists.

The other was buried deep within the labyrinth of the
middle decks, where relative gravity dictated an awkward,
bounding gait approaching that seen in old videos of astronauts
walking on the moon. Hither he would lead them after the
signing of a battery of nondisclosure agreements. Beckett would
exit the lift ahead of his entourage and bounce off down an
unremarkable corridor, turning to watch as the new arrivals
ricocheted off the ceiling a time or two before getting the hang
of it.

The group would proceed thirty or forty meters and turn a corner. Twenty meters further on was a cypher-locked door that led to another narrower side corridor. This took another turn or two before passing a security checkpoint and ending on a balcony overlooking a cylindrical shaft. A grated steel staircase spiraled down the wall to the floor two stories below. As the visitors headed for the stairs, Beckett would hop over the railing and drift down to await them at the bottom. He would pause to offer them a drink from a water fountain that sent its dribble in a magnificent arc from the spout to a catch-basin across the room.

This was the heart of Beckett's world. He would turn and give a sweeping gesture toward a pair of frosted-glass doors. They were curved to follow the contour of the walls and etched with the logo of Armagast Enterprises. He would swipe his access card on a proximity reader, and the words projected on a large screen above it would change from a red *No Admittance* to a green *Access Granted*.

"Ladies and gentlemen," he would say, "I welcome you to the nerve center of the *Argo*: its very brain, if you will." Beckett's verbal flourishes were as prolific as his manual ones. "As you know, success of the *Argo*'s mission depends to an extraordinary degree on management of the Argonaut gene pool. The crew will be isolated for millennia, and must not only survive but arrive at their destination with sufficient health and vigor to populate an entire planet: modern-day Adams and Eves, so to speak.

"Needless to say, we'll not trust entirely to the hand of God. Earth's finest scientists..." Referring to the Earth as if it were one planet among many possibly relevant ones was another of Beckett's verbal tics. "...have spent decades developing not only theoretical underpinnings of the necessary genetic science but the means to apply those findings in a practical setting. The result of that effort is quite likely the pinnacle of human achievement.

It is, as a matter of fact, the crown jewel of the pinnacle of human achievement that is the *Argo*. Ladies and gentlemen, I give you... Al in Human Resources."

This speech, or some variation upon it, would be followed by Beckett placing a hand on each of the glass doors and throwing them open with a final flourish. Wisps of mist from Al's lake of dry ice would swirl about Beckett's legs as he led forward his visitors. (A fan was arranged out of sight to the rear to create the proper effect.) Like the cylindrical vestibule, the room housing Al in Human Resources rose two stories above them. Its only light came from the core's crystalline sphere, its spotlights, a bank of computer monitors to the left, and various hooded diode lamps arranged here and there to facilitate the work of the technicians. These were also intended, one would assume, to cast shadows of a suitably dramatic nature.

Pipes and electrical conduit covered the walls where they were not hidden behind racks of humming servers. The floor was a grid of grated steel panels, below which a shaft descended into obscurity. What mist did not carry on the draft as far as the door disappeared in eddying tendrils into the depths. The ceiling, where it was visible through the dimness, was fitted with black trusses like those one might see over a stage at a rock concert. Indeed, their purpose may have been similar. They supported the ring of spotlights and various other mysterious apparatuses, one of which appeared (to a careful observer) to be a smoke machine that made visible the converging beams of the spotlights. Dividing the main cavern from the control booth was a glass partition that also served as an interface. On it was projected data which the technicians manipulated via specialized gloves strung with power cables. Blue-green luminescence of the glass panels lit the faces of those standing behind it.

It was to this lair of the beast that Skyla led Arthur and

Maisy. All three felt a flutter in their chests as they stood before the curved glass doors with their logo of etched swoops and streaks. Foolish as this made them feel, it could not be avoided. Al's aura of all-powerful mystery had been forming within them for years. It was like standing at the threshold of some ancient, vine-tangled temple buried in the jungles of the Yucatan; one need not believe in the god to feel the grip of his presence.

Skyla swiped her badge on the proximity reader. It beeped, and a light flashed red. The wall-screen continued to announce its unwillingness to admit them. Skyla knocked on the door. They waited. She glanced almost shyly from Maisy to Arthur, then back again to the door. Indistinct noises emitted from within.

It opened at last, and a wash of light fell across the rumpled head that emerged. It was a small man—a boy, really—seemingly even younger than Arthur, although this may have been the effect of a baby face still flecked with pimples. His hair had grown long past its regulation trim, and his jumpsuit was stripped down to the waist, its arms wrapped and tied in the front like a sash. Beneath was a vintage Metallica T-shirt.

He pulled a green swizzle stick from his mouth. "Hey, Skyla," he said. "What are you doing down here?" His gaze took in Arthur and Maisy, lingering briefly upon the latter. He remained unruffled.

"Hi, Warren," she replied. "Just wondering if you've got a minute. These guys had a few questions."

He paused, and his eyes drifted again over the unannounced guests. Then he shrugged and pushed the door open for them.

What they saw was not a darkened room cast with looming shadows and tendrils of mist. Rather, fluorescent tubes on the ceiling illuminated everything in harsh radiance. Al's crystalline orb was dark and its lake of mist empty. Its basin was filled with scattered detritus one might find in any office: pencils, sticky-notes, empty to-go coffee cups. The recess below the suspended grate floor was painted black so it would fade into the now-absent dimness. Its bottom was only four or five meters down and was littered with Skittles and a sticky-looking dried puddle. The glass control panels were covered in scrawls of grease-pen: everything from tic-tac-toe to a smudged mess where someone had been dabbling with a limerick.

Warren was halfway back to his magnificently elaborate swivel chair before the three of them made it through the door. This chair into which Warren settled was surrounded by a semi-circle of large-screen computer monitors that had been merged into a single sweeping view of some computer-generated world. The image was paused mid-spatter, with a musclebound enemy soldier taking the brunt of a burst of machine-gun fire. Warren tapped at the keyboard, and the screens returned to a more busi-nesslike appearance. He spun about and studied the new arrivals with vaguely irritated expectation. A half-dozen other office chairs were strewn about the floor. When it became clear Warren was not planning to offer seats to his guests, they helped themselves.

Skyla began with a glance toward Al's crystalline sphere, now dark and ordinary, hanging there in the center of the room. "Is he on?" she said.

It took Warren a moment to process her meaning. He waved it away. "That's just for show," he said. "It doesn't really do anything."

Skyla hesitated for a moment and then turned toward her companions. "Warren, this is..."

He cut her off. "Yep, got it."

"They came by my office to ask about..."

"Right, yep... I know."

Skyla was silenced.

Maisy spoke, feeling she might have better luck. "You must have heard what happened," she said, then paused. Warren was indeed more willing to listen to Maisy, although it remained unclear whether he processed what she said or was simply staring at her chest. The vague impression that his eyes were not meeting hers was felt by all present. Somewhat disconcerted, Maisy continued. "We were wondering if you could look into it a bit—see if the effects on Al's Plan are as catastrophic as everyone seems to think."

"They're not," Warren replied without missing a beat. "Anything else you want to know?"

"I beg your pardon?" said Maisy.

"Catastrophic," he prompted. "They're not. You'll be fine. We'll be fine. One divergence doesn't matter." Warren seemed to think this answered her question.

She tried again. "Can you tell us why that is?"

This gave him a moment's pause, or maybe he was still studying her chest. It was fiendishly difficult to tell. He spun around in his seat and began rapping at the keyboard. One of the screens went black, and text began to scroll over it. "Give me a name," he said.

It took the three an instant to process what he had said. Skyla was the first to do so. "Stanley Waller," she said.

Warren punched it into the computer. A new window leaped into view on a different screen. He turned the monitor on its mount, the better for them to see it. Stanley's picture was captioned with his name. There was his birthdate, occupation, hair color, eye color, and a smattering of other personal data. Warren scrolled downward until he arrived at a field entitled *Selection Criteria and Suitability Analysis*. Warren tapped the screen with a finger. "See that?"

Skyla was the closest. She leaned in and studied it for a moment. "I don't understand," she said.

"That's the stuff Al used to pick Stan," Warren clarified. "It's ranked from highest to lowest priority. The numbers to the right give the weighting criteria."

"But it just looks like a list of legal briefs," said Skyla. She provided examples, reading them from the screen: "*S. Waller v. Polk County Board of Education... S. Waller v. Artuno's Pizzeria... S. Waller v. State of Rhode Island*. What do they have to do with anything?"

Warren tapped at one of the listings and pulled up the document referenced. "It looks like Stan sued his high school over..." He read some more. "I don't know... standardized testing or something?" He clicked into another. "This one is about an icy sidewalk... broken arm..."

"But what do they have to do with anything?" Skyla pressed. "Where is his gene sequence?"

Warren went back to the main page and scrolled down further: more court cases, an employment record, a few blog posts about where to find rare vinyl records. An entry read *Biologics*. Warren clicked on it. Onto the reference window sprang a spidery network diagram. "Here it is," said Warren, as if this would explain everything.

Arthur spoke. "I thought Al analyzed gene sequences."

Warren spun back around to face them. "He does," he said. "At least, that's where it started. At first, he just looked at genetics. But Corporate decided to factor in professional experience. Then came criminal records. Social networks. You get the idea. We broadened the algorithms every time someone at Corporate got a new bright idea. Pretty soon we stopped playing their little game and just set him loose. He found whatever he could and ran his simulations based on all of it."

"Simulations?" said Arthur.

"Right," Warren replied. "That's how he decided who should come along. He found whatever data he could and dropped it into his model: played it out for a hundred... a thousand... ten thousand years. Ran it again and again and again. Monte Carlo simulation, we call it. He figured out which people, which characteristics... which combinations were most likely to produce the best outcome."

It was Maisy this time. "So, he didn't even use our genetic sequences?"

"Oh, he used them," said Warren, "but some were weighted more heavily than others. Mostly he just checked to make sure there weren't any obvious disorders down in the recessives. See here..." He pointed to the criteria list. "Stan's biologics had only a 12 percent weighting in his overall score. All of them together produce a composite ranking... here: his Argonaut Suitability Score. He was a 46 percent match. That's not bad... middle of the road, actually."

"Forty-six percent?" said Skyla. "What does that mean?"

"Someone with a genetic disorder would be a zero: no chance of being picked. Most of the population we analyzed was in the single digits. Once you get above 30 percent or so, you become a candidate. Then it comes down to combinatorics and simulations—which people work best together. I'm only a 37, but I've got a specialized skillset that made up the difference. They go as high as 60 or 65 percent, as far as I've seen. Those are the Command Staff and the astrophysicists and suchlike."

"So, what's this business about needing a crew of five thousand?" Maisy asked. "Why all the talk about genetics? Why not just have a smaller crew and a smaller ship if none of that really matters?"

At this Warren shrugged. "That I don't know," he said. "No one does. If it were just about genes, Al could certainly do it with a lot less than that. But none of those smaller samples led to viable paths. They *could* survive, theoretically speaking. But they wouldn't. At least not with any reasonable degree of probability."

"I still don't understand what a lawsuit with the Polk County Board of Education has to do with it," Skyla said.

"I've no idea, Sky," was Warren's reply. He repeated it for emphasis. He had seen this done and liked how it sounded. "No idea."

Maisy pressed. "But why would Beckett lie about it? Why would everyone lie about it?"

"Why do you think?" Warren said. He paused, but no one stepped in. "I'm guessing legal exposure. Genetic sequencing was esoteric enough that he could pass it off. Science and all, right? No one really cared much, and even if they were uneasy, they understood the need. But Al was everywhere. He was stealing everything."

"I want to see me," Skyla said.

Warren brought up her file. Al had pulled old report cards, her doctoral dissertation, academic journal publications. Her biologics ranked relatively strongly at 32 percent, and Al's network diagram showed her nearer to the top of the hierarchy, rather than down in the indistinguishable tangle where Stanley had been found. She had been an early pick. Skyla scarcely contained her pleasure at the sight of her Argonaut Suitability Score: 57 percent.

"What about me?" said Maisy. "Can I see mine?"

Warren studied her for a moment—or maybe it was her chest—and then shrugged again as if he would not stop her if she insisted upon doing something foolish. He typed in her name.

There was Maisy's picture, her name, her birthdate: everything. *Social Media Influencer*. Her nostrils flared. That was a long time ago and surely was not how she would be forever remembered? Warren scrolled down. Under the heading *Selection Criteria and Suitability Analysis* there was but a single entry: *Biologics*. Weighting factor: *N/A*.

Warren gave a low whistle and clicked in. Maisy's network diagram sprang into view. Stanley's diagram had been an inexplicable tangle of lines and nodes. Even Skyla's icon had lines coming in and lines going out. Maisy's was different. Her icon was alone, off by itself at the top of the field, with half a dozen branches diving down into the nest of squiggles and intersections below. Warren looked from the image to Maisy and back again. Then back to her.

"What does that mean?" she said. "Where's the rest of it?"

"That's all there is," Warren replied.

"Why's that? Al didn't pull my occupation, my social media feeds?"

"Oh, he pulled them," said Warren. "He may have even used them, later on—assigning jobs and whatnot. He just didn't use them to pick you. All he used for selection processing was your genetic code. And he didn't use that to pick you. It was already done. He used your DNA as a baseline to pick everyone else."

They waited for him to go on.

"You were the seed," he said at last.

"The seed?" said Maisy. She had begun to understand but subconsciously fought against the realization of what Warren had said.

"Al's not magic—sorry to disappoint you. He's got a lot of processing power for sure, but the algorithms are pretty straightforward. All of his calculations are relative. First, he checks for disorders. Once that's ruled out, he looks for attributes the crew needs. Then he looks to see whether everything in the profile fits together with all the others. That process has to start somewhere. Any one person is only a good pick in relation to everyone else. There has to be a seed: a profile against which everything else can be compared. It builds from there. That's you. The seed."

Arthur was watching his wife's face. Its color was draining, and she looked as if she could not summon the words she wanted to say—the questions for which she needed answers.

"So, someone picked her, and it wasn't Al," Arthur said.

"That's right."

"Who would that have been?" Arthur asked.

The question hung in the air. It did not need an answer.

Maisy found her voice. "But he's my father. The plan needs genetic diversity. If I was already on the list, then Beckett..."

Warren twisted his face into an ironic mask: vaguely humorous, vaguely surprised. He clearly felt bad but was incapable of expressing it in appropriate words. He was not good at empathy. "Yeah, maybe Mr. Armagast wasn't so hot on coming along after all," he said.

Arthur had never before been in a ladies' room. Wei handled those emergencies. Like so many of the new places he had visited over the preceding years, it had an eerie feel to it: familiar, but not quite right. Where were the urinals? No, of course there would be no urinals. It made sense, but still it felt wrong. How did everything stay so clean? What was with all the lotions and Q-Tips and tampons arranged in neat little bins and stacks on the countertop? Why was there a lounge with easy chairs and a coffee table that one walked through to reach the stalls? Who would want to sit back for a chat while on a trip to the toilet?

Whatever Arthur's bewilderment, Maisy had indeed made use of a loveseat upholstered in imitation leather. She sat upon it, perched on the edge with her face buried in a hand, and sobbed. She had been icy calm as she inquired of Warren after the location of the ladies' room. It was only after she had been gone for five minutes that Arthur suggested he might go and find her. He had paused at the door to consider whether it was appropriate for him to enter, but the hallways in this sector of the ship were all but empty and he could hear her crying through the door. He pushed it open and found her there. He sat and pulled her close. She went on crying, scarcely acknowledging his arrival.

He had seen her cry before, but it was not like this. Then it had been an act, or at best the stringing along of an emotion that had run its course. At the time he had thought the whole affair surprisingly manageable. This was not. It rattled him. She cried deeply and heavily, with sobs that shook her. A bubble formed over a nostril and popped before she could wipe it with a sleeve.

Without warning, she spun about as if she would burrow into Arthur's body, pushing him back into the cushions with her face thrust into his chest. She pulled her feet from the floor and curled her legs beneath her. He wrapped her in his arms and could think of nothing to say.

There was nothing to say; everything had become clear, and there was no changing it. As Maisy clung to him crying, the vision of her past opened before Arthur like an old-fashioned road map that could never again be properly folded away. She had been part and parcel of Beckett Armagast's rise to power, propelling him from just another mid-tier CEO scrambling for attention into a celebrity in his own right. The fame that had come with his beautiful and magnetic daughter had introduced him to the ranks of not just the wealthy but the famous and the powerful.

In perfect symbiosis, they had fed upon one another: Beckett's money opening opportunities for Maisy, Maisy's fame a free-of-charge advertising juggernaut for Armagast Enterprises. But all had run its course. She could propel him no further, at least not back on Earth. Like a drowning man pushing his rescuer into the depths as he struggles toward the surface, Beckett wrung from her the last shred of value she could offer. Only Beckett was not a drowning man. Not by a long shot.

Arthur knew not how to comfort his wife. He had no claim to empathy with her situation after a life spent with Mr. and Mrs. Pifflethorpe—with William. But he knew how to love her. This he did with all his might. He held her close even as her nose smeared its shiny smudge wider over the front of his uniform. He gazed into a face that was a twisted caricature of its usual poise and beauty. Her mascara ran down toward an ear, and stray lipstick reddened a cheek. He stroked at hair tangled into knots and clumped with sweat wrung from her skin by uncontrollable spasms.

It was another five minutes before the sobs subsided into snuffling heaves and another five until she was calm enough to speak. "They gave me a choice," she said. "I chose him over Mama."

Arthur listened.

"He had the money. He's the one who took me where I wanted to go. I figured I could see her anytime, but I never did. Not often, anyway. I never read most of her letters."

Arthur watched her, curled in his arms and staring off at the ceiling tiles.

"I deserve it, I guess," she said.

"You deserve everything wonderful that might happen to you," Arthur said. "This too. This adventure... the *Argo*... us... our family... it *is* wonderful. I know you think that. I know I do."

She did not seem to hear him. "Al didn't even pick me. No

one picked me. Or, I guess, one person did. He picked me so he could send me away forever."

Arthur held her tighter and whispered, "I picked you."

"I don't know why you did that."

"Yes, you do."

They were silent for a while. Maisy's sniffles continued to subside until they were gone.

"We could go back," Arthur said. "The *Argo* could go back. We're not past the point of no return. We can talk to Admiral Demarion, tell him what happened."

"What?" said Maisy. "Tell him little Maisy changed her mind and wants to go home? Turn the car around..."

Arthur at last managed a look that silenced her. "We tell him this whole thing was thrown together as a vanity project. A publicity stunt. We tell him how dangerous it is to go on with it."

Maisy pulled away and sat upright next to him. Together they stared at the back of the restroom door. She said, "For him, it was a publicity stunt. Armagast Enterprises wasn't just Beckett Armagast. Thousands... hundreds of thousands of people poured their lives into this project. It's not perfect, but it's no sham. I'll never go back. We'll never go back. We're going to make it work. We're going to leave forever." She hesitated and then looked at Arthur and said it again: "I'll never go back."

Arthur nodded. Whatever Maisy wanted was fine with him, so long as he was there.

Maisy cleaned herself up with the restroom's stock of beauty supplies. She chatted with Arthur under the stall as she peed. He found it mystifying. But her mood had swung for the better as rapidly as it had swung for the worse. He went along with it. She looked better with her makeup washed off and her hair back in a ponytail. He knew better than to tell her this.

By the time they returned to Warren and Skyla, the only

sign something had been amiss was Maisy's lack of makeup and a wet spot on Arthur's chest. Skyla responded to their knock at the door. She had been watching Warren slaughter enemy soldiers with what appeared to be an M60 machine gun mounted on the turret of a Humvee. He once again paused the game and switched over the screens.

"Listen, it's really fine," said Warren as they took their seats. He was doing his best to make Maisy feel better. It was as if he felt some culpability for it all. He was not the sort of boy to make girls cry, and certainly not girls like Maisy. "Your kid's not going to make a difference. Al makes his recommendations, but there's huge margin for error. It's all just probabilities—best guesses. Nothing's guaranteed."

Maisy nodded and smiled in response. She was finished talking about it. Arthur sensed this.

"I want to see mine," he said.

Warren looked at him, gave another ironical smile, and spun around. He called up Arthur's record and scrolled downward. The *Selection Criteria and Suitability Analysis* slid into view. Arthur realized his mistake as soon as he read the first entry: *Subject: Hey there!*

He recognized the subject line of an email. It was a very old email, but not one he would forget. He knew all the email subject lines listed one after another after another. Warren scrolled on and on, past line after line of Arthur's old love letters. It seemed Al had found them all. *Subject: Miss you! Subject: See you soon!* Why, oh why, had Arthur felt the need to use so many exclamation points? Warren's double-click seemed to reach Arthur's ears in slow motion.

"Wait..." was all he got out before the text sprang into view.

We must apologize to the reader, for we cannot bring ourselves to divulge more widely the contents of Arthur's most private communications. It was enough that three sets of eyes devoured the musings of that sensitive and tender young spirit. Fear not, they will never be classics. Over a lifetime, he had corresponded with girl after girl, each of whom he had, at the time, been convinced beyond doubt was his everlasting soul-mate.

He did his best to avert the disaster. He protested, he demanded, he even tried a comically unsuccessful bout of rage, all to no effect. Maisy giggled. Skyla blushed. Warren clicked gleefully through the trove of love letters that Al had stolen from Arthur's private files. Soon Maisy elbowed Warren out of the way and took command of the mouse. She clicked and read, clicked and read. Her sorrow vanished and was replaced with unadulterated delight.

Arthur was no William Shakespeare. He was no John Donne. What he lacked in style and technique, he made up for in heartfelt, wide-eyed faith—faith in his beloved, faith in himself, faith in love. He had faith that the weather would be fine and the water warm. He had faith that his girl (whichever girl it was) shared a fervent love of telescopes and Franklin W. Dixon. It was an unquestioning faith that took his correspondent's affection utterly for granted.

What did he talk about? What do thirteen-year-olds talk about with girls? He talked about movies, about football games, about preadolescent gossip. He opined on the uniqueness of his correspondent's beauty and the insight of her discourse. He delved into topics as risqué as who was going with whom, the girl who got her period during social studies class, and the boy who found a naughty magazine in the neighbor's trash bin. His grammar was rife with unnecessary punctuation, *your* instead of *you're*, and big words with meanings that were not quite right. There was an *irregardless*. There were run-ons and comma splices and far, far too many adverbs.

These had truly been the outpourings of Arthur's soul. In

talk of family reunions and Sadie Hawkins dances, he laid bare the foundations of his heart. He had imagined he was, with suave assurance, steering his young crush down the path toward inevitable love. She was putty in his hands. Never would she notice the thread of ardor woven through Arthur's subtext until it tangled her forever in hopeless, passionate romance. He had tried so hard—yet inevitable failure screamed from every line. Sitting there in Al's control room before the love of his life, he saw himself so foolish, so trite, his tone so dripping with thinly veiled and baseless adoration.

He gave up trying to pull his cherished Maisy away from the horror that unfolded before her. He slumped in his chair, he stared at the floor, he flushed a deeper and deeper shade of red until it gave way to ghostly pale. How many times had he been in love? How many times had he stormed the gates and been thrown back in abject defeat? That story—the story of his life—was spelled out for all to see. Did he have no self-respect? No common sense? Was he the hatchling forever wandering from one girl to the next: *Are you my mother? Are you my mother?* The questions rolled over him one after another like surf driving him under.

Maisy turned back to him at last, her face glowing with radiant joy undimmed by mascara and rouge and lipstick. "If I'd only known..." she said. "I wouldn't have wasted all that effort putting up a fight. I had no chance."

It was less her words than the look on her face that pushed the beginnings of a smile onto Arthur's lips. He squeezed them tight, fighting it back.

"Who said you weren't the crew's biggest ladies' man?" She tickled his nose.

He made a show of batting away her hand and refused to meet her eyes.

"Hey..." she said. A pause. "Hey..." She put a hand on his chin and pulled him back. "Look at this."

She laid a finger on the screen. Above its manicured fingernail was a number: it was Arthur Pifflethorpe's Argonaut Suitability Score. It said 94 percent.

Chapter Twenty-One

There is falling in love, and then there is loving. We glamorize one and disparage the other, in practice if not on principle. Once gloriously fallen, we slog onward into the business of loving: of shedding illusions that harried us into the plunge. Falling would seem an act of gravity; loving a noble act of will. Yet it is falling that captures our imagination. Is love the falling or is it the doing? Is it both? Neither? Perhaps, so difficult to define, it is simply a cocktail of chemicals devised by evolution to spur us into ill-advised procreation. Perhaps it is God Himself. Perhaps love is coming to terms with regrets and failures and inadequacies: everything we cannot have but imagine we could in some alternate reality just beyond our fingertips.

Arthur Pifflethorpe fell in love. He was forever falling in love, even after he had settled once and for all upon his Maisy. For Arthur, falling in love was not a collection of memories to contrast with what his life had become. It was a state of being: a weekly, daily, minute-by-minute occurrence in which he spent a lifetime pursuing all that was worth loving. He loved all of it—

all of her—with a conscious, active embrace of beauties along-side unmentionables alongside horrors. It was new every moment, and every moment he threw himself into it. He had no more wish for it to be easy than an athlete would wish to win by forfeit. Love was his life's work: his masterpiece. Masterpieces are composed for symphony orchestras, not for tin whistles. Maisy Armagast was no tin whistle.

For Arthur, loving and falling in love were one and the same. As he discovered each new facet of his beloved, he studied it, embraced it, and folded it into his conception of love. He would no more wish to strip away her tendency to peevishness (inevitably arising when she imagined her bottom growing thicker and embarked upon a campaign of semipermanent, nagging hypoglycemia) than he would wish to strip away her dusting of secret freckles or the little jerk she gave as she fell asleep in his arms. Washing her clean of irritants would be akin to washing his palette clean of blacks and browns and yellows and painting with only his favorite colors.

To say Arthur at last found his great love is not to say he ceased falling in love. Maisy was forever new; he, forever carried away by this or that fanciful notion and needing to be pulled firmly back to reality. He never ceased luring his wife to the banana plantation, even long after she stopped wearing a bikini under her uniform and took to minding the ravages of ultraviolet radiation. He daydreamed over their youthful microgravity acrobatics even as she reminded him, time and again, that they had had to stop when she threw up into the garbage chute. When he arranged picnics for her in the cherry orchard, she emphasized that, try as he might, there would be no frolicking about like nymphs and satyrs. Still he chased. Arthur loved the mood swings and the morning sickness and the stretch marks. He loved being taught to behave like an adult of the species, even if he never got it quite right. He loved being made to put on a fresh uniform when heading off to work in the morning, even if it made no sense.

"But they're all the same. No one will know."

"I'll know."

A moment of consideration, a flash of defiance: "Maybe I won't do it."

"Maybe I'll sleep in *my* room tonight."

And Maisy loved her Arthur. She loved that every day he was born new. She loved that he loved the things about her she could never love about herself. She loved that he tried so hard and that most of the time he got it so wrong. He was ingenuous. He was unaffected. He veered from profound wisdom into profound foolishness without seeming to recognize the difference.

We once inquired after the origins of Arthur's propensity to love. Did it arise of some disruption in the normal course of emotional development? Was he forever seeking what as a child had been torn from him? This is quite likely; but does it matter? Who among us has experienced a normal course of emotional development? Who among us is not a mishmash of idiosyncrasy and dysfunction? Arthur's propensity to love could no more be separated from the deaths of William and Mr. Pifflethorpe than Maisy's need to achieve could be separated from the megalomania of Beckett Armagast. He was no less a man for it, she no less a woman.

As for their marriage, it settled into a marriage much like any other but for the fact that together they sped off toward their deaths somewhere out in the fathomless vacuum of interstellar space. Irritations were no less irritating for being, at some level, valued. There were misunderstandings and irreconcilable disagreements and fights that woke the neighbors. There were insurmountable cataclysms that, in the morning, were found to be neither insurmountable nor cataclysmic. Arthur learned as never before how often he could be wrong. Maisy learned the most effective ways to make him aware of this. They learned together, they grew together, and—in every sense that matters—they were happy.

Make no mistake, all was not forgiven when Arthur and Maisy faced the inevitable confrontation with the command staff. What was so long delayed could never be permanently escaped. How to carry on from that moment of epiphany in the bowels of the Human Resources Department? The question never occurred to Arthur and Maisy. Nothing seemed to matter beside Al's revelations. They returned to Arthur's room in Squadron Four and slipped back into life as if nothing were amiss. Exhausted by the stresses of the day, they changed into their pajamas and fell asleep together in a bed made for one. There was no more resistance, no more imagining dragons. They knew the truth. They were awakened early the following morning by a polite rapping on the door and escorted to the brig through still-empty corridors.

It took hours for the command staff to finalize their decision. News went out, and schedules were rearranged. Conference was held. Minutes were transcribed and distributed, decision points documented, and relevant regulations and authorities identified and cross-referenced. Arthur was just finishing his lunch, carried to him on a tray from the cafeteria, when Maisy was brought into his cell. The first officer arrived a few minutes later.

Lane Beauregard had a delightful ability to play the part of disappointed father. He cracked the door, peered inside, and paused. After sizing up the situation, he stepped through and turned with absolute firmness of purpose to close it behind him. He stood for a moment looking down on the pair and waiting for the upturned faces to take on an appropriate air of contrition. Then he sat across the table from them.

"I'm happy to see you've come to realize the senselessness of trying to hide," First Officer Beauregard said. "We're all one team here: one mission, one set of rules. It's a difficult situation you've put us in."

"I might say the same," came Maisy's retort. Arthur took her hand under the table and squeezed it.

"Mmm. Indeed." The first officer's look suggested he was either conflicted or suffering from indigestion. His was a difficult face to read. Perhaps it was the secret to his professional success. "It seems you disagree. You understand, of course, that a free-for-all when it comes to... these matters... is out of the question? Perhaps you'd like to offer an alternative plan? Perhaps you feel yourselves exceptional in some respect from the rules that govern the rest of us?"

"We've been to see Al," Maisy said. "There's no reason for all of this. Especially not now, with Beckett's public-relations agenda no longer a concern. It's time to tell the crew. It's time to move on. Al can play his part. He doesn't need to dictate everything."

"No reason... mmm." Lane let silence hang for a moment before he said, "Please... go on, Ms. Armagast."

"Mrs. Pifflethorpe, if you please," Maisy said. She squeezed Arthur's hand back before continuing, "Al isn't using genetics... or not primarily. His analysis is behavioral. Five thousand is well beyond the minimum size for a viable population. Why not let him validate instead of dictate: check for problems instead of micromanage? There's no reason for him to prescribe every match. I'm sure there are plenty who wouldn't mind skipping over the relationship part. Let him choose for them."

Again, Lane's deep-set eyes studied her. They flicked to Arthur and then back to Maisy. "The command staff is aware of all this, I assure you. We're also aware of broader challenges which you don't seem to have considered. Do you suppose reproductive procedures are the only important factor in building a functioning crew? A functioning society? Do you suppose considerations of sociology—considerations of discipline—should be allowed to proceed at random?"

"What does our relationship have to do with discipline?" Arthur said. "It doesn't have to. You made it that way."

"Quite the contrary," said the first officer. Then he paused, seeming to reconsider what he was about to say. "Let me ask you, what's the single biggest factor that's led to strife—to war—throughout human history? Let me tell you. It's competition: for food, for natural resources... for mates. Do you have any conception of what it takes to plan out a society that will survive for a thousand years? That's what this is, you know. It's not just a crew. It's a society, a new world of its own, self-contained and self-dependent. Do you suppose we can just set everything in motion and hope for the best? Maybe make a fun little reality-television show out of it?

"No. Discipline is everything. Logical reasoning is everything. Things like emotion—love—will get us killed, and it won't be a pleasant way to die. Think of history; how has it gone for the human race so far? Faction, conflict, warfare, famine and population collapse; now how does that look with five thousand people sealed up in a tin can floating through space?"

There was a moment of silence that invited response before he went on.

"Young man... young lady... you don't understand it all yet. Believe it or not, I was there once, too. It all seems so simple at your age; the answers seem so obvious. Well, they only seem obvious because you don't know what you don't know. Some things can only be learned through painful experience.

"What I've learned is that people aren't nice. People aren't logical. They're petty and emotional and vindictive. And let's be honest: much of the command staff's authority comes from tacit acceptance by the crew, or at a minimum their inability to agree on a better system. What do you think is going to happen when the *Argo* closes its comm links? When the streaming services shut down and the pre-stocked food runs out? When the sun is a distant memory and we're living on soybean paste and oatmeal? How do you propose we maintain order?"

Again, he paused to let them ponder it.

"Let's set aside social dynamics and genetic engineering and artificial intelligence. Absent all of that, how would you propose we handle this? The first time our rules are challenged, do you suggest we roll over? Admit defeat? What would that do for order and discipline on the ship? I'll tell you: it would lead to chaos."

He stood to deliver the final message. "The command staff has reached its decision, and that decision stands. We welcome your willing participation, but if necessary will carry it out without your consent. Are we clear?"

He received no response and turned to leave the room.

A lump had formed in Arthur's throat that choked off whatever words tried to form. He was numb. When the door closed behind the first officer, he at last summoned the will to look at his wife. Even in tears, he had never seen her look so defeated. It was not sorrow; it was not rage. It was an empty brokenness that, for perhaps the first time in her life, could find no expression.

Arthur hated himself. Of all the times when he had been lost for words—all those crises he had thought so important— none of them produced the boiling contempt he felt for his own impotence in that moment. Why could he not speak when circumstances demanded? Why could he never rise to the occasion?

If he could have the moment again, he knew exactly what he would say. He would say there was more to all of this than discipline. There was more to it than cold logic. There was everything that made them human; everything for which they had sacrificed and would sacrifice. Would they save humanity by crushing out everything that made a human life worth living? Was humanity's contribution to the universe to be a police state entirely lacking in personal happiness? What sense did that make?

But he would never be able to say this. The first officer was gone, and Arthur was still Arthur. Perhaps it is better he never had a chance to speak his mind. These things never turn out as we imagine they will. Do not feel bad for him (at least not so bad as he felt for himself), for he would likely have come off worse for the outburst than he did from remaining silent. Triumph is not the sole province of the uninhibited.

And triumph Arthur and Maisy did. Cataclysms are rarely so cataclysmic as we think at the time. Tempers cool, rhetoric meets the cold blast of common sense. Structure and control meet the irresistible forces of entropy. In this case, it came down to Petty Officer Third Class Stanley Waller, who in his all-consuming indignation once again took matters into his own hands. Apprised of the situation by his sweetheart, he marched straight to the Legal Department and filed a lawsuit. Arthur and Maisy were violating his rights by threatening the long-term viability of the Argonaut population. Anyone willing to counte-nance their misbehavior was complicit. By God, he would not stand for it.

In their cells in the brig, Arthur and Maisy received a visit from Stanley's legal representation. They procured counsel of their own. This lawyer, in turn, recommended not only counter-suit for defamation of character but floated the possibility of suing the command staff itself. Maisy's treatment at the hands of her father was unconscionable. Given the lack of legal precedent aboard the *Argo*, the sky was (figuratively, of course) the limit. Amid all of the relevant meeting minutes, decision points, regulations, and authorities was fertile ground for litigation. In the teeth of judicial proceedings, execution of Al's plans slowed to a crawl. Soon the Argonaut rumor mill got wind of unfolding events. At that point, keeping Arthur and Maisy in the brig became counterproductive.

Little Mabel was long since born before the matter was settled to the satisfaction (more or less) of all parties. As a matter of fact, Mabel's little brother was on the way as well, although even Arthur was not yet in on this bit of news.

The command staff managed to score one small victory, however Pyrrhic it may have been. Arthur and Maisy's request to cohabitate on a permanent basis was roundly disapproved. They would pass many years of remarkably happy marriage before beginning to suspect that Lane Beauregard had played an outsized role in this decision and that his intentions were not entirely malevolent. Behind those inscrutable eyes, Arthur had always suspected some modicum of sympathy and a deep understanding for the vicissitudes of married life.

In the years to come, the turbulence to be expected at the formation of any new regime settled into its version of normal. The command staff imposed its discipline and was obeyed or ignored according to the vagaries of human will. Conflict over the production of little Argonauts sorted itself out as we would expect; one could no more deny human beings their passions than one could deny suns their heat or space its cold. Many elected to abide by Al's recommendations. Many did not. Punishments were meted out and stern talkings-to administered. In the end, they arrived at some approximation of a happy medium that allowed for tempestuous concupiscence alongside realization of concrete hopes for those of a more inward bent. Disciplinarians raged, libertines shrugged. Most just soldiered on. There was senseless conflict, although not to the degree feared by First Officer Beauregard. There was senseless oppression, although not to the degree feared by Petty Officer Third Class Pifflethorpe.

What, then, was the intent of Al in Human Resources, if he could be said to have one? Was it management of the Argonauts' stock of deoxyribonucleic acid? Was it ensuring the required number of astrophysicists, nuclear engineers, and waste-management technicians? Was it order? Was it love? It would seem the result of all his striving, all his calculation and cogitation and probabilistic modeling, was none of these. It would seem the result was a hopeless muddle. If we believe humanity is hidebound to backwardness and incompetence, this will come as no surprise.

But if we believe in the efficacy of human beings to order and manipulate their world, at least to some degree, we must arrive at the conclusion that a hopeless muddle is the best Al could arrange. He managed the chaos. He walked the tightrope. Avoiding the extremes of autocracy and anarchy, of rationality and passion, of science and art, he did the best he could. The Argonauts strived, they succeeded, they failed. They put their eggs in as many baskets as they could find and prayed a few would survive the remorseless and implacable vacuum of space. To each, Al provided validation and disappointment in appropriate measure. He raised the meek and humbled the mighty through the awesome power of untidiness.

Years passed, and the Point of No Return approached. The engine fired, and the *Argo* accelerated into the gargantuan gravity well of Saturn. Some wag in the Department of Information Technology pushed an operating-system update that superimposed a doomsday clock onto desktops throughout the ship: its numbers clicked relentlessly down toward the minute and second when the *Argo* would be forever committed to leaving behind its home planet and setting off toward no-one-knew-what. Something needed to be done to commemorate the occasion. Chief Steward Sasaki planned an ice-cream social.

Still, no one had gotten around to dismantling the observation deck, although its doors had long since been barred and chained beyond the best efforts of the Waste Management journeymen. The chief steward convinced the admiral to allow one last extravagance. They unbarred the doors and reset the thermostat. They swept the dust and carried down tables and chairs. They set up a disc-jockey table and a mirror ball and smoke machines. The Department of Childcare Services arranged cribs, playpens, and tubs of toys in an adjacent conference room. Sheets of construction paper hand-painted with peppy slogans began to appear in hallways. Tension built with some peculiar mixture of terror and anticipation from which there was no extracting the component parts.

The night arrived. Crewmembers ransacked storage rooms and rummaged through duffel bags for long-since-misplaced tie pins, strapless brassieres, and patent-leather pumps. In dark, dusty, and forgotten nooks across the ship, stills ran down to the final moment, producing vast quantities of hooch. Corridors of the *Argo* buzzed with preparation as laggards hustled from quarters to showers and back again in various states of undress. Ladies borrowed lipsticks and hairsprays. Men fastened one another's cummerbunds and arranged one another's bowties. Maisy ran late, and Arthur stewed. All was well for the Argonauts.

At long last, one and all were dressed in their finest formal attire with hair coiffed, shoes polished, and ribbons affixed. The hour approached, and doors swung open. Corridors clogged with laughing, chattering, milling throngs. They queued at lifts and streamed down back stairwells. They hollered at friends and admonished bewildered children. At long last, they filed through the observation deck's final set of emergency doors into the vast transparent dome that vanished far underfoot into a spangled firmament.

Maisy led the precocious Mabel by the hand. Arthur held wide-eyed little Arlo in his arms. Making their way to the center of the floor, the crew stood dumbfounded—adult and child alike —as the great orb of Saturn rose below the steel hull of the ship. It swelled to fill the sky below their feet, streaked with its churning bands of cloud and cast half in shade by the sun's distant speck. The gas giant's magnificent rings spread out toward them until the ship seemed to skim along past the nearest bits of debris. One could feel their speed. One could see the planet spiraling away, the bands of its rings passing like highway stripes beneath the wheels of a car. A panoply of moons dotted the heavens in every size and color imaginable. Beyond, swirling bands of the Milky Way painted a backdrop of white fire.

Only slowly did the spell break. It began, as these things will, with the children. They babbled to their mothers, shrieked for attention, and ran wild amid the forest of legs. Herded into the waiting clutches of the Department of Childcare Services, they soon lost interest in planets and moons and distant suns they had never known. Far more important was being first to make a run at the toys. Far more important was securing the Play-Doh station next to pretty little Mabel Pifflethorpe.

The crew milled and chatted in low voices that rose higher and higher as refreshment attendants worked their way through interminable queues. The disc jockey took up his station, and music pulsed through dim recesses lit by spotlights that dipped and swooped and played over legions of glowing faces and flashing eyes. The view below was misted over with smoke that crept out over the empty expanse of dance floor. It was understood Maisy would be first, and thither she led her Arthur. They danced, and in twos and threes and fours, more came to join them. Soon inhibition and awe melted into the camaraderie of common struggle and common purpose. For Arthur, there was no more hesitation, no more diffidence, no more self-scrutiny.

He danced, he laughed, he talked. He relinquished his wife to the general urging of the crew and watched with glistening eyes as she sang for them, for him. He watched her work the room as he chatted with Dexter, who expected at any moment an end to the festivities as the order was passed to abort and return to Earth. Planning for his presidential campaign continued apace. Arthur caught Maisy's eye, and she returned to him, skin glowing and hair in coiled braids that were the talk of the room. He held her close, and they danced slowly over their spot on the floor, now empty of its nest of sofa cushions.

A speech from the admiral was soon forgotten, and a toast from Father McIntosh was long remembered. He introduced his first batch of single-malt and apologized for the truncation of its aging process. "Never fear," he said through a wide smile and slurred speech. "The first completed batch of Argobeg, born of the amber waves of our very outer ring, will arrive on shelves by Neptune."

It was a night of new beginnings. It was a night of remembrance. Arthur thought of Mr. and Mrs. Pifflethorpe. He thought of William. He thought of Sloane and Isabel. He thought of nights out on a dock with waves lapping at the pilings and the *Argo* a mysterious speck of light plying the skies. He smiled at memories of a familiar voice carrying over the water and of Mr. Weiss's Maserati and of all-consuming consternation over cups of Pcpsi. He smiled that he could smile over these things. As never before, memories warmed him like the rancid hooch Ramon kept pushing into his hand.

At last, the music fell, the admiral called for attention, and the countdown flashed onto a screen behind the disc jockey's table in numbers six feet high: one minute until the Point of No Return. The admiral patched in the bridge, and the scratchy voice of the pilot projected over the loudspeakers. All systems were nominal, the order to proceed received.

Forty-five seconds.

Friends sought out friends; lovers, lovers. Maisy slipped into Arthur's arms, and he held her close, looking down at a face that looked up at him, superimposed against the breathtaking panorama. The colossal moon Titan spun past, its veering course against the line of the hull nearly inducing vertigo among those who watched.

Thirty seconds.

Those children old enough to understand had been released by their minders. Arthur watched Mabel in her jumper making her way across the floor, leading her brother by the hand. Mabel was engrossed by the vision of her mother; Arlo, by the view below his feet. His eyes followed the spinning disk of rings down, around, and up until the shifting perspective nearly toppled him off his feet. They arrived just in time, and he clung to his father's leg, engrossed in the scene. Mabel pushed her way between her parents and stared about in wonder at the lights and the glamor and the radiant faces.

Ten seconds.

The final countdown was shouted out by voices boisterous and solemn, drunk and sober, exhilarated and heartsick. Arthur's family clung to him, and his wife stared into his eyes. Neither wanted to blink and miss it. His heart flopped in his chest, for joy or trepidation.

Five.

Four.
Three.
Two.
One.

The End